A NOVEL

BILL MASKE

authorHOUSE®

AuthorHouse™
1663 Liberty Drive
Bloomington, IN 47403
www.authorhouse.com
Phone: 833-262-8899

Published by AuthorHouse 05/07/2021

ISBN: 978-1-6655-2484-1 (sc)
ISBN: 978-1-6655-2491-9 (e)

Library of Congress Control Number: 2021909225

Print information available on the last page.

This book is printed on acid-free paper.

For my wife,
Our children,
and
Grandchildren

CONTENTS

ABOUT THE COVER ART

The cover imagery was specifically created for this book by Abstract Entity Art by Justin Pritchard, LLC. The cover of "2039" captures a blend of ideals made up of both science and religion. The known and the unknown. The center of the design nods toward binary code, including all colors of the 7 major chakras, the Star of David, the Yin and Yang, the wheel of life, along with hints of sacred geometry. The archaic look is to bring forth consideration of a new approach for a new-aged understanding globally as Moses did with the Ten Commandments. In the center of the symbol is a symbol of peace combined with the mathematical expression $E=mc2$. All these elements formed together indicate a suggestive functional guide for peace and a higher understanding. As above, so below, with wonders of a multiverse and reincarnation.

PROLOGUE

It is 2039. The world is engulfed in catastrophic change. For over one-hundred-fifty-years, humanity has played fast and loose with geo-political positioning, religious fanaticism, and Mother Nature. Now the people of every continent are embroiled in challenges beyond imagination.

The Industrial Revolution changed the very nature of life. Industries powered by fossil fuels churned pollutants into the air, land, and water as a byproduct of mass production. The minerals found deep in the earth as well as those found deep in the ocean became valued acquisitions for industrialists, and the nations they represented. As industrialization evolved, the well-being of the industrialist and the nation became one in the same. In time, nations went to war based on what they called National Security, code words for securing and protecting valuable resources for the industries which drive the economy.

Eventually the economy became paramount. Industries which drive the economy became too big to fail. Big corporations grew into mega-corporations with the financial where-with-all to command the political process by controlling the media, message, and elected officials. It all occurred very subtly beyond the eye of public suspicion.

Evil is like a snake. It slithers around quietly and undetected waiting for the right time to strike. Evil is alluring and seductive. It is indeed the taste of the forbidden fruit.

Progress is not necessarily evil, but there is much unseen behind the wizard's curtain. Out of the sight of an unsuspecting public, the industrial machine pillaged the Earth, destroying the environment. At the same time, the public became addicted to the lifestyle industrialization made possible.

As the industrial age gave way to the technological age, the Titans of Industry and politicians discovered a new source of power. Help people feel like their lives are relevant through something called social media. They discovered that just as a person cannot walk past a mirror without looking at themselves, most people have a narcissistic tendency when it comes to social media. An interesting phenomenon called "Selfies" convinced those of power that as long as people had access to such self-indulgence, they would have a false sense of efficacy with the world at large.

By 2039, the vast majority of people in the United States and Europe are indifferent to the warnings coming from the scientific community. Scientists are portrayed as nothing more than Chicken Little crying out that the sky is falling.

It is as if a new Dark Age has descended upon the Earth. Crazy theories spring up like weeds in a garden. People cast aside common sense for crazy ideas and unfounded conspiracies in a world gone mad.

In the United States, there are twelve individuals with the knowledge, expertise, and determination to confront the gargantuan problems facing the world. These individuals come from a common background and upbringing which instilled in them a sense of purpose and responsibility. The older ones of this group have been outspoken for years attempting to educate people to the dangers that lurk ahead. The younger ones have followed close behind determined to do their part. Now, in 2039, their journey brings them together in a most unexpected way.

CHAPTER I

THE AWAKENING

"Jack, this is Noah. We need to visit; I have made some startling discoveries which require your attention!" Noah, has always had a penchant for all animals. As a young boy growing up in Northern Iowa, he nurtured his interest by watching animal planet and the discovery channel with his younger brother Edison for hours at a time. Noah feels a deep kinship with creatures large and small. Even as a young child, he understood the importance of keeping the earth habitable for all living things.

When not watching and learning about animals, Noah ventured outside into the Iowa countryside to observe, photograph, and learn about Iowa's creatures and their habitat. Walking along a steep creek embankment near his home in Rockwell, he could see how agricultural practices were creating erosion hazards to the creeks natural flow and the habitat of beaver, muskrats, mink, and other animals that make the creek their home. Spending time on river sand bars, Noah discovered all of the places where field drainage allowed harmful chemicals from herbicides, pesticides, and anhydrous ammonia to leach into the streams which fed the rivers and lakes. Noah questioned everything, and when he raised questions about human activity harming wildlife, he discovered the same response from those of authority, "It has been determined that what is occurring falls within the guidelines of not being harmful."

"Remember Noah," his teachers in school would say, "There are laws protecting our environment." Based on his observations, Noah did not find this all that reassuring.

Noah remembered his grandparents telling him stories passed down from previous generations about how at one time Iowa served as home to so many different animals including wolves, bear, moose, and mountain lion. As Iowa became more settled, and the food sources were eliminated, many of these animals moved to other areas where food was plentiful. As a result of this migration, there was a time when deer, coyote, beaver, wild turkey, Bald Eagles and otter were rarely found in Iowa. However, conservation efforts turned things around, so as a young boy, Noah found it easy to study deer, and with care and patience, he found ways to study all of the animals.

One day in 2019, while visiting great-grandmother Annie in Peterson, Iowa, to celebrate the Fourth of July, Noah and his brother Edison decided to take a canoe trip on the Little Sioux River from Linn Grove to Peterson.

Linn Grove founded in 1877 and named for a grove of Linden trees reached its maximum population of 433 people in 1920. A ten-foot dam on the Little Sioux River bordering the north edge of town made Linn Grove a popular fishing spot and earned it the designation as the Catfish Capital of the World. Near Linn Grove, archeologists discovered the remains of a village inhabited by native Americans over one-thousand years ago.

The first white settlement at Peterson was established in 1856. The town is named for an early settler Adlie Peterson. In 1860, ten votes were cast to make Peterson the county seat of Clay County. Fort Peterson was built in 1862 to protect against Dakota Sioux attacks. Resting in the valley of the Little Sioux River which borders the town to the south, Peterson became known as the Scenic Nest of Iowa's Northwest. The large looming hills encircle the town with a thick forest of trees and native vegetation. It is a wonderous feeling to enter the town via the steep declining roads which reach the valley floor from every direction. In the case of Highway 10 coming from the east, the valley road serpentines the hills and then makes a blind inclining curve to the right, and you are in town. While the population of Peterson is small, the abundance of squirrels, rabbits, birds, and deer is like Time Square on a busy day.

The Little Sioux, once a mighty river now represents a rather shallow muddy river ranging from twenty to sixty feet across. The river between Linn Grove and Peterson nearly triples the seven mile - as the crow flies, distance - due to its twists and turns. Once on the river, modern day explorers can imagine themselves in the dense wilds of a great forest due to the riparian woodlands of cottonwood, ash, maple, and walnut trees. Noah and Eddie envisioned themselves as Native American Sioux who used the river long before the white man ever knew such a continent existed. They recalled the stories of the Sioux Chief Inkpaduta and his band of renegades as they passed through this valley on their way to the Spirit Lake Massacre. As the story goes, the settlers at Peterson fed the Indians and provide them with shelter from the cold and snow of late winter. During their time in the Peterson area, Inkpaduta and his band displayed no signs of hostility.

Inkpaduta was a Dakota Sioux Indian Chief with a reputation of being friendly with white settlers. In fact, there are a number of first-hand reports indicating that Inkpaduta and his tribe traded with the settlers of Iowa and Minnesota prior to the Spirit Lake Massacre. In 1852, Inkpaduta's brother and nine of his family were murdered by a drunken white settler. Inkpaduta attempted to seek justice by appealing to the U.S. Army, but nothing was ever resolved. In 1857, under the duress of a severe winter which left his tribe starving, Inkpaduta and his band of warriors launched raids against the white settlers at Spirit Lake. Almost twenty-years later, Inkpaduta joined up with Sitting Bull and Crazy Horse where two of his son's took part in the Battle of the Little Big Horn.

Noah and Edison consider the history of this great valley and how the outlaw Jesse James may have camped along these very banks as he and his gang used the seclusion of the river and woodlands to make their way north to Minnesota.

※※※

During the American Civil War, Jesse James and his brother Frank operated with Confederate guerrillas in Missouri and Kansas. After the war and maintaining sympathy with the defeated South, Jesse and Frank took to a life of crime. Organizing gangs, the James Brothers along with the Younger Brothers of Cole, John, Jim, and Bob went on a spree of train and bank robberies ranging into Iowa and Minnesota. On June 3, 1871, the James Gang made a daring bank robbery in Corydon, Iowa. A little over two years later on July 21, 1873, the gang pulled off the world's first robbery of a moving train near Adair, Iowa. At one point, it is believed the gang traveled along the Little Sioux River on their way to Northfield, Minnesota in 1876.

※※※

Noah and Edison haul their canoe in a pickup to Linn Grove. Their Father and Grandfather will get the pickup later and drive it to their destination. Their Dad and Grandfather envy the boys for their adventurous nature.

Arriving at a launching place below the Linn Grove Dam, Noah and Edison do a final inventory to be certain they have all the supplies necessary for the trip.

"Did you bring the cooler like I asked you too?" Noah inquires expecting his brother forgot this simple chore.

"I not only brought it brother, but I checked to make sure we have plenty of Mt. Dew and Dr. Pepper," responds Edison knowing his brother, like himself, values the opportunity to indulge their favorite beverage without a judgmental eye.

"Did you bring the camera Noah?" Eddie counters offering Noah the same hint of suspicion that he might have forgot.

"I brought the camera, telephoto lens, and the water proof case," Noah shoots back in a defiant manner.

"Do we have the all-important cell phone?" Noah retorts thinking he might have caught his brother on this one.

"Yes, we do, I think Grandma must have told me to remember it a dozen times," Edison proclaims. Both boys have a good laugh. They love their Grandmother, and they love her persistence in looking after them.

Their Grandmother Carole, Great-Grandmother Annie's daughter-in-law married to Annie's son Bill, is in Peterson with the entire clan for the big celebration. Peterson has a long history of celebrating the 4th of July with Horse Shoe Tournaments, baseball games, Watermelon, and fireworks. Grandma is in the midst of a long history of looking after her grandchildren.

Noah and Edison are not only brothers but friends. They have been raised to be confident and competitive, and they enjoy the give and take of brothers. It is always in good fun, and sometimes it gets a bit too aggressive, but not today. Today they are on an adventure and they must work together.

The boys portaged the canoe along the river bank to a low laying sandbar which creates a bend in the river. The river is narrow and shallow at this point and offers Noah and Edison an opportunity to launch the canoe without capsizing.

Laying the canoe on the sand with the front extended into the water, the boys feel confident their journey is about to begin.

"Well, I think we are set to sail. I'll get in and you shove us off," Noah instructs as he jumps into the canoe and steps to the front.

Eddie grabs the back of the canoe and gives a push, but the weight of the canoe combined with the soft sand holds it in place like a suction cup to a window. "This thing is not going to move," Eddie grunts as his feet dig into the sand.

"Don't be such a wimp Eddie, put your shoulder and weight into it," Noah challenges as he smiles from the front of the canoe. Sitting in the front, Noah realizes none of the canoe is floating yet. The soft sand is holding onto the canoe like a mother does her newborn child.

"Give it the old college try Eddie," Noah implores. Noah has heard his Father and Grandfather refer to great effort as the – old college try. Someday as a college student, he would realize the true meaning of this saying.

Eddie leans into the canoe with all his might, but finds the only thing moving are his feet deeper into the soft sand. "You're too much weight Noah, this thing isn't going anywhere."

"I guess I will have to help," Noah says as he steps from the canoe. "I will pull the front of the canoe into the water until it is floating, and then we can both hop in as we set it off into the river. Try not to capsize the thing," Noah suggests hinting that if it does capsize, Edison will be responsible.

Both boys are wearing water shoes, and Noah notices that the river bottom becomes rockier and firmer as they move away from the sand bar. With the front of the canoe floating, Noah says, "On the count of three, give a push and hop in the canoe as gently as possible. One, two, three," Noah makes a clean leap into the canoe, but Eddie faces a different situation. By now his feet have sunk into the soft sand up to his calves. As he pushes and leaps, the suction of the sand remove his water shoes from his feet and leave him dangling from the canoe. With the canoe listing to the left side nearly tossing Noah into the water, Eddie half in the water regains his feet on the rocky bottom and lunges into the canoe.

The canoe rocks back and forth with both boys fighting to regain their balance. Finally sitting upright, the canoe is afloat and the boys can begin their day's adventure. Eddie is a bit wet from the waist down and Noah suggests he might have wet his pants. Edison uses an oar to give Noah a big splash. "Alright, I am just teasing, so knock it off," Noah pleads. "Let's get on with this adventure."

Little did Noah know this would be the day which would determine his life's devotion to the study of invasive species? As the boys float the river, they are constantly pointing out and photographing wild life, scenery, and environmental pollution. They cannot believe the tiling they found which intentionally delivered run off from fields directly into the river. In places where the run-off meets the river, the water took on an oily and rusty colored appearance. In places, a putrid smell rose up from the river. Noah and Edison have studied the effects of spreading liquid manure from concentrated animal feeding operations (CAFO) across the fields on the water table and tributaries. The American Farm and Agriculture Institute, and other big farm organizations spread propaganda saying this pollution does not occur or is within the tolerance of the environment. But as they experience this run off first hand, they know the truth is not being told.

As Noah and Edison approach a large tree, they noticed a huge Eagle nest high in its branches. They are amazed at how the tree can support so much weight. "I read where an Eagle nest can weigh more than three hundred pounds," Noah tells Eddie. "Wow, it is something how a tree can support that much weight," Eddie responds in amazement. A little further down the river two Bald Eagles pose on a tree branch as if they know full well their position as the national symbol. The boys grab a branch from an overhanging tree to steady themselves as they watch a mink on the other side of the river crawl out on a limb over the river and then pounce into the water after a muskrat. The water boils from the ensuing battle, and then the mink surfaces and returns to shore as the muskrat escaped its doom. "Did you get a picture of that Noah?" Edison asks. "I sure did, how cool!" Noah responds.

As the boys come around a bend a half-mile further down the river, Noah has just set down his Mt. Dew, when he spots something on the sand bar ahead warranting caution and further investigation. Noah reaches for the binoculars as he quietly instructs Edison to reverse their motion and get behind a tree extending into the river from shore.

"What is it Noah, what do you see?" Edison asks anticipating something exciting.

"Be quiet Eddie, let me take a look," Noah responds in a whisper. "Hold us steady Eddie" Noah says as he puts the binoculars to his eyes.

As Noah gazes at the sandbar about a quarter mile away, he cannot believe what he is seeing. He takes the binoculars from his eyes, wipes his eyes with his sleeve, and returns to his observation in disbelief.

"What is it Noah, let me have a look," Eddie implores sensing Noah's excitement.

Quietly Noah takes the binoculars from around his neck and hands them to Edison. Eddie takes a look, "Holy shit, is that what I think it is?" Eddie whispers as his heart begins to pound louder than his voice

Noah places his forefinger to his lips and urges Edison to move closer to him. "That is a mountain lion with a deer carcass at the river's edge," he says nearly out of breath from the excitement.

"What do we do?" Edison asks.

"Let's see what the lion does," Noah suggests.

Hiding behind the log, Noah and Edison watch as the mountain lion takes a drink from the river and then returns to the deer carcass. Lying down by the carcass, the mountain lion seems quite content with the world.

"Eddie, do you see that pile of brush on the other side of the river about half way between us and the mountain lion?" Noah whispers.

"Yea, I see it," Edison says in a barely audible voice.

"Do you think we can drift to that pile of brush to get a closer look and maybe some great pictures?" Noah asks.

"I don't know Noah, what if the mountain lion spots us?" Edison asks his hands trembling as he struggles to hold onto a tree branch.

"I don't think it will if we just float to the brush. If it does, it will probably run away," Noah adds for assurance.

"Okay," Edison says, "But, I am not sure this is a good idea."

"This is the chance of a lifetime Eddie; we can't pass this up," Noah insists.

After taking a minute to get the camera ready and calculate the degree to which they will need to push the canoe into the current to reach the brush pile, the boys are ready.

"Now remember Edison, we must be totally quiet. We must let the river float us to our destination or we could spook the lion," Noah instructs. Noah's biggest concern is losing an opportunity for some great pictures. Eddie's biggest concern is becoming the lion's next meal.

"Are you ready Eddie," Noah asks for assurance.

"Aye, Aye Captain Noah!" Edison responds trying to maintain a sense of humor and disguise his lack of confidence.

"On the count of three let's push as hard as we can to get to the other side of the current," Noah quietly commands.

"One-two-three," and with a big push, the boys sail across the river catching the far side current.

Catching the current they silently drifted toward the brush pile. However, they did not calculate the uncertainty of the current, and as they get to within ten feet of the brush pile, the current sweeps them back to the middle and downstream toward the mountain lion.

No longer concerned about being quiet, Edison says, "What do we do now Noah?"

"Paddle Eddie, paddle hard to keep us as far from the sandbar as possible while I take pictures," Noah responds as he grabs the camera and begins clicking away.

"What the hell Noah, you're going to take pictures when we could be killed by that lion?" Edison nearly screams.

As the boys rapidly flow down stream, the mountain lion notices them and stands by its supper. Noah, hoping he has gotten some good pictures, grabs a paddle and tells Edison to paddle like hell to get past the sandbar. As they reach the sandbar, the mountain lion watches them from no more than twenty-feet away.

As they clear the sandbar and are well out of reach of the mountain lion, the boys put down their paddles and look at each other with eyes wider than an early evening moon.

"Wow," Noah exclaims putting his hands on his head.

"Wow," Edison responds putting his hands over his heart.

Looking back at the sandbar, they notice the mountain lion has laid back down to continue its meal.

Feeling exhilarated and safe, Noah gives out a war whoop mimicked by his younger brother. "That was amazing!" Noah exclaims.

Arriving at a sandbar near the Wanata Bridge, Noah and Edison are met by their Father and Grandfather.

⸺⸺⸺◈⸺⸺⸺

Noah and Edison's Father supports them in whatever endeavor they choose to pursue. As an educational leader, Abe knows the importance of encouraging the natural curiosity of his children. He is proud of their interest in animals and nature. When Noah and Edison were younger, frequent trips to the zoo always captured their imagination. Abe often took his family camping which helped the boys develop a firsthand relationship with nature. As a result, Noah and Edison always amazed family and friends with their knowledge of all kinds of animals and their habitat.

———≫◈≪———

Noah and Edison cannot wait to share their tale of adventure with everyone. Back at Great-Grandma's house, Noah pulls out the camera to reveal the truth of their story. There on the camera are some magnificent shots of a mountain lion eating its prey on a sandbar along the Little Sioux River. Right then and there, Noah announces, "I know what I want to do with the rest of my life!"

CHAPTER 2

GROWTH OF LEADERSHIP

CURRENTLY 36-YEARS-OLD, NOAH DID HIS dissertation on invasive species in 2028, earning a doctoral degree in Environmental Science from the University of Michigan in Ann Arbor. Since that time, Noah has been observing and chronicling the spread of invasive species across the North American Continent. He has put together a most impressive video documentary of his observations for the senator.

"Tell me Noah, what is it that has you so anxious?" Jack asks in his booming voice over the phone.

"This is too important to talk about over the phone Jack. I am flying out to D.C. in the morning. I will be at your office by noon. Please set aside plenty of time for this, it is beyond belief," Noah pronounces setting a tone of mystery and urgency.

Jack grew up in the small southern Iowa town of St. Charles, just twenty-five-minutes south of the State Capital of Des Moines. St. Charles is joined together with Truro and New Virginia to form the Interstate 35 School District which got its name from Interstate 35 which snakes through the hilly southern Iowa district. Jack was an excellent student and star football linemen for the Roadrunners.

Jack's journey to the United States Senate seems meteoric in many ways. In 2029, he graduated with a law degree from Columbia University, specializing in environmental law. Following graduation Jack went to work for the Environmental Protection Agency. In 2032, he was elected to the United States Congress. He served three terms before being elected as a United States Senator from Iowa in 2038.

There is no secret as to why Jack felt the calling to public service and a life in politics.

"Dad," young Jack Joseph called out, "Do you need to be gone to Washington D.C. again?" At 13, Jack understands, but he doesn't like the void created in his father's absence.

"Jack, you know I hate to leave, but it is only for a few days, and before you know it, I will return home. I have important work to do for the hard-working people of this country," his father reminded his young son.

"But Dad, Ainsley and Ivey will drive me nuts," Jack says in exasperation.

Jeremy can hear his very gifted daughter Ainsley upstairs playing her guitar. Ainsley is an aspiring musician, and Jeremy is confident she will be a star one day. As for now, it bothers his son that she gets so much attention for her musical talent.

"You will be fine Jack," Jeremy says as young Ivey runs by with all the energy of a high-octane kid. "Learning to deal with your sisters will pay off for you someday," he says with a smile.

Jack's father works for the Social Security Administration; however, it is his union work which pulls him away from home. As a senior officer for the American Federation of Government Employees, Jeremy makes frequent visits to the nation's capital city for a variety of reasons. He tries hard to instill in his son a feeling of public service. Jeremy's father instilled this in him and he wants to pass it along.

"Jack," Jeremy tells his son, "Life is not about serving yourself. There are too many people who pursue only their self-interest without consideration for the public good. It is an honor to be in public service, and it often requires a great deal of personal sacrifice."

Jack admires his father. He also takes pride in the fact that his father often works in close proximity to men and women of great power. He likes to hear his father's stories about different men and women serving our nation.

Jack's father, Jeremy, committed himself to the principles of the Democratic Party before he even graduated from high school. Jeremy believes in courageous leadership and feels there is no room in public service for those seeking personal gain. To Jeremy, it does not matter the political party. If you are in it for the wrong reason, it is just plain wrong.

A few years later as a junior in high school, Jack accompanied his father on one of his trips to Washington D.C. He recalls the excitement and pride he felt as his father made the nation's capital his place of work.

"Jack, tonight I am going to take you to some awe-inspiring places. I want you to constantly keep in mind that these places, while often memorializing a man or woman, really stand for the ideals, integrity, courage, and service they provided this nation."

"I understand Dad. I am so glad to be here with you. So where are we going to go?" Jack can hardly contain his excitement.

"Let's start at the Washington Monument and then go to the Jefferson Memorial, Lincoln Memorial, Roosevelt Memorial, and finish with the Kennedy Grave site at Arlington Cemetery. How does that sound?"

"I can hardly believe I'm here," Jack says anxious to begin this exploration of the nation's capital.

"Believe it, you are son," Jeremy assures.

"How long will we be here Dad?" Jack asks hoping it will be long enough to get to know the city.

"We will be in D.C. four days Jack. For two days, we will spend our time on Capitol Hill where you will get a firsthand look at the sacred halls of representative government. I have several meetings scheduled, so there is a good chance you will get to meet some members of Congress and the Senate."

"This seems too good to be true," Jack exclaims.

"There are lots of good things about this city and our government Jack, but it does not come without a price. On our last day here, we will visit and reflect at the war memorials. Hundreds of thousands of young men and women have given their lives serving this country. We will take time to sit on the Mall where we have a good view of the White House, Capitol Building, and Lincoln Memorial. We will reflect on the power in the executive and legislative branches of government that allow them to send young people off to war.

"Take a good look at the Washington Monument Jack," his father implores as they stand near the base of this great monument.

"How tall is this monument Dad?" Jack asks while craning his neck to see the top.

"The Washington Monument is an obelisk constructed in memory of George Washington and stands just over 554 feet tall making it the tallest stone structure in the world," Jeremy informs his son. "An interesting tidbit about the Washington Monument is that Vice President Al Gore made a sudden stop here on election night in 2000 to take a call in the lower level of the monument. The caller told him not to concede the election due to questionable returns in Florida."

"That didn't turn out so well for Gore," Jack reminds.

"Let's walk over to the Lincoln Memorial at the west end of the reflecting pool," Jeremy suggests.

"This is sure a big open area surrounded by a lot of buildings," Jack notices.

"This is the National Mall, and like everything here, it belongs to the people. The National Mall has been the site of many important gatherings and protests. Just imagine this entire area filled with people for a protest or a Presidential Inauguration," Jeremy challenges his son. "Dr. Martin Luther King Jr. gave his famous "I have a Dream" speech from the steps of the Lincoln Memorial to thousands of people on the Mall."

As they ascend the stairs to the Lincoln Memorial, Jack's eyes are transfixed on the gigantic sculpture of Abraham Lincoln seated inside the memorial. He feels like he is entering a holy shrine, so he enters quietly and reverently.

"This was a great man Dad," Jack whispers.

"Yes, he was son," Jeremy responds. "Abraham Lincoln was elected to the presidency at a perilous time in our nation's history. From the inception of the nation, slavery was an insidious wound on the fabric of a free society. Lincoln, hailing from the free state of Illinois made his feelings about slavery clear throughout the presidential campaign. The southern states so economically dependent upon slavery felt a Lincoln presidency threatened their very existence. In the south, blacks were not considered fully human. They were considered property. Add to the mix the issue of state's rights, and you have a very volatile political environment. Every president since Washington has done things to strengthen the power of the Federal Government. The South saw Lincoln as a diehard Federalist with no time for state's rights. So, when Lincoln was elected president, South Carolina immediately succeeded from the union and thus the die was cast for the Civil War. Lincoln's entire time as president was spent devoted to saving the union during a bloody and brutal war in which hundreds of thousands of Americans (north and south) were slaughtered. As costly as the Civil War was, it provided the opportunity for Lincoln to emancipate the slaves and usher in the 13th Amendment to the Constitution of the United States which abolished slavery. In the end the union was victorious with Lee's surrender to Grant on April 9, 1865. A few days later on April 14, 1865, Lincoln was assassinated."

As they turn to leave the Lincoln Memorial, Jack is caught up in the view of the National Mall from the top of the stairs. He can visualize the Mall filled with excitement and enthusiasm as people gather to celebrate or make their feelings known. He is struck by the power of a free society.

"This is a great place Dad; I want to work here someday myself," Jack reveals.

It is a long walk across the Arlington Memorial Bridge to Arlington Cemetery, but it is a beautiful day, so Jeremy and Jack make the journey on foot. As they near Arlington Cemetery, Jack is overwhelmed by the endless rows of white tombstones. "This place is huge Dad," Jack exclaims as he looks up and down the rolling hills.

"Arlington National Cemetery is a 624-acre military cemetery containing 400,000 graves of mostly young men and women who gave their life for their country. There are also many famous people buried at Arlington of which President John F. Kennedy is one of them. If we walk up this hill, we will find his grave," Jeremy informs Jack.

As they walk the concrete path leading up the hill, they arrive at a level spot surrounded by a single chain at about knee level accentuated with the Eternal Flame. The sight is simple, but the feeling it invokes is profound. Jack immediately finds the head stone marking the President's Tomb. He stands in silence for the longest time while pondering the significance of this man, his life, and his death.

"Who are these other people buried here Dad?" Jack asks thinking he knows Jacqueline Kennedy but less sure of the smaller markers.

"Jacqueline was the President's wife and First Lady," Jeremy says adding, "She was a young woman of thirty-four when the president was assassinated. The story of her life is tragic in many ways. The smaller markers are the graves of their infant son Patrick to the left of the President's grave, and their stillborn daughter Arbella to the right of Jacqueline's grave."

Jack continues to gaze at the grave site as if in a trance. He then turns and begins to read the inscriptions on the semi-circular granite wall just below the grave site. The inscriptions come from President Kennedy's Inaugural Address of 1961.

"How come no one speaks like this anymore Dad?" Jack says impressed with the eloquence of J.F.K.'s words.

"Kennedy had a wonderful speech writer and J.F.K. was a master in the delivery of a speech. Kennedy and his team believed an effective message required a bit of poetry. Words are power, and Kennedy made them powerful. This is part of what made John Kennedy so inspiring," his Dad shares.

"I understand that Dad, but it seems like no one gets that today," Jack adds.

"Perhaps you are right Jack, let's walk around the hill where we will find JFK's brothers buried," his Dad suggests.

As they walk the short distance to the Robert and Edward Kennedy grave sites, Jack becomes intrigued by the mansion sitting at the top of the hill.

"Why is there a mansion on top of this hill Dad?" Jack inquires as they stop to gaze upon this brilliantly white house and its imposing stature atop the hill.

"That is Arlington House, Jack. That mansion once belonged to Confederate General Robert E. Lee and his wife Mary Anna Randolph Curtis, a granddaughter of George and Martha Washington. During the Civil War, the Federal Government confiscated this land and house for the purpose of a National Cemetery. Later, Arlington House became a museum for Robert E. Lee," his Dad reveals.

Now Jeremy and Jack arrive at the grave sites of Robert F. and Edward M. Kennedy. Jeremy shares the inspiring and tragic story of Robert F. Kennedy. He explains to Jack that Robert Kennedy inspired millions of people to public service. Like John Kennedy, Robert's demise came at the point of an assassin's gun.

"What about Edward Kennedy?" his son asks.

"After Robert's death, Teddy became the lone surviving Kennedy brother. Once a powerful trio, two assassins and perhaps unrevealed conspiracies brought about their downfall. Teddy continued to serve in the United States Senate until his death in 2009," Jeremy states with sadness in his voice.

Jack wants to know more, lots more, but the sun is going down in the west and they need to be heading back to their hotel. Before departing, Jack and his Dad pause to take in the awe-inspiring view of the capital city from that hill at Arlington. The sunset sheds a brilliant hue across the marble edifices and buildings which represent the cradle of our national existence.

"Isn't it interesting that during the Civil War, the only thing that separated the Southern States from the Union was the Potomac River flowing right in front of us," Jeremy remarks.

The two of them stand silently before moving on down the hill.

Jack remembers this trip with his father as a defining experience in his life. After this trip, Jack became determined to follow his father's footsteps into public service. This single experience set him on a path to law school, the environmental protection agency, Congress, and now the United States Senate.

Leaning back in the comfort of the overstuffed leather chair behind the magnificent walnut desk in his office, Senator Joseph turns his attention to Noah's pronouncement. Noah is world renown for his work with invasive species. In fact, other nations have been seeking Noah's services for years. Noah's devotion to the North American Continent is admirable, but even Jack believes Noah's talents need to take on a much larger perspective.

Picking up the phone Senator Joseph declares, "Nora, clear my schedule for tomorrow afternoon."

Nora has been Jack's personal secretary since his first election to congress, "But senator, you are expected at a strategy session of the leadership at two o'clock. The minority leader will not be happy should you miss this meeting."

"Nora, you tell the minority leader that the senator from Iowa will not be present, and I will make it clear why later."

"As you wish senator," Nora says as she picks up the phone to deliver the message.

CHAPTER 3

AN OMINOUS VISIT

B ACK AT THE UNIVERSITY OF Michigan, Dr. Abraham calls in Dr. Contessa Margery. Contessa Margery worked with Dr. Abraham as a doctoral assistant during her doctoral study. He now seeks her assistance in getting ready for his meeting with Senator Joseph. Contessa's parents, who attended Iowa State University, were not happy with her decision to attend the University of Michigan. Contessa on the other hand, could not pass up the opportunity to work with her cousin Noah while seeking a double Doctoral Degree in geology and geo-politics. She recently received her degrees before her 25th birthday. Contessa knows no one as knowledgeable and capable as Noah. His leadership and guidance were critical to obtaining her degrees and embarking on a career.

———≫◆≪———

Contessa's interest in geology sprung forth from many family trips as a young girl in which the examination and photographing of rocks documented the places they visited. Contessa's parents treasured the National Park system, and they took time to explain to Contessa and her sisters the importance of respecting the resources of the National Parks.

During her childhood, Contessa visited incredible geographic places such as Yellowstone, Glacier, the Black Hills, Devil's Tower, the Grand Canyon, Zion, and Yosemite. Contessa's parents wanted their girls to experience as many of nature's places of wonder as possible.

Contessa grew up appreciating the fact that her parents made travel and exploration a part of their family's experience.

She remembers her Mom and Dad picking up rocks at every stop and discussing the uniqueness of each rock to the area. Once they had examined, discussed, a photographed a rock, her parents would return it to the spot from which it had been taken. She recalls mimicking her parents and picking up just any old rock. Tiffany and Steve would humor their girls and made sure pictures recorded each and every discovery.

Tiffany and Steve were always in education mode teaching their girls about this unique blue ball, called Earth, and how, we share it with all living things. Their investment was key to instilling in their girls an interest in the unique history of the Earth. Through the years, Contessa developed a geological knowledge of the United States even before pursuing it as a career.

Contessa's fondest memories are of Yellowstone National Park. While they made the journey to Yellowstone on a few occasions, her favorite trip occurred when she was fourteen.

"Dad, is it true that Yellowstone National Park is actually a volcano?" Steve has told the girls this fact before, but Contessa finds the story fascinating.

"Yellowstone National Park is not only a volcano, it is a supervolcano" he reminds Contessa and her sisters.

"What is the difference between a volcano and a supervolcano?" Contessa is on the edge of her seat for this great story.

"A supervolcano is a large area that when it erupts, it does so with incredible force. If the Yellowstone volcano were to erupt, it would send rocks, dust, ash, and smoke for miles into the air. The molten lava from such an eruption would run like a wide river of fire for possibly hundreds of miles" Steve tells his girls as they sit with wide eyes looking about.

"I don't want to go to Yellowstone!" Gemma proclaims, "I'm scared."

"There is nothing to be scared about Gem," Tiffany reassures. "The Yellowstone volcano has not erupted for hundreds of thousands of years, and it is not going to erupt now, Right Steve?"

"If it's dangerous, why do we come here?" Stella wants to know.

"It is not dangerous Stella; it is a beautiful place to visit with lots of wonders to see and explore," Tiffany stresses. "There is so much to learn at Yellowstone."

"Just think about it girls, when Yellowstone erupted over six-hundred-thousand years ago, it brought to the surface rocks that are millions of years old," Steve adds with excitement.

"Look over in that meadow girls, a herd of buffalo," Tiffany is redirecting their attention.

"The females have calves! Also, they are called bison," Contessa nearly yells. "Can we get out and watch them?"

Tiffany smiles and chuckles to herself at Contessa's correction. Her girls are very smart, and she is very proud of that fact.

"There is a pull-off just ahead, we will stop for a little bit. Just remember we all stay together, and we do not approach the animals. These are wild buffalo, or I mean bison. We must keep our distance from them," Steve reminds his family as well as himself. Steve loves to get pictures, and sometimes he forfeits safety for a great picture.

As they travel up the road, they pass a sign which says, "Yellowstone Caldera."

"What is a caldera?" Stella has an inquiring mind.

"I know, I can answer this one," Contessa has her hand up as if wanting the teacher to call on her.

"Go ahead Contessa," Tiffany nods. "You don't have to raise your hand sweetheart, but thank you anyway."

"When a volcano erupts, it gets rid of all the pressure and hot stuff inside. With the loss of this pressure and material, the middle of the volcano falls inside the volcano to form a floor called the caldera," Contessa is beaming. "How did I do?"

"That was excellent Tess," Steve says followed by a Hurrah for Tessa.

"I don't feel like I am inside a volcano," Gemma says with disbelief.

"That is because the Yellowstone volcano is so big. The diameter of the caldera is about 30 miles by 45 miles. This is a huge area, so we don't really notice it unless we look at the mountains around us, or," Steve stops in mid-sentence.

"Or what Dad," Contessa demands.

"Or, we see a geyser, or thermal pool like the ones just ahead" Steve points to a stream of steam rising above the ground in the distance.

"Can we go see?" Stella is as anxious as a kid awaiting a ride on a Merry-go-Round.

"Slow down Stella, we will go in that direction," her Mom assures. "However, when we get there you must listen and not go close to these things. They are extremely hot and dangerous. You must stay beside Dad and Me."

"I love geology," Contessa declares. "It is so interesting!"

———————◆———————

"Contessa, did you organize the research for my presentation in Washington tomorrow?" Dr. Abraham asks looking over his reading glasses from behind the computer on his desk.

"Yes, Dr. Abraham, the presentation is on your iMicro 11," She notes.

———————◆———————

Microsoft and Apple merged in 2032 in a trillion-dollar deal made possible by a Republican Congress and president seeking to undo all laws opposed to monopolies. At that time, predatory capitalism was in vogue, and the dogs of unbridled corporate power were in full assault. Thanks to the pendulum, which swings from one side of the political spectrum to the other, democrats seized power in 3026 just in time to slow corporate domination, but much damage was done.

At the current time, the government hangs in the balance with a split House of Representatives, a Republican Senate, and a Democratic President. For the past several decades, a government in gridlock has become all too familiar. Over the years, the people have come to accept the inevitability of a government incapable of getting things done.

———————◆———————

"Sit down Contessa, I want to go through this presentation with you. I need your honest feedback. I plan to use the hologram presentation mode to convey the significance of my findings. What do you think?" Dr. Abraham asks.

"I cannot imagine using anything but the hologram mode. What you have discovered is truly earth shattering, and you need to capture the full attention of Senator Joseph," Contessa stresses with a sense of urgency.

"While my audience is going to be our cousin, Senator Joseph, and, I could have captured his interest over the phone, I want this to resonate to his very core. I need him to be a fervent messenger to the powers in Washington that we may be nearing the point of no return," Noah says in near desperation.

"If this does not shake him to the very core, we are all in deep trouble," Contessa says grabbing Dr. Abraham by the arm. Dr. Abraham is a strong man. He ran four years of cross country and track for St. Ambrose University before transferring to the University of Michigan. He is still committed to a running regime of several miles a day. Still, Contessa's determined grip offers a reminding sting about the importance of his mission.

"Thank you, Contessa for all of your help, I shall see you when I return. Wish me luck," Dr. Abraham says with sincerity.

"You don't need luck Noah, just stay with the presentation and speak with all of the conviction in your heart," Contessa advises.

Contessa leaves Noah alone in his office to ponder the serious nature of his journey.

<hr>

Global climate change has been around for several decades, and people have grown accustom to the idea of living with increased catastrophes. As predicted twenty-five years before, the great ice masses of the Arctic, Antarctic, and Himalayan Glacier Basin are rapidly disappearing. The oceans are warming as the ice masses of the north and south diminish in size altering the oceanic currents of cold and warm water. Shrinking ice masses along with increased tropical storms and hurricanes has brought about a rising of the sea level by several meters in many areas of the Earth. Venice, an important center of trade and culture for centuries, no longer exists. Many places in India,

China, Southeast Asia, Egypt, the Netherlands, and the United States are submerged resulting in millions of displaced people and trillions of dollars in lost assets. Given enough time, many places once alive with civilization and commerce will be regulated to the mythological sunken city of Atlantis.

Despite the warnings from environmentalists, people are being sold a bill of goods about "these times like all times will pass." People in modernized nations have grown accustom to the idea of catastrophe as a way of life. They have also grown to accept the necessity of war. Indifferent to the sacrifice of young blood and treasure, people have come to accept war as a means of self-preservation. As long as war occurs beyond our shores and the territory of our allies, we are content to keep them there as a means of security.

But war does more than provide a false sense of security. It provides prosperity for those who profit from the marketing of death. For the pure capitalist, war is just another means to an end in obtaining power. The United States, the very country that proclaims exceptionalism, is in fact the architect and merchant of death. So, the wealthy and powerful sell the idea of waging war as a means of keeping death from our very shores and doors. It is an ugly argument, but it works, and that is all that matters.

In the early 21st Century, it was predicted that the rapidly disappearing Great Himalayan Glacier Basin would lead to war between the most populated areas of Asia. Then, in 2025, war broke out between China and India over this rapidly vanishing water supply. Over the past 14-years, the war has resolved little and resulted in the loss of millions of lives. Washington has done nothing to broker peace. Population is a real threat to the human race, and what better way to curtail population than to allow the nations with the greatest population to kill each other. The prevailing thought is if they are fighting each other, they have little time to be a threat to anyone else. Furthermore, the nation's economy booms from the demand for our greatest national resource, weapons. In essence, the United States sells trillions of dollars of weapons to China and India, as well as all over the world. The United States holds the crucial scales representing a balance of power around the world.

The industrialists, technologists, capitalists, and politicians know that people can be easily sedated with prosperity and nothing brings prosperity like the sale of weapons. As long as the nightly news brings the horrors of death and destruction into the living room from parts of the world far removed from the comfort of the American home, all seems well and good. Furthermore, people have been desensitized to the horrors of war by graphic television, movies, and electronic gaming. There is nothing war can present that has not already been presented in abundance through electronic media. So, politicians promise safety and security, and after all, in a world gone crazy, what more could people want: Safety, security, and comfort; to hell with life, liberty and the pursuit of happiness, a far too dangerous notion.

As Noah boards the plane for Washington D.C. on this May 30, 2039 morning, politicians all across the nation are making political hay off of this national day honoring those who have served the country. Noah recalls the pageantry and solemn ceremonies of Memorial Days gone by. He thinks of his great-grandfather's service as a Marine storming the beaches of Iwo Jima during World War II.

Once on the plane, Noah's mind drifts back to years before when he first became interested in animals of all kinds. He remembers sitting on a stool in his grandparents four season room watching just about anything he could on Animal Planet. He thinks about all of the amazing creatures he has learned about of the past and present. He smiles recalling all of the praise and encouragement he received from his parents and grandparents about his knowledge and interest in animals. Most of all, he remembers that canoe trip down the Little Sioux River.

As his plane leaves the ground and gains altitude, he looks out the window and wonders if anyone suspects what he knows. From thirty-five thousand feet, the Earth below doesn't look much different than it did ten-twenty-thirty years ago, but if you get closer, the similarities disappear. Burying your head in the sand cannot hide the fact that the world will never be the same again. Noah feels a tear rolling gently down the side of his cheek. The tear reveals the fear and sensibilities Noah feels for the time ahead.

"Hey mister, hey mister, can I have a look?" came the call from the young boy sitting beside Noah.

Startled from his trance, Noah finds a young boy who reminds him of Opie Taylor from old re-runs of the Andy Griffith Show. "What, oh sure, here trade me seats."

"You don't need to do that," his mother sitting on the far side of the boy insists.

"It is no problem; it is a view every young boy should have an opportunity to enjoy," Noah graciously slides the boy over his lap and into his seat, as he slides over next to the boy's mom.

"Thanks, that is very kind of you," his mother offers. "Might I ask what you do?"

"I am a Doctor of Environmental Science with a specialty in invasive species," Noah responds. "By the way, my name is Noah Abraham."

"Nice to meet you, my name is Nancy Ingersol."

Noah finds himself enamored by the attractive and friendly nature of his traveling companion. Her light brown hair and prominent cheek bones give her a Jennifer Garner appearance. She definitely smells nice, just a hint of Chanel No. 5. Her soft breathy voice combined with deep blue eyes and a warm smile have him captivated. Struggling to say something, he finally speaks.

"And what is it you do Nancy?" Noah asks.

"I am a single parent living with my Father in Ann Arbor until I can get back on my feet," Nancy says somewhat hesitantly.

"So where might I ask are you going?" Noah inquires.

"We are going to Washington D.C. so Langdon can visit his father, Howard, who works for the state department," she answers.

As they both turn their attention to the ten-year old boy totally engrossed with the view outside the window, Nancy adds "Langdon is absolutely crazy about animals."

"Your Mom says you like animals Langdon," Noah inquires.

"I do; do you know the fastest animal?" Langdon asks.

Playing along, Noah says, "I am not sure, can you tell me?"

Noah has made himself a friend for the rest of the flight. Langdon is relentless. He knows so much about animals, and he can rattle off facts with great ease.

"Langdon, why don't you let this nice man have his seat back, he would probably like to rest" his mother suggests.

"It is fine Nancy; he reminds me a great deal of myself at that age," Noah assures.

As the captain of the plane announces their imminent landing, Noah reminds himself of the task which lies ahead. Sitting with Langdon and his Mom has been a nice diversion. For a short bit, Noah felt like everything might be normal. Now, he has returned to reality, and he remembers the importance of his mission to all people, including his traveling companions.

As the plane rolls to a stop at the terminal, Noah thanks Nancy and Langdon for the company. He encourages Langdon to always keep his interest in animals. Grabbing his bag from the overhead compartment, he quickly makes his way down the aisle leaving his new friends behind.

As he exits the terminal, he looks for an available cab. Then he feels a tap on his shoulder. Turning, he finds a tall distinguished looking young man smiling, "Dr. Abraham?"

"Yes, I am him."

"I am Senator Joseph's Chief of Staff, Arnold, he told me to pick you up and bring you directly to his office," the young man pronounces.

"Well, I thought I might check into a hotel and freshen up a bit before seeing the Senator," Noah responds.

"No, I don't think so. The Senator is anxious to see you, and he will not be kept waiting. Besides, he said you would be staying with him at his Georgetown apartment," the young man informs Noah.

"Well then, let's be on our way!" Noah proclaims.

Hopping into the black limousine, Arnold instructs the driver to flash through the lights. With this, Arnold activates the flashing lights on the car which allows them free passage from the airport to Senator Joseph's office.

Noah feels as if he has entered an entirely different world. He and Jack are close cousins and associates, but he has never experienced this kind of VIP treatment. Settling back into his seat, Noah realizes he is on a very special ride.

CHAPTER 4

DESCENDING DARKNESS

As Noah zooms across Washington D.C. to the Senate Office of his cousin, his younger brother Edison Jude is deep in the swamplands of what was once Miami, Florida. At 33, Edison Jude has a doctorate in Aquatic Science from the University of California-Berkley. Dr. Jude is a world-renowned expert in reptiles. His published articles and books about the devastation of Global Warming are well read, but not well received. He is currently working on a Theory of Reptile Evolution.

What once served as a world hub for commerce gave way to swampland four years before as the ocean rose faster, and to a much greater degree than anticipated. With the warming sea water came increased storm activity, and Miami became the target of monster hurricanes. The intensity and longevity of these storms left Miami Beach and Greater Miami in ruins. The Florida Keys are gone, and any land barrier which may have existed between the Miami region and the Everglades has disappeared.

When such catastrophe occurs, it does not take long for the creatures of the sea and swamp to rule. Anyone visiting the area formally known as Southern Florida will engage a ghoulish experience at best. The water depths vary to the point that some sections of Miami and Miami Beach are well submerged, where other areas are covered with ten to twenty-feet of water with no indication of it receding. Low tide offers no opportunity to salvage that which the sea has claimed as its own.

A view from the air or at a distance reveals what appears to be a city rising up out of the water. Miami is home to over three hundred high-rise buildings. The downtown area is a cluster of some of Florida's tallest buildings such as the Financial Center, Marques Residences, Wells Fargo Center, and Miami Tower. The sea has claimed everything below street level and in many places, everything two and three stories high. This means there is a great deal above water, but the challenges are beyond comprehension. The most difficult challenge involves the daily battering of the sea which wears down the very foundation supporting these tall structures. The waves roll in only to crash down on the foundations of these buildings. It is a rhythmic battering over and over like some giant sledge hammer jarring and weakening the structure until it finally surrenders to the sea. Over the four years since the sea laid claim to this area, several foundations have given way and the buildings have simply collapsed.

The most ghoulish aspect of the entire scene reminds a person of the oil still seeping from the USS Arizona at Pearl Harbor nearly 100-years after its sinking. The difference with Miami involves what is seeping to the surface. All aspects of human society continually drift upward as the sea loses its bond to that which once represented an important part of the mortal world. This includes thousands of corpses trapped inside the edifices of human existence as they are released when buildings yield to the forces of the sea.

Even more ghoulish are the coffins which when liberated from their concrete entombment float to the surface as if looking for a second chance at life. Miami and Miami Beach have hundreds of cemeteries, and none of them were constructed to withstand the battering of a relentless ocean. Every effort has been made to retrieve the bodies and the coffins, but there is not enough time or manpower to get it done. It is not known what just floats away, getting lost to the sea, and what becomes food for the creatures of the deep.

Capitalism never rests, and an entirely new industry of corpse recovery spun off the already lucrative undertaking business. These businesses mine the sea for corpses as aggressively as an old forty-niner mined for gold. Once harvested, the business uses state of the art technology for identification. Once identified, the closest of kin is contacted, and a deal struck for the return of the body. The costs involve a recovery fee, finder's fee, and identification fee all adding up to a handsome amount.

Only the bravest or the stupidest of divers enter the waters of Miami. The waters are infested with reptiles and sharks. Over the years, the Great White Shark has grown to incredible proportions, and Miami provides an excellent environment for these predators. Most humans such as Dr. Jude enter these waters in the protection of a submergible craft. Once under the water, the unbelievable horror is tempered by the minds self-defense mechanism to perceive it as a bad dream, or something out of the movies.

As Dr. Jude looks out the submergible window, the scene is surreal. The streets are lined with cars and trucks patiently waiting for their owners to drive them away. All structures are covered in corral and other sea vegetation. The submergible slowly works it way through the debris strewn waters. Everything which had at one time been living now lay silently at the bottom, trapped in cars and buildings, or silently floating bloated beyond recognition, and in most cases half eaten. Ironically, the sight of a sunken cemetery has little impact on the visitors to this nether region, for the entire area of Miami and Miami Beach has become a cemetery.

Dr. Jude has done all of his reptile research in southern Florida, other than the six months he spent in Africa, South America, and Asia. As a doctoral student and now a practitioner, all of his research focuses on his Theory of Reptile Evolution. Over the past few years, Dr. Jude has carefully measured the incredible growth of reptiles in Southern Florida. His findings are published in several scientific journals, and receive recognition from the world's scientific community. Unfortunately, his work has had little impact on politicians, the people who make the laws which are destroying the environment.

Despite Dr. Jude's warnings that crocodiles, alligators, snakes, and sharks are rapidly growing to enormous size and density, very few people in power pay attention. Dr. Jude has made it clear that these creatures pose a real threat to people living in or visiting the Southern part of the continental United States. Despite his warnings, politicians guarantee the people it is of no real concern. If necessary, the politicians say they will call out the National Guard or activate Federal troops to deal with this menace. In a moment of brilliance, someone even suggested building a fence.

As the limo pulls along the curb in front of the Senate Office Building, Senator Joseph's Chief of Staff gets out and opens the door for Dr. Abraham. As Noah steps forth upon the hallowed turf of generations gone by, he feels a sense of nobility of purpose. Perhaps the city is not dead.

Noah brings with him a small electronic device carrying all of the information he needs to make the power brokers in the nation's capital take notice. He wants to do this in the most dramatic and yet appropriate manner. His cousin, Senator Joseph, is well respected, and if he were to command attention, maybe, just maybe there might be hope. Most politicians consider Dr. Abraham a bit of a fringe thinker. Noah is fortunate to have a connection in Washington who not only loves him, but believes in his work.

Entering the Senator's office, "Noah, my dear cousin, how are you? What brings you to Washington?"

"As I mentioned on the phone, I have information absolutely critical to our survival as a human race," there is urgency in Noah's voice.

"Well, I am certainly interested in the survival of the human race. I think?" responds the Senator giving his cousin a wink.

Looking about the room, the senator sends everyone out of the room to provide him and Noah time alone. Actually no one is ever alone in Washington, the city is a surveillance center. At least the air of privacy promotes an open conversation. Senator Joseph truly knows the game well and employs the services of the most tech savvy staff. He also hires the services of former CIA operatives to make sure all attempts to spy on him fail.

"So, Noah, how is your Dad? What do you hear from your brother and sister? We are all proud of Kennedy's selection as the head of the United States Olympic Committee," the senator declares.

"My Dad is enjoying retirement. Dad is involved in an AAU senior's program which keeps him constantly on the go. He likes to keep busy if you remember," Noah shares about his father.

"Oh, I remember your Dad was very sacrificing when it came to his kids and sports. I have lots of love for Uncle Abe. I am glad he is doing well," Senator Joseph says as he pours a drink at his office bar. "Would you like to wet your whistle, Noah? I imagine it was a long flight."

"No thank you, I need to freshen up before I loosen up," Noah responds.

"So, tell me how are things with Kennedy and Edison?" the senator asks.

"I haven't heard much lately, but the Olympics just gained a real asset. Kennedy is a marvelous choice to head our countries Olympic Program. As for Eddie, I worry a great deal. He has chosen for himself a life among the vermin of the world. To this day, I believe he watched one too many episodes of Turtle Man," Noah says with a chuckle.

Kennedy Kay exited West Fork High School loving to run. To her father's delight she attended the University of Northern Iowa earning a B.A. in Art Education. Kennedy then followed in her Grandmother and Aunt Tiffany's footsteps, earning an M.A. degree in Business Administration. While Kennedy did not run collegiately, she committed herself to a running regime which would challenge any college athlete. Upon graduation from the University of Northern Iowa, she began preparing to qualify for the 2024 Olympics. After qualifying for the 2024 Olympic Team, she met with an unfortunate injury when she stepped in a gopher hole while training, and tore her medial cartilage on her left knee. With no time for repair and rehabilitation, she had to drop from the team as a runner, but her devotion to the sport earned her a position as a coach. She has worked as an Olympic coach and administrator ever since and now has been appointed Head of the United States Olympic Program.

"Well, l I just heard from Edison last week" the Senator boasts.

"What the hell, I don't quite know what to say" Noah responds in exasperation.

"Cheer up Noah – Eddie and I have been communicating for years regarding his observations in Southern Florida. His cries from the water wilderness of what once was a thriving metropolis reminds me so much of John the Baptist, I just hope he doesn't meet a similar fate," Jack says with real concern.

"Come on Jack, you know Edison is as credible a scientist as you will find. He does not see reptiles in the same manner as most people. To him they are just another animal needing to be carefully studied. We should be grateful to have scientists, who like undertakers, select a rather peculiar profession," Noah suggests with tongue in cheek.

"Don't take me wrong Noah, Eddie and I have a very professional and caring relationship. I find his observations astounding and well worth serious consideration. But the problem is not me, the problem is all those political horse's butts who not only do not want to listen, but just do not want to hear it," Jack says while pacing and waving his hands overhead.

"Well, you may not want to hear what I have to present. I am only going to offer you the most disturbing information you have ever heard or been asked to consider," Noah warns.

"I would not expect anything less from our family. We are a family that wants to make a difference. We are the fourth generation since Annie and Grandpa, Grandma Martha and Grandpa Jerry. They wanted us all to be happy, and perhaps if we consider the Greek definition of happiness "the pursuit of excellence", we are nearing the golden ring" Jack says with a laugh.

"Oh, what the hell, I guess all I can do is give it to you. Please lower the lights and I shall begin," Noah requests taking a primary position in the room.

"Just a second Noah, let me get another drink. Do you still like Grandpa's old favorite of JD and Coke?" Jack says as he turns to the office bar.

Knowing his cousin will not accept no as an answer a second time, Noah responds, "JD and Coke would be just fine."

Returning with the drinks, Jack says "Here we go, let's see what you've got?"

"I brought my exhibits as holograms in the event you would like to interact with them," Noah informs Jack in a challenging manner. Noah really wants Jack to interact with the holograms.

"Well let's see what you've got," Jack insists.

"Here is hologram one, it is of northwest Ontario near Red Lake at a longitude of 94 degrees and a latitude of 51 degrees in January, 2014. Just take a good hard look at the picture. Don't leave one thing unnoticed," Noah commands as he sits back and allows the senator to manipulate the picture to view it from every angle.

"Here is the second hologram; it is of northwest Ontario near Red Lake in January of this year. It is the very same area as in the first picture. Notice anything different?" Noah asks.

"There doesn't seem to be as much snow in the second picture," the senator says.

"Take your finger and move the picture around for a different perspective," Noah urges. "Now what do you notice?"

"It seems rather green," the senator recognizes.

"Look closer" Dr. Abraham implores. "Take your time and tell me everything. Look deep into the picture."

"I see what looks like alfalfa and I see some small flowers. Wait on that flower I see a spider and I believe under that log I see a snake," Senator Joseph reveals.

"Look over there, Jack" Noah points in the direction he wants his cousin to look. "Do you see the skunk foraging? What about here, can you see the wood chuck?" Noah asks.

"I see them now Noah, but why is that so significant. I remember sometimes seeing a skunk in Iowa during a warm December day," the senator reminds his cousin.

"Jack, the average January temperature in this area was between 9 degrees and a minus 13 degrees Fahrenheit in 2014. Today, the average temperature is between 30 degrees and 52 degrees Fahrenheit. Those flowers are warm climate Bastard Toadflax and Bell Flowers that never grew in this area of Ontario twenty-five years ago. All of the insects, reptiles, and animals you see should be hibernating. Historically, they never reveal themselves until April or even May twenty-five years ago," Dr. Abraham stresses.

"I get it, Noah, climate change is real and having a profound impact on our planet. How is this anything new?" the senator says.

"I know this did not just happen overnight, but what I have shown you is just a lead into the big revelation," Noah says preparing his cousin for what is about to come.

Jack remains silent because he is not sure what Noah expects him to say and he is still trying to make sense of Noah's presentation.

"Now, take a good look at this northwest Ontario Mountain Lion in 2014, and now what appears to be a lion in this same area today," Noah urges.

"Well, I certainly see the difference in the second picture. Has the second picture been doctored to look prehistoric?" Jack asks Noah. "It appears to have fangs."

"No, the picture has not been doctored Jack. In the second picture you are looking at the resurgence of Smilodon, the Sabre-Toothed Tiger, a mammal extinct for over eleven thousand years."

"Bullshit, that is impossible. This must be a doctored picture. This beast is massive!" Jack exclaims in disbelief.

"Use your finger to manipulate the hologram Senator. As you move around the beast, notice the muscular structure particularly in the neck," Noah wants his cousin to get a real sense of this animal.

"It doesn't look any bigger than a regular lion, but it sure looks strong," Jack acknowledges. "What is it eating?"

"Don't be fooled by its size," Noah asserts. "This animal is about the same size as a lion, but it is far stronger than anything you have ever seen. Despite the short legs, the Smilodon is quick and those neck muscles allow it to sink its eight-inch canine teeth deep into its prey. Believe it or not, what it is eating is an adult male moose."

"That looks like a pretty big moose Noah. So, this lion must be a scavenger?"

"Over the years Moose have flourished in number and size. Twenty-years ago, an adult Bull Moose stood about six to seven feet at the shoulders and weighted around 1,500 pounds. The bull moose this Sabre-Toothed Cat is eating probably stands eight to nine foot at the shoulders and weighs 2,500 pounds," Noah reveals. "And this cat killed it!"

"Where are the other Sabre-Toothed Tigers?" Jack asks.

"This is very interesting Senator. While we know the Sabre-Toothed Tiger lived in small prides, this is the first picture we have of one. We have seen no others, and while they are known to hunt in groups, we believe this huge moose which is also very fast, may have been brought down by this one cat," Dr. Abraham suggests.

"Take a look at another hologram Senator, what do you see?"

"I see a large bird, perhaps an eagle," responds the Senator.

"Now look at this one. What do you see?" asks Dr. Abraham.

"Well, it certainly looks like another large bird," replies the Senator.

"Large bird my ass, take your finger and pull the bird in for a closer look Senator. That bird is carrying a full-sized male deer in its talons!" exclaims Noah. "Look at the wing span and size of this bird. Think of the strength required to carry an animal that weighs no less than one hundred and fifty pounds."

Noah goes on to show Senator Joseph a number of pictures depicting wolves, bears, and wild boar as they were in 2014. He follows this with pictures of enormous Dire Wolves, Short-nosed Bears, and Hell Pigs that have been found in the Canadian wild in 2039.

"This is very interesting Noah, but what makes this such a big deal?" asks the Senator.

"The deal is massive covert activity occurring at the micro level, and the evident changes at the macro level convince us we are experiencing a traumatic shift in the balance of nature," Noah asserts. "I can give you example after example which suggests we are on a rapid track to oblivion."

"Just how fast is this occurring?" Jack asks hoping the answer is not very fast.

"What I have shown you is happening everywhere. Edison's findings from the depths of Florida substantiate this fact. My God Jack, does Miami and Miami Beach not resonate with anyone here in D.C.," Noah says in exasperation.

"How fast Noah, give me an illustration?" Jack demands.

"The Earth is changing at warp speed, and it is not changing in favor of human existence. It is changing faster than the ability of the United States or any other country to find a solution let alone respond," Noah almost shouts. "I have given you visual evidence made available to no one else as of this time. I come to you because you are one of us. We are in deep shit!" Noah adds.

"Take it easy Noah; I have been fighting for environmental causes all my adult life. I have worked tirelessly for a common-sense approach to the environment. Every time you have notified me about a new concern, I have taken it up with my colleagues." Jack argues back.

"I know you have! Jack, you are one of the good guys, but we need to keep fighting or we may very well be finished on this planet," Noah asserts.

"See Noah this is where I run into trouble. Even those who offer a listening ear get concerned when I speak doomsday scenarios. No one wants to believe this. But the real problem is the fact that most elected officials on both sides of the aisle are beholden to big money. It is big money that is pulling the strings of decision-making in Washington," Jack says in frustration.

"Okay Jack, if your colleagues and the big money people don't want to deal with this on a scientific level then share this thought with them. They might be pulling the strings, but we have proof that a resurgence of gigantic predators is occurring in North Central Ontario. These predators have unquenchable appetites, and unless we do something, they will increase in numbers. As these predators increase in numbers stretching the food source in the North, they will begin to move elsewhere for their food supply," Dr. Abraham says. "Tell the people who matter that this region in Ontario is only 170 miles from Winnipeg, and 106 miles from International Falls, Minnesota, U.S.A."

"What do you suggest we do Noah?" Jack inquires.

"This is not a conversation for just you and me. You need to get the attention of the people who matter so we can broaden the scope of this conversation," Noah says with earnest.

"The world is changing; it has always been changing. People living at sea level have always known they sit in the path of the sea should she want to reclaim the land? Most people see it as all part of Mother Nature," Jack asserts.

"But is it Mother Nature acting of her own accord? Or, is it Mother Nature fighting back against the abuses of humans for well over a hundred-fifty years? Why can't we get some sense out of Washington?" Noah says bringing his fist down on the table.

Before the Senator can respond, Noah notices he has a call coming in from Contessa. He knows she would not be calling unless it was urgent.

"Excuse me Jack, Contessa is calling and I need to see what's up."

"Absolutely Noah, you can take the call here, I will step out into the outer office. Just let me know when you are done," Jack informs him.

"Hello, this is Dr. Abraham."

"Noah, this is Contessa. I am sorry to interrupt your meeting with Senator Joseph, but I have some startling information," Contessa says while attempting to catch her breath from the anxiety brought on by her discovery.

"Go ahead Contessa, take your time, what is it?" Noah asks trying to calm an obviously nervous caller.

"You are aware that one of my doctoral dissertations focused on geological changes over time," she asks.

"Yes, I am," Noah assures her.

"Well, I just received preliminary proof that the Canadian Tar Sands are receding," Contessa says with a sigh.

"Of-course they are Contessa, humans have been mining the Canadian Tar Sands for the past three decades," Noah says in a matter-of-fact manner.

"No Dr. Abraham, this is entirely different," Contessa proclaims.

Noah knows that Contessa is very serious when she calls him Dr. Abraham. When she took on the doctoral assistant position with Noah, he made it clear she was to call him Noah. After all, they are cousins.

"Then tell me, I am waiting," Noah prompts her on.

"The Tar Sands are receding of their own accord. It is a geological phenomenon unlike anything anyone has ever seen. Just as the Tar Sands evolved over time, they now seem to be receding along the same path at a more rapid rate," She says.

"Are you certain Contessa, this is a huge discovery if it is indeed true," Noah asks.

"I have to run further studies, but if this holds up, it could be the very first signs of what we have been talking about recently," she notes.

"Devolution," Noah says. "My God is it possible? Thank you for calling Contessa. Start going over all of the data immediately and do not stop until you have a definitive conclusion," Noah orders before hanging up the phone.

Standing in Senator Joseph's office, Noah is in a trance. It is all too clear, and yet so many people are unwilling to see. It is especially dumbfounding how those in a position of leadership refuse to lead. They are in the back pocket of multinational corporations and blinded by their decadent lifestyle. Noah shakes himself out of his trance and opens the door to the outer office.

"Well, I hope you had a productive conversation," Senator Joseph says as he steps back into his office.

"I just got off the phone with Contessa Margery, I think you might want to sit down," Noah suggests.

"What's up Noah?" Jack asks.

"You know those pictures I showed you? The changes I tried to get across involved how the land, and in particular the animals have changed in twenty-five years to resemble something which we have not seen on Earth in thousands of years," Noah points out.

"Well, that should be good shouldn't it? You environmentalists have been telling us we are killing the planet, and certainly it must have been healthier thousands of years ago, so perhaps all will be okay" Jack suggests fully knowing the answer.

"Jack, do you remember our conversation while playing eight ball at Grandma and Grandpa's last Christmas? And by the way, I believe Kennedy Kay won that tournament," Noah says with a smile.

"I believe I do Noah. Is that where Hannah Rae made some comment about something called Devolution?" Jack wonders.

Hannah Rae is a Professor of Agricultural Science at Iowa State University. Hannah's father was a career teacher and coach, but his love of animals led to raising cattle and baling hay. Her father, Robert, did not believe in using genetically modified seeds or feed. He believed genetic modification was unnatural and harmful to the land and humans. Hannah believed her father, but she wanted to learn more and find out answers for herself. This background on the farm, and her natural curiosity directed Hannah's post-high school education.

Dr. Rae's area of specialization is genetics. She did her dissertation on the impact of genetic alteration of crops and livestock on air, soils, waterways, and fisheries. While her dissertation was hailed as a masterpiece in the environmental community, big agricultural business called it a farce and scare tactic. The United Farm Association, the mouth piece for mega-farms and corporate farms, actually attempted to keep Hannah from receiving her doctoral degree. Then, when Iowa State made her a Professor of Agricultural Science, big Agriculture threatened to withhold their financial support for the university.

Dr. Rae's dissertation contended that should farm practices, so opposed to healthy land and animal husbandry be continued, the laws of nature would repel and reject such abuses through non-productivity. Her theory asserts that genetic alteration, concentrated animal feeding operations (CAFOs), chemicals, and putrefied animal manure are environmentally offensive. Such practices are leading to agricultural ruin. Hannah termed such a rebellion on the part of nature - Devolution.

The journey we have made in the forty-three years since the introduction of genetically modified seeds (GMCs) are plants whose DNA has been engineered to withstand an onslaught of pests and disease while producing an abundant yield. Little consideration was given to the long-term impact such genetically modified crops would have on the land.

"As Hannah once told me when having such a conversation," Noah inserts, "Humans think they know better than nature."

"I remember," Senator Joseph proclaims, "Hannah stated that Devolution is a process by which the Earth reclaims itself. Those attempting to refute Dr. Rae's hypothesis said such reclamation on the part of the Earth would only make the ground more fertile and therefore be a boom for production. Dr. Rae argued that the reclamation would involve a total rejection by the Earth of current farming practices. She claimed that as the Earth became unhealthier, food sources and availability would decline dramatically unless farming practices returned to an Earth friendly process. For the past several years, she has been calling for a voluntary scaling back in the use of genetically altered crops and animals, with an eventual cessation in hopes of avoiding a full-scale environmental rebellion on the part of the Earth. She has lobbied congress on several occasions to pass laws which would lead to an organized scaling down which might save our planet. Unfortunately, agriculture, like everything else, is all about money."

"By God there is nothing wrong with your memory senator. Devolution is exactly the word. Well, my phone call from Contessa suggests that Devolution may be a universal phenomenon. Her doctoral dissertation which asserted the Canadian Tar Sands would recede is now actually occurring," Noah says looking directly at his cousin Senator Joseph.

"I am not sure how that is relevant. We have been pulling crude oil from those tar sands for the past quarter of a century with no signs of them drying up. So now you are telling me they are drying up on their own," Jack says a bit mystified.

"I am telling you that they are drying up, and I am suggesting to you that oil fields around the world are beginning to dry up of their own accord. The Earth is beginning to rebel against the abuses it has suffered at the hands of the human race," Noah bellows with both hands raised in the air.

"Noah, just last week Congress received a report which stated that the oil and natural gas reserves around the world are healthier than predicted 30 years ago. While we still strive for renewable sources of energy, we will not run out of fossil fuels for decades and perhaps centuries to come," Jack fires back.

"Come on Jack, you don't believe all that bullshit you receive from the big oil conglomerates. They would sell their parents and children down the river for big profits. In fact, what they are doing is selling civilization down the drain, and you know it," Noah insists.

"What am I to do Noah? I have been fighting for better environmental practices for years, and the only thing it gets me is a tough challenger for re-election. One of these times, big money will win, and I won't be much good to you at all," Jack notes realistically.

"All I ask is that you give us a voice in the United States Senate. If you get a chance, take it to the President," Noah implores.

"I will do all I can Noah. Trust I am on your side of this issue, and I shall try to make it resonate throughout the government," Jack assures. "Now let's get out of here and go home for some relaxation. I don't know about you, but I could use some food and beverage."

As they make their way to the senator's Georgetown Brownstone, they talk about family and all the good times they have had throughout the years.

"So where is Ainsley Annabelle these days?" Noah asks.

"Actually, Ainsley is doing a concert at the Rose Bowl in Pasadena this very night," Jack informs.

"The Rose Bowl is a rather large venue," Noah notes.

"It is huge, and she will pack the arena. Her message for world peace and a return to simpler times is resonating on college campuses across the country and around the world. She is at the forefront of Rock and Roll artists calling for a new hippie renaissance," Jack boasts. "I think she is having a much bigger impact on things than I am as a U.S. Senator."

"I have several of her productions, and I am proud of her message. She is calling on young people to do the right thing and focus less on material possessions and more on relationships with each other and their planet," Noah adds proudly. "She is doing important work."

<hr />

Ainsley has been playing guitar and performing for so long that it seems like she might have been born performing. She has never been hesitant to get in front of people. In second grade, she got in front of the entire family and juggled. She taught herself how to play the guitar and write music. While in high school she performed at events in Des

Moines including the 80/35 Concert. She was a part of Girls Rock in Des Moines. Ainsley's personality brings out the best in people. Combine her intelligence, talent, and personality, and everyone knew she would be a star.

Ainsley Annabelle attended college at the University of California in Berkeley and earned a doctoral degree in Music. Even prior to graduation in 3026, Ainsley signed a recording contract with High Flying Studios in Nashville. Working closely with Justin Timberlake, Ainsley honed her song writing skills in blues and rock and roll. Berkeley provided the setting in which Ainsley found her voice and conscience. She loved to make music, but she wanted to make music with a message worth following.

For the past fifteen years, Ainsley has been recording and performing live to share her message of world peace and environmentalism with whomever might listen. Now, in 2039, Ainsley's message is resonating on college campuses across the country and world. She has a massive following to her message of activism. She will soon embark on her Save the Planet Tour.

⟫◆⟪

That night, after Noah retired to bed, Jack makes a call to Ainsley in Pasadena. With a three-hour time difference, he is able to catch her before her big show.

"Hi Sis, are you ready for a big night?" Jack asks.

"Little brother it is good to hear from you. How are things in the chaotic and corrupt city of Washington?" she inquires.

"Listen Ainsley, Noah has spent the better part of the day with me. He has shown me some holograms which are rather startling. Then, while he was in my office, he received a call from Contessa regarding a regression of the tar sands in Canada. He linked it to that bizarre conversation we had at Christmas time about something called Devolution," Jack shares.

"I remember the conversation Jack. It was quite freaky," Ainsley remembers.

"Well, they feel rather confident the Earth may be moving in that direction. I am telling you this because of your ability to reach people.

If there is any hope of change, it must come from the people, there is no chance it will come from Washington," Jack adds with urgency.

"Jack, I promise you every night I put all of my energy and effort into communicating a message of change. It is difficult beating back the forces of materialism, but I sense young people are starting to realize the truth, and when they do, we will make the 60s look like a county fair," Ainsley announces.

"Well good luck tonight Sis, let's hope we're not too late."

"Thanks, little brother, keep your eye on the newspaper tomorrow!"

As Jack heads to bed, he wonders how he ever allowed himself to get involved in politics. Whoever said politics was about leadership had their head up their ass. Jack has served at the state and national levels and he finds it all to be about bullshit. Leadership is about doing the right things, and politics is about doing things right so you can get re-elected. There is too much compromise in politics, and it is usually in the wrong direction.

As Jack mentally surveys the past one-hundred-years, he realizes that anyone who took an unwavering stance on issues usually suffered character assassination or actual assassination. He also knows such assassinations were the result of conspiracies emanating from the inner circles of big business and big money where the real power resides. Tackling such a foe is far greater than a David and Goliath showdown.

As Senator Joseph drifts off to sleep, he does not realize his life is about to dramatically change. During the course of his slumber, his subconscious turns the tumblers in his mind until it unlocks the determination to walk into the fire. When he wakes, Senator Joseph is done playing Washington political games. He has an urgent message, and he will be heard.

The next morning, Noah rises before the senator. Leaving a note of appreciation and encouragement, Noah takes a cab to the airport and hops a plane back to Ann Arbor. He is anxious to talk with Contessa about her findings. There are so many things to explore. There is so much work to be done. He just hopes it's not too late.

As he lays back in his seat for the flight home, his thoughts turn to Nancy Ingersol and her son Langdon. These two people personalized the entire dilemma and the challenges ahead. Tired, Noah soon drifts off to sleep.

CHAPTER 5

RESURRECTION

D R. THOMAS HENRY IS A Quantitative Paleobiologist working on a project with the Smithsonian Institution of Natural Science. Thomas is seeking to determine the genetic and environmental disposition for a resurgence of dinosaur life on Earth. At 27 years old, Dr. Henry is what might be termed a genius in the area of Paleobiology. As a high school student, he entered a science fair project based on original research involving the DNA structure existing in a dinosaur fossil he found while attending a Paleontology Camp in Utah. His hypothesis centered on the regeneration of such material, believing if it could fossilize, then certainly it could regenerate. His project won him national and international acclaim, as well as a full ride scholarship to Virginia Tech, where he fast tracked his way to a PhD. in Quantitative Paleobiology in four years.

Dr. Henry is a field practitioner, and he has spent the past five years digging in the Heart of the Canadian Badlands in Alberta, the Sahara Desert, the Valley of the Dinosaurs in Argentina, and currently Mongolia's Ukhaa Tolgod (Brown Hills) in the Gobi Desert. Dr. Henry is a world renown Paleontologist, and the world's foremost thinker in Quantitative Paleobiology. Dr. Henry contends that given the right conditions, fossils could regenerate into living tissue and bring about the resurrection of dinosaurs from their stone-cold grave.

While paleontologists around the world regard Dr. Henry as a brilliant mind in the area of paleontology, most scientists of other disciplines look at his theories as foolish nonsense. Thomas Henry is not deterred by such ridicule. Most people do not understand the molecular structure of a cell and the power of DNA. Given the right conditions, the mighty can be brought low, and the lowly made mighty.

———————————

Thomas Henry was always a high energy kid with far more questions than answers. His love of dinosaurs began at an early age, and his collection of toy dinosaurs was the envy of everyone his age.

Thomas would spend hours organizing his dinosaurs for just the right kind of setting needed for battle. This meant he required a great deal of uninterrupted floor space. His two sisters, Hannah and Olivia, were not always so cooperative.

"Hannah, stop touching my dinosaurs! You are ruining things, get out of here," Tommy would explode whenever Hannah thought she might join in his fun. No one was quite sure if Hannah at two years older wanted to play, or if she just wanted to get under Tommy's skin. "Leave," Thomas would demand.

"What's going on in there?" his mother would yell from the kitchen.

"Hannah is touching my dinosaurs. She is ruining everything," Thomas would answer.

"I am not, I just want to play too," Hannah would plead.

"Hannah, you know how particular your brother is with his dinosaurs. Why don't you find something else to do?" Alyssa suggests.

"I'm so tired of him taking up the entire floor," Hannah would respond with a foot stomp. "He doesn't own the floor."

As Hannah stomped her way up the stairs to her bedroom to play, Olivia, Tommy's twin sat on the couch watching the drama. Olivia was quite content to do her own thing.

As he got older, Thomas Henry discovered a gift for math. His father, a math teacher challenged Thomas' math ability at every opportunity. Robert enjoyed playing chess, and he taught Thomas the rules of the game. As a result, Thomas became a chess wiz while in elementary school. His math and problem-solving skills spilled over into science, and his passion and curiosity for dinosaurs did the rest.

———————————

As Thomas Henry greets the Mongolian morning, he lays on his cot under a canvas tent with his hands behind his head looking up at the drab green material. His thoughts drift to all the important things going on in the world which are paid little attention by the press and people in power. He knows the Earth is moaning from the duress it has suffered at the hands of human beings. He thinks of his cousins, all engaged in important work to save the planet and humanity from the folly of itself. He prays someone will listen before it is too late.

His thoughts drift to the unique and special nature of his family. Closing his eyes, he returns to the farm house living room where his Dad and Mom nurtured his interests and curiosity. He can see all the dinosaurs big and small that he would spend hours organizing on the floor using his imagination to bring them to life. Then, like some meteor striking Earth, which may have contributed to the dinosaur's demise, one of his sisters would run through the room laying all his work to waste. Oh, how he would get upset when this happened. Now, he thinks of his sisters, missing them, and hoping they are doing well.

"Dr. Henry," one of his associates yells emphatically as he runs into the tent. "Dr. Henry, you need to see this!"

Jolted from his daydreaming, Dr. Henry jumps from his cot, throws on his clothes, pulls on his boots, grabs his hat, and exits the tent in seconds flat. "What is it Reza?"

"Come quickly," Reza says as he runs backwards stumbling over his own feet in excitement.

In a run resembling a 100 yard sprint, Dr. Henry arrives at the large research tent which houses all of the most important artifacts. Throwing open the front flap of the tent, "What is it that has Reza in such a state of excitement?" he asks as he sees four of his top assistants huddled around a well-lit table.

"Come over here doctor," one of his assistants urges.

Approaching the table, Thomas Henry sees one of the dinosaur eggs from the nest they discovered three weeks before laying on the table under an intense heat lamp. Dr. Henry and his team discovered a treasure trove of fossilized Oviraptor bones and nests. Being just bigger than a human being, the Oviraptor was a rather small dinosaur from the late Cretaceous period. At one time, the Oviraptor had been thought to diet on eggs (thus the name), but a closer study over time revealed the Oviraptor to eat mollusks, clams, small animals, and reptiles. Therefore, Dr. Henry and his team are dealing with a carnivorous and a rather aggressive dinosaur.

"Look at this Dr. Henry, tell us what you see," Reza insists.

Taking a position at the table directly in front of the egg, Thomas begins to look at every angle. He carefully rolls the egg to get a good look at the entire oval. He gently picks it up and brings it closer for inspection. He holds it up to the light to remove all shadows. "I see one of the eggs we found three weeks ago gentlemen," Thomas announces. "Is there something I am missing?"

"Do you remember asking us to establish the age of this egg?" Reza asks.

"I do, and what did you determine?"

"Well, this is all preliminary, and it is based on the most current and somewhat controversial methods of dating, but we believe this egg is 50 million years younger than anything discovered in this region," pipes in one of the assistants.

"Seriously, and what about the other eggs we found alongside this one?" Thomas asks.

"We have focused on this one doctor. We cannot comment on the others," Reza says.

"Well then I suggest you do so," Doctor Henry pronounces as he turns to exit the tent.

"Wait doctor that is not the most interesting observation about this egg," Reza says causing Doctor Henry to stop and turn.

"What do you mean Reza, tell me what you have observed," Dr. Henry insists.

"When we discovered this egg and cleaned it all up, it had distinct cracks running from this point along one end, to this point on the other end. It also had distinct cracks running around the oval. When we started studying this egg three weeks ago, we put it under this intense heat lamp to heighten our observation. This morning when we approached the egg for observation, we noticed that all of the cracks are gone," Reza shares with the excitement of a young child showing something to their parents.

"So, all the cracks are gone?" Thomas asks, "What about the dating of the egg; when was that completed?"

"We just got the results back this morning," An assistant interjects.

"So, we have no idea what the date of the egg might have been three weeks ago?" Thomas continues his inquiry.

"None whatsoever," Reza responds.

"This is very intriguing and certainly could be something huge," Dr. Henry notes. "What I want you to do is get the other eggs, and get them all dated. Then I want you to subject them to the same intense heat lamp as this one. Let's see if we arrive at similar observations."

As Dr. Henry exits the tent, he is followed closely by Reza. "Dr. Henry I am disappointed in your response. I thought you would be elated at what may clearly be a sign of regeneration," Reza says a bit bewildered.

"Come into my tent for a moment Reza so we can talk," Dr. Henry directs. "Reza, what you shared with me this morning is unbelievable. If this observation holds up with the other eggs, we will truly be traveling uncharted territory. However, I do not have the latitude of emotion. If I were to do anything but remain calculated about this, I could personally impact the way we see things. We must now follow through objectively to assure our results and conclusions are solid."

"You are right Doctor. I will personally see that the other eggs are handled consistently with the manner in which this one was handled. Thank you."

"Thank you, Reza, I am going to spend the rest of this morning in my tent writing. Please see I am not disturbed unless it is something highly significant."

<hr />

Dr. Thomas Henry has a secure wireless channel to his sister Dr. Hannah Rae in Iowa. He is quite excited about the observations with the egg. He believes the egg may prove that regeneration is not only possible, but probable considering the environmental conditions around the world. Thomas recalls the conversation at Grandma and Grandpa's last Christmastime, and he believes Hannah's idea of Devolution as it applies to the Earth, may actually apply on a more holistic basis.

"Hello, Thomas is that you?" Hannah inquires.

"Well, I certainly hope no one else is using this channel Hannah. How are you Big Sis?" Despite their frequent adversarial relationship growing up, Hannah and Thomas enjoy a close and loving relationship.

"I am doing well Thomas, where are you at these days?" she asks.

"I am leading a team of researchers in the Gobi Desert," he responds.

"Mongolia, my God Thomas is there anywhere you won't go in search of the lost chord?"

"I would travel to the ends of the Earth as long as there are discoveries to be made. Speaking of discoveries, I think we have found something rather important." he shares.

"Please do tell," she begs.

"Are you certain this channel is secure and no one other than you and me has access?" he demands.

"I am certain Thomas. Not the CIA, NSA, BBC, or DNN could break the lock on this channel. I know how important it is for us to talk in confidence," she assures.

"Hannah, I think we have stumbled upon an actual case of regeneration. We have found dinosaur eggs that seem to be going through a state of reparation. I have no idea where this may lead. We are doing follow up studies on other eggs found at the same location, but if it holds up, your whole notion of Devolution may apply to far more than the farm land of Iowa," he insists.

"How long will this study take?" Hannah asks anxiously.

"It will take three-weeks just to arrive at the same point we are with the first egg. However, we will continue to observe the first egg over the same period of time to see what occurs," he informs his sister.

"Thank you, Thomas, please keep me posted. I love you brother, take care!"

"You also Hannah."

—————◆————

As Thomas puts down his communication device, he takes time to re-read Hannah's dissertation on Devolution. He begins to write in his log the circumstances of the egg. He adds his own addendum to Hannah's theory by suggesting that devolution applies to all of nature, because at the most micro point there is atomic activity in all things. Thomas now realizes that what they are seeking may not be a sum of parts, but actually a coordinated shift of the Earth to a new paradigm of existence. Such a revelation would change the way people not only perceive the world but themselves.

CHAPTER 6

INTO THE DEEP

I VEY ISABELLE IS AN ASTROPHYSICIST with a doctorate from Harvard. After receiving her doctorate in 2035, Ivey took a position with the University of Tokyo at the Atacama Observatory in the Atacama Desert in Chile. At 18,500 feet, the sky is crystal clear. The Atacama region is actually one of the driest deserts in the world at an extremely high altitude enclosed by the Andes on the east and west. There are several large volcanoes running north-south along the eastern side of Salar de Atacama which include Lincancabur, Acamarichi, Aguas, Calientes, and the most active Lascar. Due to its dryness, high altitude, and non-existent cloud cover, combined with very limited light pollution and radio interference, Atacama is one of the best places on Earth to conduct astronomical observations. The observatory houses the most powerful optical and infrared telescopes in the world. Because of the elevation, the observatory is self-contained including air pressure and oxygen. People and supplies only arrive or depart via a high-flying helicopter. The observatory is equipped to house five people at a time. Ivey only leaves the observatory to return home for special occasions. Dr. Isabelle can't explain it, but there is something powerfully compelling about sitting at such a high altitude gazing out.

While seeking her doctorate, Ivey interned with the Van Allen Institute at the University of Iowa. Dr. Isabelle specializes in the dynamics found throughout the Universe. For the past four-years she has been looking for an alternate theory to the creation.

On this particular night, Ivey is peering into the heavens when overcome with a heavy feeling of gloom. She cannot explain it, but there is something more to what she is looking at than meets the eye. She has looked at this sky well over fourteen-hundred times over the past four years. The marvel of looking into the cosmos in such an intrusive manner feels a bit like subterfuge. Is it possible there are things going on in deep space which people were never meant to see? It is too late for Dr. Isabelle; she is hooked and could not stop if she wanted. The fact she's lived in this isolation for four years with only one escape back home during that time testifies to the incredible hold this place has on Ivey.

Ivey loves her parents and is incredibly proud of her brother and sister. She knows her Dad and Mom worry about her being cut off from the rest of the world. She wishes they would realize it is not only okay, but for now, what she wants and needs. She lives to be at the telescope looking into the farthest reaches of the heavens.

"So why this feeling of gloom when I am sitting here doing the very thing I desire," Ivey thinks to herself as she gazes at the screen transfixed on something yet to be detected. "Nothing," she admits, "I see nothing that should give me a feeling of anything but excitement and exhilaration." It has been a long night, and Ivey finally can look no more. Telling one of her co-workers to wake her if anything note worthy should occur, she now seeks rest. Ivey is not worried she will miss anything, the magnificence of the sky has been there for ages, and it will be there when she awakes.

Lying down on her bed in the small dorm style room, Ivey rapidly drifts into a deep slumber. Sleeping at this altitude is more than dreamy. She has never yet awoke feeling anything but rested. Her dreams always take her on a wonderful journey. At Atacama, everyone's vitals are monitored while they sleep. Working for extended periods at this altitude despite all efforts to create a normal environment can be stressful. The monitoring of vitals is a health precaution which everyone agrees to and understands the importance.

In the observation room, Dr. Amanda Stardust is monitoring Ivey's vital signs when she notices a rise in heart rate and blood pressure. Some fluctuation is normal, but not for Ivey. Dr. Isabelle is always so composed and stable. When Dr. Stardust calls a colleague to witness her observation, Ivey's heart rate and blood pressure make another jump.

Rushing into the small room, Dr. Stardust and Dr. Galileo find Ivey rocking back and forth on her bed. She appears to be asleep and she is not making a sound. They decide the best thing is to awaken Dr. Isabelle. Touching her shoulder and saying "Doctor, Doctor . . .," Amanda wakes Ivey. Dr. Isabelle is startled, "Why are you in my room?" she asks Dr. Stardust and Dr. Galileo.

"Please leave," she emphatically tells her two colleagues who rapidly exit the room. "Dr. Stardust, I think it is best if we explain this to Dr. Isabelle in the morning," suggests Dr. Galileo. "Good idea," Dr. Stardust responds.

Sitting on the edge of her bed, Ivey wipes her forehead realizing she has been sweating. "What is going on, I still feel the . . .," all of a sudden Ivey is struck with an epiphany. "Sure, everything looked the same, it always does, but last night I observed an unusual and subtle movement which caused me to have a feeling of gloom," she thought to herself. Ivey knew that seeing and feeling something once hardly provided evidence of anything. She must see if this holds true over a period time.

For the next two-weeks, Dr. Isabelle observes the same thing and experiences the same feelings. Each night, she dreams in such a manner as to elevate her heart rate and blood pressure. Each morning she wakes feeling as if she were being made privy to something ominous.

At the end of the two-week period, Ivey knows she has not gathered enough empirical evidence to support a conclusion, but she has reached a conclusion. It is a conclusion she cannot share with anyone, and yet she must share it with someone.

"Olivia, this is Ivey on a separate and secure channel, do you have time to talk?"

As a young girl, Olivia was always fascinated with bugs, especially butterflies. Her and Grandma use to chase after insects and butterflies trying to catch them for observation. Olivia found butterflies most interesting because of their colors and erratic flight pattern. Olivia even studied chaos theory in college because of the "Butterfly Effect."

On the small acreage where Olivia grew up, there were many opportunities to chase and catch bugs. There were many types of bugs in the Cedar Grove north of their house. When the Holly Hocks were in bloom, they attracted lots of butterflies, but the best place for butterflies was the alfalfa field when in bloom. There were also some Milk Weed in the pasture which attracted Monarch Butterflies. Then it happened, the butterflies began to die off. Making the demise of butterflies a high school science fair project, Olivia was introduced to microorganisms and the dangers they present. This was an "aha moment" for Olivia. Little did she know that microorganisms would become an important part of her life.

"Ivey, how are things at such a lofty altitude at the bottom of the world?" Olivia says in greeting her cousin and good friend.

Ivey is two-months older than Olivia and they spent lots of time together growing up. All those times at holidays, campouts, and the many other family gatherings, Ivey and Olivia developed a unique and close friendship. They can never talk without remembering those fun times.

"Well, I would certainly prefer to be scooting across the water on Big Mable with my dear cousin and friend," Ivey retorts.

Big Mable was the cousin's favorite tube to ride on behind Grandma and Grandpa's 1991 Bayliner Capri. Mable allowed the kids to sit with a back rest to lean against while zooming across the water. Mable's large base provided the stability the kids wanted when speeding outside the wake of the boat. Sometimes they would hit a large wave and go sailing in the air. As long as they stayed balanced, Mable would always land flat on the water and never flip.

Ivey and Olivia shared a good laugh when recalling how their cousin Noah often tried to do all kinds of acrobatics on Mable. They laughed even harder remembering how Edison tried to imitate his brother. These two cousins always loved to laugh, and on this occasion, they could almost see the tears in each other's eyes as their laughter became more intense.

"Remember," Ivey begins but can't get the words out because she is laughing so hard. "Remember," she struggles, "How Hannah thought it was a great trick just to hang her foot over the edge of Big Mable. My

God, I can still see her grin as if she had just performed an amazing feat of acrobatics," Ivey shares.

Now the two are sharing one of those silly moments they came to treasure while growing up. "Oh Olivia, I do so yearn for those simpler days in our lives," Ivey reveals.

"Don't kid me," Olivia counters, "You love your work."

Olivia is right; Dr. Isabelle can sit at the telescope for hours never thinking about anything else. As she gazes into deep space, she encounters wonders most people will never see in their lifetime. Oh sure, pictures in magazines, but to be gazing at the great beyond in real time consumes the body and soul.

Ivey has studied the NGC 6744 spiral galaxy which is 75 percent bigger than the Milky Way and exists 30 million light years from Earth. It is such a marvelous wonder with an ever- present eye, as if it is some extraterrestrial hurricane. She has been transfixed by Galaxy M83 or the Southern Pinwheel which is half the size of the Milky Way at 15 million light years from Earth. This galaxy offers Ivey a most brilliant show of light and colors involving birth and death. The sight of a dying star, expelling its outer layers, creating a sensational Helix Nebula, is mesmerizing.

Sometimes, Ivey wants to study something closer to home, so she focuses on the Milky Way, home to her own solar system and planet. The Milky Way spans 100,000 light years, so it certainly has much to offer. She enjoys the sighting of a ghost star which involves hot dust and gas from a supernova which may have occurred as recently as 7,000 years ago. She becomes spellbound by celestial sculptures involving beautiful ribbons of hot gas and dust. She frequently looks for Zeta Ophichi the runaway star hurtling across the cosmos creating a visible wave in front of it much like a boat speeding across the water.

"Okay Olivia, you're right, I do love my work, but how about smores around a campfire with all those other knuckle heads," Ivey says referring to her cousins with great fondness. "It doesn't get any better than that does it?"

"Oh, I remember the one thing you liked to do the most when camping, you liked to get away from the campfire and the trees, and just look up at the sky. Do you remember all the conversations we had about space and time?" Olivia asks.

"I do remember quite well. While I have looked at some marvelous things though a telescope, those days of star gazing were the best," Ivey divulges with a hint of melancholy in her voice.

Picking up on Ivey's mood swing, Olivia seeks to change the subject, "How about playing a game of pool at Grandma and Grandpa's House? Did you ever win the pool tournament?" Olivia teases knowing the answer.

"No, but my name is on the tournament plaque for a number of things," Ivey says with a laugh.

"The memories are rich Olivia, and I am so glad to be talking with you. You have such a calming influence on me!" Ivey shares with her cousin.

"I always thought it worked the other way around," says Olivia continuing to sense something in Ivey's voice. Besides, Ivey never called her Olivia unless it was serious.

"So, what is on your mind Ivey?" Olivia asks curiously.

"I don't know Olivia, perhaps I should just forget it," she says with the sound of exasperation in her voice.

"Spill the beans Ivey. We are on a secure channel, and you know the word is "mum" with me," Olivia assures her cousin.

"Okay, but bear with me. You know I am addicted to my telescope. I sit here for hours upon hours gazing into the vastness of space not certain what I am looking for but hoping to see it" she says trying to convince her cousin.

"You don't need to convince me Ivey, I know what you're talking about. While you may be looking into the vastness of space, I spend hours looking at the infinite world of microorganisms through a microscope. We are in the same boat; we are just looking in different directions," Olivia says emphatically.

———※◈※———

Dr. Olivia Kae is every bit as married to her work as Dr. Isabelle. In the last three-years, Dr. Kae has focused on the microorganisms associated with Cholera, Malaria, and other diarrheal diseases. Recently she added the Bubonic Plague to her list of concerns. Rising global temperatures has expanded the tropics far beyond their range of 25 years ago. Mosquitoes, ticks, fleas, spiders, and other small insect carriers of Microorganisms, flourish in tropical regions. While the diseases on Dr. Kae's list have been predominately under control due to safety precautions, vaccinations, and treatment, Dr. Kae has witnessed a resurgence of these diseases as a warming planet acts as a petri-dish for mutations and variants.

———※◈※———

"You cannot utter a word of this to anyone Olivia," Ivey says knowing she need not be worried.

"Get to it girl, I don't have all day," Olivia presses.

"Two-weeks ago, I got the feeling of doom while gazing through the telescope at the outer reaches of the universe. This might seem insignificant, but I never get this feeling. I was unable to shake the feeling, and I woke up that night in cold sweats. I never wake up at night, and I always enjoy a wonderful slumber," Ivey shares.

"Go on, I believe there must be more," Olivia encourages.

"As I sat on the edge of my bed, it dawned on me that I saw something the night before, a subtle movement at the edge of the Universe unlike anything I had experienced. I decided to do a longitudinal study of this before drawing any conclusions. So, I have been looking every night for the past two weeks, and every night I see the same thing and get the same feeling of doom," Ivey shares.

"Well Ivey," says Olivia, "Two-weeks hardly makes a longitudinal study."

"I know that," says Ivey, "but the feelings have been so intense. I have not had one good night's sleep in two-weeks. Each night I become more and more convinced at what I am seeing, and yet, I cannot share my observation or draw a conclusion with anyone else without being told I just need some rest," Ivey shares in frustration.

"So, what do you believe you are seeing dear cousin?" Olivia asks hoping to relieve some of the stress she hears in Ivey's voice.

"Until two-weeks ago, the outer fringes of the Universe revealed the same signs of an expanding universe. Two-weeks ago, it stopped," Ivey says abruptly.

"What?" Olivia asks incredulously.

"I wasn't certain at first, but I have no doubt now. The Universe has stopped expanding," Ivey says again.

"Is it retracting?" inquires Olivia.

"I don't know, that will take time and serious study to determine. What I do know is as of right now, any expansion of the Universe has stopped," Ivey says.

"Wow," Olivia exclaims, "This could be a huge discovery. Has anyone at other observatories or with access to powerful space telescopes reported anything similar?"

"Not a thing. If someone has made a similar observation, they are remaining quiet and perhaps for the same reason as me," Ivey suggests.

"So, what are the possibilities Ivey?" Olivia solicits from her cousin.

"As much as it is causing me great emotional duress, I must continue to carefully observe what is going on each night. This could be a momentary blip and things will return to normal any night, but I highly doubt it. This could mean the Universe has been stretched to the limit, and in that case one of two things could happen; the Universe like a balloon stretched beyond its limits could burst, or it could retract. In either scenario, it could take millions or billions of years to know the outcome," Ivey divulges.

"I don't know what to say Ivey," Olivia reveals helplessly.

"You don't need to say anything dear friend. I just needed to share this with someone who would listen without passing judgment. I knew I could count on you. I need to go, please take care and all my love," Ivey says in closing.

"My love to you too dear cousin, my love to you too!" Olivia closes.

Olivia tries to wrap her mind around what Ivey has shared but finds it insurmountable. There is so much happening on Earth, and now add the specter of not only space but the Universe, is just too difficult to comprehend. "Could there be a direct relationship between the Earth and universe?" she wonders. Answering her own question, "How could there not be a relationship, it would be no different than the relationship between her micro-world and the macro-world on Earth. God help us all" she mutters to herself.

Like so many scientists around the world, including her famous cousins, Dr. Kae has tried to warn politicians and the government to take steps to avoid what could one day be a pandemic. Her warnings that new resistant strains of these diseases are emerging has been met with recommendations to develop new ways to combat these new strains. For decades, scientists and people of good conscience have been calling for radical changes in the way humans treat the Earth, only to be met with a deaf ear and indifference by people who just don't seem to want to be bothered.

It seems that people who could make a difference have no interest or concern for the billions of people who live in harm's way, what Olivia calls the "cusp of disaster." Most people live with little defense against the assault of nature. With the world teetering on the brink, everyone is at risk.

A concern by the science community for the impact of human activity on the Earth's climate has been around for a couple hundred years. However, it was only fifty-one years ago in 1988 that Dr. James Hansen testifying before a congressional committee, offered the first assessments that human-caused warming had already measurably affected global climate. Since that time, the wealthy have perpetuated the ruse that global climate change is a myth while preparing for the inevitable. The wealthy have expended huge amounts of resources to build elaborate mansions and compounds completely based on renewable sources of energy, and secured from the dangers of an ever-changing climate. They have gone to great lengths to create impenetrable gated communities with all of the security of an armed nation. They have done this in the name of capitalism suggesting that such things are available to anyone with the initiative to rise above their current station in life. It is a message so ingrained in the people of the United States that they cannot even comprehend the wealthy have an ulterior motive. The wealthy have bought up all of the prime land in the most geographically secure parts of the country to create their own modern-day fiefdoms. In some places, they have begun constructing gigantic domes capable of protecting all those inside with a self-sustaining environment. Olivia knows what this is all about, but she also knows for the sake of humanity, the impending dangers must be confronted like a linebacker confronts a running back with a full head of steam.

———————

Just as Ivey needed someone to speak with, Olivia now finds herself needing someone to talk to. She knows she cannot speak of her conversation with Ivey, and she is not interested at this point in talking shop with anyone. She needs a diversion, something to take her mind off it all. It is now her turn to pick up the phone.

———————

"Hello, this is Dr. Caroline, special assistant to the United States Ambassador to the United Nations on the Environment, can I be of assistance?"

"Well since you are an assistant, I would imagine after an introduction like that you should be able to be of assistance," comes the voice on the other end of the phone.

"Oh my God, is that you Olivia!" Stella yells into the phone with excitement.

"It sure the hell is me Stella, and I am calling to get an update on your work with that hunk of a U.S. Ambassador Leonardo DeCaprio," Olivia teases.

"Now listen up Olivia, the guys 40 years my senior and I am his assistant," Stella retorts in defense of her dignity.

"Forty-years your senior or not, the guy is as handsome now as he was at thirty-five. For goodness sakes Stella, you work for a handsome movie star, international celebrity, and powerful advocate for the environment. How about acknowledging that fact," Olivia challenges.

"I will not deny the spotlight is fun and interesting, but between Ambassador DeCaprio and me it is all business," Stella assures.

"Okay, Stella, I believe you, it is all business, but the question is, what kind of business, monkey?" Olivia won't leave it alone.

"What do you want Olivia, why are you calling?" Stella asks trying to redirect the conversation.

"I just need to talk to someone who might lighten my heart. The world just seems so heavy, and while your work is incredibly important, you seem to get some form of diversion. I thought you might share some of the lighter moments with me," Olivia pleads.

Stella Caroline is just 23 years old. She entered UCLA following high school graduation from Waukee High School in West Des Moines, Iowa, and continued her studies until achieving a doctorate degree in Atmospheric and Oceanic Science. Upon graduation, Stella received an appointment to be a special assistant to the U.S. Ambassador to the United Nations on the Environment. She later learned that her appointment by the President of the United States to this position had transpired from the recommendation of her cousin, then Congressman Jack Joseph.

Like her cousins, Stella inherited an outgoing personality, solid work ethic, and desire to enjoy life. As the next to youngest, all of the older cousins used to tease her, and as a result she perhaps developed the best sense of humor. Now she finds herself on the world stage gaining the attention of some of the most powerful, wealthy, and intelligent men and women in the world. Stella doesn't seek out this attention for any reason other than to leverage her knowledge and ability to advance the cause of environmental issues.

None-the-less, Stella's intensions matter little to the Iranian Ambassador's son, the British Prince, or the French charge d'affaires who all seem intent on gaining her favor at social events that require her attendance. Stella finds the attention flattering and condescending at the same time. She did not work so hard in college to simply become an object of admiration. If Stella had her way, which she does not, she would spend her time working on diplomatic solutions to important environmental issues.

"I have but a moment Olivia. I am getting ready for a social at the Plaza Hotel this evening, and Ambassador DeCaprio is picking me up in forty-minutes," she reveals.

"Oh my," Olivia says with a hint of sexuality, "DeCaprio is picking you up."

"You do realize Olivia that I am his special assistant, and there is mandatory attendance at this event," Stella shoots back.

"Are we getting a bit defensive Stella? You know what my Dad always said about getting defensive don't you?" Olivia asks.

"Yes, I do, he always said a person wouldn't get defensive unless they had something to hide. Well, I do not have anything to hide. Do you hear me; I have nothing to hide!" Stella asserts with a stern note to her voice.

On the other end of the line Olivia begins to laugh uncontrollably. She is tickled to have struck a nerve with her young cousin. As she wipes the tears from her eyes, "Stella, I knew you would be the best medicine. Just talking with you puts such a big smile on my face. I do love you so much! So, who will be attending this shindig tonight? Please do tell me."

"Olivia, if I did not know better, I would think you were the star gazer rather than dear cousin Ivey. For your information, I did get a peak at the guest list, and there are going to be a few very interesting young people on hand for this event. But you know I dare not share such classified information" Stella teases.

"Stella if you do not tell me who you are talking about, I will make you pay next time I see you. So, come clean with the goods, and I mean the goods," Olivia demands.

"Okay, my time is short, but here is what I know. The Oscar winning actress Mia Talerico will be present in all of her beauty and long blonde hair spender. She loves Gucci fashion, so I imagine her dress will be stunning. McKenna Grace is on the list. She is such a marvelous personality. I have met her before, and I hope to spend some time with her tonight. Quvenzhane Willis will be present. She has established herself as such a powerful advocate for environmental issues."

Before Stella can add to her list, Olivia cuts in with urgency, "What about young men Stella, what young men might be present to seek your attention?"

"Olivia, I do not attend these functions to seek the attention of anyone other than people Ambassador DiCaprio tells me I must speak with. While it all seems like fun and games, it is a working function for me," Stella reminds her cousin.

"Fine," Olivia retorts, "Now tell me what I want to know!" Olivia needs this kind of diversion from her work and the recent phone call with Ivey. It is not that she cares all that much, but Stella lives in a different world removed from the stress of research.

"Alright, the Princess Eleonore of Belgium, and Charlotte of Cambridge, Britain will be in attendance. Nothing lends a regal air to an event like royalty. I have met them both, and if they were not playing the role of princess, you would never know they held a title," Stella informs.

"What about men Stella, what young men will be attending?" Olivia demands.

"There are two young men on the list who should captivate your interest. Zachary Arthur, the very accomplished actor and environmental activist will be present and sitting at our table. Ambassador DiCaprio likes Zachary seeing a bit of himself at a younger age. Also, Prince Abdul Muntaqim Bolkiah of Brunei from the Island of Borneo in the South China Sea will be present," Stella reveals, "And that is all I have to share."

"So, Zachary Arthur is 32 years old. He is such a dream boat with his long black curly hair. You're a lucky girl, I will want a full report on this," Olivia informs her cousin.

"That's the door Olivia, I must go. Talk with you later. I love you!" Stella closes.

"Bye Stella, I love you!" Olivia responds but it is too late, the phone is dead and the conversation is over.

Olivia decides to sit for a moment and consider the night ahead for Stella. She wonders what it must be like to live in New York City, and work with such an important person. Stella gets to experience not just the finer but the finest things in life. She tries to place herself in Stella's shoes being surrounded by dignitaries, celebrities, and most of all handsome young men. Zachary Arthur, the name softly comes from her lips as she closes her eyes and envisions Stella sitting at the same table, and perhaps right next to this dashing young man. Then it dawns on Olivia, she didn't even ask Stella what she might be wearing to this event. In fact, she didn't really ask Stella much about how she was doing. Olivia swings her hand in front of her face as if wiping away the thought. Good Lord, how could Stella be doing anything but fantastic under the circumstances?

CHAPTER 7

THE WARNING

As Dr. Caroline climbs into the Limousine that will carry her to the big event at the Plaza Hotel, she is unaware that 636 miles north west at the University of Michigan in Ann Arbor, her sister Dr. Margery is reviewing some startling data.

As Dr. Abraham enters the room upon returning from his trip to Washington D.C., Contessa turns to welcome her cousin back. "Noah, it is so good to have you back, how was your visit with Senator Joseph?"

"I thoroughly enjoyed the time with our dear cousin, but politics in Washington is the same old same slow process" Dr. Abraham says with a sigh of relief to be back in his familiar surroundings. "I am convinced Senator Joseph will do everything in his power to bring the startling revelations I shared with him to the attention of his senatorial colleagues and the President."

"How could our governmental leaders not sit up and take heed at what you shared?" Contessa asks quizzically.

"It is Washington D.C., Contessa, and most of these men and women have their head so far up their ass they can't even see daylight. Furthermore, our revelations are in Canada, and you know how dismissive Washington is of Canada," Noah says as he sits in a nearby chair leaning his head back and looking at the ceiling. "So how are things here?"

"It is good you are sitting down. Noah, I have something of deep concern to share," Contessa says taking a seat next to him.

Sitting up as to shake off the burdens of his recent journey, Dr. Abraham turns his keen intellect to Contessa. He knows that Dr. Margery does not make dramatic proclamations easy. "What's up?" he asks.

"As I was working in the geology lab this morning, I noticed some strange data coming in over the digital broadband seismometer from along the Mid-Atlantic Ridge. The readings were less than four on the Richter scale, but they caused me concern. I contacted the National Earthquake Information Center in Denver to report my observations. They made note, but they did not share my concerns. It is not uncommon to have minor seismic activity along the Mid-Atlantic Ridge, and it exists so far from any populated areas," Dr. Margery shares with anxiety to her voice.

"So why are you concerned Contessa?" Dr. Abraham asks recognizing her state of alarm.

"The digital broadband seismometer has been in use for a long time. This instrument is sensitive enough to pick up the motion of wind blowing through trees, or cows walking in fields, so it must be observed and interpreted carefully. It is often too easy to dismiss vital information as some kind of anomaly," Contessa states.

"So again, why are you concerned?" Noah inquires.

"I am concerned for the very reason the NEIC is not. The Mid-Atlantic Ridge is known for seismic activity, but mostly along the northern and southern part of the ridge. But the readings I am seeing run along the entire 10,000 miles of the ridge!" Contessa proclaims while leaning forward in her chair.

"I am not a trained Geologist Contessa, but if I remember my geology classes at all, minor earthquakes are hardly uncommon," Dr. Abraham recalls, "And this seems to be a minor event."

"You are correct Noah; there are over 1.5 million Earth rumblings of a 2.5 on the Richter scale or less each year. I might add that this is an increase of 600,000 from the 900,000 per year 25 years ago. There are 90,000 between 2.5 and 5.4 each year, which is an increase from 30,000 that occurred 25 years ago. Other than what traces we see on the Seismograph, no one ever knows about most of these unless they are a precursor to something bigger. I am concerned this might be the case with what I am observing in the Mid-Atlantic," Contessa says folding her hands together as if about to pray.

"I truly hope I am wrong Dr. Abraham, but if I am not, the east coast may be poised for a catastrophic event," Contessa declares.

Noah knows Contessa is serious. She very seldom calls him Dr. Abraham unless she is certain about the things of which she speaks. "What can I do Contessa, I am not a geologist, and I do not have the ear of any one at the NEIC?" Noah enquires. To these people, I would be the proverbial man howling into the wind.

"Noah, Stella is in New York City, Jack is in Washington D.C, Olivia is in Atlanta, Edison is in Miami, and Ivey lives 18,500 feet above sea level at the Atacama Observatory in Chile. If I am correct, they are in grave danger. We must inform them of our concern," Contessa pleads.

"Did you ask the people at the National Earthquake Information Center to run the data through their Earthquake Early Warning System? Certainly, the algorithm would detect whether the P Waves indicate further or serious seismic activity," Noah inquires.

"I did, and they said the system showed nothing of concern," Contessa admits, "But I am still convinced something unnatural is going on. I think we must let my sister, your brother, and our cousins know what we suspect," Contessa tells Noah as she rises from her chair. "This could be a matter of life and death."

"We must not cause a panic Contessa. We are working outside our realm of expertise and authority," Dr. Abraham reminds her.

"We might be working outside our realm of authority Noah, but geology is my area of expertise. We have seen far too many times when those in position of responsibility fail to uphold their duty to the public trust. I know we cannot issue a general warning, but at least we can try to make a difference," Dr. Margery pleads.

"Okay Contessa, you contact Stella and I will get on the phone with Jack," Noah nods as he rises and moves toward his office. "After that, I will call Edison, and you contact Olivia and Ivey."

In New York City, Stella Caroline has arrived at the Plaza Hotel and completed her journey through the receiving line of dignitaries. As she approaches the cash bar to get one of her favorite Gin and Tonics, Zachary Arthur gently catches her by the arm "Well good evening Dr. Caroline, I had hoped you might be at this event."

"You knew full well I would be here Zach, in fact, I am sure you know we are sitting at the same table," Stella retorts with a smile.

"Now what would make you think I would be interested enough to check the guest list or seating arrangements?" he responds.

"Ever since I met you last month, you have been incorrigible about leaving messages on my cell phone. I don't suspect the calls are all business," Stella says.

"Well how would you know? You never returned any of my calls," Zach challenges.

"I've been quite busy, but if I must, I will make it up to you by allowing you to buy me a drink," Stella's smile adds a twinkle to her eye.

As Zach hands Stella a drink, her cell phone rings.

"I thought we were expected to turn those things off at these events?" Zach says mischievously.

"Excuse me for a minute Zach, I need to take this," Stella pronounces while turning to find a quiet place.

"Hello, is this you Contessa?" Stella asks with excitement and anticipation.

"Stella, this is Contessa. Please listen to me carefully, this is important," she begs.

"Sure, what's up, you sound anxious and out of breath," Stella says before falling silent to listen to her sister.

"Stella, I cannot say with 100 percent certainty, but I have good reason to believe that the entire eastern seaboard is going to be rocked by a horrendous earthquake. I am not talking about a little shaking; I am talking about a monster that could rein havoc across New York City. Please, where ever you are at, identify a place now where you will be safe," Contessa implores her sister.

"Why have we not received a general warning?" Stella questions.

"There has been no general warning because the National Earthquake Information Center does not share my concern. Please don't ignore what I am saying, this could be a matter of life or death. I beseech you, don't wait, take action now," Contessa appeals to her sister.

"Hello, this is Senator Joseph's office, may I help you," the Senator's secretary asks.

"Nora–"

Before Dr. Abraham can go on, "Well hello Dr. Abraham, are you still in town?" Nora asks recognizing his voice since Noah and the senator sound so much alike.

"Nora, patch me through to the senator, this is urgent," Noah demands.

Nora has known Dr. Abraham for a number of years and she has never known him to be rude. Whatever the reason for his call, it must be important to come with such urgency.

"I am sorry Dr. Abraham, but the senator is at the White House," Nora reveals.

"Patch me through to the White House Nora, I must speak with Jack now!" Noah nearly shouts.

Now Nora knows the call is serious because Dr. Abraham never refers to the senator as Jack to her or anyone else. "Hold on Dr. Abraham, I will see if I can get through to the president's secretary."

"Mr. President, there is an urgent call for Senator Joseph. Can he step out to take it?"

"Hello, this is Senator Joseph, what can be so important as to draw me away from the President of the United States?" he says in an accusing manner.

"Jack, this is Noah."

"Noah, I just arrived to visit with the President about the things you revealed to me. What could ever be so important now?"

"Jack, Contessa is seeing seismic activity all along the Mid-Atlantic Ridge. She believes a major earth quake is imminent. The entire eastern seaboard could be at risk," Noah announces.

"Are you certain? Why have we not heard anything about this from the National Earthquake Information Center? What you are saying is serious, and how imminent are you talking about?" Jack asks in rapid succession.

"We are not certain. The National Earthquake Information Center does not agree with us. Yes, this could be catastrophic. And imminent means it could occur very soon," Noah reveals with candor and seriousness.

"What do you expect us to do about it if we have not received notification from the federal agency entrusted with issuing earthquake warnings? We cannot declare an emergency situation and risk a panic based on one person's opinion even if I trust that person emphatically," the Senator says revealing the obvious.

"This is not just any person Jack. Dr. Margery is an expert in geology. I trust her knowledge, insight, and opinion without reservation. If I didn't, I wouldn't be making this call," Noah's indignation is obvious. "What I expect you to do is be prepared. If a major earthquake occurs along the entire ten-thousand-mile fault line of the Mid-Atlantic Ridge, the result will be unprecedented."

"Thank you, Noah, I appreciate your warning, and I will act accordingly," Senator Joseph assures.

Going back into the Oval Office, the president can tell that Senator Joseph is a bit shaken. He invites the senator to sit so the two can talk. He is not prepared for what the senator is about to share with him regarding his phone call with Dr. Abraham. After listening, the President knows if this is true, everything along the Atlantic seaboard is in jeopardy.

Dismissing the senator, the president calls in his Chief of Staff and orders him to check with the National Earthquake Information Center. He then calls in his top-secret service agent and orders him to prepare for a rapid response should an earthquake occur.

The president is not about to start a mass panic based on the call from Dr. Margery. The president does not know Dr. Margery like Noah or Jack. He has no way of knowing how her credibility is greater than that of his closest advisors or any federal employee on this subject. Even if it is true, what can he do? There is not enough time to begin any kind of evacuation. All he would do with any kind of proclamation or warning would be to create chaos.

Senator Joseph quickly returns to his office and advises Nora and his staff of the impending situation. He then contacts the leadership of the Senate and House to apprise them of the potential situation. He reaches out to anyone who may be in a position to save lives in the event the scenario to which he has been made privy transpires.

———————>»◆«<———————

Back in New York, Stella has rejoined Zachary Arthur. Pulling him aside, she shares the nature of her phone call with him. He suggests they find Ambassador DiCaprio and bring him up to speed on this potential situation. Asking the ambassador to join them in a room off of the Imperial Ballroom, Stella reveals what she has been told by her sister.

The ambassador tells Stella and Zach to remain quiet about this to avoid what might be an unnecessary panic. He assures them that he is going to look into this and take necessary precautions. He tells them how important it is that they remain calm and act normal.

As Stella and Zach return to the Imperial Ballroom, Ambassador DiCaprio pulls out his cell phone and calls the direct line to the White House. Talking with the president, the ambassador is told to quietly make arrangements for an emergency but at the same time realize there is no valid reason for the government to be issuing a warning. More than likely, the president reminds the ambassador somewhat unconvincingly, that this is nothing of concern.

Getting off the phone, Ambassador DiCaprio contacts the head of security for the event and directs him to prepare for an emergency should a quake indeed occur. Returning to the Imperial Ballroom, the ambassador prepares to offer his opening remarks to the assembly of distinguished guests.

———————>»◆«<———————

"Hello, Contessa, to what do I owe this call," says Olivia.

"Olivia, listen carefully, I know you are 160 miles from the Atlantic Coast, but if what I fear occurs, you will be greatly impacted," Contessa reveals.

"Whoa, slow down cousin, what are you talking about?" Olivia inquires pushing the phone tight against her ear so not to miss a thing.

"I suspect a major earthquake is going to happen soon along the Mid-Atlantic Ridge," Contessa prophesizes.

"Why have we not heard anything of this through official channels?" Olivia wonders.

"Because the people running the official channels have their head up their ass," Contessa uncharacteristically spouts with a huge sigh. "You need to pay heed Olivia and take steps to do what is necessary to be prepared."

"When is this supposed to happen?" Olivia asks.

"It is imminent, Olivia, now just assure me you will take this seriously and do whatever you can to be prepared," Contessa is shouting into the phone as if her voice needs to travel the 708 miles from Ann Arbor to Atlanta. Before her cousin can respond, "I must go; I need to call Ivey now!"

As the telephone goes dead, Olivia stands stunned at the conviction with which her cousin has delivered this dire information. "How do you prepare for something catastrophic in a matter of seconds, minutes, or hours?" she wonders. "I cannot do this a lone, I need immediate help to prepare and secure this place."

"Hello, this is the National Underwater Oceanic Observatory in what was once beautiful downtown Miami," comes the voice on the other end of the phone.

"I need to speak to Dr. Jude immediately," Noah says with obvious urgency in his voice.

"I am sorry, but Dr. Jude is currently making observations from a submergible. We have instructions he is to not be disturbed. I can . . .," the voice on the other end of the phone cannot finish.

"I don't give a rat's ass what instructions you have, I am his brother, and I am telling you this cannot wait. Contact him immediately, this is serious!" Noah commands.

"Dr. Jude, this is Walter, you have a phone call . . .," Walter is interrupted before he can finish.

"Walter, I left specific instructions to not be disturbed. I am observing some amazing things; I do not have time for a phone call," Dr. Jude commands.

Feeling caught in the middle, Walter says, "Sir, it is your brother. I told him your instructions, but he insists you speak right away."

"Well, why didn't you say it was Noah, patch him through," Dr. Jude says his voice softening.

"Edison, can you hear me?" Noah says seeking confirmation.

"I hear you loud and clear brother. What makes your call so important?" Edison asks.

"Contessa and I fear there will be a major event along the Mid-Atlantic Ridge which could be devastating to the entire eastern seaboard," Noah shares adding his name to increase the sense of seriousness. "Contessa has observed seismic activity which she believes is a precursor to something big."

"Brother, the Mid-Atlantic Ridge experiences thousands of minor seismic events every year. Of all the plates on Earth, those contiguous to the Mid-Atlantic Ridge have been the most stable for thousands of years!" emphasizes Edison.

"This is not a time to be academic Edison. I know you are a relentless explorer, and you often throw caution to the wind, but this is not the time. Please pay heed. Get the hell out of the water and prepare for something big," Noah implores.

"Now that you mention it brother, I have been observing something unexplainable. The ocean is always in motion, but recently I have observed an unusual sort of washing occurring along the bottom when diving at 1000 feet or more," Edison observes.

"We can talk about this later Edison. Just get the hell out of the water and prepare for something big," Noah repeats his command.

"Okay, Noah," Edison assures as he radios into Walter at the Observatory. Noah can hear his brother's communication, "Walter this is Dr. Jude. We are making an immediate return to the observatory. I need you to gather up all digital records with the intention of taking them immediately to the surface with ourselves and all other personnel. Do you copy?"

"I copy," comes the response from Walter.

"Are you satisfied brother?" Edison asks.

"Thanks Eddie, I will talk to you later. Good luck!" Noah says in closing.

"Hello this is Dr. Isabelle, who is calling," Ivey questions over her short-wave radio system which she relies on when other types of signals are unavailable.

"Ivey, this is Contessa in Ann Arbor, Michigan, how are things at the bottom of the world?"

"Contessa, what is this family reunion week? I just spoke with Olivia a few hours ago. How are things? I guess you folks in the north would say they are pretty upside down for us," Ivey offers with a chuckle.

"I wish this was a pleasure call, but I need to apprise you of something we think is imminent, but more than likely will not impact you," Contessa says.

"What's going on Contessa?"

"I know you are closer to the Pacific Ocean than the Atlantic, and I also know you are somewhat enclosed by the Andes Mountains, but we have reason to believe a major event is imminent along the 10,000-mile Mid-Atlantic Ridge. We also believe such an event poses a serious threat to the entire North and South American Atlantic seaboard," Contessa reveals.

"So how does this impact the Atacama Observatory?" Ivey inquires.

"Since you are in a part of South America where the distance between the Atlantic and Pacific Oceans is minimal, you could experience a shaking similar to the waging of a dog's tail," Contessa suggests.

"That sounds rather serious," Ivey notes with a bit of anxiety in her voice. "However, I do believe we are built to withstand earthquakes of a significant magnitude."

"I am not so concerned about earthquakes for you as I am volcanic activity. Depending on the event, it could spur on otherwise dormant volcanoes, and I know you have a few of those in your area. Please be prepared to evacuate should any unusual volcanic activity occur," Contessa urges.

"I will meet with the others, and we will take every precaution. We have a helicopter always available to us, and we are all licensed pilots. If necessary, we can be out of here in a matter of minutes," Ivey assured her.

"Good, let's hope none of this is necessary. You take care, and I will keep in touch," Contessa closes.

With that, Contessa is off the air. Everyone that needs to be notified has received word. This is of little help to the millions of people who live along the eastern seaboard of North and South America. Sitting back with Dr. Abraham, Contessa feels an awful sickness in her stomach. She sips a drink Dr. Abraham brought her, and the cool flavorful liquid has a settling effect. She is so grateful to have the support and friendship of her cousin. She feels so helpless, the powers controlling the emergency and rapid response networks all across the country do not believe she knows what she is talking about. She can only hope they are right. Only time will tell now, and for now, she and Noah have done all in their power.

Noah sits in silence with Dr. Margery. As he sips his vodka and lemonade with a shot of grape juice, one of his grandfather's favorites, he wonders how this has all come to be.

For the past two-decades, the world has been assaulted by environmental calamities. Science and scientists have issued warning after warning about the impact of unregulated human activity on the environment. Despite the attempts of education to create a scientifically literate population, a large segment of the citizenry of the United States continue to deny that which science proves.

The great irony is that science helped deliver humanity out of the dark ages. The enlightenment based on philosophy and science is responsible for creating the foundation for modern government and society. The product of science is everywhere making modern life too easy.

However, anything can be like a heroin addict's inflated need for more. As a result, science finds itself in a catch 22 situation. Science brings forth new and glorious advancements in all areas of life. Science also finds itself warning against excess. The addict's compulsion for more.

The scientific community which is almost unanimously in agreement on the impact of human activity on the environment can issue warning after warning, but, if people don't want to hear it, they will not listen.

Noah picks up a copy of the "Earth in the Balance" by then Vice President Al Gore. He has read this prophetic warning so many times, he can recite pages as testimony to the dark deliverance of the world to human abuse.

Throughout the past several decades, science has fallen victim to evangelical Christians as it fell victim during the Renaissance to the Pope. It is all part of the never-ending battle between God and science, faith and fact. How is it that even in the face of doom people cannot accept that science may be a tool provided by God for the redemption of the world. If only we could find the answer to our deliverance.

CHAPTER 8

ASSURING SAFETY

B ACK IN WASHINGTON D.C., THE President's Chief of Staff Andrew Peet contacts the head of the Environmental Protection Agency about the ominous warning. The EPA head tells Peet such a seismic event along the Mid-Atlantic Ridge is highly unlikely due to the rift valley which exists between the North American Plate and the Eurasian Plate, and the South American Plate and the African Plate. The Mid-Atlantic rift is caused by the plates moving a part. Such movement which is at about the same speed as the growth of a finger nail, may cause minor tremors of which most of them go undetected. This kind of tectonic movement is not the cause of significant earthquakes.

Peet reports his findings back to President Armstrong, but reminds the president that history holds testimony too many instances when ignoring such warnings has resulted in calamity. Being the political animal he is, Peet urges the president to cover his ass in the event something occurs.

The president has personally met several members of Senator Joseph's illustrious family. While the corporate world and most politicians attempt to discredit the unique scientific work of these individuals, the president recognizes the merits of their work. He also knows Senator Joseph as a man of integrity and common sense. As a former Eagle Scout, the president believes in the credo "be prepared."

After giving it further thought, President Armstrong instructs his Chief of Staff to place FEMA, the Army Reserve, Coast Guard, and National Guard along the east coast on high alert. President Armstrong commands Secretary of Defense Bluster, Chairman of the Joint Chiefs of Staff General Randolph, National Security Advisor Shady, and other top cabinet members to report to the situation room at the White House immediately.

It is 8:00 p.m. eastern time when everyone finally arrives at the situation room. "Thank you for arriving so quickly. The matter before us is of the most serious nature. I have received information from a highly credible source that a major event along the Mid-Atlantic Ridge is eminent. This information suggests the event could result in a violent earthquake along the eastern seaboard. I think everyone in this room knows the serious implications if such an event should occur," the president announces as he makes eye contact with each person sitting around the table.

"Mr. President, are you certain about the credibility of such a warning? Of all the places on Earth where a major quake could occur, the Mid-Atlantic Ridge is the least likely. These tectonic plates are moving apart, not converging." states National Security Advisor Shady.

"Mr. Shady, do you remember the earthquake of August 23, 2011 which shook the entire east coast?" the president asks challenging his National Security Advisor on the topic.

"I do Mr. President, and if I remember correctly, that quake measured 5.8 on the Richter scale, with the epicenter being about 3.5 miles below the state of Virginia. The quake of August 23, 2011 as well as the many other minor quakes since are not a result of the Mid-Atlantic Ridge, but rather minor fault lines located below the east coast," Mr. Shady responds. "How is this relevant?"

"The relevance is we do not have the luxury to debate the likelihood of such a scenario. We are going to treat this with all seriousness, and I need everyone around this table to do their job," the president commands, "Is that understood."

Everyone around the table mumbles ascent and nods in agreement. Some look at each other in disbelief, but they know, they serve at the pleasure of the president.

"We must take every precaution to protect our citizens and our vital national interests. Every naval station along the Eastern Seaboard must do everything possible to be prepared to deal with what may come. I want as much of our air power along the coast moved inland as quickly as possible. I want all military bases prepared to lend emergency assistance as well as population control. Should this occur, it could be a real disaster, but nothing compared to the disastrous impact of chaos and panic," President Armstrong demands.

"Can you be a little more definitive with our roles and responsibilities Mr. President?" a rather foolish cabinet member asks.

"We don't have time for such bullshit as roles and responsibilities. You each have a job, and I expect you to do it. Furthermore, I expect you to work together as a team in addressing anything that may need to be done," the president asserts.

Just as the president completes his statement, the group hears a rumble and feels movement in the room. It is mild, but it is real enough that everyone takes heed.

"Move ladies and gentlemen, move now and get things in motion before it is too late," the president orders.

Over in the Senate Office Building, Senator Joseph has ordered his staff to go home and take care of their families. Arnold, the Senator's Chief of Staff is a bachelor and has no family. He insists on remaining with the senator who is determined to oversee the evacuation of the Capital Complex.

Using their digital devices while moving through the hallways from office to office, the two insist people go home and seek safety until any prospect of danger has passed. Stopping in the security office, the senator finds the Majority and Minority leaders working collaboratively with security to implement an evacuation process. The senator is hesitant to break up the party since these two politicians hardly ever work together, but he knows they have families and he does not. It takes some convincing, but he eventually wins the day assuring them that he can do the job they are doing. They need to get home to their wives and kids.

All along the eastern seaboard the rumble and shaking registered with 140 million people who no matter what they are doing, stop and take notice that something unusual occurred.

At the Plaza Hotel in New York City, Leonardo DiCaprio is at the podium making his welcoming remarks when the rumble interrupts him in mid-sentence, and follows with a minor five-second shake. In that brief moment, he is glad to have spoken with security about being prepared should something occur. In the next moment, he knows it is time to activate security and opt for safety.

"Ladies and Gentlemen, please remain calm. What just occurred was a minor event, but perhaps an important warning for us to call it a night. While we are not certain, sometimes such minor events are followed by something more significant. Security is prepared to help us evacuate in an orderly manner. They will start with the back tables and work to the front. If we all cooperate, we should all be on our way home in a matter of minutes," the ambassador instructs. "Please, as you return to your home or wherever you feel safest, please exercise caution and good judgment for your safety and that of your family. While we hope nothing further occurs, it is best to presume it will."

Sitting at one of the front tables, Stella Caroline and Zachary Arthur remain calm awaiting their time to exit. They both know about Dr. Margery's warning and hope what they just experienced is all there is to it. Stella fumbles with her water glass displaying the nervousness she feels inside.

"Relax Stella, it will be alright," Zach assures.

"I am trying Zach. My Dad often told me to be like a duck, all calm and composed above the surface, but paddling like hell underneath. It is good advice, but right now I am struggling just a bit," Stella discloses with a nervous smile.

At about that time, Ambassador DiCaprio appears at the table, "Stella, I need you to come with me."

"What about Zach?" she asks not wanting to leave her table companion behind.

"Bring Zach along, I just need you to follow me," he says.

With security guards in front and behind them, Stella, Zach, and the ambassador head to the staircase. "This will be a bit of a climb," one of the security guards informs them, "but keep moving."

As they get to within three floors of the roof, they encounter a line of people heading in the same direction. Pushing the line to the side, the security guards hurry the three past everyone else to the roof top door. As they exit the door onto the roof, Stella can hardly believe her eyes. There are helicopters everywhere like a swarm of humming birds darting back and forth, but always staying clear of each other.

On the roof top sits a helicopter, "This one is yours Mr. Ambassador, please get seated and buckle up quickly for departure!" comes the instructions from the man coordinating the landing and taking off process. "Thank you, Marvin," the ambassador says to the man as he hurries Stella and Zach aboard.

In a flash they are airborne going straight up until clear of everyone else before moving away. Stella notices that they have hardly left the roof top and another helicopter lands, loads, and departs. It seems dangerous as helicopters rise from the roof top in a continuous column. Speechless, she stares out the window in amazement at the mastery of coordination and piloting required to allow this to occur without incident.

Turning to Ambassador DiCaprio, "Where are we going?" she asks.

"We are heading inland to the University of Syracuse. I am good friends with the President of the University, and she has agreed to put us up for a few days. We will be able to work out of the President's mansion while we monitor and assess anything that may occur," the ambassador answers.

"What about all of those other people and helicopters, where are they heading?" Zach asks.

"Everyone has a designated place to go either of their choosing or arranged by the Department of Homeland Security. No one is allowed to leave by motor vehicle, and within a matter of minutes, everyone will be on their way to safety," the ambassador reveals.

"How did this all happen so quickly?" Stella inquires.

"As soon as you told me about the warning from Dr. Margery, I implemented a protocol which is always in place in the event of certain types of emergencies. Once the protocol was implemented, security stood ready to act on a moment's notice. When that rumble occurred followed by the shaking, no matter how mild, I had no intentions of waiting any longer. Even before I made the announcement, security put all aspects of the plan in motion," the ambassador said with a cross between a frown and smile.

"What if that is all there is, what if there is nothing more to it?" Zack wonders.

"That, Zach, would be the best of all results. However, we cannot take any risks. If that rumble and shake were just coincidence in the wake of Dr. Margery's warning, we should all be glad. In the meantime, we need to take time to see if there is more to come," Ambassador DiCaprio reminds the other two as he places a folded piece of chewing gum in his mouth while offering Stella and Zach a stick of gum.

"What about the millions of people in New York City and all along the eastern coast? What will happen to them?" Stella asks with alarm in her voice and eyes wide as a young fawn.

"Stella, we all live at the mercy of Mother Nature. People who live on the east coast, or anywhere else for that matter, do so knowing Mother Nature may rear her ugly head at any moment. You and I know better than most that this has become increasingly a fact of life as humans continue to place their self-interest over the interests of a healthy planet," the ambassador says affirming what Stella and Zach know to be the truth.

As they zoom across the sky toward Syracuse, Stella leans back, closes her eyes, and prays.

In Atlanta, Georgia, Dr. Kae is too far inland to hear the rumble or feel any movement. Since getting the warning from Contessa, Olivia has been busy coordinating and securing everything that needs to be tied down in the lab and storage facility. She is confident they can avoid a breach of any kind with appropriate precaution.

Returning to her office to ensure no important messages have arrived during her absence, she notices that DNN (Digital News Network) is reporting on the rumble and shake which just occurred all along the east coast. The news is reporting it as a minor event unaware of Contessa's concern. Up until the rumble and shake, they received no information from the National Earthquake Information Center, and even now it is being reported as an insignificant event.

Feeling a bit overwhelmed, Dr. Kae sits for a moment in her high back chair and takes a sip from a cold cup of coffee. She wonders why the NEIC hasn't at least put out a warning urging people to take some basic precautions. She realizes they must act prudently. Anything other than this could spark wide spread panic, which would result in mayhem and chaos. It is such a precarious situation when there is no certainty anything of serious proportion will occur. Finishing her cold coffee and taking a bite from a previously ignored chocolate chip cookie, Dr. Kae returns to the work at hand.

In the lost city of Miami, Dr. Jude surfaced from the water in time to hear the rumbling and feel the movement. He is a seasoned professional. He knows immediately this is something totally different than anything they have experienced before. There is something going on along the Mid-Atlantic Ridge that is unnatural and ominous. Most people hear the rumble and feel the movement, but Dr. Jude senses things nobody else can feel. Perhaps it comes from all his years of studying and working around reptiles, but he knows things when others have no clue.

Picking up his digital device, he quickly has Dr. Abraham on the phone. "Noah, I thought I'd better contact you and let you know, I am out of the water and at the surface," he tells his brother.

"Good, Edison, now get yourself to a safe and secure area," Noah directs.

"Oh, don't worry brother, we are securing our area, grabbing our data, and getting the hell out of here," Dr. Jude informs.

"Do you know more than I do Eddie?" his brother asks.

"I always know more than you do," Edison shoots back in a playful manner.

"This is not the time to be a smart-ass Eddie, what do you know? Tell me now," Noah decrees.

"It is not what I know Noah, it is what I feel. As you probably already know, there has been a rumbling and movement along the east coast. Most people don't see it as anything significantly different from what has occurred occasionally in the past, but I do. What we have experienced in the past results from a sudden movement of the Mid-Atlantic Ridge in certain places as it separates. What occurred less than an hour ago was different," Edison reveals.

"How so Eddie, be more specific?" Dr. Abraham requests.

"I have experienced an earthquake caused by subduction before Noah, and this felt like that. I don't think the rift valley of the Mid-Atlantic Ridge increased; I think it decreased. If this is the case, Contessa's warning may be totally justified and something big is about to occur," Edison shares with obvious alarm in his voice.

"Then get off the phone and get the hell out of there Edison so I can talk to you later," Noah implores.

"I hear you, big brother, I will be in the air in less than 30 minutes. Talk again soon," Edison says as he closes out the conversation and returns to the work of evacuating.

<hr/>

In Ann Arbor, Dr. Abraham walks down the hall to Contessa's office. It is 7:45 p.m. Central Standard Time, but they both have no intentions of stopping work anytime soon. Ever since Contessa detected the movement which gave her concern for the east coast, they have been closely monitoring data and trying to convince people to take precautionary action.

"Contessa, I just got off the phone with Edison," Noah announces as he enters her office.

"Is he secure and safe?" she asks turning in her chair to see a look of alarm on Noah's face.

"He is still in Miami, but he is working to get out of there as-soon-as possible. He heard the rumble and felt the motion reported all along the east coast. He is certain you are correct in your assessment that something big is going to happen," Noah reveals shaking his head in disbelief.

"Why, what could cause an oceanographer to agree with me?" she wonders leaning her head to the side with a quizzical look.

"He said, what he just experienced was unnatural for the Mid-Atlantic Ridge. He said, a rumbling and movement caused by the rift widening is discretely different from what he experienced. What he heard and felt resulted from subduction in his opinion," Noah shares.

"Subduction would make sense if it didn't defy millions-of-years of the earth's development. But it would explain my concern for what I have been observing and interpreting. How is this possible?" Contessa pauses to consider her own question. She rubs her forehead like a magic lamp hoping for an answer.

"What if it is all part of a coordinated pattern Contessa? Think about what has transpired in the past couple weeks. We are observing some very strange and rather rapid animal transformations in Canada. You believe the Canadian Tar Sands are retracting of their own accord. Hannah's observations regarding the farm land of the mid-west. Edison has reported a significant increase in the size of sea creatures in the Miami graveyard. The rising sea levels and the manner in which they seem to be reclaiming the land cannot be dismissed. What if Hannah's idea of Devolution is real? What if it is occurring on an all-encompassing level?" Noah supposes.

What Noah does not know are Dr. Henry's discovery in the Gobi Desert, Dr. Kae's revelations about insects and disease, and Dr. Isabelle's encounter with the Universe. If he were able to add these to his consideration, his all-encompassing assessment of Devolution becomes all too real.

"If this is true Noah, the plates along the 10,000-mile Mid-Atlantic Ridge may be reversing course and coalescing," Contessa surmises, "The implications are beyond comprehension."

"What is most riveting Contessa is the possibility that all of this is occurring as a result of some conscience intent on the part of something we cannot see nor understand. What if all of this is inevitable? What if it is beyond our ability to interfere and prevent the things of which we are most concerned?" Noah wonders aloud with distress in his voice.

"I believe it is time for us to convene a meeting of our cousins to determine what we are facing, and what we might do to be a part of the solution," Contessa asserts pointing to a group picture sitting on her desk of everyone from last Christmas at Grandma and Grandpa's.

"I think you are right Contessa. Let's see if we can make this happen," Noah affirms reaching into his pocket to retrieve one of his favorite tootsies.

Tootsies have long been Noah's comfort treat. As a youngster, Noah would consume hand fulls of tootsies at his Grandparent's home. Grandma always kept all flavors of tootsies in full supply in a jar on the kitchen counter. His Grandma and Grandpa use to smile when discovering a stash of wrappers hidden to conceal Noah's consumption. Grandma would chide him to no avail to use the garbage can.

Now, he tosses the wrapper onto the credenza in Contessa's office.

CHAPTER 9

SLEDGEHAMMER

A s NIGHT FALLS ALL ALONG the east coast, everything is anything but quiet. The low rumbles and groaning coming from the Mid-Atlantic Ridge continue without increasing in intensity. Most of the movements are undetectable at the surface, but every-once-in-a-while a noticeable shift occurs. The authorities have used every media source possible to urge calm. However, it is difficult to ignore the increased presence of FEMA, the Army Reserves, Coast Guard, and National Guard, especially when the news media leaves no stone unturned and ignores the request for discretion by local, state, and national authorities.

The one thing the authorities want to avoid is a mass panic. Few things could be as nightmarish as millions of people trying to flee in panic. Under such a scenario, all avenues for evacuation and assistance would be quickly clogged by the surge of humanity. As far as the authorities know, nothing of significance is going to happen. The National Earthquake Information Center has not issued any kind of warning. In fact, authorities are being told by everyone but Dr. Margery and Dr. Abraham that the Mid-Atlantic Ridge will not result in a major earth quake, and if there were an event, it would not negatively impact the eastern coast of North or South America. It is only because of the president's high regard for Senator Joseph and his cousins that any level of preparation is underway. The rumbles and small shaking have also given the president reason to act.

The authorities can only hope that this will all pass without incident.

They know that a major quake could cause catastrophic devastation. They have learned over the past couple decades to be prepared.

It is just past mid-night when the entire east coast is hit with a deep rumbling and shaking which causes the lights to flicker. At the White House, Chief of Staff Peet is taking a phone call from the head of the National Earthquake Information Center, Nevelle Quiver.

"Mr. Peet, we clearly noticed that last event, and it is truly something of concern. We have never seen anything like it along the Mid-Atlantic Ridge. It is our advice that you get the president to a secure location and out of Washington if possible," urges the man on the other end of the phone.

"I will notify the president immediately!" Peet responds.

Rushing from his office, Peet knows he will find the president in the Situation Room monitoring the orders he has thus far issued. Entering the Situation Room, he finds the President, Attorney General Blithe Loophole, and Secretary of State Ronald Globalseer huddled together in conversation.

Looking up over his glasses, the president notices Peet enter the room. "Did you hear and feel that last shake Peet?" the president asks while knowing full well the answer.

"I just got off the phone with the head of the National Earthquake Information Center Mr. President, and he says there is reason for serious concern," Peet reveals with his arms crossed and shaking his head. "I am always amazed at how the experts finally get it right when we're in the fourth quarter of a situation."

"Well, I'll be go to hell," the president responds, "Do they really think we should be concerned now?" he adds with the cynicism of Antisthenes, the Greek student of Socrates who is considered the father of cynicism.

"They advise that you need to get to a secure location Mr. President, or get out of Washington all together," Peet continues.

"What are they saying Mr. Peet? What is it that now has them so concerned?" asks the president.

"I do not know specifics Sir; I just know they now believe we could be in for a major event," Peet asserts.

"Peet" the president calls out as his Chief of Staff is about to exit the room, "We need to get a warning out all along the east coast in a way not to cause a panic, but to get people to take every safety precaution."

Turning to his Attorney General the president commands, "Get a hold of Senator Joseph and tell him to get his ass over here immediately!"

Since Dr. Margery first contacted him, the senator has been busy seeing to it that the Senate Office Building and Capital Building are evacuated. He has been telling everyone to leave and seek a secure and safe place. As usual, he has met resistance from naysayers who leave him dismayed at their careless stubbornness. However, the last rumble and shake were note-worthy, and caused even the most stubborn S.O.B. to take action.

"Senator Joseph, this is Attorney General Loophole. The president would like you in the Situation Room immediately!"

"Tell the President I am on my way," the senator responds.

Senator Joseph has done all he can to warn people and evacuate Capitol Hill. Standing 6'3" and weighing 225 pounds, Jack Joseph still possesses the physical stature he did as an undergraduate linebacker for the University of Northern Iowa Panthers thirteen years ago. Senator Joseph exits the Capitol Building with Arnold close behind and hurries down the steps to Pennsylvania Avenue. Running as fast as a person can in dress shoes, he traverses the 2.1 miles to the White House in just under 15 minutes. Hustling to the basement of the West Wing, the Senator enters the Situation Room.

"Senator Joseph, I see you are as fit as ever," the president greets. "Please join us at the table."

Sliding up to the table on his first ever trip to the Situation Room, Senator Joseph sees the monitors around the room are focused on Boston, New York City, Charleston, Jacksonville and a satellite feed of the eastern seaboard. "Everything looks peaceful and quiet Mr. President," the senator observes.

"The calm before the storm senator, the calm before the storm," the president announces.

"You seem certain about that Mr. President," the senator says hoping he is wrong.

"I have been pretty certain since your cousin Dr. Margery offered her words of warning. Haven't you? I am now more certain than ever after receiving word from the National Earthquake Information Center that something ominous is occurring," the president reveals giving a huge sigh.

"Should we remain here Mr. President?" the senator asks.

"This is the most secure area in the White House compound," the Secretary of State assures, "This room was built to withstand just about any kind of assault even from Mother Nature."

The Secretary of State no sooner offers his assurance when the most God-awful rumble sounding noise, much like a person standing in the room hammering on kettle drums, occurs. The four men in the room look at each other as the room literally begins to buckle and heave like a mechanical bull attempting to throw them from their chairs. All they can do is hang on and hope it passes quickly.

When the rocking and rolling stop, the men have no idea how long the quake lasted. They are in the dark, but they are okay. The president assures the others that the White House has several emergency backup power systems, and as soon as the computer locates the right one, power will be restored. Almost prophetically, the lights blink on, the monitors come back to life, and the room shows little sign of such a violent assault.

The monitors on the wall show something totally different. Pictures of Boston and New York show a skyline once tall laid low. There are fires burning everywhere. These two cities look as if they have been hit by an atomic bomb. Turning their attention to Charleston and Jacksonville, the scene offers little hope that any part of the east coast has been spared.

Taking a look at the satellite feed of the east coast, the four men notice something disturbing. Running along a line north to south, it looks like a huge disturbance moving east and west in the Atlantic Ocean. About this time, the door to the Situation Room swings open and the bruised and bloodied Chief of Staff Peet bursts through.

"Thank God Peet you are alive," the president proclaims.

"Mr. President, we have no time to waste. The earthquake triggered a tsunami which is expected to reach the east coast in three hours. We are all in grave danger. I have a helicopter ready on the south lawn to take you and the others to safety," the Chief of Staff informs. "We must move quickly!"

As the men depart the Situation Room, they make their way to ground level using the stairs. As they reach the top of the stairs and enter the corridor adjacent the Cabinet Room, they witness the walls breached and the room caved in over the Press Secretary's Office and the Roosevelt Room. They hurry to the Oval Office to find furniture turned over, priceless pictures and statuary strewn across the floor. The windows to the south, out of which many presidents have spent time reflecting, are shattered with glass everywhere. Ceiling debris litters the President's desk. The president halts as if to get something from his desk, but his secret service detail shove him toward the door leading to the south lawn.

Hustling outside and onto the awaiting helicopter, the president, attorney general, secretary of state, Senator Joseph, and Arnold take their places and buckle in for a quick take off. The president yells for Peet and the secret service agents to board the helicopter, which they do just before the door slams shut and the ground quickly fades in the distance.

As the helicopter rises above the trees, the panorama which awaits these air-borne hostages is surreal. The Washington Monument, which once stood tall at the center of the Mall now lay across the ground like the ancient temple of Zeus in Olympia, Greece. The Lincoln Memorial stands like some uncompleted project with missing pillars and an incomplete roof. Senator Joseph recently traveled to Greece, and the sight of the Lincoln Memorial reminds him of the ruins of the ancient Parthenon. All along the Mall the buildings look like someone has taken to them with a giant sledge hammer. At the far eastern end of the Mall, the dome of the United States Capitol Building has collapsed, taking with it much of the west front of the building, and filling the Great Rotunda with 4,500 tons of iron and steel. The partially collapsed Senate and House wings of the Capitol stand separated as a stark reminder of Lincoln's warning about a house divided. The most poignant sight for the president is what little remains of the White House. The people's house, the house first occupied by John Adams, second President of the United States, lay in ruins.

Before the helicopter turns to head west away from the city, the men get a good look to the east toward the Atlantic Ocean. The men are surprised to see an ocean which looks serene and calm. Sensing their puzzlement, the pilot offers a lesson about tsunamis, and what is expected to hit the east coast.

The pilot tells the men that a tsunami is an underwater disturbance. In this case, the tsunami was set off by the earthquake. tsunami waves can move at 500 miles per hour, and they seldom manifest themselves until they near landfall and shallow water. It is at this time that the surface water traveling at an incredible speed gathers up and forms a sea wall which can hit with a very destructive force.

"Where are we headed pilot?" the president asks.

"We are headed for your retreat outside Nashville. A command center is being set up at this time, Sir," the pilot responds.

"How can I assess the extent of the damage from Nashville? I need to be in Philadelphia or somewhere closer to the east coast," the president asserts.

"I am just following orders Sir; I am sure there will be someone at the retreat to address all of your questions," the pilot says.

"Let me turn on the monitor so you can see what is going on Sir," the co-pilot offers. These pilots have trained all their careers for such an evacuation hoping to never put their training to use.

The monitor in the cabin flickers to life with scenes out of some kind of sci-fi movie. The first report comes out of New York City where the entire borough of Manhattan lay in ruins. The reporter is talking about devastation beyond imagination. Sky scrapers came tumbling down destroying everything and killing everyone in their path. The destruction from the earthquake set off fires determined to eradicate any evidence of civilization. The fires illuminate the night providing important visibility to emergency vehicles and personnel. However, the fires are releasing toxic gas which threatens not only people still alive on the island, but with a breeze coming in off the ocean, anyone living within a 20 mile radius. The Lincoln Tunnel collapsed as did every bridge to the island with the exception of the Tappan Zee Bridge. The Army Reserves have commandeered the bridge, not allowing anyone to leave the island, so the bridge can be used exclusively for emergency purposes. Miraculously, the Statue of Liberty still stands in New York Harbor.

The reporter turns her attention to Long Island. While the damage is great, it is much more contained on this island, still considered the playground of the wealthy. The main concerns for the people of Long Island are the fact that the Queen Midtown Tunnel is flooded, and the Williamsburg, Manhattan, and Brooklyn Bridges all leading to and from the island have been destroyed. This means any access to and from the island is restricted to the Verrazano-Narrows Bridge and Highway 478 in the south, and the Ed Koch Queensboro Bridge and RFK Triborough Bridge in the north.

The National Guard has commandeered the Verrazano-Narrows Bridge as an indirect access to Manhattan via Highway 478. The guard is prohibiting anyone other than authorized vehicles to use Highway 478 because it goes into Manhattan. The bridges to the north are open to traffic, but they are congested and slow. As for the remainder of the city, it is in a state of emergency, and the roads are packed with people trying to flee the horror.

The biggest concern for the people on Long Island is the oncoming tsunami which could devastate this island. Long Island is 118 miles long and 23 miles across at its widest point. Historically, at the turn of the 20th Century, Long Island served as home to the great industrialists, financiers, and robber barons. Over time, the general population took over Long Island until 25 years ago, the population of Long Island was nearly eight million people. Today, after years of struggle and take over, Long Island has returned as the home to some of the wealthiest families in the United States. These people of great wealth have invested millions if not billions of dollars in building fortified compounds for security and safety. Now, in the wake of this great earthquake, these elaborate compounds stand vulnerable to the horror that is coming. The distance from Long Island to the closest point of the earthquake along the Mid-Atlantic Ridge is 1,686 miles. With the tsunami traveling in excess of 500 miles per hour, it is predicted to reach Long Island shortly after 3:00 a.m. with wave heights reaching 250 plus feet above sea level.

"Mr. President, I have General Randolph on the line for you Sir," the copilot says.

"General, are things as bad as they look on this monitor," the president says praying for some sign of hope.

"Mr. President, things are worse than you could ever imagine. I have set up a command center in the Hudson Highlands just west of New York City. The place looks like the site of Armageddon. Manhattan is ablaze, and frankly we cannot get rescue vehicles close enough to do any good. We are going to send in airtankers to drop water in the hope of curbing the fires. The down side is we have no way of removing or shielding people from such drops. Hell, Mr. President, we have no way of knowing how many people may be alive or dead in Manhattan" the general proclaims.

"Listen general, you do whatever is needed to put out those fires so emergency crews can get into Manhattan. I realize the danger of water drops on civilians, but I also know if we do not put out those fires, people who could possibly live may very well burn to death," the president commands. "Now tell me, what do we know about the rest of the east coast?"

"We know that every city along the coast from Jacksonville, Florida to Portland, Maine has been devastated by the earthquake. We know that the bigger cities are very much in the same shape as New York. Boston is a mess as well as a burning inferno. We are exercising the same approach to Boston as New York," the general adds.

"What about our naval fleet, how much damage has been done?" the president inquires.

"I believe the fleet weathered the earthquake well enough, but the oncoming tsunami may be a different story," the general reports.

"How about our planes? What is the status?" the president probes for more information.

"With the advanced warning, we got about 50% of our planes out of harm's way. I have not received an assessment of the damage done to the remaining planes, but it does not sound good" the general notes.

"Keep me posted general," the president orders in closing.

"Mr. President, I know you have a lot on your mind, but may I make a suggestion?" Senator Joseph asks.

"Most certainly senator, I can use all the help I can get," the president says with true humility in his voice.

"Mr. President, once you arrive at the retreat outside Nashville, you need to order the establishment of a provisional capitol in Nashville as the operating seat of government. Once you have done this, you need to address the people of the United States and the world on television. You need to provide leadership and assurance to everyone that things are going to be okay," the senator offers more as a directive than a suggestion.

"Are things going to be okay senator? You saw the same thing I did as we flew away from the Capitol. You have heard the same reports I have coming out of New York and the east coast. We are in a most dire situation," the president laments.

"There can be no denying the gravity of the circumstances facing the nation and world Mr. President, but you do not have the latitude to do anything but give the people of this nation and the world a reason for hope," Senator Joseph emphasizes. "You must display the strength of leadership expected of a president, and that means doing things to show a functioning government remains in place," the senator stresses with a forcefulness of determination. "Mr. President, you need to order all members of Congress to convene in Nashville as soon as possible."

You offer me sound advice senator; I appreciate your leadership and assistance at this most tragic time for our nation," the president responds.

Upon arriving at the Presidential retreat outside Nashville, Tennessee, the president, Senator Joseph, Attorney General Loophole, and Secretary of State Globalseer discover that the earthquake also brought devastation to the west coast of Europe and Africa. Furthermore, the earthquake resulted in a tsunami moving east and west across the Atlantic. The tsunami is just beginning to reach landfall all along the eastern seaboard of North and South America as well as the western seaboard of the British Isles, Spain, Portugal, and the Africa. Despite the delay between the earthquake and the tsunami, no one has time to prepare for the worst.

CHAPTER 10

PAYING THE PIPER

I N NOAH'S OFFICE AT THE University of Michigan in Ann Arbor, Contessa and Noah are monitoring the devastation on a bank of televisions. Even as far away from the epicenter of the quake as they are, they felt rumblings and minor ground movement. Most of the reports coming across the networks are supposition because no one can get out of or into the areas most impacted by the earthquake. Furthermore, the Army Reserves and National Guard have isolated the entire east coast due to the eminent arrival of a monster tsunami.

As Contessa reviews the data coming from the seismograph, it becomes apparent that the earthquake along the Mid-Atlantic Ridge hit in excess of ten points on the Richter scale. She explains to Noah how earthquake magnitude is computed on a base ten, which means each whole number of the Richter Scale is equal to an amplitude of the ground motion by ten times. She asks Noah to consider an earthquake of 6.1 to 6.9 as strong and characteristically causing lots of damage in populated areas. An earthquake of 7.1 to 7.9 is ten times as violent, and with each increase in whole numbers, the violent nature of a quake increases ten times.

Noah is transfixed by the reports coming across the air waves. How could the National Earthquake Information Center not have picked up on this very dangerous situation? Sitting with his head in hand, Noah's eyes are glassed over from the tsunami of tears rolling down his cheeks. This objective man of science is overcome with emotion knowing millions of people have perished and millions more languish in a state of despair just beyond the reach of help. He wonders if anything could have been done to avert the horror of it all?

"Why did no one pick up on this impending catastrophe?" Noah wonders aloud. "Why did no one pay any attention to your foreboding about this situation?"

"You know all too well the answer to your question cousin. For how many decades now has no one paid any attention to all of the warnings regarding global warming, climate change, and pending doom coming out of the scientific community?" Contessa inquires of Dr. Abraham. "Besides, our warning may have saved the lives of our cousins, the president, and many other people. For this we can be grateful."

"What do you think is going on Contessa? Is there no hope for our future? Have we crossed the point of no return?" Noah asks seeking assurance that there is always hope.

"I suspect there are changes going on right in front of our very eyes which we fail to see. I wonder how long the rift valley of the Mid-Atlantic Ridge has been compacting without notice. The Earth is in rebellion Noah, and perhaps after something as catastrophic as this, the warnings of the scientific community will finally receive the attention so long overdue. As for hope, there is always hope as long as we are able to fight," Contessa assures Noah.

"Is Devolution actually occurring? Is the Earth fighting back against more than a century of abuse by humans? If this is the case, what can be done to return the Earth into balance?" Noah asks rhetorically.

"It has all happened in the blink of an eye cousin. Before the industrial revolution, humans had only a marginal impact on the planet. Then modernization brought on by unbelievable scientific, industrial, technological, and medical advances created a global paradigm shift. Civilization found itself in an entirely new world without an instruction manual. Humanity became materialistic junkies. The more people had, the more they wanted. Use became abuse, and so many things which appeared to be blessings now appear to be a curse," Contessa surmises.

"You are right Contessa, we evolved without any forethought to the consequences of that evolution. Driven by money, power, and a lust for all things material, we as a human race created a scenario of doom," Noah adds shaking his head as if it is all a bad dream turned nightmare.

"Everything we have seen and heard supports Hannah's Theory of Devolution on a global scale. The Mid-Atlantic Ridge earthquake could be but the first of many such super calamities to beset the world. We must prepare ourselves to not only respond to these incredible disasters, but we must seek an answer with all urgency," Contessa proclaims.

"So, what do you think occurred along the Mid-Atlantic Ridge?" Noah asks his cousin trained in geological matters.

"This is only supposition, but I believe it to be faulting. Faulting is when strain along the edges of enormous crustal plates release causing a series of small jumps. I believe we detected, and people along the east coast felt this faulting as rumbles and minor shaking. This was our warning to something bigger. What then occurred was subduction. Subduction is when an oceanic plate and a continental plate converge causing the denser sea plate to take a dive and plunge back into the earth's interior. This was the initial earthquake which would have been bad enough, but I believe this subduction was followed by a collision which is when two continental plates converge. This caused the sustained earthquake on the surface, and it is difficult to say what occurred under the surface of the ocean," Contessa shares.

"You certainly have an incredible knowledge of geology," Noah is more than impressed with Contessa's knowledge and understanding.

Contessa reminds Noah of all the times Uncle Robert brought geological items as Christmas gifts. They think about how everyone even the adults found this novel and educational approach to a Christmas gift as engaging and fun. They recalled how Grandma and Grandpa allowed them to have a big container of water in the family room where everyone sifted and mined their bag of treasures. It often got messy, but that gesture of turning a Christmas gift into an adventure captured everyone's imagination. Contessa reveals how those gifts and many experiences with her parents helped trigger her interest in geology which led her to this particular time and place.

Contessa and Noah discuss the manner in which childhood experiences impact the development of adults. They reflect on how fortunate they were to have parents and grandparents who supported and allowed them to explore their interests. Noah chuckles remembering the framed collage of Turtle Man that Grandpa made for Edison. Eddie kept that collage hanging in his bed room all through high school and even took it to college with him. That was Eddie, give him a reptile and he was happy.

Contessa brings up her little sister Gemma. As the youngest member, Gemma enjoyed the full advantage of a dynamic family. She listened to many family debates on topics of importance, and developed a sense of wonder for ideas. Now, as a university junior, she is in the thick of ideas pursuing a degree in philosophy.

Noah and Contessa's journey down memory lane is shattered as breaking news comes across their television screens. The tsunami struck the east coast with more violence than ever imagined.

The major coastal cities of Portland, Boston, New York, Norfolk, Charleston, and Jacksonville were all hit by waves 250 feet tall. The flooding has turned these cities reeling from the destruction of the earthquake into lakes littered with debris, rubble, wreckage, corpses, and the fragmented remains of metropolitan centers. The waves extinguished much of the fire at ground level, but the burning infernos go unattended and out of reach.

No one knows the death toll, but it must be in the millions. Most of the people inhabiting these cities perished with no warning, no means for getting out of harm's way. They vanished under the rubble or the all-consuming sea. The east coast of the United States has become a desolate, watery, fiery grave.

One thing about a disaster of this magnitude is that it does not discriminate for any reason. The extremely wealthy, who live in plush estates and gated communities on Martha's Vineyard, suffered the full extent of the earthquake and the tsunami. Whole swaths of low-lying land including beaches, salt marshes, roads, and homes were simply washed away. The Chappaquiddick shoreline has been reclaimed by the sea. The Felix Neck Wildlife Sanctuary is gone. What has not been destroyed by the earthquake or washed away by the tsunami lay in unrecognizable ruins.

In Boston Harbor, Old Ironsides along with hundreds of other boats, ships, and yachts are sunk or half-submerged having surrendered to the onslaught of destruction. The swell of water from the Tsunami flooded the entire downtown of Boston including most of the Freedom Trail all the way beyond the old Boston Commons. The Big Dig is engulfed in water. The Charles River knows no bounds spilling over into the city all the way to Cambridge and Harvard University. The city lay in architectural ruins. Nothing along the coast line of Massachusetts is spared. The John F. Kennedy Library and Museum are gone. The tombs of John and Abigail Adams and John Quincy and Louisa Adams in the crypt of the United First Parish Church in Quincy are now underwater graves. The unknown is the death toll, and the injured beyond the reach of assistance creating a ghoulish nightmare.

In New York, It will be decades if not longer before the people can begin to reclaim Long Island and Manhattan Island. The Statue of Liberty which withstood the earthquake, washed away under the force of the tsunami. For all their money, the wealthy with their kingly estates on Long Island have perished along with their earthly paradise. Some of the tallest structures ever built have been reduced to rubble. Trump Tower, the narcissistic edifice to a human ego of the worst state, lay in ruins with the once elegant penthouse a fiery inferno only a few stories above the water level. To think that not long ago, a desperate, confused, and self-indulgent people elected Donald Trump as President of the United States. Trump, who thought himself bigger than any person or deity, did more as president to throw the world into chaos than any leader before or since. Only the century old Empire State Building remains standing tall above all the carnage. One thing seems certain, a concentrated population has given way to a concentrated death toll, and hundreds-of-thousands of people in need of rescuing remain out of the reach of help.

The earthquake turned thorough fares, turnpikes, and bridges into twisted ruins of steel and concrete resembling some bizarre David Smith creation. Any land access to Manhattan and Long Island lay as impenetrable as the Cheyenne Mountain Complex, leaving stranded those waiting and willing to help. With the onslaught of the tsunami, air and water emergency crews had to patiently wait for the wall of water to pass. Even then, the emergency response paled in the face of such great need.

In Norfolk, Virginia, half of the naval force has been destroyed. In Charleston and Jacksonville, the situation is no different from Boston or New York. All of the beaches and homes along the coastline are gone. The earthquake reduced them to rubble, and the tsunami swept them into the sea.

Once the tsunami subsides, rescue units all along the coastline assault the carnage as if to retaliate against the horrific blitzkrieg of nature. With little access by land, the emergency crews use a swarm of helicopters to airlift emergency personnel, vehicles, heavy equipment, and supplies in an attempt to bring relief to those clinging onto the hope of survival. Emergency boats and ships of all sizes not destroyed by the earthquake or tsunami are commandeered for the emergency effort. Many of the larger vessels are turned into floating hospitals and others as floating morgues.

Many of the dead lay under tons of debris which will take months and years to clear away. The retrievable dead are returned to the mainland where forensic experts make every attempt to identify the remains before sending them to make shift crematoriums and mass graves. In the case of such a disaster, time is of the essence in the disposal of the dead.

It is not a matter of disease, but more out of consideration for the living. Human corpses are not incubators of disease unless they are infected by disease at death. Otherwise, the biggest concern is the gruesome nature of a decaying human body. The stench created by a decaying human body is overwhelming, and once in the olfactory system, it is hard to escape the memory. Furthermore, animals which could carry disease feeding upon the dead presents a real problem.

The massive nature of this disaster requires the President of the United States to declare a state of emergency and consider putting in place Martial Law for the impacted areas. The eastern seaboard of the United States is home to over one-hundred million people. Once the air clears from the earthquake, tsunami, and the fiery inferno, it becomes obvious the death toll could rise to millions of people.

Sitting in the conference room at the compound outside of Nashville, President Armstrong is considering a recommendation made by his Chief of Staff, Peet, and supported by his National Security Advisor, Shady, to declare martial law all along the east coast.

"Mr. President, I understand the essential need to use the military in the rescue effort and in maintaining order, but I believe a declaration of martial law is ill-advised," warns Senator Joseph. "You have called for a convening of the United States Congress at the provisional Capital in Nashville. I recommend you wait to confer with the leadership of both parties before making such a drastic decision."

"Waiting is what got us in this position Mr. President," Secretary of Defense Bluster injects. "Now is not the time for waiting, but decisive leadership."

"Mr. President" intones Attorney General Loophole, "Martial Law is a concept in direct contradiction to democracy as well as the Constitution of the United States. To implement Martial Law without at least conferring with legislative leaders is a breach of faith."

"For God's sakes have you, Senator Joseph and Attorney General Loophole, not been watching the same calamity as I?" Mr. Peet asks in a mocking tone.

"Mr. Peet, might I remind you that martial law is in effect a dictatorship of which this nation is not. The president has already pressed the Army Reserves and National Guard into action for emergency relief purposes," the attorney general acknowledges.

"Martial Law is heady stuff Mr. President. I do realize that these are unusual circumstances, but even during the Civil War, President Lincoln did not impose martial law without congressional authorization," reminds Senator Joseph.

"Mr. President, this is a matter of national security. You do not have the latitude to wait for congress while the East Coast burns. If you need a Presidential precedent, then look to Andrew Jackson's imposing of martial law on New Orleans during the War of 1812," suggests Advisor Shady.

"Excuse me Mr. Shady, but Andrew Jackson imposed martial law on New Orleans as a U.S. General not President. Furthermore, Old

Hickory had little time for the Constitution if it didn't suit his fancy," argues the Attorney General, "Jackson was a dictator by nature."

"I serve at the pleasure of the President, but I feel it would be remiss to not remind you Mr. President, as well as the other distinguished members of this council that the Intolerable Acts imposed by the British, and a leading cause of the Revolutionary War, were a form of martial law. Such action by you could have unwanted ramifications," Secretary Globalseer adds.

"General Randolph, my biggest concern about declaring martial law would be the overreach of the military, as well as the militaries unwillingness to stand down from martial law when so ordered," the President announces. "What say you, Sir?"

"Mr. President you are the Commander-in-Chief. The military will exercise our role and responsibility to the extent you so desire and no more. When you order us to stand down, we will stand down," General Randolph responds.

"Mr. President, in one of the last proclamations of martial law which occurred during World War II, from December 7, 1941 to October 24, 1944, in what is now the State of Hawaii, the Army went beyond the governor's decree and set up an unlawful military government. After the war, a federal judge for the Islands condemned the conduct of martial law saying the military threw the Constitution into the garbage bin and set up a military dictatorship. The military might say one thing Sir, but can they be trusted?" Senator Joseph wonders begging caution.

"How dare you question the loyalty of the United States military you commie liberal," General Randolph spouts out before being cut short by the President.

Accessing a map, the President begins, "Gentlemen, I respect every opinion in this room. I consider you all great patriots, but I must make the final call." Now pointing to the map, "General, I am ordering the establishment of martial law beginning at the 28.083333 latitude and fifty miles west of the 80.608333 longitude. Now here is where it gets tricky general. I want you to establish martial law within a line running 50 miles west of the beginning point to Jacksonville, FL at 81.6558333 longitude, Charleston, S.C. at 79.930923 longitude, Norfolk, VA at 76.285556 longitude, Washington D.C. at 77.032 longitude, Philadelphia at 75.1641667 longitude, New York City at 73.935242 longitude, Boston, MA at 71.0602778 longitude, and Portland, ME at 70.255833 longitude to the International Boundary just north of the 45th latitude". The president is a master of cartography. "General, I am counting on you to connect the dots in a responsible manner which ensures we are covering an area of necessity but not overreaching. Is that understood?" the president directs.

"It is clearly understood Sir," General Randolph responds.

"General, this is not to be a hard sell. I do not want this action resulting in any kind of revolt. I want the people to see this as a protective and precautionary measure intended for their own safety. I want you and the Joint Chiefs to directly oversee this action, and I expect daily, if not more often, reports on all aspects of this operation," the president orders.

"Yes Sir!" responds the general.

Regardless the president's directive, the enforcement of martial law requires a large military contingency and a heavy hand. Martial Law is never popular. Amidst the disaster, people up and down the east coast frantically search to find family and friends. Under martial law, people are met at every turn by a U.S. military armed and commissioned to keep people out and maintain order.

The biggest challenge for the authorities attempting to control, manage, and monitor the areas of devastation is the media. Promises to provide limited access and full information as things transpire is not enough for a hungry press. Using every tool available to them, the press attempts to outmaneuver and dodge authorities along an impossible line of defense running from Maine to Florida. The press engages a clandestine strategy of making their way onto helicopters and ships to gain access to the truth. Despite warnings of prosecution and severe penalties, the Fourth Estate is not about to give up the Constitutional guarantee of a free press or their obligation to create an informed public.

On the other hand, the press is in a feeding frenzy. Despite the ruination of network and publication headquarters up and down the east coast, the major news agencies remain very much alive and well in their combat to be first in breaking news. Being first means viewers; viewers mean advertising, and advertising means money. In situations such as the current calamity, being first does not equate to accurate reporting. The government knows that in such situations inaccurate reporting can lead to public reactions which are far from helpful.

CHAPTER II

UNITING

"M R. PRESIDENT, I WOULD LIKE to take my leave for a few days," Senator Joseph requests.

"Senator, do you not remember that I have called the entire Congress to Nashville for a joint session. This seems like an odd time to request a leave," President Armstrong proclaims.

"Mr. President, as a Senator from the State of Iowa, I do not need your permission. I have lobbied you and your administration as a Congressman and Senator regarding the dangerous course we as a nation have charted in the face of climate change. I warned you of this impending disaster. I helped evacuate the capital, and I have tried to provide wise council. I now need some time to visit with my sisters and cousins. If you need me, call and I shall return post-haste," Senator Joseph announces.

"Senator, might I remind you that to disobey a direct order from the President of the United States amounts to an act of treason," Chief of Staff Peet intones.

"Peet, you're a son-of-a-bitch! I do not now nor will I ever take orders from the likes of you. From the very first day of this administration, you have ill-advised President Armstrong. Why the hell he listens to you I will never know. He should have sent you packing a long time ago. Now, if you will excuse me, I have an important journey to make," Senator Joseph says as he turns and exits the room.

As the senator departs, everyone else in the room stands looking at each other dismayed by Senator Joseph's bold actions. Angrily, Chief of

Staff Peet commands the President to send one of his security guards to apprehend and arrest the senator for treason.

"Mr. Peet, I am the president and I do not take orders from you. It is in no one's interest to do as you suggest. The senator said he would return if needed, and I shall take him at his word," President Armstrong reveals.

"If you allow him to just walk out, you will lose all control. This is not the time to be weak-kneed, you must be decisive," Peet counters still angry from the senator's rebuke.

"Shut the fuck up Mr. Peet before I take the Senator's advise and send you packing," the president responds out of frustration. "General Randolph, catch up with the Senator and see he gets a military plane to wherever it is he is going. Make arrangements for that plane to stay with the senator and be available for his return when needed."

"Noah, this is Jack, how are you doing?" Senator Joseph is calling to let his family know he is on the way to Ames.

"Jack, we are pretty on edge here. This whole calamity along the east coast may just be a prelude to future events," Noah shares.

"How soon can you and Contessa be on a plane to Ames?" Jack asks.

"We can be on a plane within a couple hours Jack, what's up? Noah's interest is peaked by the request.

"I think it is high time we have a meeting of the minds. I would like to bring all the cousins to Ames for a round table discussion about the Armageddon we face," Jack reveals.

"Ironically that is exactly what Contessa and I have been discussing. We have all been working independently and observing very similar phenomenon. All our independent efforts to change public policy in this country and around the world have been for naught. It is past time we pool our knowledge, experience, and expertise in a collective effort to save the planet and humanity," Noah says without even realizing the full implication of his words.

Contessa sitting nearby overhears Noah's end of the conversation and she is greatly moved by the idea of saving the planet and humanity. After all this time, they are no longer looking at providing warnings, data, and information about protecting the planet, but rather saving the planet and humanity. It all sounds so ominous, and yet, Contessa knows it has truly come to this.

"Noah, will you contact Kennedy and Edison and have Contessa contact Stella and Gemma about immediately coming to Ames? Tell them to depart now!" Jack commands with all urgency.

"I will do that as soon as we hang up," Noah assures. "What about the rest?"

"I will let Hannah know we are heading in her direction and ask her to contact Olivia and Thomas. I will also ask her to make arrangements for our lodging and a place for us to meet. I will contact Ainsley and Ivey myself," Jack continues.

"I will see you soon cousin," Noah says as he hangs up.

"What was that about Noah?" Contessa asks suspecting she might have an idea.

"We are going to Ames. Senator Joseph is calling for a meeting of the cousins," Noah reveals the obvious.

"It's about time," Contessa says in relief. "Many minds are better than one or two, and it is about time we put our heads together and hope it's not too late."

"Contessa, call Stella and Gemma. Let them know what's up," Noah directs.

"Stella, this is your Big Sis, it is great to hear your voice. I am so glad you are well clear of the dangerous situation on the East Coast," Contessa struggles to not reveal her emotion. "Senator Joseph is asking for us to convene the cousins in Ames immediately! We need you to catch a plane ASAP."

"I will run this by Ambassador DiCaprio. I am sure he can help me get a flight out of Syracuse, and I will be in Ames before you know it," Stella responds.

"Hello Gemma, how is my Minnie Me?" Contessa has always been proud of the similarities between her and her littlest sister.

"Is this you Contessa? Why are you calling me while the east coast burns?" Gemma likes to hear from her sisters, but she is puzzled by the timing of this call.

"Listen carefully, we need you to make arrangements to come to

Ames. I know you are in the midst of your studies, but we could really use your help," Contessa makes her case.

"Sure, Biggest Sis, but what's up?" Gemma cuts to the chase.

"No time to explain. Senator Joseph is asking all the cousins to meet in Ames straight away. Please don't delay!" Contessa emphasizes.

"Okay, I'll be there. No worries," Gemma assures as the call ends.

"Kennedy, this is Noah."

"How are you Noah, could you feel anything from that earthquake, are you alright?" Kennedy asks.

"I'm fine! Look Kennedy, we need you to immediately fly to Ames for a meeting of the cousins. We are facing something we didn't think would occur for decades, if ever, and we need your help," Noah pleads.

"How can I be of help Noah; I am not a scientist like yourself," Kennedy asks puzzled by the prospect of being needed.

"Senator Joseph wants us all there. He feels that only by working together is there any hope of finding any answers or solutions. Please just get on a plane and be in Ames quickly," Noah implores.

"I'll be there, little brother, see you soon," Kennedy agrees.

"Hannah, this is Jack."

"Jack it is good to hear your voice. I was so concerned with you in Washington D.C. and everything. Are you alright?" Dr. Rae sounds quite relieved.

"Hannah, I am going to put you under the gun. I am calling a meeting of all the cousins to occur in Ames. I am asking our cousins to be there as soon as possible which means some will arrive within the next few hours. We will need lodging and a secure conference room where we can meet. Can you do this?" Jack asks.

"It sounds like I had better do this, and of course you know I can, or you wouldn't have put this ball in motion," Hannah responds. "So, what's up?"

"Devolution is up Hannah, Armageddon, Apocalypse, the end of days, all the things you have theorized and more look to be validated by our worst fears. We need to bring our collective knowledge, experience, and critical thinking skills together in hopes of finding an answer and a solution. Let's hope it's not too late!" Jack declares. "Oh, one other thing, be sure to call Olivia and Thomas!"

"Olivia, this is Hannah and I don't have much time. Please get on the first plane out of Atlanta for Ames. We need you here as soon as possible for a meeting with all the cousins. Will you do this?" Hannah says in haste.

"I will, I will be there" Olivia responds.

"Ivey, this is Jack, how are you doing at the bottom of the world?"

"We've been shaken up a bit brother, but everything seems to be holding together. Obviously, our altitude protected us from the tsunami. Our greatest concern is the impact of the earthquake on what have been up-to-this-time inactive volcanoes," Ivey reveals.

"Can you get out of there and find a way to Ames? We need you in Ames as soon as you can possibly get there," Jack urges.

"If our lone helicopter is operational, I can get to Puerto Aisen where a small plane can take me to Santiago for an international flight. With any luck, I can be in Ames within 24 hours," Ivey predicts.

"Well get going, and I hope to see you sometime tomorrow little sister," Jack says in closing.

"Hello, Thomas is this you," Hannah shouts over the shortwave radio.

"Hello, this is Thomas Henry, is that you Hannah or Olivia?" Thomas asks knowing it is a secure channel reserved for his sisters.

"Thomas, this is Hannah. We need you to come to Ames now!"

"What is the urgency Hannah, I know there has been a catastrophe along the eastern seaboard, but Ames should be isolated from that disaster," Thomas notes.

"We are gathering all of the cousins to form a council of consolidated thinking around the recent events and the possibility of further calamities. We need your help!" Hannah pleads.

"Hannah, I need to give my assistants proper instructions before I leave. I can do this tonight. I will then take a jeep to the nearest Trans-Mongolian Railway to Jining. From Jining I can catch a flight to Beijing where I can pick up an international flight. It could take two days or more to arrive in Ames, but I will be there," Thomas assures.

"Thank you, Brother, travel safely," Hannah closes.

"Ainsley, this is Jack."

"Oh, thank God you must be alright. I have been worried about you.

The news has been so inconclusive about everything. Please tell me you are fine!" Ainsley begs.

"I assure you I am fine, but things are not fine. I need you to temporarily postpone your tour and come to Ames. I am calling a meeting of all the cousins to see if we can discover a way out of this environmental mess. I need you to do this!" Jack beseeches.

"Sure, whatever you say Jack. My manager will not be happy, but she will just have to get over it. How long do I need to postpone my tour?" Ainsley wonders.

"Indefinitely big sister, until we have come up with a plan, we will need to stay huddled together in Ames," Jack reveals. "I will see you tomorrow."

"Edison, this is Noah. What is it like there in Southern Florida?"

"It's gone Noah; it has all been washed away. It is a mess, a real nightmare! Everything north to Cape Coral and across to West Palm Beach is submerged. All of the east coast beach front is gone. Thank you for the warning or I would not be talking to you. The devastation is unreal," Edison proclaims in a very unusual show of emotion.

"Where are you now Eddie?" Noah asks.

"I'm safe in St. Petersburg on the Gulf side of the peninsula. In a couple days we plan to venture out and survey exactly what exists," Edison declares.

"I have a change of plans for you Eddie. We want you to come to Ames and join the rest of your cousins in a council aimed at devising a plan to deal with what is happening and the things we believe are yet to come. We would like you in Ames as soon as possible," Noah says.

"I will need to alert my team regarding my change of plans. I will also need to give them careful instructions regarding any further activity on their part. This has become an extremely dangerous place and I still insist on safety first. As soon as I have taken care of this business, I will be on my way," Edison commits.

While Dr. Rae sets to work making arrangements in Ames, her cousins begin crisscrossing the nation and world for their rendezvous with destiny. Hannah makes arrangements for each person including herself to have their own room at the Hotel Memorial Union. The rooms are not big, but the location and accommodations are perfect for keeping the group in proximity to each other and the Great Hall, which Hannah has commandeered for their meetings.

The Great Hall is much bigger than needed, but Hannah believes such a place is required for the work ahead. Furthermore, she knows the Great Hall has special meaning for Dr. Margery, Dr. Caroline, and Gemma, because their Mom and Dad were married in the Great Hall. In making arrangements, Hannah has tables with built in wireless presentation capability arranged in a circular pattern in the center of the room around which everyone can sit. On both ends of the room, she arranged for a jumbo screen to accommodate sharing. This arrangement will allow everyone to sit around the table and never have to turn their backs to each other. In one corner of the room, there will be a refreshment table continually stocked with a variety of foods and beverage. To the side of the room, a bank of flat screen televisions are in place to allow the group to stay connected to what is occurring around the world. On the other side of the room, a bank of tables contains all of the equipment necessary for the reproduction of material for sharing. Dr. Rae has made arrangements for four fulltime associates to be available to offer assistance whenever they may be needed. There are restrooms located just outside the hall.

The stage is set for the convening of the most important conclave in human history. No group of people has ever endeavored to answer or find a solution to so many enormous problems. No group has ever carried such a weight on their shoulders knowing that the fate of the Earth and the human race are at stake.

CHAPTER 12

CONVENING IN AMES

I T SEEMED LIKE FOREVER, BUT two days after making the call for everyone to converge at Iowa State University for this incredible challenge, the morning to begin arrives. Getting to the Great Hall early, Dr. Rae makes sure everything is perfect to greet her brother, sister, and cousins. As she stands pouring herself the first of what would be an ocean of coffee, Dr. Rae hears a voice from behind, "Hannah, it has been far too long," as she turns to see her brother, Thomas Henry, approaching wearing his desert fatigues and broad rim hat in hand.

Her eyes immediately fill with tears of joy as she embraces her brother. "Oh Thomas, it is so good to see you! I am so glad you had a safe trip."

"The trip was safe and very interesting! We flew directly over the North Pole, and from 35,000 feet it is easy to see the polar cap in retreat. However, the view of something ominous occurring in the North Atlantic caught my attention," Dr. Henry shares. He is about to continue when the door opens wide followed by a flood of family.

"Welcome, Welcome," Hannah shouts as she joins in the hug fest.

Since their earliest days, this group of brothers, sisters, and cousins learned how to hug. They could all relate to the massive hugs of greeting and goodbye given by Grandma and Grandpa. Grandma and Grandpa wanted their family to be close, and they felt that hugs were an important demonstration of affirmation and affection. In this family there are no one arm hugs or side hugs, only genuine hugs of a full embrace.

As the greetings turn into conversations, Hannah senses the need to offer some direction "If I can get your attention for a moment, I have a few basic instructions. I know you all have much to share, and I guarantee there will be plenty of time for just that. Let me direct your attention to the side area where you will find an abundance of refreshments. Please help yourself at any time. You notice we will be sitting in a circular arrangement, so sit wherever you would like. Take a little time to wrap up your current conversations, visit the refreshment table and bathrooms, and find a seat so we can get started."

Everyone appreciates Hannah's attention to detail and order. They all know the business at hand is of the utmost importance, and yet, they have such an affinity for each other it is hard to put an end to their conversation.

As Senator Joseph takes his seat at the table, Dr. Jude quickly slides in beside him. Going around the table from Dr. Jude are Dr. Rae, Dr. Abraham, Ainsley, Dr. Kae, Dr. Caroline, Dr. Henry, Dr. Margery, Gemma, Kennedy, and Dr. Isabelle. With the group still chatting away, Dr. Rae interrupts again, "If we could get started, I have a few things to explain," she says and silence falls upon the group. "Thank you everyone, I know this is far more formal than our normal gatherings, but I also know you fully understand the seriousness of the business before us. I want to thank each of you for promptly answering the call to come to Ames. I know some of you traveled great distances (Thomas and Ivey) to be here. Before I turn things over to Senator Joseph, I would like to make you aware of the room arrangements. And, of great importance, outside the doors to the left near the reproduction equipment are the rest rooms. Also, I have four of my research assistants available to assist at any time. I am now going to turn things over to Senator Joseph."

"What an illustrious family we have become. Yet, despite our knowledge, training, experience, and accomplishments, we find ourselves in the very world we have been trying to avoid. Now, after decades of slowly evolving calamities, we have experienced what to date is the granddaddy of them all. The east coast is in ruins, the government forced inland to Nashville, a weak President abdicating to the darker side of reason with martial law, a Congress still mostly in denial, and no answers in sight. I left the president in Nashville, and came here to meet with what I know are the brightest and best in our scientific and humanitarian communities. Thank you for coming, our task is nothing short of astronomical, and the very fate of humanity is at stake," the senator concludes.

"Jack, what is the government doing to address any of this?" Thomas asks.

"Thomas, the government has been dysfunctional from gridlock for decades. Nobody can, nor wants to agree on anything. Everyone is looking out for themselves. Big money controls the levers of government, and as long as they can turn a buck, they don't give a shit what happens to anyone else. We have not had a strong, decisive, visionary president since John F. Kennedy. Right now, the president is under the influence of control freaks. Under their influence, he has chosen to respond to the horrendous situation along the east coast by declaring martial law without the advice or consent of Congress. The stage is set for total war between the executive and legislative branches of government, while the east coast burns and drowns at the same time. Even when confronted with such massive destruction, unity cannot be achieved," Jack shares.

"Can I get the floor," Eddie asks looking around the table, "I've got something I would like to share."

Everyone around the table nods in approval, but Dr. Jude hesitates to move. Looking at Senator Joseph, he leans his head to the left and says, "Well?"

"Oh, sure Eddie, the floor is all yours, I didn't know you needed my approval," the Senator injects.

"Well, someone has to run this meeting, and I just thought it would be you," Eddie says with a smile. "Let's see how this projection equipment works. These pictures represent the area prior to the recent Earthquake and Tsunami which have made it impossible to reach."

Firing up the projection equipment the jumbo screens come to life. Dr. Jude flashes a picture of a crocodile nested in the ruins of the Perez Art Museum. "Look at this beautiful building which once housed a fine collection of 20th century and contemporary art defining the cultures of the Atlantic Rim. By 2030, this magnificent building designed by Swiss architects Herzog and de Meuron was engulfed by 25 feet of water caused by rising sea levels due to global warming. Today, this building and much of the extraordinary art it housed is in ruins, and the museum a haven for a host of reptiles and sea creatures."

Moving to the next picture, Edison shows Biscayne Bay as it existed a week before the recent earthquake and tsunami. The bay once a pristine blue, is a putrid brown littered with garbage and sewage. "This bay, once a gorgeous ocean front of incredible property and recreation, fell victim to rising seas which washed out wastewater-treatment plants, chemical collection centers, city dump collection centers, and every other kind of human waste, turning it into a bay of trash."

Dr. Jude's next picture shows a large water wasteland with buildings and dead trees rising above the surface. "This is the vicinity of Flamingo Park in what used to be Miami Beach, Florida. Ten years ago, the rising seas reclaimed this entire area. For us the significance of Flamingo Park is where our Grandfather and our great-uncle Dan gathered with thousands of others to protest the Republican National Convention and the Presidency of Richard Nixon in 1972."

"It is a long story, but at twenty-two (if you can imagine Grandpa at that age), he dropped out of Wayne State College, left behind his Phi Sig brothers, and went to Reno, Nevada with a group of friends. After eight months in Reno, most of the group along with a few others traveled to Miami Beach, Florida via Peterson, for the Republican National Convention. In Peterson, Uncle Dan joined the group much to Great-Grandpa and Annie's disapproval. Once arriving at Flamingo Park, the group set up camp and joined in the protesting of the Presidency of Richard Nixon. Three days into the protesting, Grandpa was arrested and spent the night in the Dade County Jail. He was put in a large holding cell which also included Rock Legend Carlos Santana. The next day with the convention over, Grandpa was released. He quickly joined the rest of his group and they made their way back to Iowa."

"Ironically, Nixon turned out to be one of the good guys on the environment. In 1970, he signed the National Environmental Policy Act into law."

"I could show you more devastation, but you get the idea. Please take a close look at this final picture. This is the Turkey Point Nuclear Power Plant. The rising seas and disastrous storms eventually did exactly what we had warned against by destroying several of the reactors and releasing radioactivity into the atmosphere. Today the entire area lay in ruins," Edison says with a sigh of exasperation.

"Let me switch gears to my favorite subject, reptiles and sea creatures. Very few people have seen these pictures. They are relatively new, but also highly classified by the government. Since the government has mostly ignored decades of warning about impending doom, and Washington D.C. now lay in ruins, I don't feel too compelled to be concerned about the government," Dr. Jude asserts glancing at the senator. "No offense intended senator."

"No offense taken, cousin, I have been howling into the wind just like the rest of you. I have tried to provide positive leadership from the inside out, but it has been an exercise in futility," Senator Joseph interjects.

"Okay, here we go, hang on to your hats," Dr. Jude proclaims. "What do you see in this picture?"

"I see a rather large snake," Thomas Henry announces. "A snake that looks rather pregnant."

"This isn't a rather large snake, Thomas, this is a huge snake. This is a Burmese Python, and as you may recall this invasive species took over the Florida Everglades 20 years ago. Burmese Pythons originally grew to about 12 feet in length and fed primarily off of small animals. This particular Burmese Python is 24 feet in length, and its large belly is due to eating an adult deer. Nothing is safe from these very strong and aggressive predators," Edison notes. "It should also be mentioned that when mature at four to five years old, female Burmese Pythons lay 50 to 100 eggs each year. With climate change and more tropical weather moving north, so do these predators."

"Invasive species are a big part of the problem we face," Dr. Abraham adds. "Invasive species come in all forms from the Kudzu which forms dense monocultures in which reptiles thrive, to the Spiny Waterflea which preys on fish and yet fish cannot prey on it. In fact, there are more invasive species in the United States and throughout the world today than there are species indigenous to any particular region."

"If we are going to talk about the devastation brought on by invasive species, we must acknowledge the most invasive species of all – human beings," Ainsley declares. "It is after all human civilization, if that is what you want to call it, which spread invasive species around the globe on ships and planes. It is humans themselves who invaded and destroyed the environment."

"Show us another picture brother," Kennedy requests attempting to keep the group focused on Dr. Jude's presentation.

"Most animals like the Great White Shark, and reptiles such as alligators and crocodiles have grown to enormous size. As they increased in size, they increased proportionally in aggressive behavior. The Great White has become the most pervasive and vicious predator in the sea. As for alligators and crocodiles, these enormous creatures also increased their quickness and speed. As climate change results in a more tropical environment to the north, these reptiles expand their territory," Dr. Jude emphasizes.

"Bear with me as I make my point in this last picture," Edison asks. "In this picture you are looking at four different sea creatures. In the upper left you see a Sarcastic Fringehead, a rather frightful creature even when it was smaller and regulated to the Pacific Ocean off the coast of the United States. Today, the Sarcastic Fringehead grows to ten feet and is found in the Atlantic off the southeastern coast of the United States. In the upper right is the Giant Oarfish which once grew to 36 feet but now is commonly 60 feet long. In the bottom left is a Giant Squid once found at 40 to 50 feet long now taking on the dimensions of the mythical Kraken at over 100 feet long. In the bottom right is the devilish looking Black Dragon Fish. This ugly fish once regulated to the deep at five-to-seven thousand feet below the surface has grown in size reaching 20 feet in length and adapting to shallower murky waters," Edison shares. "My point is that as the environment changes so does the size, aggressive nature, and territory of sea creatures and reptiles."

"What has been your most surprising discovery?" Stella Caroline asks.

"My biggest surprise has been the reaction and response of the government and people of influence. The economy seems to be the most invasive of creatures. When facing dire situations, it is always the economic impact which commands the most attention. Upon the loss of

Southern Florida to the sea with ten-million people dead or dislocated; the biggest concern remained economic. Even today in the face of such a disaster along the eastern seaboard, the talk is dominated by the economic impact. I fear it is too late," Edison concludes.

CHAPTER 13

KNOWLEDGE BUILDING

As Dr. Jude concludes his presentation, Arnold, Senator Joseph's Chief of Staff darts into the room and whispers into the senator's ear. Attempting to remain calm, it is apparent Arnold is anxious about something.

"Hannah, can we get DNN on the jumbo screen? We need to direct our attention to breaking events just occurring," the senator insists. Several years ago, CNN (Cable Network News) transitioned to DNN (Digital Network News).

Cable Network News (CNN) was founded and owned by the Turner Broadcasting System division of Time Warner in 1980. In the beginning, CNN provided valuable news information to people across the United States and around the world. However, as the corporate hand began to squeeze and package the news to fit a predetermined agenda, and ensure a healthy bottom line (money), CNN became known as the Corporate News Network. Over time, any integrity in the reporting of events fell victim to anchors and reporters more interested in making a name for themselves, and promoting their own point of view, rather than creating an informed public. As CNN lost all public trust, it was often referred to as Corrupt Network News.

In 2030, facing almost certain financial ruin, CNN was bought up by Digital Network News owned jointly by Microsoft, Google, and Facebook. Merging together on this project, these three technological giants brought to viewers the most technologically sophisticated programming. Upon taking control, DNN immediately put the old guard of CNN out to pasture, but ironically replaced them with their children. With new young blood, and a fresh approach to the news, DNN rapidly returned to dominance in news market shares.

As everyone turns their attention to the jumbo screen, Coyote Blitzer, son of Wolfe Blitzer of CNN fame, comes on the screen. Coyote looks like a chip off the old block but that is where the similarities end. Where Wolfe was very dull and calculated in his presentation, Coyote brings flair and personality to his reporting.

"It has just come to our attention that there are huge volcanic eruptions occurring across Iceland along the Mid-Atlantic Ridge which runs through Reykjavik to central Iceland before turning north. The volcanoes in full eruption include but are certainly not limited to Hekla, Katla, Askja, Herdubreid, and Krafla. We do not have pictures; the entire area is far too treacherous. Our scientific contributor tells us this certainly is bad news for Iceland, and these eruptions could impact global climate as ash and gas are spewed into the atmosphere and troposphere to be caught up in the northern polar jet stream. Because the jet stream flows from west to east, the initial ash and gas will be dispersed across northern Europe and Asia. However, if these eruptions continue for a sustained period of time, we could experience fallout across the northern part of the North American Continent."

"God, I hate reporters," Olivia declares, "They never tell you anything of substance. I know it would be suicide to send people into this region, but there are scientific experts who can analyze the situation far better than some scientific contributor."

"Listen guys," Contessa jumps in to comment, "If all of these volcanoes are in full eruption, Iceland and the people of Iceland are toast. The Earth is returning Iceland to a very primitive state. Furthermore, if these eruptions reach the Volcanian stage which is a five or six on an eight-point scale of severity, northern Europe and northern Asia are in for a serious gas and ash bath which could kill millions of people. If these eruptions reach the Plinian stage which means the eruptions are tossing the gas and ash six plus miles into the troposphere, we could be in for a long cold winter."

Once again Coyote Blitzer announces breaking news, "We have received word from a short-wave radio operator living just north of the

Iceland capital city of Reykjavik that all hell has broken loose. What was not destroyed by the earthquake is now sure to fall victim to the volcanic activity. As far as the radio operator can determine, the city of Reykjavik is gone along with nearly 200,000 inhabitants. The operator said the air is very toxic with the ash fallout coming at three inches an hour. Before signing off, the operator said farewell leaving little hope for anyone on this Island nation."

"What we need are reports from Europe and around the globe. We do not know the extent to which the earthquake and now these volcanic eruptions are impacting the rest of the world?" Noah remarks. "I think we need to take some time and get up-to-date on what is going on before we continue our deliberation."

"I agree, I need to check in with Washington, oops I mean Nashville to see what information they may have to share," says Senator Joseph.

"Let's take thirty minutes and contact any sources we may have which can help us determine the extent of these unfolding disasters," Noah suggests.

Arriving back in the room, everyone is abuzz with information. As they find their place around the table, it is easy to tell that Senator Joseph is rather annoyed.

Noticing her brother's unsettled temperament, Ainsley Annabelle asks if he can report back to the group first. "What seems to have you in such a bitter state brother?"

"I called Nashville to speak with the president, but I couldn't get past his asshole Chief of Staff Peet. I am so tired of that egotistical son-of-a-bitch acting as power broker between the president and everyone else," Jack shares in an angry tone.

"Well, what did he say? What was his assessment of what is going on?" Olivia Kae inquires.

"That is the other thing which is so damn irritating. This man has no moral core. He does not think of things in terms of humanity, but rather power and economics. Every time I ask him about the extent of the disaster, he talks about the cost, the trillions lost, the collapse of Wall Street, and economic upheaval. He talks about the need to control everything through the expansion of martial law across the country," Senator Joseph shares nearly reaching shouting range.

"What about the people on the east coast? What about the people in other parts of the globe?" Thomas Henry pleads.

"That is just it, Thomas, this bastard Peet doesn't think in terms of people. He is a pure political animal and sees everything as a political situation to be controlled. When I finally demanded, what about the people Peet, what about the people? He said oh hell senator, everyone is dead," the senator reports burying his head in his hands.

"Did you ever get to talk with the president?" Kennedy Kay asks.

"No, I did not. I kept insisting to speak with the president, and Peet told me to go to hell. They would call me if and when I might be needed. Go to hell, can you imagine, I just saved his sorry ass the other day, and now he tells me to go to hell," Senator Joseph says shaking his head back and forth as if he were a bobble head doll.

"We all share your frustration Jack," taking a pause for empathy to set in. "Who would like to share next?" Dr. Rae asks knowing the group needs to keep moving. Time is of the essence.

⋙◆⋘

"Please let me tell you what I have discovered," Dr. Abraham volunteers. "I was going to share this in a presentation, but I believe now is the time. Contessa Margery and I discovered a resurgence of the Sabre-Tooth Tiger, Giant Short-Faced Bear, Dire Wolves, Hell Pigs, and gigantic Eagles in the forests of north central Ontario. These carnivores have been feeding on an abundance of moose, deer, elk, and other large mammals. As I recently shared with Senator Joseph, these incredibly large, strong, and vicious animals have remained isolated to north central Ontario because of the abundance of food. However, the greatest fear is a lack of food will cause these animals to find their way into populated areas."

"How could these extinct beasts come back to life?" Ivey wonders aloud.

"I will let Dr. Margery explain her theory," Dr. Abraham yields to Contessa.

"I recently discovered that the Canadian Tar Sands are receding of their own accord. I have tried to find some explanation for this, but the only thing I can think of is Devolution. What if Hannah's Theory of Devolution is correct in an all-pervasive manner? If this is true, the Earth is in revolt, and making possible that which would for all practical purposes seem impossible. As the Tar Sands recede, the remains of once extinct animals are exposed to air, sunlight, water, and everything else essential to life. It appears that as quickly as these animals became extinct, they are now on the rise," Dr. Margery reveals.

"So. if they stay in the north central Ontario forests, people should be out of harm's way," Kennedy Kae suggests.

"Not necessarily so sister," Dr. Abraham interjects, "During our thirty-minute break, I learned that the recent earthquake spooked the herbivores of the forest so that a large number have migrated south into closer proximity with Dryden, Kenora, Geraldton, and Hearst. If this migration causes these vicious predators to move south, these population areas are in grave danger!"

"Can't these animals be killed before they become a danger?" Ainsley suggests.

"Yea, fat chance," Dr. Jude spouts out in reaction to Ainsley's question.

"Ainsley, these are more beast than animal. They are highly intelligent and cunning. They are fast and strong," Noah emphasizes. "Let me make an illustration. Many of us have heard the stories told by Grandpa about how difficult it was to kill a raccoon back in the day when they trapped. Grandpa said that these tiny animals possessed a disposition, a will to live which made it nearly impossible to kill them. As gruesome as it sounds, they would shoot the raccoon several times in the head, or beat it with a club, and still the animal often refused to die. Well, the animals I am talking about are a hundred and maybe a thousand times more difficult to kill."

"So, what exactly are these animals? I have heard of the Sabre-Tooth Tiger before, but none of the others," Inquires Dr. Isabelle.

"Well, the Giant Short-Faced Bear or Arctodus Simus is a real bully. This bear stands eight to ten feet tall at the shoulders and twelve to fifteen feet tall when standing on its hind legs, and weighs between 2,500 and 3,500 pounds. During its previous time on Earth, few other animals would challenge this bear. This bear is among the most terrifying predators ever to appear on the North American Continent.

You name the carnivores past and present, and they would all give way to the short-faced bear. This bear is not just huge it can run reaching speeds as high as 40 miles per hour. A resurgence of the Giant Short-Faced Bear represents a real threat to populated areas should it ever come out of the woods. The bear could easily rip down doors, crash through windows, and slaughter humans at will."

"Dire Wolves or Canis Dirus are about the same size but heavier than the Canadian Timber Wolf. They are extremely fast and unbelievably vicious. A Dire Wolf has large teeth with great shearing ability and bite force. These wolves are pack hunters and very cunning. In a populated area, no one is safe."

"Hell-Pigs or Entelodontidae are not really a pig. They possess a bulky body, short, slender legs, and a very long muzzle. These carnivores stand seven feet at the shoulders and weight a thousand pounds. Hell-Pigs are ugly with a heavy bony lump on each side of their head. They have incredibly powerful jaw muscles for working large canine teeth, heavy incisors, powerful molars, and dangerous tusks. Hell-Pigs are vicious, always hungry, and indiscriminate in what they kill and eat. Most important of all is they eat anything, and I mean anything."

"The gigantic eagles which I have witnessed carrying off a full-sized deer are something not previously known. Our limited observations indicate they fly at extremely high altitudes which represents a dot in the sky to human vision. With a wing span of over 20 feet, and weighing in excess of 500 pounds, these birds can dive at over a 150 miles per hour. They strike before their victim even knows they are present. So, if these predators get near a populated area, the entire population is in jeopardy," Noah proclaims.

"These sound like Pterosaurs or Pterodactyl," proclaims Thomas.

"I know, but those were reptiles, and these are clearly birds," insists Noah.

"Thomas, where are you going?" Hannah calls out as her brother quickly jumps from his seat and heads for the door.

"I must make a call to Mongolia immediately," Thomas responds, "I will be back as soon as possible."

Dr. Thomas Henry has visited Iowa State on many occasions and is familiar with the short-wave radio community in Ames. Leaving the Great Hall, Thomas rushes to a nearby fraternity house where one of its members is a short-wave radio operator. Entering the house, Thomas quickly gains access to the HAM radio for his transmission.

Amateur radio operators are also known as radio amateurs or hams. Ham radio operators are granted a license by a governmental regulatory authority after passing an examination on applicable regulations, electronics, radio theory, and operation. Hams are assigned a special call signal used to identify themselves. In 2039, there are approximately ten-million Hams around the world. When all other communication fails, Hams can often get the message through. As Dr. Henry knows, a Ham in Ames can communicate with his Ham in Mongolia.

"Dr. Henry to Reza, come in Reza. Dr. Henry to Reza, come in Reza," Dr. Henry calls out over the radio. "Dr. Henry to Reza, come in Reza."

In Mongolia, Reza, Dr. Henry's top doctoral assistant is just returning to the communication tent. Ever since Dr. Henry departed for the states, Reza has been hoping to hear from his boss.

"Dr. Henry, this is Reza, do you read me?"

"I read you Reza; it is good to hear your voice. How are things going?" Thomas asks.

"Dr. Henry, we have been carefully observing the other eggs as you instructed, and we are witnessing the very same changes as in the first egg. It is as if the eggs are going through a process of reparation," Reza shares with excitement.

"What about the first egg Reza, what changes if any have you observed?" Dr. Henry inquires.

"That is the strange thing Dr. Henry, it seems like the process has slowed down a great deal with the first egg," Reza reveals.

"Listen carefully Reza, here is what I want you to do. Take the first egg and put it in water. Do not immerse it in water but have it set half covered in water under normal conditions at night. However, during the day I want you to place the egg still in the water in the direct sunlight where it is hottest. Do you understand me Reza?" Dr. Henry asks insistently.

"I understand Doctor, I will do exactly as you say," Reza responds.

"Good! Reza, keep a close eye on this egg, and I will check back with you in a couple of days. This is Dr. Henry signing off."

Hurrying back to the Great Hall, Dr. Henry returns to his chair to find the group still engaged in a conversation about Noah Abraham's beasts.

CHAPTER 14

ON THE BRINK

WHILE INTRIGUED BY THE CONVERSATION about the great beasts, Stella Caroline sits quietly taking it all in as she awaits her turn to speak. Anxious with reservation, Stella learned far more than she wanted to know during her 30 minutes of inquiry. Unlike Senator Joseph's sources, Stella's were quick to share everything they knew.

What she will not tell the group involves her brief conversation with Zachary Arthur, her table companion at the Plaza Hotel. When she placed the call to Ambassador DeCaprio, now at Syracuse University, she secretly hoped she might get a chance to talk with Zach. Her brief conversation with Zach gave her great joy in an environment and at a time when joy seemed all but lost.

"Stella, Stella," Dr. Rae called out attempting the bring Stella Caroline out of her trance. "Stella, are you with the rest of us?"

Shaking her head in an effort to toss off her thoughts of Zach, Stella struggles to come back to life. "Yes, I am here, what is it you want?"

"We were wondering if you had anything you learned during your time of inquiry to share with the group," Dr. Rae inquires looking quizzically at Stella over her glasses.

"Oh, I'll bet she has something she could share but won't," Olivia hints while raising her eye brows in teasing her cousin.

"You be quiet Olivia or I will never talk to you again," Stella retorts gritting her teeth.

Olivia lets out a laugh followed by a giggle knowing she has struck a vulnerable spot with her cousin.

"Girls, your banter is all well and fine, but can we stay on topic? We don't have the liberty for foolishness," Hannah reminds her sister and cousin."

"It seems some foolishness is just what we need Hannah, as we may all be doomed. Unless you have forgotten, governments and society at large have been ignoring the signs of the times for decades. Now, it appears we may be facing the actual end of times," Olivia shoots back at her sister.

"That will be enough Olivia; we need to hear from Stella if she has anything to report," Hannah redirects her attention back to Stella.

"I do have things to report, but they only build on the calamity we know already exists. I spoke at length with Ambassador DiCaprio who currently resides at the University of Syracuse. He told me that the entire eastern seaboard was lost in the quake and the tsunami which followed," She says in a nearly inaudible voice.

"We all suspected this might be the case, but what exactly does that mean?" asks Dr. Jude.

"The Ambassador says it means, of the millions of people who lived along the east coast, there are very few if any survivors. He said it means that 2,069 miles of coastline, and 28,673 miles of tidal shorelines have been reclaimed by the sea. The East Coast as we knew it is gone. All the major cities along the east coast including Bangor, Maine, Boston, Massachusetts, New York City, Washington, D.C., Charleston, South Carolina, Jacksonville, Florida, and all of south Florida are beyond recovery. They have all officially become part of the Atlantic Ocean," Stella notes as tears roll slowly down her cheeks.

"We know this is difficult Stella, but we all need to know whatever it is you have to share. Can you continue?" Hannah asks.

"We tend to focus on the United States, but there is a much larger portion of the world that was impacted by the earthquake and Tsunami. Nassau, the Bahamas, Cuba, Haiti, Puerto Rico, the Dominican Republic and all of the unprotected Islands of the Caribbean region are shattered and in ruins. Millions of people have perished," Stella informs the group who sit in silent horror.

"Your news is awful," Contessa says while fighting back tears of her own. "We all know and are close to many people who have been lost. It seems like our meeting here may be an exercise in futility."

"It seems you have more to share Stella," Hannah asks insightfully. "I know it is difficult, but what else have you learned?"

"It appears the destruction runs all along the east coast of South America. The reports Ambassador DiCaprio received indicates that Caracus, Venezuela, Georgetown, Guyana, Sao Luis, Brazil, Rio De Janeiro, Brazil, and Montevideo, Uraguay have all suffered the same fate as our east coast cities. Everything south of Uruguay has been shook up but seems to have been spared," Stella concludes.

———————◆———————

As the group waits in stunned silence for the next person to volunteer information, Gemma leans toward her older sister. "I had no idea the depth and breadth of the things all of you have been dealing with. I feel a bit foolish spending my time on philosophy when reality comes crashing in. Why am I here?"

"A great man once said, "Some people see things as they are and ask why; I dream things that never were and ask, why not? You are our dream weaver dear Gemma. We need you here," Contessa says knowing we all need affirmation.

———————◆———————

Before anyone else can speak, the jumbo screen flickers to life with large red words "Breaking News," followed by the face of Coyote Blitzer. "We now have news from the eastern side of the Atlantic, and it is not good."

"How about making an understatement you Jack Ass," Dr. Jude yells as if the person on the screen can hear him.

"The famed Rock of Gibraltar is no more," Coyote reports in dramatic fashion.

Before he can continue, Dr. Jude shouts at the screen, "My God man, millions of people are dead, dying, or in distress, and you report on a God Damn rock."

As if hearing Dr. Jude, Coyote goes on, "The Rock of Gibraltar is not actually a rock, but a monolithic limestone promontory which stands 1,398 feet on the southwestern tip of the Iberian Peninsula. The recent earthquake along the Mid-Atlantic Ridge has caused the Rock of Gibraltar to render itself to the sea."

"In Christ's name man, give us some news of significance," Dr. Jude pleads to the screen.

Ignoring the request, Coyote adds to his report, "The significance of the Rock of Gibraltar goes back ages when it was one of the Pillars of Hercules. In ancient times, the rock on the European side and the Jebel Musa on the African side of the strait marked the limit to the known world, a myth originally fostered by the Greeks and the Phoenicians."

Just as Dr. Jude pleads to Hannah to shut the damn thing off, the big red words "Breaking News," reappear on the screen.

"Let's see this report," Olivia requests, "Maybe we will actually learn something of significance."

Once again Coyote Blitzer appears before the group. "We cannot fully substantiate this, but we have good reason to believe this to be true. Scandinavia is currently experiencing an ash and gas bath which could literally bury much of these nations and asphyxiate the combined population of over 20 million people."

"That is a hell of a thing to report without full substantiation," Senator Joseph says.

Coyote's report continues, "We can now substantiate that while the west coast of Ireland suffered great damage from the earthquake and tsunami, the British Isles remain largely undamaged. It seems the natural barrier created by the Islands protected the major cities of Dublin and London, as well as Paris, Amsterdam, and Brussels. We are sorry to report that the nation of Portugal and the capital city of Lisbon lay in ruins."

"Well, it looks like some parts of Europe may have gotten lucky on this one. What do you think is the case for the west African coast?" Kennedy wonders.

Coyote Blitzer now brings up a huge map of the world, "Let's take a look at this map" he suggests, "As you can see, we have drawn a dark red line from the far northern part of eastern Canada through the eastern seaboard of the United States and down across the eastern seaboard of

South America. Everything to the east of this line lay in ruins. There is no way of knowing how many millions of people have perished, and we may never know as the recovery of bodies may be impossible."

"Good heavens," Ivey exclaims, "The map of the world has been changed forever."

"Now focus on the eastern side of the Atlantic," Coyote requests, "The line cuts across western Ireland down across Portugal and then follows the western coastline of Africa impacting Morocco, Western Sahara, Mauritania, all the way down to the southwest tip of Liberia. The beautiful city of Casablanca, Morocco lay in ruins, as do the cities of Dakar, Senegal, and Freetown, Sierra Leone."

"This is all beyond unbelievable," Ainsley Annabelle says her voice breaking from emotion. "For how long have we, as well as generations before us, tried to warn people about the dire consequences of abusing this Earth? For how long have we tried to convince people and nations to work together for the good of humanity? For how long have we advocated peace? This is like taking part in some horror movie."

"For too long it has been about nothing but economics," Dr. Jude interjects. "The great nations of the world are all dominated by the wealthy, who will not relinquish one-inch of their dominion for the good of this planet or the benefit of others. For the past six Decades people, including our grandparents, parents, and ourselves have warned about the dangers of unbridled human activity, wealth inequality, and uncontrollable militarism. And yet, today these are the essence of the problem. And so, the rich get richer, the poor get poorer, and the Earth suffers from every kind of abuse."

"There is a kind of sick justice in much of this," Dr. Abraham solemnly inserts. "Over the decades, the powerful and wealthy have built their plush and heavily guarded estates on some of the best and most expensive property along the east coast of the United States. Today, as we gather here, much of these kingdoms lay in ruins."

"That is true Noah, but many of these people were able to escape the devastation while millions of lesser means perished," Dr. Jude reminds the group. "These rich and powerful people will learn nothing from all of this. They will only see it through the eyes of money and power. They are not sitting somewhere bemoaning the great loss of life, they are thinking of ways to recoup their wealth and retain their power. We know this is true, we have seen it time and time again. Even as Miami sank into the sea, the wealthy plotted ways to save their fortunes."

"Hannah, may I speak for a moment?"

"Certainly Olivia, what would you like to say?" Hannah asks her sister.

"For the past couple of years, we have been observing and tracking the spread of a highly repellant resistant mosquito in the tropics of South America. These mosquitos have grown in size and number. Mosquitos are possibly the most dangerous creature on Earth in their ability to carry and transmit diseases. While this is not a new phenomenon, we are seeing new strains of old diseases that are more lethal and resistant to any form of treatment," Olivia shares.

"Why is this significant now?" Gemma wonders.

"Gemma, these creatures are following the growth of the tropics with increased global warming. With the recent disasters, we could see not only a spread of the tropics, but an infestation of mosquitos. Mosquitos thrive in warm, damp areas," Olivia reveals.

"So, what can we expect Olivia?" Thomas asks.

"The deadliest diseases in the tropics today are Malaria, Dengue Fever, Yellow Fever, and the West Nile Virus. Malaria attacks the liver destroying blood cells which lead to kidney failure and death. Dengue Fever leads to serious hemorrhaging and death. Yellow Fever starts off as nose bleeds, bloody vomit, and abdominal pain which then results in high fever and eventual death. The West Nile Virus attacks the brain and central nervous system which leads to convulsions, coma, and death. In the tropics, diseases are out of control. They are untreatable, and the survival rate is less than 30 percent" Olivia notes.

"Well, this is certainly depressing," Kennedy exclaims. "There are enough problems to go around, so what do we have for solutions? When do we start brainstorming the actions we might initiate, take, or be part of which might pull civilization back from the brink?" As an administrator and organizer, Kennedy is anxious to see things put in place that will result in things getting done.

"We have crossed over the brink Kennedy," Senator Joseph proclaims somewhat desperately. "While we focus on natural disasters and disease, we cannot forget the carnage occurring in Asia and on the sub-continent of India as nations slaughter each other for control of the limited fresh water coming from the ever-shrinking Great Himalayan Glacier Basin. Over the past 20 years, untold millions of people have died in these wars. Thank God, they have exercised the wisdom to not use nuclear weapons which has far ranging implications on all levels."

"The issue of fresh water has now taken on new meaning in the United States, South America, Europe, and Africa," Hannah proposes to everyone. "These recent events threaten to contaminate and restrict the availability of fresh water in all of these areas. If the nuclear power plants in these regions become corrupted like those in South Florida, we could experience a freshwater shortage of the greatest magnitude."

⟫◆⟪

"Might I make a suggestion?" Kennedy asks. "We have now spent the better part of a day dealing with numerous catastrophic situations of which any one would drain the emotional strength of a normal person. I know we are all trained and equipped for such conversations and situations, but I think we need a break to allow ourselves time to renew."

"I think this is a great idea" Ainsley adds. "Might I suggest we take the remainder of the day to engage an emotional and spiritual renewing activity?"

"What do you suggest?" asks Gemma.

"Hannah, can you get access to the university Music Department?" Ainsley wonders.

"I believe I can," Hannah responds.

"Music soothes the savage beast, so how about letting it soothe us. We all have musical backgrounds and ability. I suggest we have the necessary instruments delivered here to the Great Hall so we can play some music," Ainsley says with her indomitable smile.

"I know it seems odd in the face of such calamity, but we need a diversion to keep our minds sharp. I think this is a grand idea," Noah adds. He has not picked up a trombone since his high school schedule caused him to give it up, but he likes the notion of having a go at it.

Kennedy, who gave up the trumpet while in high school, knows she will need to be the resident critic, so she plays along. "I think it is a good idea, I can conduct. But I will only do so if after we make some music, we head to Hilton for some basketball. Physical activity is also a great reliever of stress."

Just the mention of music and basketball diverts everyone's attention from the ordeal at hand and begins to lift their spirits. They all remember the importance of music and basketball to their grandparents and parents. They recall the Rock and Roll Bar at Grandpa and Grandma's house and how music was being played on the stereo all the time. A spontaneous laugh comes across the group as they simultaneously remember those times Grandpa tolerated their little hands turning the dials on the stereo receiver and CD player. They recall their own love of music, and their experience in learning to play an instrument. They recollect the Christmas weekends at Grandma and Grandpa's when they were invited to perform as part of the festivities. Most of them stayed with an instrument through high school, but only Ainsley made music her career.

Dispatching her assistants, the instruments are soon being rolled into the Great Hall on several carts. It took one cart alone to bring in the trap set for Edison. Another cart held the amplifiers and microphones which would be needed to raise the roof. They all agree if you are going to make music, make it loud.

Looking over the carts, Ainsley, Hannah, and Ivey find guitars. While she prefers the rhythm guitar, Ivey agrees to play the bass for this session. Noah and Jack locate trombones, Thomas and Contessa grab trumpets, Olivia picks up a saxophone, Gemma discovers a clarinet, and Stella gets a hold of a flute. Kennedy, noticing a conductor's baton on one cart, positions herself to take the lead whether she knows what she is doing or not. She knows no one will be paying attention to her anyway.

"Alright everyone to your places!" Kennedy commands as the others are still setting up.

"Testing one, two, three, four," Ainsley says into a working microphone. "Testing one, two, three, four," she repeats.

"We know you can count Ainsley, stop showing off," Kennedy yells to be heard over the beating drums, bellowing horns, and guitars.

Edison, who always loved the feel of drum sticks, hammers on the trap set as if in some mad race to the finish.

"Eddie, knock it off," Kennedy screams being reminded of all those times she had screamed at her little brother during their youth. She smiles taking notice of the handsome and accomplished young man now working over a trap set like Animal, the drummer for Dr. Teeth and The Electric Mayhem.

Just as Edison begins to slow down on the drums, Noah and Jack decide to let the trombones blare for no particular reason. These two guys made the Great Hall echo the return of the great dinosaurs. Thomas picking up the sound, delivers his own primitive blast, and Contessa joins in.

"Everyone quiet down so we can make some music," Kennedy pleads knowing full well she will be the only one not making music. It then dawns on her that these instruments and this noise have already made everyone forget the gruesome reality of the world around them.

As Kennedy stands in silence, everyone realizes she is no longer annoyed and begin to soften until silent. "Okay, now that is better," Kennedy announces.

Just at that moment, Olivia who still plays the saxophone in her leisure time delivers the most soul wrenching squeal followed by some very unusual sounds. She eggs Gemma on to join in with her clarinet. Everyone breaks out in laughter. Olivia and Gemma, long held to be the quietest of this band of cousins are acting out of character and everyone loves it.

Even at his age, Jack is a bit envious of Olivia. He always wanted to play the Sax, but his parents and the band instructor at I-35 decided the Trombone was better suited for Jack. Jack always suspected his parents went along with the band director's need for Trombone players, and he became the sax-rificial lamb.

"Alright, does everyone have it out of their system now?" Kennedy asks.

With this, Stella offers an almost angelic rendition of the melody for "Sgt. Pepper's Lonely Heart Club Band."

Standing in the front line of the group, Ainsley speaks into the microphone, "Thank you Kennedy for a masterful job of bringing this illustrious group to order. Lead on dear cousin!"

"We have no sheet music folks, so what songs might you all know?" Kennedy asks.

Stepping to the microphone in front of her, Hannah reminds everyone, "We are all blessed to have inherited the ability to play by ear from our Great-Great Grandmother Addie. We were also all exposed to the same music over and over every time we visited Grandma and Grandpa's house in Belmond. I suggest we start there and see how it goes."

"Great idea Hannah" let's try something like 'Day Tripper' by the Beatles," Kennedy suggests.

Before she can raise her baton, Ainsley reminds every one of the song by playing the incredible guitar riff marking the beginning and so many segments of the song.

"Thank you, Ainsley," Kennedy says. Raising her baton, she says, "a one, and a two, and a three."

Before anyone can play a note, Ainsley comments, "Well look who can count now," which evoked everyone's laughter.

"Let's try again, only this time let's see if you guys can actually play," Kennedy smiles, "a one, and a two, and a three."

What happened next mystified them all. They all came in on time, they remembered the tempo, and it sounded quite good. After playing Beatle melodies for about 30 minutes, they really got the hang of things. To their surprise, one of the doors to the Great Hall remained unlocked, and nearly one-hundred ISU students had quietly taken up residence at the back of the room to listen and enjoy.

Entering the room, the students have no idea the significance of this group of people. It did not take long and they recognized Ainsley. They immediately become excited and a bit unsettled. A few of them who were politically astute recognized Senator Joseph. Several others identified Stella from her picture in the tabloids. As for the other band members, no one was certain who they might be. Whoever they are, this group of students knew they could make music.

For the next half hour, they play the Stones "Jumping Jack Flash" and "Exile on Main Street" where Olivia shows herself to be a saxophone virtuoso. They take great pleasure in playing the Who's "Won't Get Fooled Again". They really rock out on Harry Nilsson's "Jump into the Fire".

After an hour, they still want to play on, so Jack suggests they try a few of Ainsley's songs. Everyone agrees to give it a try.

The students at the back of the hall cannot contain their excitement at being treated to a live performance. A few of them shout out "Alright Ainsley", "Rock on Ainsley", and "Punk Rock forever!" Kennedy quickly calms them down with a stern look and the wave of her baton as if to say "quiet down or you will be out the door."

"Let's try one we should all know that I have been doing a lot of lately," Ainsley says, "Give Peace a Chance". Ainsley has recently revisited John Lennon's song, and returned it to the national anthem status it once enjoyed in the 1970s. This make shift combo of cousins next play Ainsley's number one hit compositions of "Save the Planet", "Where Love Lives", and "Keeping it Simple".

"Well, I think that is enough," Kennedy announces from the podium. With this announcement, the students at the back of the room flow as quickly out of the room as they came in.

With everyone still clinging to their instruments and the escape of the last hour and a half, Ivey steps to the microphone, "There is one last song we must do before we call it a night." With this she takes her bass guitar and thumps out a rhythm.

"Ivey is absolutely right" Contessa chimes in, "Where would we be without this song? Let's begin with youngest to oldest."

"Hurrah for Gemma, Hurrah for Gemma, Contessa's (everyone says their own name which sounds quite jumbled but it always did) in the crowd yelling Hurrah for Gemma, 1-2-3-4 who we going to yell for? Gemma that's who!"

At the end of each verse for a different cousin, Jack would give a blast on his trombone, and Edison would rattle the drums.

When they had finally completed the circuit with Kennedy, they all laughed with great joy. They all have vivid memories of the many times the Hurrah song had been sung for them for so many reasons. Now they sing it for each other knowing the huge almost insurmountable task before them.

As the instruments are loaded back on the carts and hauled away, they all agree it is too late for a game of basketball. With their spirits lifted, it is now time to get some rest. Assured that they will play basketball as a way to end their next day, Kennedy agrees.

CHAPTER 15

UNRAVELING AT THE SEAMS

As the cousins enter the Great Hall the next morning, they are greeted by the ever-serious face of Coyote Blitzer. Standing at the global map, Coyote has Rowdy King, daughter of the famed reporter John King, who used maps for years as a way of displaying the demographics and voter trends in presidential elections.

The focus this morning is on the ever-changing population density around the globe. For years, the reports focused on growth. Population seemed to expand exponentially on every continent. Then, a few years back, natural and man-made catastrophes caused populations to shrink in certain parts of the world.

"Look at this map of just nine years ago," Rowdy says directing attention to a global map on the interactive board.

"Look at these numbers for the five major continents," she says, "700 million in North America, 500 million in South America, 900 million in Europe, 1.5 billion in Africa, and 6 billion in Asia."

"It makes you wonder what the capacity of the Earth might be?" Coyote notes as he looks at the map.

"That's exactly right Coyote" Rowdy responds, "Let me show you something."

"I hope our audience is paying close attention. We have some rather startling findings to share," Coyote implores the viewing audience to pay heed.

"If you don't mind, I am going to do this in chronological order Coyote," Rowdy informs.

"Please do it in the way that makes the best sense to our audience. Viewers, please keep in mind, Rowdy is a magician when it comes to working with these maps. She is one of the reasons DNN is number one in the news business," Coyote plugs much similar to his father of CNN days.

"Let's start in the Middle East. It is no secret that this region has been embroiled in conflict for decades. Ever since the formation of the Islamic Caliphate after the takeover of Iraq, Syria, Jordan, Kuwait, Lebanon, Oman, Qatar, Yemen, and the United Arab Emirates in 2030, there has occurred cleansing and conflict. Within the Caliphate alone, 100 million people have perished as a part of the cleansing process. With Israel to the west, Shiite Iran to the east, and hostile Saudi Arabia to the south, the Caliphate continually fights for its life. Over the past nine-years, another 100 million people have lost their lives through war and terrorism, and today the population of the entire Middle East is 100 million people, when it was 300 million a mere ten-years ago.

"That is a startling fact Rowdy, and the situation in the Middle East is no better today," Coyote offers.

"That's right Coyote, the violence and hostility show no sign of abating," Rowdy agrees.

"So, what is next Rowdy?" Coyote asks.

"Take a look at Asia, the most populated continent on Earth. In 2030, Asia was home to six-billion people. This is not the case today," Rowdy informs.

"So, what has been going on in Asia to change things?" Coyote asks. Coyote knows the answers to all his questions. He is to Rowdy what Ed McMahon was to Johnny Carson.

"Coyote, do you remember 20 years ago when scientists were warning about the devastating effect of global warming on the Great Himalayan Glacier Basin?" Rowdy asks.

"I remember says Noah. As high school students we studied the geo-political impact of the shrinking Himalayan Basin on this region. No one should be surprised at the results," he says as if talking to the jumbo screen and answering for Coyote Blitzer.

"I do remember," Coyote says, "If I recall correctly, it was predicted that the shrinking glacier basin would reduce the fresh water supply all across Asia and lead to wars over water."

"That is correct Coyote. The Great Himalayan Glacier Basin also known as the Hindu Kush Himalayan Region, which encompasses an area of about four-and-a-quarter-million kilometers squared, and extends across all or part of eight countries including Afghanistan, Bangladesh, Bhutan, China, India, Myanmar, Nepal, and Pakistan," Rowdy reports.

"I thought the United Nations put in place protocols for the peaceful acquisition of fresh water for all of these nations?" Coyote inquires.

"They did, and it worked for a limited time. However, so many of the world's major nations such as China and India followed the lead of the United States in feeling that the United Nations protocols and treaties did not apply to them. As a result, China was the first to begin positioning themselves to have a greater advantage in accessing this valuable fresh water resource," Rowdy informs.

"So how did they do this Rowdy?" Coyote continues his on-air investigation.

"China took the first steps under the guise of national sovereignty to build damns to contain and access fresh water. While this brought the ire of the international community, there was very little that could be done without violating China's sovereign rights. However, at the same time, China implemented an aggressive and high-tech program to secretly siphon fresh water from beyond their boundaries through deep underground tunnels," Rowdy continues.

"Sounds like a dangerous and precarious undertaking," Coyote notes.

"When India discovered what was occurring, China had already managed to reduce the fresh water supply to all the other countries for their own benefit. While the Yellow River Basin and Yangtze River Basin flowed with plenty of fresh water, the Indus River Basin and Ganges River Basin showed signs of drying up," Rowdy explains.

"If I remember correctly, India and Pakistan first appealed to the United Nations for help in remedying this problem," Coyote says somewhat quizzically.

"Talk about a farce," Senator Joseph intones, "This all happened before I arrived in the Senate, and I am not saying things would be any different, but the United States Senate basically said let the bastards kill each other. This was such a callous response of indifference."

"The United Nations General Assembly wanted the Security Council to take action, but the United States vetoed every single resolution aimed at sanctioning China. The General Assembly finally passed a resolution without the support of the United States, the die had been cast in this explosive part of the world," Rowdy goes on. "With limited fresh water, India and Pakistan faced draught, starvation, and dehydration. Thousands of people were dying every single day when India and Pakistan declared war on China. Now today, the major rivers of Asia run red with blood. Over two-billion people have died and there is no end in sight to the carnage."

"What an awful situation Rowdy, and to think all three of these nations possess nuclear weapons," Coyote reminds. "Thank God they have shown the restraint to not unload a nuclear holocaust on each other and the world. While we have heard enough on the death front Rowdy, I do believe you have more."

"I do Coyote, and I will attempt to be a bit more succinct. Turn your attention to Africa the continent with the second highest population. Today, as has been the case for the past several decades, Africa remains engulfed in warfare between hostile nations led by evil and corrupt governments. Add to this famine, drought, and disease, and you have a recipe for death on an unbelievable scale," Rowdy points out while standing in front of a map of the African continent.

"The situation in Africa is too important to reduce to sound bites Rowdy, please take your time and help us understand what is happening," Coyote implores.

"What is occurring, is a continent ignored by the rest of the world! Don't be a buffoon," Dr. Kae shouts at the jumbo screen. "This is all madness. Africa has been a Petri dish of death for far over a century. We all grew up watching the advertisements asking people to feed an African child for fifty cents a day. The sad truth is most people were more willing to donate to the care of an abandon pet than the betterment of a human life. It is just pure madness! Actually, it is bigotry of the worst kind."

Olivia is interrupted by Rowdy continuing her report, "The population of Africa never got beyond 1.5 billion people by 2020. In the past 20 years, it is estimated that 300 million people have been butchered in war, 300 million have died from famine and drought, and another 400 million have perished from dreaded diseases such as Pneumonia, Malaria, Diarrhea, Tuberculosis, Whooping Cough, and Meningitis. The bulk of all these deaths are in the tropical and sub-tropical areas of Africa which includes Nigeria, Ethiopia, the Congo, Tanzania, Kenya, the Sudan, and Uganda."

"Such a toll in human life seems unimaginable. Where else do we see this nightmare unfolding Rowdy?" Coyote asks with his uncanny quizzical skills.

"Have you been sleeping for the last week? What the hell do you think is going on now you imbecile? The world is coming apart at the seams, and this guy asks where else the nightmare may be unfolding. God help us all!" Dr. Jude bellows at the screen.

"I think we are going to need some serious decompression time tonight after dealing with all of this horror," Dr. Rae suggests.

"You got that right," Dr. Abraham adds.

"Let me finish with a couple of things," Rowdy requests while bringing up a map of North America. "In just the last week, the population of the North American Continent has been reduced by over 100 million people due to the gigantic earthquake and tsunami." Switching to a map of South America, Rowdy continues, "In South America, a continent suffering from an onslaught of disease, borne by the deadly mosquito, the recent geological catastrophe may have cost up to 50 million lives." Now switching to a map of Europe, "For whatever reason, Europe has gone mostly unscathed from recent events, and the lives lost is marginal. However, with volcanic ash and gases spewing into the atmosphere, and being carried across the northern part of Europe, we have reason to believe millions of lives are in danger."

"So, considering all this, what is the bottom line? What is all of this telling us?" Coyote ponders.

"It is telling us we are a bunch of idiots playing a fool's game if we think life can and will go on in the future as it has in the past," Stella offers her voice cracking from the weight of the DNN report.

"It is telling us what many of us have known for a long time. Life on this planet is precarious at best. We must find a better way," Contessa agrees with her sister.

"Take one last look at the map Coyote," Rowdy urges. "Here is a map of the world with population density by continent in 2016 adding to a total of just over seven-billion people. Here is a map of the world with population density in 2030 adding to a total of over nine-and-a-half billion people. Here is a map of the world today 2039 with a population density of just over six-billion people. In the past nine-years, over three-and-a-half-billion people have perished from war, famine, drought, disease, and natural disasters. Where will it end?"

"Now there is a question to ponder," Ainsley asserts, "Where will it end, or will it end before the human race is no more?"

"Death is possibly the oldest puzzle confronting humanity. It is inevitable, there is no escape, and yet we often view it in such negative terms. The question is not necessarily about death itself, but the necessity of death. Death in such tragic ways is a consuming horror. While we can't control death, we strive to control life. Human's do not like to feel helpless," Gemma's philosophical side offers an alternative perspective.

The DNN Report consumed the entire morning. All the cousins feel somewhat distraught from the severity of what they now call the Death Report. Despite being acclimated to dealing with heady stuff, the Death Report weighed heavy on their minds. They have all been involved in efforts to save the planet and humanity for the past many years. They have fought valiantly to educate people and impact public policy in an effort to avert the very herculean challenge they face. Now, they find themselves in the midst of a world spinning ever increasingly out of control. They are anxious because they have no idea the time-table they face to perhaps turn the tide on a rapidly approaching Armageddon.

Sitting around the table for lunch, the group unusually quiet focus their intellectual capacities on identifying what is actually going on. Deep down, each one knows that unless they can put clear definition to what is going on, they will be lost down this rabbit hole of calamity with no hope of return.

With lunch over and everyone still silently sitting in their seats, Contessa stands, "I know we are all pondering the same thing. We have all been raised to know we must understand the root of the problem before we can hope to find a solution. I remember Grandpa always saying, when trying to arrive at a determination, make a "T" chart and get absolutely everything relevant out in the open where it can be seen and closely examined. I would like to suggest we make a "T" chart about what we know and understand, and what we don't."

"That is a great idea!" Thomas Henry jumps in with a response. "The sooner we get started the better."

No sooner has the suggestion been made and Dr. Rae projects a "T" Chart on the jumbo screen and stands ready with a felt tip marker, "Let's get to it," she announces, "Let's do some good old brainstorming."

"Just a second everyone, let's not get overly zealous," Noah cautions. "We still have much to learn before we can proclaim what we know and what we don't know. A "T" chart is a great idea, but let's put this strategy to work after hearing from everyone."

Nowhere in the world can you find a team of more intelligent, caring, capable, and determined individuals than the 12 cousins gathered on the Iowa State University Campus. This family is well rooted in a culture of achievement. They know if it can be defined, it can be defeated. If it can be defeated, they can save the world.

After several hours of deliberation, Thomas Henry is exhausted, "Hey everyone, I know time passes quickly, but it is time to give ourselves a break. The more we strain, the more difficult our task becomes. Sometimes we can get so close to our subject we cannot see the forest for the trees."

Before Dr. Henry can say another word, Kennedy jumps in, "Thomas is absolutely correct, we need to take time to reduce the stress which is truly a part of this undertaking."

"It's time for basketball!" Ainsley shouts with a whoop. Pausing for a moment, Ainsley adds, "Sorry for the shout of revelry, but a good game of basketball is a great tension reliever."

With this the entire group sets aside the weight of their deliberation for an alternative and yet parallel universe on the basketball court. Each one of them brings skills to the basketball court. They all love the game and they play it for keeps. There is no real dominant force on the court except the desire to excel with every move and effort. Upon arriving at the court in Hilton Coliseum, they realize there are twelve of them so who is sitting out first. Unbeknownst to them, a figure hidden in the shadows watches with interest, "How would you like to add one more player to your group?" the figure shouts out.

Without a thought, Kennedy responds "Come on down, we can always use another player." As the tall figure approaches the floor, Dr. Rae recognizes the individual, "Harrison, what are you doing?"

"Oh, I come here often to enjoy the solitude of an empty auditorium. There is something therapeutic about it in such a crazy world," he responds.

By now the rest of them recognize NBA Hall of Famer, Harrison Barnes, a former Ames High School and North Carolina Tar Heels star, and now the Cyclones head men's basketball coach.

"Okay, I guess we get Mr. Barnes," says Noah Abraham quickly.

"Hey, wait a minute," yells Ainsley, "I think Mr. Barnes should be on our team."

"Don't call me Mr. Barnes, please just call me Harrison," He insists.

"Yea, Harrison is on our team," Ainsley quickly interjects as if calling dibs.

"Alright, have it your way, Harrison is on your team," Noah agrees.

The irony is it doesn't matter if they have twelve players or thirteen, only five per team can be on the floor at one time. None-the-less, these accomplished individuals totally enjoy the proximity to such a great player of the game they all deeply admire.

The competition ensues with fury and frenzy. Many people go to the floor after the ball, and more than one collision requires minor first aid. The more they play the better they get, and the more they relish this rare opportunity. While each cousin has competency in different aspects of the game, the one thing they all hold in common is the ability to shoot!

So, they play and play on in near obscurity. Unlike the Great Hall, Hilton Coliseum does not reveal much of its character unless packed to the hilt. So, the game goes on until one by one they are pooped. Drained physically, their minds free to release powerful endorphins, these cousins are ready for a restful and revealing night of sleep. Gathering their things, they bid their new friend goodbye. The cousins now head back to their rooms to rest for a big day ahead.

CHAPTER 16

MALTHUSIAN THEORY

T HE NEXT MORNING EVERY ONE gathers around the table refreshed from a good night's sleep, and boiling over with conversation regarding new perspectives and ideas for consideration.

Dr. Rae rises to speak sporting a small band aid just above the left eye brow, "I would like to thank our youngest cousin for my black eye."

"I am sorry Hannah," Gemma Juniper apologizes for a sharp elbow causing Hannah's need for a Band-Aid, "but I really wanted that rebound."

"No need for apologies, I think we all got a bit rough in our play. We were taught to be competitive and aggressive. These traits have served us well in more ways than on the basketball floor," Hannah acknowledges Gemma's apology.

Jack shares a story in which Grandma, Grandpa, Uncle Dave, Dan, Jody, and 2nd Cousin Joel were playing on the concrete court adjacent the garage at Great-Grandma and Grandpa's place in Peterson. "Those guys played for keeps, and Uncle Dave's elbow connected just above Grandma's right eye causing a bloody gash," he makes note of the similarity to Hannah's injury. Supposedly Dave apologized several times, but they all admired aggressive play.

"You know what Grandpa taught us, there are things in life you can control and there are things outside your control. Focus on the things you can control and don't waste time and energy on the uncontrollable," Dr. Jude reminds the group. "Let's move on from the eye injury."

Using Edison's comment to return their focus to the serious matters at hand, "There is truth to that Edison, but as scientists it is our obligation to search for answers even amongst what appears to be uncontrollable situations. We must try to find a way to abate a trend which seems to be spinning out of control towards oblivion," Contessa Margery declares "We must find reasons to prevail or we may all perish."

"I have been working with diseases for a long time. It seems like every time we make a significant advancement the disease develops resistance to our efforts to control it. The fact is, disease is taking its greatest toll in heavily populated tropical regions of the globe, and these regions are expanding as the Earth warms. I remember studying Malthusian Theory of Population during my undergraduate and graduate work. I suggest we take a good hard look at this theory," Dr. Kae urges the group.

"I think Olivia has a good idea. If many of our problems are human induced, then the Malthusian Theory has merit. What is more human induced than the over population of this planet?" Ivey asks rhetorically.

"I believe we have all had some introduction to the work of Thomas Robert Malthus. Let's see what we can ferret out and if it has any meaning or relevance," Dr. Rae directs the group, "We will note everything on the jumbo screen to see what unfolds."

"It is interesting that we are accessing the thinking of someone who first articulated his views in 1798. This guy gave the world a warning 241 years ago, and a self-proclaimed intelligent people have paid them no heed. It is a wonder," Senator Joseph proclaims.

"If I remember correctly, Malthus said that the population of the Earth would grow exponentially while food production would grow at an arithmetic rate eventually creating a starving world," Kennedy injects.

"That is true Kennedy, but what Malthus did not know was the rise of genetically modified crops and animals which would increase production and food sources to feed a hungry world," Dr. Rae points out.

"Good point Hannah, but if this is true, why are there people including millions of children starving all around the world?" Ainsley notes with disgust.

"I will answer that Ainsley," her brother the Senator chimes in, "It is all about an economic system in which food is made available through government subsidies at a profit for the producers, and used as enticements to nations with starving people. These overpopulated and starving nations are ruled by corrupt leaders willing to trade mineral rights to huge multinational corporations in return for power and food. When the food is shipped to them to feed the hungry, these brutal leaders use the food to control the people. Doling out food in such a way as to keep many people alive yet miserable, and allowing many to die as a constant reminder of the ruler's authority."

"Why do we allow these brutal dictators to remain in power?" Dr. Abraham asks somewhat feeling he knows the answer.

"What a great question cousin," the Senator observes, "Why would a nation based on the high principles of the Declaration of Independence and the Constitution of the United States support a brutal dictator. Well, the reason is three-fold with none of the reasons holding much water. First, we do it because we can gain favor from the dictator when needed. Second, we do it because it avails important resources to U.S. based multinational corporations, which means money in political coffers. Third, we do it because all the leaders in these countries are corrupt. If we toss out one bad leader, we get an equally bad or worse leader, and we jeopardize any influence we have in that particular nation. It is all politics and economics. Politicians somehow turn a blind eye to the suffering; I guess it makes it easier on their conscience."

"Well Malthus' original equation may actually be quite accurate because we are seeing a decline in food production due to an organic rejection of GMOs. We could soon be in for starvation on a scale we could never imagine," adds Dr. Rae.

"Let's not forget the great idea of using food for fuel as a means of saving the environment. Seriously, the use of food for fuel is nothing more than a money scheme. It actually leads to an increase in ozone depleting gases, and reduces the amount of food needed to feed the world. It is an immoral policy if there ever was one!" Contessa adds to the conversation.

"What else do we know from Malthus?" Dr. Jude probes.

"Malthus believed there exists checks to population growth such as natural disasters, living conditions, war, famine, and disease," contributes Dr. Henry.

"Did his contemporaries think him daft?" Stella wonders.

"Well, his contemporaries weren't very impressed with his ideas, but in later years, politicians used Malthus to their advantage whenever possible," Senator Joseph adds.

"Didn't anyone take him seriously, I mean just look around," Gemma wants to know, "Why has no one been paying any attention? Why has no one listened? One can feel the abyss swirling around like some ominous force of destiny about to swallow up the whole of humanity."

"I know the answer to this one," Kennedy chimes in with an air of confidence, "After World War II, and the population boom which followed, predictions by Paul R. Ehrlich and Simon Hopkins warned of an imminent Malthusian catastrophe."

"False prophets is what they were called. When their warnings did not yield fruit, the entire theory suffered questions of credibility. It is really a bad idea to just ignore something that makes pretty good sense," Contessa Margery states waving her hands as if to sweep the idea away.

"One of the shortcomings of science is the unwillingness to accept things without proof from a longitudinal study. The scientific community said that not even decades or centuries could prove or disprove the existence of mechanisms promoting a Malthusian catastrophe. Well, I don't think you need very long to see a connection today," Dr. Isabelle points out in a rather firm declaration.

"Consider this my dear sister, brother, and cousins," Ainsley joins in. "Consider a billion people and now multiply that by nine and heck, throw in another 500 million for good measure. The strain on Mother Earth has been unfathomable. Think of the food, water, space, and energy it takes to sustain a population of that number."

"I know this is premature and off this topic, but I could swear that during my most recent visits to the deepest parts of space, I could hear a groan. I know it seems improbable, but there I was transfixed to my telescope and the most unique occurrence in deep space brings with it a groan. Malthus seems to suggest that the Earth or life itself has a singular conscience which will act to protect itself when necessary. Could there be a connection?" Dr. Isabelle reveals.

"And lets out a groan," Dr. Rae says with a big adoring smile for her cousin Ivey.

"And lets out a groan," Ivey concurs.

"Look at this quote from Malthus, it sounds quite familiar," Dr. Abraham redirects the group's attention back to the Jumbo Screen. As everyone studies the screen, they read the quote: "Famine seems to be the last, the most dreadful resource of nature. The power of population is superior to the power in the Earth to produce subsistence for man that premature death must in some shape or other visit the human race. The vices of mankind are active and able ministers of depopulation. They are the precursors in the great army of destruction; and often finish the dreadful work themselves. But should they fail in this war of extermination, sickly seasons, epidemics, pestilence, and plague, advance in terrific array, and sweep off their thousands and ten-thousands. Should success be still incomplete, gigantic inevitable famine stalks in the rear, and with one mighty blow, levels the population with the food of the world."

"What we know is humanity has suffered innumerable catastrophes over the past nine years which has resulted in a significant reduction in population back to pre-2016 numbers. All the scenarios fit into the Malthus Theory on Population. If we accept this, then we must also accept that there are some things which are beyond our control. There were many signs ignored in 2016 while the world was still somewhat stable. Now we face a 2016 population in a very fragile world," Dr. Henry points out to the group.

"However, what if it is not all population based? What if more than population is driving what is going on, what if Malthus is only partially correct and by coincidence at that?" Contessa ponders.

"If we are going to accept Malthus as being the one and final authority on what is going on in the world, we can end our deliberations and find a safe and secure place to ride out the storm. All we need to do is wait for Mother Nature to reduce the population to a manageable level and things will return to normal," Dr. Abraham says with tongue in cheek.

"Our distinguished cousin knows we are not about to accept one cause and be done with it. Malthus cannot be ignored, but now that we have examined his theory and certainly acknowledge its merit, let's move on to other theories and ideas," Stella suggests, "Let's engage a thorough discussion of Hannah's theory of Devolution after a short break. As for now, I could use some coffee and a Danish."

"Okay everyone, you heard it, break time. Let's be back in our seats in 20 minutes," Dr. Rae instructs.

"Hello, this is Senator Joseph. Mr. Peet, so good to hear your voice again, what can I do for you today?" the senator finishes with you're an old scoundrel in the back of his mind.

"Senator, the president is calling for a joint session of Congress here at the State Capital Building in Nashville in one week. He would like to see you the day before the session for a private meeting regarding what he plans to tell Congress and eventually the American people," Peet reports as a matter of fact.

"Assure the president that I will be there as requested," the senator responds in kind.

"Hello Ambassador DiCaprio," before Stella can hardly say anything else, the Ambassador enthusiastically responds, "Stella Caroline how good it is to hear your voice. How are things in Ames? When will you be returning to Albany? What news do you bear?"

Wow, Stella thinks, I have never heard the ambassador so excited to hear me, "I am doing fine, and things are good in Ames. We have covered a great deal of ground in the past three days, but we are still grappling with a number of things which are very difficult to understand. I hope to be back in Albany within a week."

"Do you have any news?" the ambassador probes.

"We don't know any more than everyone else, but we are trying to put the pieces together in a manner that will make sense and result in some plan of action. Hopefully that will happen soon," Stella offers as news.

"Hey, here is someone who would like to say Hi," the ambassador informs Stella.

Stella is amazed at how this suggestion from the ambassador makes her heart race with excitement and anticipation, "Hello," she says, but there is no response.

Then the line comes alive, "Stella is that you, this is Zach."

"I know who it is silly," she blurts affectionately without realizing such.

"Silly! So, you're gone a few days and now I'm silly?" Zack responds playfully, "You know, I wouldn't seem so silly if you were back in Albany."

"Believe me Zach, I would like to be back in Albany, but I cannot leave the work that's being done here. You know I am bias when it comes to my family, but this is a most incredible group of thinkers and doers. I am confident we will emerge with a plan of action for returning the planet to balance," Stella reveals.

"Well, I know if the rest of your family is as smart, capable, and good looking as you, you will indeed find a solution," Zach shares obviously smiling through the phone.

"Zach, how is good looking relevant? Stop making me blush," Stella smiles back.

"I am glad I can make you blush, that means your ego is in check my lady," Zach is now in full flirt.

"Oh, my ego is in check Zach. Just take a look around the globe and ask how anyone's ego could not be in check. Anyway, I need to go, Dr. Hannah Rae expects me back in my seat in a few minutes. Take care, Zach," Stella closes as she hangs up. She did not clearly hear Zach's closing of "I love you, Stella!"

Near the coffee table, Dr. Noah Abraham stands alone lost in deep thought. For some reason, the thought of Nancy Ingersol and her son Langdon popped into his mind. He remembers fondly their brief encounter on his flight to Washington D.C. He wonders how they are doing amidst all the tragedy and chaos. He wonders if Langdon's father made it out of D.C. before all hell broke loose. He reaches into his pocket pulling forth his wallet only to realize he failed to obtain her phone number. How could he have let this happen, after all, she invited him to call her sometime for coffee. Noah shakes his head in disbelief.

CHAPTER 17

THEORY OF DEVOLUTION

A S EVERYONE TAKES THEIR PLACE around the large table, their eyes immediately picked up on the large word Dr. Rae placed on the jumbo screen "DEVOLUTION".

With everyone settled, Hannah begins "Devolution is a term I borrowed based on many observations of the agricultural soil in Iowa and around the World. To devolve is to return to some former state. Many people view soil as an innate material when in fact the soil is teaming with microscopic and other organisms which make it very much alive. For centuries the ecological balance in the soil made it a perfect host for growing all forms of vegetation including food crops. Like most other life forms, the soil evolved to be healthy and fertile. Then a few years ago, I along with my assistants noticed something very unusual occurring in the soil. After decades of being abused with a full range of chemical fertilizers, pesticides, herbicides, putrid waste, and genetically modified seeds, the soil seemed to be saying "no more"! At first, we thought the soil was burning out from all this abuse, which in essence meant a loss of fertility. But as we tested various soil samples, we discovered the soil wasn't burning out, but rather rejecting the abusive practices of the past several decades. Rather than burning out, the soils biological makeup is resisting any attempt to artificially enhance productivity through unnatural means. What our tests have shown is if we eliminate the artificial practices, and return to land husbandry as it was known for hundreds if not thousands of years, the soil quickly regains fertility for natural and unaltered seeds."

"So is this when you came up with the term Devolution," Olivia asks.

"No, we needed something upon which to do a comparative study. So, we examined soil from organic farms, which do not abuse the soil with chemicals and other unnatural stimulants. We discovered this soil to be highly fertile and excellent for growing crops using non-GMO seeds," Dr. Rae testifies. "The only difference is the non-GMO seeds produce yields at a much lower level than the GMO seeds. But that doesn't seem to matter."

"Why doesn't that seem to matter?" asks Ainsley. "It would seem to me that crop yields are important to feeding a hungry world."

"You make a good point Ainsley, but what we are observing is a total rejection by the soil to anything not compatible with good soil health. I have asked that a small test plot of soil be brought in for your observation. Please come over to this side of the room where you can see for yourself," Dr. Rae urges.

Everyone gets up from their spot at the table and gathers around large elevated trays of soil. When everyone is in place, Hannah continues, "Each of these trays contain eight inches of soil which has been subjected to the abuse of chemicals, insecticides, herbicides, putrid waste, and GMO seeds for several decades."

"They all look like good rich Northwest Iowa soil,", Dr. Henry comments as he runs his hands through one of the trays of soil. Lifting a handful of soil to his nose, he takes a good sniff, "This soil smells like good loam to me, I don't see the problem."

"We will do this one tray at a time so you might see exactly what we are observing," Hannah says. "You are all receiving a gas mask to wear during this first test, and I want you to stand back a few steps. We are going to treat this tray with the same amount of anhydrous ammonia per-square-foot that would be applied to a field."

With this, Hannah directs her assistant to use the special tool for applying the anhydrous in the same amount and way it would be applied to a field. As the assistant guides the tool through the soil releasing the anhydrous, everyone leans in wanting a better look.

"I wouldn't get too close if I were you," Hannah warns. "This will take a couple minutes."

With the application complete, the soil begins to smoke with the white vaporous wisps generally associated with the application of anhydrous. In this case, the white smoke increases in intensity until it bursts into flames. The soil burns until the anhydrous is depleted.

"What the hell was that?" Dr. Jude asks incredulously.

"That was the soils rejection of anhydrous ammonia," Hannah offers.

"But Hannah, farmers have been using anhydrous ammonia for decades. I can recall trucks hauling two huge tanks of anhydrous into the field at a time. Nothing like this ever happened," Jack recalls the massive amounts of anhydrous ammonia applied to the fields over the years.

"Jack, there is a threshold for everything. We believe the land has reached its threshold for tolerating the application of anhydrous ammonia. The soil is saying, enough is enough!" Hannah expresses in a definitive and determined manner.

"So, this soil is now burnt and ruined for future production," Stella wonders.

"No, not really, the soil seems to be telling us this is not an acceptable practice any more. It is as if the soil has a mind of its own, but the soil is okay," Hannah assures.

"I don't understand how the soil is not harmed by the fire?" Ainsley admits.

"Have you ever seen a fire eater at the circus? The person places a torch of fire into their mouth and yet they are unharmed. The soil is performing a very similar trick. It is burning the Anhydrous and yet remaining unharmed," Hannah explains.

"So, what is to be learned from these other four trays of dirt?" Dr. Henry asks.

"Let's move to the next tray. Now using a similar applicator, my assistant will apply a normal dose of herbicide per-square-foot to this tray. While we are waiting, she is going to do the same thing with insecticide to the soil in the third tray," Hannah instructs. "Now let's take a five-minute break to get a drink and return to the second tray."

While getting coffee, Olivia corners Stella in hopes of obtaining some good gossip, "So Stella did you talk to Zach during our last break? Do you miss him?" she says teasingly.

"Olivia, you need to get a life. Zach and I are just friends," Stella chirps back.

"You avoid my question cousin; did you talk to him?" Olivia insists.

"Yes, I talked to him but it was no big deal. I called to talk with the Ambassador and Zach just happened to be there," Stella responds unable to hide a devious smile.

"Zach and Stella sitting in a tree," Olivia begins.

"Stop that right now Olivia, we are not elementary students, so put an end to this nonsense," Stella demands putting an angry but I love you, cousin, look on her face. "We need to get back to the second tray and rejoin the others."

With everyone back at the tray, Hannah can tell they are amazed at what they are seeing. "What do you think?" Hannah asks.

Looking at the second tray, the group sees a tray full of weeds already four or five inches tall. "What the hell is going on here?" Senator Joseph asks cutting right to the chase.

"The soil is not only rejecting the herbicide it is using the herbicide to do exactly what is not intended. The soil has converted the herbicide into weed food," Dr. Rae notes. "Now turn and take a look at the tray where we applied insecticide."

As the group turns to examine the third tray, several of them give out an audible gasp. There in the third tray under a protective cover is a tray full of insects. "I might sound like Jack, but what the hell is going on here?" asks Dr. Jude.

"What you are seeing is the same thing with insecticides which occurred with herbicides. The soil is rejecting the insecticide and actually turning it into a substance upon which the larva of insects not only thrive, but burst forth like some kind of scourge," Hannah announces.

"This is unbelievable, just totally unbelievable," Ivey mutters while shaking her head in disgust.

"Oh, we're not done yet, come over to tray four. I apologize for the foul odor you are about to experience, but we must do this to complete our demonstration. My assistant is now going to apply liquid putrid waste to this tray in the same amount per-square-foot as would be applied to a field. Once you adjust to the odor, pay close attention to the tray," Dr. Rae instructs.

Once again, the assistant chisels the liquid waste into the soil in the same manner it would be applied to a field.

"My God, you would think having grown up in Iowa I would be use to such a foul stench, but this is sickening," Kennedy asserts while holding her blouse sleeve up to her nose to soften the odor.

"I can't believe Iowans have put up with this odor for so many years. This reeks to the point of making one ill," Contessa says while trying to buffer the smell and wipe the tears rolling down her cheeks with the same scarf.

"The liquid waste seems to be absorbed by the soil. What are we expecting here Hannah?" Dr. Henry asks his sister.

"Give it some time brother, be patient and you will see what we have been observing," Hannah urges.

"Look," Ivey shouts pointing to the tray, "The liquid is bubbling to the surface and giving off a color very similar to what might be found in a very stagnant pool of water."

"It is bubbling up as if it is boiling, and the odor is worse than when it entered the soil," Kennedy says turning away and bending over half gagging from the experience.

"I think you have seen and smelled enough of this one," Hannah suggests, "Get that tray out of here. I think everyone needs to take five more minutes to get some fresh air and water before we go to the last tray. I promise you the last tray will astound you."

Outside, Ivey catches Edison standing alone, "Can you believe what we are seeing Edison? This stuff defies logic in every possible way."

"We aren't dealing with anything logical these days Ivey. There is so much going on around us which defies everything. The amazing thing is that of all the people in the world, we are the best hope for finding a reason and solution for this stuff. What are the odds that twelve brothers, sisters, and cousins would be inseparably linked to saving the world?" Edison remarks.

"Well, I am hopeful we will succeed! Knowing that you and all the others are here working to understand this mess, and find a way out of what appears to be the end of times," Ivey shares.

"Do you really believe in such a thing as the end of times? It sounds so Biblical. Do you think there could be. . .?" Edison begins to ask.

"A God," Ivey says finishing his thought.

"We better get back inside to have a look at Hannah's fifth tray. Hopefully it won't be as offensive as the last tray," Edison says as he turns to reenter the building and return to the Great Hall with Ivey at his side.

Back in the Great Hall everyone gathers around the fifth tray wondering what it will reveal. "In this final demonstration, my assistant is going to plant GMO seeds at the same depth and seeds per-square-foot as in the field. After the planting is done, we will need to return to the table for continued deliberation as it will take a couple hours for the fifth tray to reveal its results," Hannah instructs.

With the seeds planted in the fifth tray, everyone returns to the table. Once everyone is settled at the table, Dr. Abraham asks, "Hannah, are these five experiments the basis for your theory of Devolution?"

"No, despite all our soil testing and observations, we still had no idea what was going on, so we decided to check our animal records. We were missing something we couldn't quite grasp?" Dr. Rae reveals.

"Well, don't hold us in too much suspense, you have just shown us some rather incredible things?" Kennedy states anxiously.

"We discovered that a close examination of our records reveals subtle but significant changes occurring in all of our livestock. We found that cattle, chickens, hogs, sheep, goats, and other livestock are slowly rejecting all genetically modified and antibiotic feed. We came to this conclusion by measuring the amount of feed left in the feed bunks and by charting weight gain. We noticed that breeding with genetically modified sperm is yielding a significantly reduced pregnancy rate than in the past. Even when using a genetically modified bull, the pregnancy rate is way down. Interestingly, we have lately witnessed an absolute zero pregnancy rate when using genetically altered sperm or a bull with a genetically altered cow," Hannah divulges.

"This all seems rather odd, how does it fit into what you have been witnessing with the soil?" Olivia inquires trying to see the pattern if one exists.

"We discovered our animals are changing to resemble the livestock of over 150 years ago. When we work with the few animals at our disposal which have not been genetically modified, they will not eat genetically modified feed," Hannah tells the group.

"What about the genetically altered animals?" Olivia continues her probing.

"That is a good question. Even the genetically altered animals are only accepting organic feed. Furthermore, they are slowly shedding their genetically altered characteristics and returning to their original state without any kind of genetic manipulation," Hannah further claims in an incredulous way.

"So now you are at Devolution," Ainsley suggests.

"No, not yet, but the pieces of the puzzle are beginning to fall into place," Hannah tells the group.

"What more do you need?" Contessa asks, "It seems you have more than enough evidence to support your theory."

"Thanks cousin, but as you know, the scientific community is full of skeptics and it takes a pretty rock-solid case to sell a theory as fact," Hannah reminds everyone.

"What did you do next?" the senator asks.

"Water my dear cousin Jack. We needed to see what was happening with the water. After decades of pollution with chemicals and waste, our waterways are flowing cesspools unfit for man or beast. For decades, our public policies dealing with runoff from fields, CAFOs, Ethanol Plants, and other industries have been worthless in protecting our ground water including our underground aquifers. By the time people decided to take notice, the problem had advanced too far. As you might guess, there were capital investors sitting like vultures waiting to take advantage of the problem through the creation of water distilleries. This rapidly became a billion-dollar business in which everyone has to pay handsomely for access to safe water."

"Didn't this drive public policy in the direction of restoring the purity of ground and underground water so such distilleries were not needed?" the senator asks as if he doesn't already know the answer.

Hannah quickly responds on the senators inquiry, "Come on Jack, you have been in the public policy domain for several years, certainly you know the moral of this story."

"Yes, I do Hannah; the moral is never allowing anything to become a billion-dollar business unless you want to become enslaved to the dictates of such a business. It is the old too big to fail, or actually, it is the too big to defeat, and big enough to buy whatever and payoff whoever they need. In this case, the water distilleries have most of the state representatives who determine public policy regarding water in their back pockets due to legal and illegal financial payoffs," Jack acknowledges.

"You mentioned CAFOs; can you enlighten us about these initials?" Ainsley wonders.

"Sure, CAFO stands for concentrated animal feeding operation. A CAFO may encompass a square-mile of land or more involving hundreds-of-thousands of animals. Because the animals are housed in close confinement, animal health and growth are the concern. Animal health in a CAFO requires a significant use of antibiotics. Dealing with animal growth involves a high concentration of protein in the feed. When dealing with smaller animals such as poultry and hogs, these animals may go from birth to slaughter and never see the light-of-day," Hannah explains.

"This is an awful condition," Ainsley suggests.

"This is a highly unnatural condition Ainsley. CAFO's go against everything we know about good animal husbandry. Furthermore, the abusive use of antibiotics and protein has adverse effects on human health. This has been proven by the FDA, but the federal and state governments refuse to touch this issue because of the power of big farm," Hannah proclaims revealing her position on such issues.

"This is all very interesting, but can we get back to the relationship between CAFOs and water?" asks Noah.

"Certainly," Hannah responds, "The high concentration of antibiotics and proteins used by CAFOs in animal feed results in unnatural waste. The unnatural waste coming out of these animals is channeled into a huge holding pit which is deprived the oxygen needed for normal decomposition. This deprivation of oxygen causes the waste to create highly toxic chemicals and as you have witnessed a highly toxic odor. Limited regulations allow these holding pits to be constructed as cheaply as possible. As a result, it does not require a great deal of Earth shifting, which occurs seasonally here in Iowa, to cause a breach in the containment wall. Even the smallest breach which goes undetected or unaddressed allows a dangerous amount of this toxic substance to leach into the ground water over time. Larger breaches often deliver the toxic substance directly into the waterways. Today, these CAFOs are monstrosities capable of totally destroying the waterways and aquifers of their own accord. Even if the containment pits hold their integrity, this putrid waste eventually gets spread across the fields as fertilizer. Despite denials, spreading this horrific substance across the land allows it to seep into our ground water," Hannah announces.

"So once again we see a failure of public policy," Stella interjects.

"How does it feel to be a part of that whole process Jack?" his sister Ainsley prods him knowing full well Jack has been fighting the establishment on issues like this his entire political career.

"I am not proud of a system which is so corrupt that we have arrived at such a dire state for our nation and the world. The warning cries have been sounding for decades, and yet it is money which wags the tail of a system which is suppose to serve the best interest of contemporary times and posterity. I have been fighting the good fight, but it is of little consequence if you don't win the fight," Jack somberly responds to Ainsley's comment.

"What have been your observations with the water Hannah?" Noah Abraham inquires.

Hannah asks her assistant to bring in the thirty-foot long five-foot wide mock up of a river complete with continuously flowing water for her next demonstration. "What we have here is purified water which we are using for this experiment. Watch what happens as my assistant introduces toxic chemicals and waste into the water. Now remember, what we are introducing to this mock up experiment is proportional to what would come off of a field or drainage system."

As the assistant pours the toxic material into the water, the water begins to boil.

"If the toxic material does not kill all living things, the boiling does. As soon as the toxic material is introduced into the water, the water becomes useless. As the toxic material seeps into the underground aquifers, the effect is the same," Hannah shares.

"So where is the hope when it comes to water? Where does Devolution come into play?" Kennedy asks.

"There is none unless we stop putting toxic material into the water. Once people stop polluting our water, the water, given time, will become pure and capable of sustaining life," Dr. Rae proclaims.

"So, this is good news," Stella proclaims, "It is a reason for hope."

"It is good news, but it will not occur without a cost," Hannah declares.

"So here we are back at the cost, what are we talking about for a figure," Senator Joseph asks.

"The cost will not be in money, Jack, the cost will be in human lives. As the Earth reclaims itself, the world will experience food shortages like never before. We are talking about a major shift in food production. As for water, fresh water will only become available if our practices change. I also don't imagine the water distillery corporations are going to sit idly by and let the Earth put them out of business. However, that is more in your domain Jack," Hannah expands her thinking.

"So is this rejuvenation of the water just a mystery, or is there some scientific reason for what is occurring," Dr. Henry asks his sister.

"As you can imagine, the toxic water eventually put an end to all fresh water aquatic life. The water is for all practical purposes, dead. This is why you also do not find any kind of wildlife in Iowa. Anything drinking the toxic water dies. Most species of land and flying animals have moved on to other areas where the water is cleaner. However, there is a scientific reason for what is occurring with the water. The polluted water is being purified through the boiling process. When the pollution stops, the purified water comes alive with life sustaining rejuvenating micro-organisms. While we cannot scientifically explain why this is occurring, we can scientifically acknowledge that it is occurring," Dr. Rae seems to be an inexhaustible source of information. She makes it seem so matter of fact, and yet it is unbelievably complex.

"I take it we now have the basis for the Theory of Devolution?" Dr. Kae asks her sister.

"Nature is fighting back whether the soil, water, animals, tar sands, reemergence of huge predators, or whatever else is happening around the World. It is as if there is a conscious effort on the part of nature to reclaim the Earth. This is what I call the Theory of Devolution," Hannah proclaims. "Nature at war with what we call civilization. Man must surrender and return to sustainable practices in all areas of life or face the brutality of nature."

"Tomorrow it's Ivey's turn to share in detail what she has observed from her seat three-and-a-half-miles into the troposphere at the bottom of the Earth. For now, let's all make our way to Hickory Park for some good food and drinks," Hannah directs the group. Once at Hickory Park, the cousins reminisce about all the times they enjoyed a good meal and fellowship with their parents and grandparents. They laugh at how the danger of over eating is ever present. But the food is so good, and the need for sustenance so great. Sitting together, they share great stories which provoke much needed laughter, but the severity of the challenges they face weigh heavy on their minds. They know what is occurring around the globe is a result of human activity. They know there is no way of averting many of the calamities yet to come. They know their job is not to prevent, because it is too late, but if they can find ways to manage the things to come and convince civilization of the absolute need to change, they can possibly prevent the extinction of human beings from the planet.

So, they eat and drink, some of them drinking perhaps a bit more than they should, but for some it is tougher to numb the senses from a day of dealing with Armageddon. Even in their sleep, the weight of the world falls drip by drip on their minds and souls. It is an unsettling way to sleep, but the mind is a mighty machine which never stops processing and searching for the answers to questions which reside in the heart.

CHAPTER 18

THE EDGE OF TIME

Entering the Great Hall, the next morning, the cousins are greeted by the jumbo screen with Coyote Blitzer about to share "Breaking News". In the course of a couple days, DNN has reestablished a satellite link with correspondents along the east coast of the United States.

Coyote Blitzer spares no time in getting to the news, "We now go live to my brother Beaver Blitzer who is reporting from the Catskill Mountains just northwest of New York City. Tell us what is going on Beav."

Beaver Blitzer looking desperate and concerned, "In the past few days there has occurred an unbelievable push of humanity from the vicinity of New York into the sanctuary of the Catskills. This means a throng of people have come up against the National Guard and Army Reserve units attempting to maintain order and enforce martial law in this region."

"Have there been any incidents as a result of this mass onslaught of people?" Coyote asks.

"There have been several altercations where the military has attempted to hault the flow of people only to be met by a rather violent and determined mob. Look at this video just taken this morning," Beaver directs.

"It looks like a swarm of humanity. How has the military dealt with this situation?" Coyote continues to probe.

"Not very well, there have been many instances where rifle fire has occurred from both sides resulting in an undetermined number of civilians wounded or dead and a dozen or so military personnel wounded or dead. This is not a good situation for the President," Beaver pronounces.

"What kind of weapons are involved Beaver?"

"Well Coyote, we frequently hear the rapid fire of automatic weapons and on occasion we have heard explosions. We cannot confirm if this kind of force is being used by one or both sides."

"You stated an undetermined number of civilians and military personnel are wounded or dead. Can you be more specific?" Coyote probes Beaver for more news.

"If you are wondering if women or children have fallen victim to the chaos, the answer is yes. If you want numbers, we cannot provide these at this time," Beaver closes. "This is Beaver Blitzer for DNN news, the first in news."

"Well, I would certainly agree with that assessment. The place looks like a war zone. Please keep us posted as things occur. Let's now check with Poopy Cooper who is reporting from the vicinity of St. Augustine, Florida." Coyote directs his attention to Poopy. Poopy Cooper is Anderson Cooper's adopted daughter of Asian descent. Ironically, her Asian name is pronounced poopy.

"Poopy, how are things going in the southeastern part of the nation?" Coyote is anxious to know.

"Coyote, the Florida peninsula has been trashed by the Earthquake and Tsunami. From the beginning, people have been flooding out of Florida like rats abandoning a sinking ship. By the time the National Guard and army reserves arrived, people were rushing northwest by any means possible," Poopy reveals.

"So does the military have everything under control?" Coyote wants to know.

"Are you kidding, it is an absolute battle ground. As people flow northwest, the possessions they made sure to bring along were their weapons. Just take a listen." As Poopy holds her microphone up in the air, you can hear uninterrupted gunfire in the distance.

The cameraman has even captured a pickup with men in the back waving their rifles as they make their way west along Interstate 10. It looks like something out of a scene from the Middle East.

"Do you have anything to report on the dead or wounded?" Coyote continues to probe.

"No, I don't, but I can tell you that emergency vehicles are everywhere!" Poopy reveals as a convoy of ambulances with sirens blaring rush by her location.

"It sounds like mass chaos. Thank you Poopy, please keep us posted."

For decades, the tug-of-war over guns has ensued in the United States. With every tug, the gun lobby would tug back with twice the force. As a result, millions of dollars and countless hours resulted in meaningless gun control. Now, the government has implemented martial law fulfilling the prophesy of the NRA.

There you are folks, "Breaking News" from the network who is first in the news business, DNN." Coyote closes with the shameless network plug.

"My God, the president has managed to take the worst kind of calamity and turn it into something worse," Senator Joseph notes. "With that bastard Peet as his first and foremost advisor, there is little hope of the president bringing any sensible resolve to what is going on."

"Perhaps you are needed more in Nashville than here dear cousin," Dr. Jude suggests.

"Bullshit, if I went to Nashville today, that ass Peet would stonewall my access to the president. I am of a greater service here where I can gain the knowledge and understanding needed to be of service when the Congress convenes," Jack assures his cousin.

⟫◈⟪

Patiently waiting, Ivey stands at the front of the room looking over this distinguished assembly of family. She is amazed at how fast each one of her cousins, as well as brother and sister, have risen to national and international prominence in their own chosen fields. She wonders if it is by accident or some grand design that each person in the room connects like pieces of a puzzle to the task at hand. These are not just intelligent, accomplished, and distinguished people, but they are of a strong character and disposition for dealing with problems of an enormous magnitude. She feels fortunate to be counted amongst them at this most dire and unfortunate time for humanity.

"Can I get your attention," Ivey asks in her soft-spoken demeanor which is in stark contrast to her as a youth. "Thank you! As you know, I have spent the better part of the past few years perched 18,500 feet above sea level at the Atacama Observatory in the Atacama Desert in Chile. It is hard to describe the sky from that altitude at the bottom of the world, but even with the naked eye it is as if you can reach up and pluck a star from the sky. And the moon, my God, the moon looks as big as a Ferris wheel! Anyway, I spend 12 hours each day gazing into space through the lens of one of the most powerful telescopes ever created. My job is to search the distant edges of the Universe for any signs of creation."

"What have you seen?" Kennedy jumps in to ask.

"I have seen things that would make you believe science is full of shit," the usually reserve Dr. Isabelle states. "After looking at the majesty of space once, let alone hundreds of times, there is nothing so marvelous, so miraculous that could be by accident. And yet, as a trained astrophysicist, I must keep an objective eye and mind to my work."

"So, what have you seen?" Kennedy reissues her request.

"It is incomprehensible, the measure of things going on in deep space are in light years. There are fire storms which would reach from the sun to the outer limits of our solar system and even bigger ones licking at the edge of time. These events hundreds-of-thousands-of-light-years away are extremely violent and beautiful at the same time. What I observe, and what we know as the universe, is expanding all the time," Ivey tells the group.

"How does this relate to what we are dealing with on Earth?" Dr. Kae asks her dear friend and cousin.

Taking a minute to reflect on the question, Ivey pauses and walks with her hands behind her back much like her Grandmother often does. "That is a good question. I guess if we don't know where we came from, how can we possibly know where we are going?"

"How do you think your observations contribute to our effort?" Dr. Abraham asks with a rather perplexed look on his face.

"Noah, there are two things I contemplate every time I look to the sky. The first is, you become convinced that within all the chaos, there is harmony; and second is, the universe is always growing and expanding," Ivey explains. "In all my time looking into deep space, I never got the feeling I was alone. In fact, I am always overwhelmed with the feeling that the universe is not made up of separate things, but in fact is one entity in which everything else is a part."

"I am not trying to be difficult Ivey, but that is significant because?" Noah further presses for understanding.

"It is significant because you cannot look out into deep space without the overwhelming feeling that you, that our planet is, but a small part of it all," Ivey continues. "Suppose what is happening on Earth is not isolated to Earth, but indicative of what may be occurring throughout the Universe?"

"I understand what you are trying to say Ivey, but basing things on feelings and supposition is not very scientific?" Noah says a bit challenging.

"You are absolutely right Noah, usually it takes years to study and test data before we can make any kind of assertion, and then it is often a loose guess at best. But then the Universe is a different beast, and our test subjects are hundreds-of-thousands-of-light-years away. The difference for us is we don't have years to find the connection, so we must use what we have and know today," Ivey retorts becoming a little bit miffed at her cousin's challenges.

Noah senses Ivey's irritation, "I apologize Ivey; it just seems interesting that we have gone from examining things here on Earth to talking about things so unimaginably far away."

"I knew this would be hard, so I have patched into what I have observed for the past few years and arranged it into a 60 minute experience. I ask you to stay focused on the screen, and take in absolutely everything as you let everything take you in," Ivey informs.

With this, the Great hall goes completely dark and the jumbo screen comes alive with the image of deep space. Everyone falls silent mesmerized by the brilliance before them.

"I have turned the audio up so you can also hear the sound of deep space," Ivey tells the group.

As everyone gazes at the images so huge and brilliant, so violent and tranquil, so chaotic and orderly, a faint hum can be heard. It is the sound of deep space. It is not loud, it is soothing. How can a hum be soothing? Yet, it is. As the images appear before the group it gives them a feeling of being part of something much greater than anything they have ever considered before. For 60 minutes the group marvels at the violent majesty of creation. They had no idea the incredible perspective Ivey possessed on life. Where others saw violence and death, she saw beauty and creation.

As the lights come back on in the Great Hall, everyone feels blinded while their eyes adjust to keep up with the light. Soon everyone is buzzing about the marvels they just witnessed. Sure, most of them have seen pictures released by NASA, but they had never seen what Ivey revealed. These pictures took them to the very edge of the universe where time begins and continues to create. Their conversations are intense because like most adults, their youth involved a love affair with the stars. They talk about all those times camping together in which everyone sat around the camp fire and gazed at the sky searching out some star, planet, constellation, or human launched satellite orbiting the Earth.

They recall how they used to look at a particular star and talk about how the light they were seeing had been emitted by the star so many light years ago. In essence they were looking into the past. Now Ivey took them on a trip far beyond the solar system, beyond the Milky Way Galaxy, and so deep into space as to see the beginning of time.

"I certainly now know why you are sharing this with us. After that experience, I believe there must be meaning and relevance to everything going on around us. You may all recall the Robert Kennedy quote Grandpa liked to remind us of, "This time like all times is a good one but if we only know what to do with it", "well I would suggest, this information is good information if only we knew what it might mean," Noah offers as a testimonial.

"Ivey, I think you just blew my mind," Dr. Henry tells his cousin, "While I have been digging in the dirt, you have been engaging some heavenly dance with the stars. I can certainly see the relevance. Violence and harmony are simply different sides of the same coin. However, while there is little we can do regarding the happenings in deep space, we must try to find solutions for the problems we face here on Earth."

"A person has to wonder about the dualistic principles at work. For every action there is an equal and opposite reaction. Call it what you might, you cannot have the good without the bad," Ainsley announces thinking there must be a song in there somewhere.

Now that Ivey has everyone buzzing with energy gained from their deep space journey, she brings the group back to order and focus. "Could I get your attention once again, I am not done with my presentation."

It seems to take forever, but slowly and surely the room falls silent with everyone's attention focused on Ivey. "What I show you are illustrations of the things I see every day when I peer out into deep space. That is until a few weeks ago. What I am going to do now is show you again what I would see and hear prior to a few weeks ago. You will recognize this because you just experienced it for 60 minutes. Then, without any prompting, the scene will change. I want you to watch and listen carefully," Ivey instructs.

Once again, the Great Hall falls dark, and the jumbo screen comes alive with the marvels of deep space. Then, as the group watches, some acknowledging it sooner than others, something changes. Each person in the group is first overcome with an eerie feeling of hopelessness and despair. A few even begin to cry for some unknown reason. Then they notice the scene change. It is as if a wall or perhaps hand is pushing back on the expansion of the Universe. And then they hear it, the groan Ivey spoke about of which Olivia made teasing fun. For 20 minutes or more, they watch as this unexplainable force stops time in its tracks.

This time when the lights come back on, everyone is quiet with some quickly wiping tears from their eyes and cheeks.

"What the hell was that," Contessa asks as she continues to wipe her eyes.

"I have never felt anything like that before in my life," Dr. Rae proclaims.

"Ivey, I am so sorry, I never understood what you were talking about on the phone. I can't imagine experiencing that for a solid three weeks," Olivia tells her cousin almost breaking down in tears.

"The feeling; the imagery; the groan made me think I was watching someone laboring against an impossible force," Senator Joseph discloses.

"What do you think Ivey, what is it we are experiencing?" Dr. Jude asks.

Pausing again to gather her thoughts, Ivey feels the need to choose her words carefully, "What you watched is still going on in deep space. It is as if some force is pushing back on the universe in an attempt to bring order. I call it the Hand of God!"

"And so, we have born the Hand of God Theory. Here amidst a group of individuals trained and dedicated to logic and reasoning, arrives religion," Dr. Abraham denotes.

"Maybe this is not meant to be of scientific importance. We live on a planet in which billions of people adhere to some form of religious belief. In fact, many of these beliefs have led to hatred, conflict, war, death, and destruction throughout history and more so today. You have Sunni and Shiite Muslims killing each other and everybody else in the Middle East. In Israel, you have Palestinians still battling the Jews for recognition and a home. You have Buddhists fighting Hindus in India, Pakistan, and throughout Asia. There are Catholics in conflict with Protestants in parts of Europe. Frankly, religious fanaticism leads to more war, death, and destruction than any other ideology. If ever peace could be achieved within and throughout the world's religious communities, we could accomplish a great deal," Ainsley asserts.

"I found Ivey's presentation stunning to say the least. While I am a person of faith, I have not thought about it in a long time. What if there is a Supreme Being at work, wouldn't the religious leaders of the world want to know?" Kennedy wonders.

"I for one am profoundly impacted by Ivey's presentation. However, before we all jump to the conclusion of some superior being at work, we should remember Professor Stephen Hawking's take on singularity. He theorized there might be a time when a collapse of the Universe occurs," Dr. Kae suggests.

"I understand what you are saying sister, but I don't think any of us can sit here and say we did not feel like there was something supernatural, something ominous or omnipresent about what we witnessed with Ivey's last presentation. I do believe the Hand of God Theory has merit and could be a powerful force in healing the world," Dr. Henry suggests.

"Listen to us, a group of mostly highly trained scientists sounding like a gathering of theologians," Dr. Abraham snidely remarks.

"Come on Noah, you know what they say about religion and science, they both require a great deal of faith. Maybe the common denominator here is faith," Contessa chides her colleague and cousin for being a bit closed minded. "Perhaps the Hand of God and the singularity of which Professor Hawking spoke are one and the same."

"Noah is just putting up a front," Stella suggests, "During the presentation, I heard him say "Oh my God," more than once. He is not as much of an agnostic as he would like you to believe," Stella completes her comment by giving Noah a big hug.

Noah smiles, "I think Ivey is onto something very profound. I just have a hard time grasping something so elusive. I mean, the Hand of God, who are we going to sell that one to?"

Standing up, Jack puts his hand sharply down on the table, "We will sell it to the religious leaders of the world, that is who we will sell it to. If they are moved half as much as we have been by Ivey's journey into the depths of space, we might be able to enlist their help, and God knows we are going to need all the help we can get!"

"Thank you, Ivey, for something we will all long remember. I too believe your information/demonstration will be very helpful to our cause," Hannah assures. "We are running into the late afternoon folks, is there anything else we need to address today?"

"Hannah, we never did return to your tray exhibit of planted GMO seed. Don't we need to see that last experiment?" Dr. Jude reminds her.

"Of course, Edison, thank you for the reminder. The tray has been sitting over in the corner untouched or unattended other than my assistant seeing it had the necessary lighting and water. Let's go over and take a look" Hannah leads the group to the corner for a look at the tray.

As the group approaches the tray, they cannot believe their eyes.

"Has someone messed with this tray?" Contessa asks.

"No one has done anything to this tray other than make sure the appropriate lighting and water were provided," Hannah assures.

"So how can this be? We saw the seeds planted at the appropriate depth yesterday, and now today every single seed is laying on the surface of the soil," Dr. Henry proclaims. "It is as if the soil has pushed the seeds back to the surface."

"There seems to be some kind of common denominator here in the idea of pushing. With the Malthus Theory, the Earth pushes back on over population. In Devolution, the soil and water seem to be pushing back on the use of chemicals, putrid waste, GMO seeds and animal abuse. In the Hand of God, the push seems to be against the expansion of the Universe. There is something here we must find and identify if we are going to discover a resolution and develop a plan," Dr. Jude proclaims.

"I know we are all exhausted, let's knock off for the day and return refreshed in the morning. Why doesn't everyone just find the best way they can relax for the remainder of the night, see you in the morning," Hannah closes for the day.

CHAPTER 19

DIVERSION

Back in his room, Senator Joseph calls the president. As usual he ends up with Asshole Peet on the phone stonewalling his access. "Why do you think you're so important?" Peet challenges the senator. "If you want to talk to the president, you can do so just like everyone else when you arrive here in Nashville for the Congressional session."

"Peet, you're a pompous piece of horse shit, you don't even realize you're very much part of the problem," the senator shoots back. "I never could understand what the president sees in you as his Chief of Staff."

"Goodbye senator," as Peet abruptly hangs up.

Sitting back, Jack wonders if this is how it was when Rome burned while Nero fiddled. He smiles thinking there may have been an ancient Peet blocking all access to the emperor. Anyway, the world may very well go to hell while Peet stands firm as a man of power. Jack picks up the phone, "Eddie would you like to join me for a drink at the Black Raven?"

"A drink sounds excellent, how about we invite Hannah; it will be like old times at Grandma and Grandpa's house," Eddie suggests.

"Excellent idea, give her a call and I will meet you in the lobby in 30 minutes," Jack wants a little time to shower which ironically was one of his less than favorite activities as a boy. The rush of the water revives his spirit and renews his energy. As a young man, Jack discovered that a shower can be a transforming event.

Back in his room, Noah finds himself thinking about Nancy Ingersoll. He only met her and Langdon for a brief time on the plane to Washington D.C., but there seemed to be a connection he cannot explain. He desperately wants to know that Nancy and her son are alright. Nancy said she lives with her father, but she never mentioned his name. Getting out a strange pair of glasses, Noah puts them on and presses a little button to the side of the right lens. Both right and left lens come alive with a soft light. "White pages," Noah commands. "Nancy Ingersoll in Ann Arbor, Michigan," he requests. Appearing immediately before his eyes is the name of Nancy Ingersoll, associated with the name of another man with a different last name. There is a phone number, and Noah's heart begins to race wondering if this is the same Nancy.

"Connect me with the phone number on the screen," Noah commands. As he listens to the tone indicating an attempted connection, his heart moves to his throat.

"Hello," Noah hears a soft pleasant voice on the other end of the line.

"Hello, is this Nancy Ingersoll?" Noah asks.

"Why yes, it is," she replies.

"Is this the Nancy Ingersoll with a son named Langdon?" Noah continues.

"I am the same Nancy Ingersoll. Is this Noah Abraham?" she asks in return.

"It is, how did you know?" Noah is astonished.

"Well, you have a very distinctive voice, and you made quite an impression during our plane ride together, well you know not together, but sitting in the same row," Nancy seems a little embarrassed at her comment. "So why are you calling me?"

"Nancy, you and Langdon made a powerful impression on me during our short plane ride, and with everything going on in the world, I wanted to know that you and Langdon were alright," Noah reveals.

"Well thank you Noah, Langdon and I have thought about you also. Langdon really liked the man who let him have the window seat, and knew so much about animals," Nancy shares.

"Perhaps when I get back to the university, I can give you a call," Noah suggests holding his breath for the right response.

"I don't know Noah, my ex-husband recently died during the

collapse of Washington D.C., and I am not quite myself," Nancy reveals with an extra softness to her voice.

"I understand, and I am sorry to hear about your husband," Noah responds with disappointment in his voice.

"Oh, he was my husband once, but not anymore. We were close for Langdon's sake, and his death leaves a void in Langdon's life, but we will move on," she shares with Noah.

"Well, I just wanted to see how you were doing, and I am glad you and Langdon are safe and well," Noah attempts to bring closure to the call.

"Thank you, Noah, it is so very thoughtful, and please when you get back to Ann Arbor, do give me a call, I would like to hear from you again," Nancy urges.

"I will," Noah responds wondering if she can see his big smile. Oh, I most certainly will call he thinks as he says, "Goodbye Nancy."

His spirits lifted; Noah doesn't want to just sit in the room for the remainder of the night. "Thomas, this is Noah, how would you like to grab a drink with me at the Black Raven?"

"A drink sounds wonderful, how about asking Contessa to join us?" Thomas suggests.

"Great idea, call Contessa and I will meet you in the lobby in a half-an-hour," Noah informs him while thinking a power nap would be nice. Lying back on the bed, Noah drifts to sleep with thoughts of a young woman and her son running through his head.

"Olivia, this is Ivey. I'm not interested in just sitting around my room reading tonight, how about getting a drink at the Black Raven?"

"Oh! What a wonderful idea Ivey. Hey, let's ask Stella to go along so we can get the full scoop on that dream boat Zach," Olivia says with a hint of subterfuge in her voice.

"Great idea, there is no better medicine than hearing tales of how the beautiful people live," Ivey responds. "Give Stella a call Olivia, and I will meet the two of you in the lobby in a half-an-hour.

"Hello Ainsley, this is Kennedy."

"I know who it is cousin, after all these years, I know your voice very well. What's up?" Ainsley always has an air of fun to her voice.

"What do you think about the two of us escaping this place and heading to the Black Raven for a drink and a little revelry?" Kennedy asks hinting at a bit of mischief.

"I could use more than a drink dear cousin, but then, a drink is a good start and we will take it from there," Ainsley's responds. "On second thought Kennedy, as the oldest and most incorrigible members of this wonderful family, we have a responsibility to educated the youngest."

"I know exactly where you are going with this Ainsley. Give Gemma a call to see if the youngest would like to learn a few tricks from her more experienced cousins," Kennedy finishes. "Give her a call and meet me in the Lobby."

"I will call now! Let's not dally, we might miss the action. See you in the lobby," Ainsley puts down the phone, and immediately gets Gemma onboard for the excursion. Checking herself in the mirror, Ainsley grabs her money and shuts the door behind her.

In the lobby of the Memorial Union, there is a phone that Dr. Rae has made available for use in calling a taxi. Arriving in the lobby before anyone else, Ainsley picks up the phone and asks for a cab. While waiting for Kennedy and Gemma, Thomas enters the lobby.

"Tommy," Ainsley always called him Tommy when growing up. It was an affectionate habit, "What are you up to this evening?"

"Oh, not much, Noah, Contessa, and I are heading to the Black Raven for some libation," Dr. Henry announces.

"Some libation you say, sounds rather risqué for a group of scientists," Ainsley flashes that wonderfully goofy smile she uses when poking fun.

"And what might I ask you are up to this evening Ainsley? I suppose it is no good," Thomas pokes fun back.

"I have ordered a cab so Kennedy, Gemma, and I can hit the town," Ainsley says as Kennedy and Gemma arrive in the lobby. Like clockwork, a taxi pulls up to the front.

"Well don't hit it too hard," Thomas advises as Kennedy, Gemma, and Ainsley exit to the cab.

Standing in the lobby, Dr. Henry follows Ainsley's suit and calls for a taxi. When waiting in a lobby for someone, time takes on a different dimension. A second seems like a minute, and a minute seems like ten. As he is reading some of the announcements on the bulletin board, Hannah arrives in the lobby.

"Well brother, why are you in the lobby? Are you so desperate for reading material that you need to come down here and read the bulletin board?" Hannah asks knowing something is up.

"I am waiting for Noah and Contessa; we think a drink at the Black Raven will be good medicine. Hopefully our taxi will be here soon," Thomas reveals.

As Hannah and Thomas talk, Jack and Edison show up in the lobby.

"Hey Thomas, you want to join us for a drink?" Senator Joseph asks his cousin.

"Thanks, but I am waiting for Noah and Contessa," Thomas divulges.

"Okay, well you might be waiting a while, you know Contessa. She is a bit like her Mom when it comes to getting ready. I believe Grandma use to call it high maintenance," Hannah teases. "Hey look guys there is a taxi out front, let's grab it."

As they rush out the door, it is too late for Thomas to tell them they are taking his taxi. "Oh well," he thinks, "I will just call another one."

Thomas doesn't have to stand much longer when Noah arrives in the lobby. "Have you seen Contessa yet?" he asks.

Before he can state the obvious, they hear the loudest gabbing and laughing as the elevator doors open. Out charge Olivia, Ivey, and Stella. They haven't even had a drink yet and they are all jovial. On the way down the elevator, Stella spilled the beans on a couple of celebrities she has met, and the girls are all giddy about her story. They hardly even notice Thomas and Noah standing in the lobby as they walk by and out the door. Before the door can shut, they hear Olivia scream, "Look guys there is a taxi waiting for us, let's go!"

Looking at Noah, Thomas says a bit exasperated, "That is the second taxi I called that has slipped from my grasp. I shall call another, and I don't believe there are any more vultures coming our way."

"Man, Contessa takes forever, what could she be doing?" Noah says half complaining, and half knowing exactly what is going on.

As Contessa finally enters the lobby, both Thomas and Noah say in unison, "Well here she is, Miss High Maintenance."

"That's not very nice guys, a girl needs a little time. We are not like guys who don't care if they look crumpled, girls have a refined nature," She declares.

"Well, miss refined, your sisters and seven cousins have been down and gone before you. As Grandma might say, you are high maintenance," Noah tells his working partner.

"The taxi has arrived, let's get to it before someone else grabs it out from under us," Thomas insists.

As Thomas, Noah, and Contessa enter the Black Raven, they see everyone else has already procured drinks. Over in the corner huddled like a football team preparing a play are the Senator, Dr. Jude, and Dr. Rae. Over along the wall away from most people and laughing like crazy are Olivia, Ivey, and Stella. At the bar as one might guess are Ainsley, Kennedy, and Gemma working on the drinks that three young men obviously just bought them.

The Black Raven isn't overly busy, but it is abuzz, as most of the customers recognize Senator Joseph and Ainsley. At least for now they are leaving them alone with the exception of the three young men at the bar.

The cousins do not mind this kind of social segmentation. Growing up they all became very close, but Ainsley and Kennedy were always the oldest and naturally hung out together. They always felt that Gemma as the youngest was their responsibility. Jack, Eddie, and Hannah grew up like peas in a pod. While younger, Hannah always wanted to do whatever Jack and Eddie were doing. Olivia and Ivey were close in age and grew close early in life. They both loved baby Stella, so as Stella got older, the two of them adopted her as their own. As for Thomas, Noah, and Contessa, they grew up interested in very much the same things. They fell in love with animals and nature early. Looking around, they find a tall table to sit around and relax.

<hr />

"Stella, tell us what it is like to work with Leonardo DiCaprio?" Ivey inquires giving Stella a nudge.

"No, no, we don't need to know about her boss, we want to know about Zach. Tell us everything!" Olivia demands.

"Mr. DiCaprio is a very interesting person," Stella begins, "His level of intelligence and experience are challenging. He has been dedicated to environmental causes for a long time. It is an inspiration to work with someone with that kind of commitment."

"Stop it Stella," Olivia interrupts, "You know we want the entire lowdown on Zach!"

"You know I don't kiss and tell Olivia, but I have enjoyed Zach's company. The last time I talked with him, I am certain he closed by saying "I love you."

Olivia and Ivey couldn't help themselves by cooing at Stella's revelation. Stella begins to blush a bit, "knock it off you guys."

"Are you sure he said "I love you", or was it "love you" or "love ya", you know they all have a little different meaning," Olivia prods.

"I think it was "I love you", but now that I think about it, I am not so certain," Stella takes on a look of disappointment.

"I love you" or "love ya" is six-of-one or half-a-dozen of another, it is really all the same," Ivey looks to reassure her perplexed cousin. "We're just envious that you landed a job working with some very well known and important people."

"Well, it is not all that it seems to be. Well known and important people are just people too. Believe me, some have great personalities and some are repulsive. Some are beautiful and dazzling, and some are more ordinary. You take the makeup off, and everyone has blemishes. They come packaged with all the weaknesses, frailties, and problems of people in general. They just arrive with celebrity, power, prestige, and in most cases money," Stella tries to assure her cousins that, the emperor has no clothes.

"I found Ivey's presentation a little eerie," Contessa reveals to her drinking companions.

"There is definitely something there which indicates dissention within the Universe," Noah agrees. "She calls it the Hand of God."

"What if it is God? What if some mysterious force is acting at this very time to bring about the things we have been discussing? What if it is out of our hands?" Thomas wonders.

"I don't believe anything is ever out of our hands. If there is a God, and even if God is interceding to rectify the error of human ways, we still have free will," Noah asserts.

"Yea, free will, now there is a concept. It seems to me that free will may be the vehicle by which we have arrived at this destination?" Contessa counters.

———————>●<———————

Meanwhile at another table, "It seems we're in a mess senator," Eddie addresses his cousin this way when making a serious comment.

"A mess is putting it mildly Eddie. This president is guilty of a dereliction of duty. He is hunkered down in Nashville listening to his Chief of Staff, and clinging to power in all the worst ways. We have U.S. military firing upon and killing civilians in a gross misuse of martial law. The president's actions on the east coast are leading to riots in cities across the country. The economy is in shatters, and all the president does is hand over increased economic power and control to the wealthy. As you know, the wealthy will use any situation for personal gain and to hell with everyone else. I am fearful the president is going to declare martial law across the U.S. and basically make this a military government," the senator shares his consternation.

"When do you go to Nashville for the convening of the Congress?" Hannah inquires.

"Next week," Senator Joseph responds. "Next week we will see who holds the reins of power."

"What is your influence like in Congress now that you have served in both the House and Senate?" Hannah wonders giving her cousin Jack a rather stern look.

"Up to this point, my influence has fallen on mostly deft ears. It is not just the president who dances to the fiddler of the rich. Most members of congress owe a huge debt to wealthy contributors. It is a noise which is difficult to penetrate. However, considering our current mess, combined with the evidence we have outlined over the past few days, I may be in a better position to exert my influence," Senator Joseph predicts with some anticipation.

"Do you support the president?" Edison asks.

"Prior to the most recent catastrophes, I begrudgingly supported the president, despite his lack of leadership on environmental issues, but now, now, I cannot support his actions," the senator declares. "He is violating every precept of the Constitution and good government."

⟶※⟵

Finishing their drink, Ainsley, Kennedy and Gemma have excused themselves from the three young gentlemen to powwow in the lady's room. "Where do you see this going, Ainsley?" Kennedy asks once inside the closed doors of the universal gathering place for ladies strategizing their bar experience.

"Listen, we have too much going on to be bothered by these three hound dogs. However, if we play our cards right, they will buy us another drink before we give them the brush off," Ainsley says with a smile.

"Seriously Ainsley, we can both afford to buy drinks for everyone in this place, so why do we need to string these three guys along?" Kennedy asks shaking her head in disbelief.

"We came down here for a diversion from all the things we have been dealing with these past few days, and these three guys offer us a diversion. Let's play along, after all, the bar game is just another form of cat and mouse. Another drink, and we will give them the brush off," Ainsley advocates her plan.

Upon returning to the bar, the three guys buy another round and then quickly play their hand.

"What do you girls say after this drink we get out of here? I have an apartment nearby where we can continue our drinks and conversation."

Kennedy and Gemma look at Ainsley as if to say, looks like someone wants to fast track this game. Ainsley knows from the smile on Kennedy's face that the ball is now in her court. Knowing a thing or two about shenanigans, Ainsley responds, "Sure, why not, we could use a change of venue."

Gemma gives out an audible gasp and cups her hand over her mouth to muffle the sound.

Kennedy begins to stutter shocked at her cousin's response. Ainsley looks at Kennedy with a sly smile as if to say the ball is now in your court. Kennedy is frantically looking for a response when Ainsley decides she has made her cousins suffer enough. "Oh wait, I forgot we have an important meeting early tomorrow morning. We will have to take a rain check on your offer."

The guys recognize the classic brush off, and decide to cut their losses. Ainsley and Kennedy begin to giggle uncontrollably as Gemma just shakes her head in disbelief. Now, they watch these three young bucks make their way to the next table of available women.

"I could just kill you Ainsley," Kennedy says as her giggling evolves into a laugh. "You can be so naughty."

"I couldn't pass it up cousin, and the look on your face, perplexed and anguished, was priceless. But you must admit, I didn't make you suffer too long before I came to the rescue," Ainsley says through her laughter which makes her difficult to understand.

"You guys are unbelievable," Gemma says while finishing off her drink. "Don't you think your game could be a bit dangerous?"

"The game Gemma, requires a certain degree of care. First, you never play it alone. Second, you never initiate the game. Third, you don't play it with someone who has had too much to drink. Drunks are no fun and very unpredictable," Ainsley advises. "Actually, the best advice is to not drink with anyone you don't know or trust. Tonight, we made an exception in an effort to cast off the burden of the day."

"Let's have one more drink and head back to the dorm," Kennedy suggests.

"Good idea, I am a bit tired, and morning will come too quickly," Ainsley agrees putting her arms around her two cousins and having one last chuckle.

CHAPTER 20

CONSUMED BY EVENTS

O VER THE PAST FEW DAYS, the group adapted to being greeted by breaking news on the jumbo screen. This morning is no different. Everyone is certainly renewed by their diversion at the Black Raven the previous night. As they enter the Great Hall, each one heads immediately for some coffee and pastries. One-by-one, they begin to fill in their seats around the table. Looking up, there in front of them is the giant image of Coyote Blitzer.

"Good morning, it is 9:00 a.m. Eastern Time, and during the night we had some developments stateside and around the world," Coyote declares as the screen goes to big red letters "BREAKING NEWS".

"At 1:00 a.m. Pacific Time, the National Earthquake Information Center in Denver reported seismic activity along the San Andreas Fault which runs along much of the west coast. While the activity was mild and only minor tremors were experienced, it could be a warning of things to come," Coyote Reports. "Let's go live to Bluster Cuomo reporting from San Jose, California, just south of San Francisco. Can you hear us Bluster? What is going on in California?"

"I can hear you loud and clear Coyote. As of this time, people are just beginning to hit the morning commute. Last night the entire west coast experienced minor tremors. Under normal circumstances, this might not be of much concern, however, with the recent devastation along the east coast, people living along the San Andreas Fault are just a bit skittish."

"What is the status of everything now?" Coyote probes knowing he could use something better than that for breaking news.

"All I can say is everyone seems to be on pins and needles. I spoke with several people as they made their way to work, and frankly, they are scared. The uncertainty and anticipation of a major earthquake is somewhat unbearable," Bluster shares.

"Is there any indication that people are looking to get the hell out of there?" Coyote seeks to add drama to the situation.

"Interestingly, the people are being assured that last night's seismic event was nothing more than a usual California rumble. The State and Federal Government are doing everything possible this morning to keep people calm. But let me tell you what I have noticed, and what I heard from a ranking official with the governor's office. They do not want a mass exodus which could result in freeways being clogged. Such a situation could give way to rioting and violence. The governor has requested military assistance from the president to maintain order and discourage people from trying to make a mad rush for safety," Bluster reveals.

"Is it working?" Coyote looks for more.

"Listen Coyote, I don't know if I should report this, but it is the news. The same official with the Governor's Office told me there are more helicopters in California than anywhere else in the world. Anyone who is anybody has access to a helicopter or private plane, and they will be allowed to depart via air space. I must admit, I have noticed an increase in air traffic this past hour."

"Very interesting Bluster, and yes, this is important news. People have a right to know what is going down," Coyote asserts. "Thanks for the report."

"This is Bluster Cuomo for the number one source in news, DNN."

"What a bunch of shit!" Ainsley echoes off the walls of the Great Hall. "The fat rats escape, and all the others are left to be swallowed up by an unforgiving Earth."

"At least the National Earthquake Information Center wasn't ignoring this seismic event, however, unless people are systematically evacuated, we could be in for a large death toll," Contessa notes.

"How do you systematically evacuate millions of people?" Dr. Abraham wonders.

"You do it one person at a time, and you do it sooner rather than later. I am fearful the military is not present to help evacuate, but rather contain people and hope for the best," Senator Joseph adds.

"We are receiving breaking news faster than we can keep up," an exasperated Coyote Blitzer tells viewers. "We have just learned that the president has placed the entire west coast including California, Oregon, and Washington under martial law. National guard, army reserve and even regular army are being moved into these states to maintain order and enforce the law."

"This is exactly what I feared, the president has gone into panic mode. With the guidance of that worthless Peet, the president's top priority will be control. His actions will do more to cause panic on the west coast than any seismic event," Senator Joseph declares. "Just watch, before the end of the day all hell will break loose in Los Angeles, San Francisco, and Seattle as people attempt to escape calamity and doom. The exact thing we don't want to happen is people panicking which will lead to rioting, violence, and altercations between civilians and the military. For God's sake where will this end?"

"We are just getting word that Mt. St. Helens is releasing large amounts of smoke which could be an indication of a pending eruption," Coyote shares. "We do not have a reporter on the scene, but we do have a live feed from local station KWTF out of Portland. Just look at the plume of smoke coming from this volcano, it does not look good."

"It not only doesn't look good, but it looks like this volcano is going to experience a major event soon. If I were the governors of Oregon and Washington, I would be telling people not to panic, and begin making an orderly evacuation of at least 100 miles around Mt. St. Helens," Contessa pleads with the jumbo screen standing and holding her hands outstretched and upward. "With this new activity along the west coast, it is a wonder there are no indications of activity within the Yellowstone Caldera."

"It won't do the governors any good to suggest evacuation with the military in charge. The people of this area are stuck between a rock, the volcano, the military, and a hard place. This could get ugly!" Senator Joseph comments.

So far, the Yellowstone Caldera shows no sign of unusual activity. This is good considering it is the largest volcanic area in the world. It has been six-hundred-and-forty-thousand-years since the Yellowstone Caldera last erupted. If this area should go active and result in a major eruption, global civilization can kiss its ass goodbye," Contessa declares.

"We have breaking news on the international front," Coyote once again commands the groups attention from his prominent location on the jumbo screen. The nation of Israel has launched a massive military strike against the Islamic Caliphate capital of Damascus, Syria, and its stronghold in Bagdad, Iraq. We are being told by sources close to the Israeli Defense Minister that an armada of drones aimed at strategic targets is being followed by a barrage of rocket fire to be followed by massive air strikes and a full ground invasion. I am going live to Kitty Harlow who is currently in Jerusalem."

"Kitty, what do you know about the breaking news coming out of the Middle East?" Coyote pleads.

The jumbo screen flickers and a faint image comes into focus. Within seconds, this incredibly beautiful blonde, looking much like her famous mother appears on the screen. Kitty Harlow is very much a model of female television reporters. She is young and drop dead gorgeous with long flowing hair, and sporting more than enough cleavage to make viewers take notice. She speaks distinctly using her lips to accentuate every word through perfectly aligned teeth. Every viewer to a fault fanaticizes about the true promise of those lips.

"Coyote, Jerusalem is in air raid mode anticipating a great deal of retaliation from the Islamic Caliphate. My source close to the Israeli Prime Minister said the drone strikes on Damascus and Bagdad began just before dawn. This is a surprise offensive intended to catch the caliphate off guard, and give the Israelis a strategic advantage to inflict significant damage before the caliphate can mount their own response," Kitty reports.

"This is not only a surprise for the caliphate, but this is a surprise to the world. Why this, and why now, when the caliphate seems to have its hands full with the Iranian Shiites and the more moderate Sunnis in

Saudi Arabia? The internal struggles within the Islamic world seem to insulate Israel from hostilities," Coyote states with a sense of confusion.

"I do not know the underlying reason for Israel's actions. I do know that Israel has declared the existence of the Islamic Caliphate as geographical neighbors an impending and unacceptable threat to their nation. Israel does not accept the caliphate's interest in the Palestinian question, and believes the Palestinians are receiving military hardware from the caliphate. What is most unusual is the blatant surprise of Israel's actions. Past military actions by the Israelis have always been preceded by bellicose rhetoric from the Prime Minister and other high ranking government officials. The drone strikes this morning and the aftermath amount to an unprovoked attack by Israel," Kitty declares. "Coyote, we have air raid sirens going off all across the city. I think it's time for us to find shelter. This is Kitty Harlow reporting for the number one source in news, DNN."

"Thank you, Kitty! Definitely find shelter and remain safe," Coyote urges. "Folks we will keep you informed on the hostilities taking place in the Middle East. For now, let's turn to our map wizard, Rowdy King, to help us better understand what is going on in the Middle East."

"Thank you, Coyote, I think our viewers know the geographical layout of the Middle East, but let's do a quick review. Looking at the map, you can see that the Islamic Caliphate controls the land all along the eastern border of Israel from the Golan Heights along the Jordan River to the Dead Sea. The distance from Jerusalem to Damascus is 218 km or 136 miles as the drone flies, and the distance from Jerusalem to Baghdad is 878 km or 546 miles. "This is a very confined and highly populated geographical area. This is a dire situation," Rowdy explains.

"I must be honest, Rowdy, I am completely dumbfounded by the Israeli hostilities," Coyote proclaims.

"The irony of all this is that no matter who is fighting who, they are using U.S., Russian, and French weaponry sold by the merchants of war. Money is the root of all evil, and weapon merchants have been raking in the gold for years. Look at this map overlay which shows the concentration of foreign weapons across the Middle East. This overlay illustrates the indiscriminate sale of weapons by all entities across the region. It is as if there has been a mad rush to Armageddon," Rowdy unveils an overlay which clearly illustrates this point.

"It is important for our viewers to know that a lot of U.S. weapons in particular have fallen into the hands of the Islamic Caliphate as they have defeated opposing forces and taken control of the territory, or when a U.S. friend turns foe. Russia has also raked in billions from arms sales to Iran and the Caliphate. Israel is almost exclusively armed by the U.S. and France as is Saudi Arabia. While nations preach peace, they continue to make money off of the weapons of death and destruction," Coyote adds. "Thank you, Rowdy, don't go too far away, we may need more of your map magic soon."

Once again, the screen goes blank for a minute only to light up with more "Breaking News". Several people around the table give out a sigh knowing that the news or breaking news could consume the better part of their day. While it is important to stay abreast of events, there must come a time to work toward a solution.

"My God, I do hope this is the last of the breaking news stories this morning so we can continue our deliberation," Dr. Henry blurts out.

"I agree; we need to get to work," Dr. Kae responds.

"We have just learned that hostilities between China, India, and the surrounding nations of Asia and the Indian Sub-Continent have escalated with major rocket strikes all across the region. The diplomatic talks regarding the water dispute broke down when the Chinese refused to discontinue their tunneling for water in the Great Himalaya Glacier Basin. India struck first, raining ICBMs down on major Chinese cities including Beijing, Shanghai, and Hong Kong. In retaliation, China responded with ICBMs to New Delhi, Mumbai, and Calcutta. With the borders of China and India lined with massive troops, the missile attacks quickly escalated into a full out ground assault. Hundreds-of-thousands of Indians and Chinese are being brutally butchered as they, along with allies across the Asian Continent, struggle for dominion. Meanwhile, the military machines of both nations lob incredibly destructive missiles at each other which are killing thousands upon thousands of innocent civilians," Coyote reports. "We can take heart that neither nation has yet, and hopefully will not, resort to a nuclear response."

"I am more than exasperated by all of this," proclaims Dr. Edison Jude. "Honestly, can we do anything about this, or are we engaged in an exercise of futility?"

CHAPTER 21

THE PLAN

"WE HAVE LEARNED A LOT over these past few days, and now, we know a lot. It is time for us to put forth a plan of action. We have not just been drawn here together out of our kinship, but out of the fact that we represent the best hope for the world. It is certainly unique that we are of the same family background, but it matters little if we do nothing. It is time to develop a plan and move forward before it is too late," Dr. Noah Abraham announces. "I ask you my dear brother, sister, and cousins, where do we go from here?"

"I am moved by what was revealed from Ivey's deep space experience. And so, I propose we appeal to the great religious leaders of the world to meet and experience the very thing Ivey has to offer. The world needs faith and hope. If we can unite the world's religious leaders behind a common cause to save the planet, it would be an important step in turning away from Armageddon. This I believe is our first front," Contessa suggests.

"I believe Hannah Rae along with the testimony of Noah, Contessa, Edison, and Thomas present us with irrefutable theories of Devolution and Reptile Evolution. I believe the Earth is rebelling against the abuse of humans, and unless humans change the manner in which they relate to and deal with the Earth, things will continue to spiral out of control until all hope is lost. I urge us to take aggressive action in educating the world about Devolution and Reptile Evolution. We must do everything in our power to bring balance back to the Earth's ecosystem," proposes Kennedy. "We must be the catalyst for change!"

"We must find cures for the great afflictions of humanity," demands Dr. Olivia Kae. "A warming planet is being overrun by disease, especially those spread by the mosquito. Even if everything else succeeds, if we do not find a way to combat deadly afflictions, the people of Earth will surely perish."

"The worst affliction suffered by human beings is self-infliction," interjects Stella. "In my limited experience, I have seen firsthand the degradation that humans can inflict upon each other. We must face the truth that of all animals, none are more savage than humans. If anything can bring sanity to a world gone insane, it would be the unification of religious leaders behind a common cause. We cannot pass up the opportunity provided by the "Hand of God."

"While I am in agreement with Contessa, Kennedy, and Stella, I believe our most dangerous challenge is the Mosquito. With tropical warming occurring all across the Earth, the geographical range of the Mosquito is rapidly expanding to threaten all human life," Olivia continues to hammer her point. "If we do not find a way to control these insidious little dive bombers, humanity will soon suffer the most unimaginable and horrific physical and mental afflictions with no possible recourse."

I know there is hypocrisy in what I am saying, but we need money and lots of it. I believe we need to convert money into a message which raises the consciousness of people all around the world if we are to prevail. None of us are or will we ever be controlled by money, but if we are going to get the word out in a meaningful and substantial way, we need money that will enable us to control the medium and the message. At the same time, we must command the high ground in convincing people that things must change, and if they do, we can and will bring the Earth back into balance," Ainsley proclaims. "We must put together an extravaganza which will capture the attention and imagination of people in a manner that leads to a change in behavior."

"Human behavior is tricky. It has been determined that there are four basic personality types: Optimistic, Pessimistic, Trusting, and Envious. These types are pretty evenly distributed among the human race. As you might infer, Optimistic and Trusting offer avenues conducive to a change in human behavior. Pessimistic and Envious are a different story.

It will require a carefully constructed message and campaign to raise consciousness and change human behavior," Gemma asserts revealing wisdom beyond her age.

"As much as I abhor the sound of it, and I believe money is the root of all evil, we must be resolved to raise money and use it for good," Dr. Margery asserts. "We not only need to raise money to control the medium and message, but we must raise money to help those in need. We certainly know the governments of the world will be of no help."

"I believe we need leadership. We need someone who can and will lead this nation and the world away from the abyss and towards a new and sane world. A leader with popular appeal who will toss aside the influence of big money for sound judgment. Someone who will hold sacred the best interest of all people and posterity. I believe this leader is my cousin, Senator Jack Joseph. We must accept the political realities of our dilemma and stand firmly behind our cousin for President of the United States," declares Dr. Edison Jude.

"Hold on Edison, I appreciate your voice of support, but much of the world's problems are due to politics. To make a political campaign a part of our mission, makes our mission look disingenuous and opportunistic. Such a campaign will have an adverse effect on the very things we are trying to accomplish, and play right into the hands of those who will oppose our efforts. We must put politics on hold," Jack insists.

"So, what is our plan?" demands Dr. Rae"

"The plan is we use our unique talents, determination, and relentless energy to work together in an effort to effect a positive change in the existence of humans on Earth." declares Dr. Henry. "If we choose to do nothing, the fate of all mankind rest on our idle shoulders."

"I suggest we focus on four things: One, is an effort to unify the religious leaders of the world behind the Hand of God. Two, is to clearly articulate and share the Theory of Devolution and Reptile Evolution with people around the world. Three, is to find an answer to the mosquito problem and the spread of disease. Four, is to put together a grand extravaganza to raise money and change the beliefs and behaviors of all people around the world," Dr. Thomas Henry proposes.

"I couldn't agree more," Kennedy proclaims rising from her chair to accentuate her support.

"If this is our focus, how do we make it happen?" Ivey asks knowing it is easy to say what you want to do, and it is another thing to actually do it.

"I don't know?" Contessa inserts, "But, we must make the effort. I truly believe what Ivey has to offer could bring unity and a common purpose to the world's religious leaders."

"What we must do," Kennedy extols from her years of organizing, "Is personally reach out to each religious leader to join in a common cause. Ask them to come together for the salvation of humanity? Ask them to put aside their differences long enough to make the effort? Show them the Hand of God!"

"How can we go wrong?" Ivey shouts, "I cannot imagine a more dreadful situation from which to make such an appeal. But I cannot do this alone."

"You will not have to do this alone Ivey. I will be part of your team!" Stella volunteers.

"I too will work with Ivey and Stella to bring the religious leaders of the world together. I am convinced we can make this happen. The three of us will make an invincible team," Senator Joseph proclaims.

"We shall set forth on such an endeavor immediately!" Stella offers. "So, where does Devolution fit into our consideration?"

"Devolution, in and of itself is huge," the senator suggests. "There must be an all-out campaign to educate people about the rapidly advancing ecological and environmental apocalypse if things are not changed!"

"Profound my cousin," Edison offers tongue in cheek. "You certainly don't take a back seat to Yogi-isms."

"With all seriousness," Dr. Rae attempts to keep everyone focused, "What we have is just a beginning. It will be a struggle to get beyond the accusations of the crazed-out fanatics our mission threatens the most! As Gemma noted, pessimistic and envious people will be a hard sell."

"Oh, I think you are underestimating the true desperation of a people wandering without leadership," Stella asserts. "They are not only ready, but willing to hear the truth. With disaster all around them, they are ready, yes indeed, they are ready for leadership."

"But leadership is more in Senator Joseph's bailiwick," enjoins Dr. Abraham. "We need to talk about this!"

"Just a second Noah," Dr. Henry cautions. "We were talking about Devolution and leadership. They are not mutually exclusive. Leadership is exactly what is needed to combat Devolution, and we need a franchise of leadership, not a monopoly. Jack is a great leader, but if this endeavor is to succeed, we must all see ourselves as leaders."

"Thomas is correct, we are all leaders and as such, we must set forth within our own sphere of influence and know that while we are segmented, we could not be more united," Senator Joseph proclaims with a raised fist.

"If I might suggest, I see myself along with Noah, Contessa, Edison, and Thomas teaming up to tackle the challenges of Devolution and Reptile Evolution," Hannah offers hoping the others agree. "In this area, we can and will take the lead."

"What Ainsley, Gemma, and I can do is raise human consciousness to the true nature of our work. We can organize, promote, entertain, and raise funds. We can help raise the funds needed to drive all other endeavors. We can control the medium and the message," Kennedy acknowledges.

"We can fill stadiums with spectators to witness the beauty and truth found in music, performance, reflection, and unselfishness. Between the three of us, we can bring together the greatest of all talents to march as an army on a sacred crusade to save the world," Kennedy announces with the determination of General Eisenhower addressing his troops before Normandy, or General Harry Schmidt's command at Iwo Jima.

'I cannot argue with my cousin of such passion. I think she has just provided me with the context of my next song. There is something that rings true about a sacred crusade," Ainsley offers in a melodic tone hinting of the music to come. "However, stadiums will not hold the mass of people we will bring to the cause."

"I stand alone, but feel the unity of our cause and the determination of our effort," Dr. Kae says from the sidelines. I have a mission to complete. I must return to my team in Atlanta and push forward with all haste. The war we wage with the demonic menace of doom must be won before it is too late."

"Absolutely, there could be nothing more immediate than the challenge before you Olivia. We would all like to help, but none of us possess the knowledge, skill, or talent needed to combat the affliction facing your area of expertise," intones Ainsley.

"You are so brave Olivia, and we are all with you 100 percent because we know the mind-boggling obstacles in your path, but it is a cross you must bear alone. You can do it; we all believe in you!" Stella affirms what Oliva and everybody else knows to be the truth.

"I will do my best cousins. I know with the help of my research team it can be done, and if we have the resources necessary to complete our research, I believe we can win this battle sooner rather than later," Olivia offers in her sometimes-quiet manner as she reflects on the enormity of the challenge before her. Humankind has been far too long combating the evil dangers of the winged demon."

"It seems we have all come to an understanding of the task at hand, and the roles we each must take in our common cause to avert the final day," Hannah says with right hand raised as if offering a blessing. "Go forth, report forth, push forth, and usher humanity into a new Garden."

CHAPTER 22

THE WINGED DEMON

O LIVIA HEADS OUT KNOWING THE immediacy of her mission, and never feeling alone because the family's circle of love is ever present. Olivia was a quiet child never to be confused with shy. She has always known and felt things very deeply, and her relationship with her brother, sister, and cousins grows closer and stronger as the years pass.

Not one of the eleven others envy the task confronting Olivia. She is at the lead of cutting-edge research into ways to combat the most dreaded monster on Earth. Over millions-of-years of evolution, the mosquito has become the conveyor of doom. It carries its dastardly deed to any and all regions of the Earth despite the duration of opportunity. While this demon of Satan is a present and ongoing danger throughout the world, the mosquito is an infestation, carrying the venom of hell on Earth especially in areas of squalor.

Olivia knows the enemy must be confronted where it is most potent and vulnerable. The mosquito must become the preverbal bark being worse than its bite, or humanities fate is one of enduring misery. These pesky and toxic pests must be dealt with at their delivery system. The idea that such an infectious pest could be eradicated is more than fool hardy.

For centuries, humans focused on repelling this villainous foe using all types of sprays, fogs, oils, and other substances to ward off this devil with wings. When the mosquito won out and disease ensued, humans worked to find serums and vaccinations which actually fought the disease, rather than the deliverer of doom.

For what seems like forever, humans have tried to control the mosquito by using insecticides which are aimed at the larva. It seemed reasonable to believe that the threat would go away by killing the larva. Nothing is further from the truth. The resilience of this pest and its ability to live on is well established.

Dr. Kae understands the urgency of her mission. Should she fail, all the efforts of the others will be moot. The Earth is on the cusp of a mosquito infestation so far reaching that humanity could cease to exist. Dreaded diseases carried by millions of small dive bombers, delivering their version of hell, could render humanity helpless.

Up to this point, the war between humans and mosquito has been a feeble attempt to reduce the inevitable. Despite all efforts, the mosquito comes forth when the conditions allow, and these conditions are rapidly expanding around the globe. The mosquito is an aggressive creature with no consideration for the inhumanity it brings.

Arriving back in Atlanta, Dr. Kae is picked up by an agency chauffer who spares no time in returning her to the lab and her colleagues. Work at the lab has been churning non-stop in pursuit of Dr. Kae's brilliant theory about how to neuter the mosquito.

Long before achieving her doctorate, Olivia Kae felt a calling to deal with the most insidious creature ever conceived. She has been devoted to the study of this winged devil for most of her adult life. Recently, her study uncovered a vulnerability which if attacked could render the mosquito a harmless pest.

Olivia concludes that we must learn to cohabitate, which means the mosquito must not be capable of doing any harm! Probing deep from every angle and perspective, Dr. Kae's team is working to develop a vapor approach to altering the DNA structure of the mosquito. If her idea works, it will render the mosquito incapable of carrying or transmitting disease. The experiments at the lab are fast tracked which means, "What can we see and what do we know now!" These experiments were well along when Olivia departed for Ames. None-the-less, the things Olivia saw, heard, and discussed in Ames created a profound urgency. She arrives back at the lab anxious and determined to find a successful answer.

Entering the lab, Dr. Kae gets right to the point, "What do we know, do we have any indication that our vapor can change the genetic code of the mosquito in a way as to render it impotent as a carrier?"

"Our studies have yielded positive results Doctor Kae," her top assistant researcher reports.

"What does that mean?" Dr. Kae wants specifics.

"It means that the most recent study group of mosquito larva exposed to our vapor hatched as harmless and incapable of carrying anything. Furthermore, Doctor, since the female mosquito lays eggs every few days, we have been able to determine that once rendered harmless, the female passes on mutated DNA which render all subsequent generations harmless and incapable of carrying anything. You have done it Dr. Kae, you have taken on the most insidious creature ever conceived and won," the assistant proclaims.

"Don't get ahead of yourself," Dr. Kae warns. "This is certainly great news, but until we have taken it out of the lab successfully into the real world, we have little to celebrate. None-the-less, call the team together and let's break open a bottle of champagne. It is important to celebrate even the slightest bit of hope."

As the team celebrates their recent breakthrough, Dr. Kae feels it is time to reveal the next step in the battle. There are 3,500 known species of mosquito, and they are taking a deadly toll on human and animal life. While the focus is saving human lives, they cannot ignore the impact on livestock. The mosquito is a real threat to the already stretched food supply. If this vapor causes the restructuring of the mosquito DNA as the research suggests, humanity will also benefit from the protection of livestock.

"May I have your attention," Dr. Kae requests of her team. "I am going to schedule a meeting with the head of the CDC, Mayor of Atlanta, and Governor of Georgia to request using our DNA altering vapor here in Atlanta as a first step in the elimination of the mosquito as the devil's workhorse. I realize we could go many places in the world to test our results, but as you know, Atlanta is one of the most mosquito infested places in the United States. I cannot see traveling a great distance to do what can be done right here at home."

"Doctor, are we certain this vapor will not have an adverse effect on humans or animals?" a member of the team inquires.

"Dr. Rooh, five female members of this team including myself have been secretly exposed to the vapor as it has been developed to ensure there is no adverse effect on humans. We have been working closely with a DNA expert who has routinely tested our DNA structure as well as those of our eggs to ensure there is no change. We have received a clean bill of health," Dr. Kae reveals to a surprised group.

"What about animals Dr. Kae?" another team member asks.

"I am sorry Dr. Mason, but we had to do this in a rather clandestine manner, and I hope you understand. We have a secret kennel of animals and livestock which have also been exposed to our vapor as it has been developed. These animals and livestock have all passed DNA tests," Dr. Kae announces.

"Dr. Kae, if what you say is true, you have violated some serious ethical rules when it comes to the testing and application of experimental substances," a rather hostile team member proclaims.

"What would you have done Dr. Pompous, we have just made a break through with our vapor research, and if we had not simultaneously done the human and animal testing, we would be months, if not longer away from the application stage. The world is on the cusp of a deadly assault, and you are concerned about ethics and protocol?" Dr. Kae challenges.

"I have no choice but to report you to the ethical committee here at the CDC," Dr. Pompous declares. "We cannot allow such a mad scientist approach to research and development."

"You won't have to report me to any committee Dr. Pompous; I plan full disclosure to the head of the CDC, Atlanta Mayor, and Governor of Georgia. So, if you wish to dismiss yourself from this team, I would be glad to accept your resignation. However, let me remind everyone that what we have done in secret is no different or less urgent than the research and development of the Manhattan Project in the 1940s. Furthermore, if this works, we will save far more lives. Now if you will excuse me, I must make some very important calls," Dr. Kae is fiercely determined to make this work.

As Dr. Kae leaves the room, Dr. Pompous finds himself standing alone among a team of very loyal and admiring colleagues of Dr. Kae.

Each person in the room knows the dangers and risks Dr. Kae has taken on in the campaign against the deadly mosquito.

"Listen Dr. Pompous," Dr. Rooh says squaring up with his colleague face to face. "Without Dr. Kae, we would never have reached this point in our quest. She has never asked any of us to do more than she has been willing to do herself. You need to shut your trap and get on board, or get the hell out of here!"

"I am not excited about the secrecy, but I understand. No one has risked more on this project than Dr. Kae," Dr. Mason interjects. "We all know the urgency of our battle. The world is getting warmer and wetter, and geographical events are wrecking havoc around the world turning every nook and cranny into a cesspool of mosquito infestation. Death tolls due to mosquito carried diseases increase many times over every year. We know without any doubt that such an increase in disease and death will soon become exponential unless something is done. If Dr. Kae had not taken this initiative, the epitaph for humanity may very well be "They are no more but at least they were ethical.""

As her team firms up their support for Dr. Kae's leadership, she is in her office attempting to make arrangements for a meeting that very same day. As you enter Dr. Kae's office, you immediately focus on all of the books and piles of papers which are constantly in use. As you sit in the chair across from her desk and survey the walls, you discover a picture of her parents framed by pictures of herself, Brother Thomas Henry, and Sister Hannah Rae. Closer examination reveals pictures of her Grandma and Grandpa, uncles, aunts, and cousins. On one isolated wall is a large abstract painting of a mosquito in a circle of sacred geometry by the famed artist Justin Pritchard.

As Dr. Kae picks up the phone to make her first call to the head of the CDC, she surveys all the pictures and smiles. This is her family which is inseparably linked in the struggle to save humanity. She finds each face and the memories bring inspiration and courage. She smiles as someone brings the other end of the phone to life.

"Hello, this is Dr. Masterson's office, how may I help you?" the secretary asks.

"Matilda, this is Olivia Kae, is Dr. Masterson in?"

"Why yes Dr. Kae, I will put you right through," came the response.

"Olivia, how is my favorite researcher doing today?" Dr. Masterson greets. Dr. Masterson is a big man of about 60 years of age with long hair he sometimes wears in a pony tail. He maintains a neatly shaved beard which accentuates his frequent smile. Dr. Masterson manages a huge responsibility with the friendly demeanor of a small-town merchant.

"Dr. Masterson, I truly believe we have unlocked the vault to the mosquitoes' DNA which allows us to render them nothing more than a pest. I would like to meet with you, the mayor, and governor immediately."

"My Lord Olivia, this is quite a pronouncement. But why would you want to meet with the mayor and governor?" Dr. Masterson asks knowing such revelations are usually shared with him first as a preliminary step.

"Please, just set up the meeting, and I will share every detail. We are on the cusp of something big, and we have no time to waste," Dr. Kae pleads.

"If it were anyone but you Olivia, I would probably be hesitant, but I know you would not make such a request lightly. I will call you back as soon as I have spoken with the mayor and governor," Dr. Masterson shares.

"Thank you, Paul," Olivia uses Dr. Masterson's first name. Not many people can call the director by his first name, but Olivia has a special place in Dr. Masterson's heart. He lost a child named Olivia, who would have been Olivia's age, to a mosquito borne disease.

Hanging up the phone, Olivia can feel her heart racing with excitement and anticipation. Her team has worked relentlessly to find the key to defeating this blood sucking, disease spreading, foe of humanity. Leaning back in her chair, she ponders the best approach in meeting with these three powerful individuals. She knows that all of her work, and the work of her team is for not, if she fails to convince these leaders to take the right course of action.

Dr. Kae is confident she will quickly gain the support of the director. He is a highly intelligent man who has closely followed the work of her team. However, he does not know about the secret testing. The mayor lives with the mosquito infestation in Atlanta, and bears the burden of dealing with morgues filled with the dead and hospitals filled with the dying. She is a person of great compassion, and the people of Atlanta are fortunate to have such a caring leader at the helm. Char King is the granddaughter of famed Civil Rights Leader Martin Luther King Jr. Raised in Atlanta, she knows the wickedness of this pesky bug they are trying to defeat. She has been the mayor for eight-years, and is universally loved and respected by the citizens of Atlanta. As the mayor, Char does not hesitate to buck the establishment to do what is right for her city. None-the-less, Dr. Kae will be asking permission to use a vapor on her city for which she has no assurance other than Olivia's word that it will be safe and do what is intended. Governor Hickenlooper's family actually has Iowa roots. His Grandfather Bourke served as governor and a U.S. Senator from Iowa. True to his Grandfather, the governor is a moderate republican. He is up for re-election in one year, so engaging something like Olivia is proposing, will be tough for him, despite the increasing horror brought on by the monster of misery.

"Olivia, this is Paul, I have arranged a meeting with Mayor King and Governor Hickenlooper in the penthouse suite of the Carlton Hilton in the morning. I have apprised them of the topic, and they have asked that we keep this low-key, which explains the Carlton Hilton. We can all arrive inconspicuously, so I would like you to travel to the meeting with me. Please meet me in my office for a 7:00 a.m. departure."

"I will be there!" Olivia responds.

It is already three o'clock in the afternoon, and Olivia can feel a bead of sweat building across her brow. She cannot blow this opportunity, but then again, how can these three leaders dismiss the possibility of such a breakthrough. Olivia is a scientist and a researcher, not a politician. She wonders "What is the best approach?"

Picking up the phone, she calls the one person she trusts for this kind of advice. "Hello, this is Nora at Senator Joseph's remote office in Nashville, can I help you?"

"Nora, this is Dr. Kae, may I speak with the senator?"

"Olivia, how are you dear?" Nora is very fond of the senator's family and she has a special place for Olivia. A few years ago, Nora's husband Albert suffered from a life-threatening ailment, and Olivia offered advice, comfort, and guidance which saved his life. "Yes, I will connect you with the senator immediately."

"Hello Olivia, it is good to hear from you again so soon. What can I do for you?"

"Jack, I don't have time to go into details, but we have made a critical breakthrough in our fight against the mosquito. I have a meeting with Dr. Masterson, Mayor King, and Governor Hickenlooper in the morning. I need to convince them to accept my recommendations, and I am not certain of the best approach."

"There is only one approach Olivia, and that is to be straight forward, honest, and transparent in what you have to say. Our nation and the world are in this current predicament because there has not existed truth and honesty in government for decades. Everyone has an ulterior motive, and as a result, the prevailing mode of operation is dishonesty, corruption, and self-interest. I urge you to be refreshingly honest, and you will hopefully get the response you seek."

"Thanks Jack, I will give it my best," Olivia responds.

"Be yourself Olivia, if you are, they will see the truth and urgency in what you have to say," the senator encourages.

"Thanks Jack, you are the best!" Olivia tells her cousin.

"Good luck, and I will be anxious to hear how it turns out," Jack closes.

Hanging up, Olivia knows Jack only confirmed what she herself believes, but it's always good to hear it from someone who walks the walk every day.

CHAPTER 23

MEDIUM AND THE MESSAGE

K ENNEDY, AINSLEY, AND GEMMA DEPART Ames and head directly
to Chicago to meet with the world-renowned promoter Ansel
Colioso. As they board the plane out of Des Moines for the short flight
to Chicago, they are convinced more than ever that their mission is to
convince the multitudes worldwide that change is not an option but
an absolute necessity for the survival of the human race. They are also
convinced that they are the only ones capable of raising the kind of
money needed to finance the challenges faced by their brothers, sisters,
and cousins.

These three cousins agree that they must mount a global tour of
colossal proportions if they are to reach enough people around the world
to alter the course of governments entrenched in serving the wealthy.
All three are putting their respective endeavors on hold to tackle this
incredible challenge. They, as well as others dedicated to joining the
cause, must be willing to donate all proceeds to the work of dealing with
the ecological, environmental, religious, and political fire storm racing
around the Earth.

Never in human history has such an undertaking been attempted.
Considering all the developments of the past few years, and in particular
the past few weeks, it would seem to be an easy sell. However, the
wealthy have had their talons in the world media and political systems
for so long, they could sell sand to a thirsty man.

While the United States and allies defeated Nazi Germany in 1945, it has sometimes been questioned who won the war. Around the world, the political establishment adopted the philosophy of Joseph Goebbels "If you repeat a lie often enough, it becomes the truth. If you tell a lie big enough, and keep repeating it, people will eventually come to believe it." Following the Second World War, leaders had an opportunity to chart a new and promising course for humanity. Unfortunately, the self-serving nature of humans led to the formation of a powerful triumvirate between the worlds wealthiest, the news media, and politicians. In many cases, they are one and the same.

John and Robert Kennedy may have been the last politicians to speak with true candor to the American people. As a result, they were silenced, and the world has never been the same. Sure, there is always opposing viewpoints, but when it comes to the rubber hitting the road, it has all been about serving the few. The people in the United States and around the world have been saturated with lies upon lies until no one can tell or even know the difference.

Even amidst horrendous global disintegration at all levels of existence, people of low socio-economic status who are victimized the most, grab hold of the lies like a life raft on a turbulent sea. The triumvirate has been selling them snake oil for so long they don't even recognize the poison.

Flying over the Midwest United States at 35,000 feet, the world looks rather peaceful and serene. At such a view, there is no evidence that Hannah's Theory of Devolution is at work. It would be so easy to dismiss all of the concerns, but Kennedy, Ainsley, and Gemma know better. They have seen the evidence and they know the horror of the past is but an indication of things to come unless they can convince humanity to change course!

Upon arrival at O'Hare International in Chicago, Kennedy, Ainsley, and Gemma are transferred to Ansel Colioso's helicopter and taken to his penthouse suite at the top of Willis Tower, some 1,400 feet above street level. As they are greeted by the butler at the penthouse door, the three cousins enter into a large living area filled with evidence of Ansel's success as a promoter. There in a prominent place to the left side of the room sits the white grand piano upon which John Lennon composed Imagine. On the right side, in an equally prominent spot, is the piano upon which Beethoven composed his 5th Symphony. Throughout the room are ancient Greek and Roman artifacts. Ansel is a collector, and he likes to show off his ability to purchase the best. As they walk to the middle of this large room, they are overwhelmed by the view of Lake Michigan and the Chicago skyline. The entire northeast side of the suite is floor to ceiling windows.

"Enjoying the view girls?" Ansel asks as he walks briskly into the room giving Kennedy and Ainsley a hug. This is the first time he has met Gemma, and he is quickly enthralled by her youthful beauty and charm. Gemma has a smile which could light up a room on its own. Gemma makes mention of an ancient Greek sculpture of Socrates sitting on a nearby table. Ansel is impressed she recognizes the philosopher, and they share a moment discussing Socrates significance to Western culture.

Ansel Colioso has known Kennedy and Ainsley for several years. He is a big fan of both and has a track record of supporting the endeavors of each one. However, he is not prepared for what they are about to present.

"The view is amazing," Ainsley assures, "From here, the world looks very peaceful."

"Yes, it does, and I am so glad I did not make New York my home," Ansel announces with a sigh of relief. "Please have a seat and tell me what I can do for you."

"Ansel, did you know we are cousins?" Kennedy asks looking for any sign of surprise.

"I did not know that, but I can see the resemblance now that you mention it," he responds sitting up to take a closer look at the three. "Yes, it is quite evident in your eyes and smiles."

"Then you do not know we have brothers, sisters, and cousins who are the world's foremost authorities in their particular fields of endeavor," Ainsley reveals.

"I did not know that my dear, please tell me more," Ansel requests moving to the edge of his chair and leaning forward with interest.

"We have just spent a week in Ames, Iowa in closed meetings with my brothers Dr. Noah Abraham, an expert in environmental science specializing in invasive species, and Dr. Edison Jude, an authority in aquatic science specializing in reptiles. Ainsley's brother Senator Joseph of Iowa was present as well as her sister Dr. Ivey Isabelle, a world class Astro-Physicist. Gemma's sisters Dr. Contessa Margery, who has doctorate degrees in Geology and Geo-Politics, and Dr. Stella Caroline, special assistance to the U.N. Environmental Ambassador, Leonardo DiCaprio was on hand. Our cousins, Dr. Hannah Rae, a leading authority on Agricultural Science and genetics, Dr. Thomas Henry, a Nobel Prize winner in the area of Quantitative Paleobiology, and Dr. Olivia Kae, the lead researcher in Microbiology and infectious diseases at the CDC took part in these meetings," Kennedy reveals. Name dropping has always been a good strategy with Ansel.

"My goodness girls, you do indeed have an impressive genealogical connection. I am also impressed with your New Age approach to names. It would take an astute observer to discover the connection. So, what is the significance of your visit?" Ansel asks now sliding back into his chair.

"Ansel, the world is on the cusp of oblivion, and people are not listening. During the past week, we saw convincing evidence that we are approaching the end of days. If we do not act, we may very well fall victim to the end of the human race on Earth," Ainsley shares with a flare of dramatics.

"Do you have a projection room Ansel?" Kennedy asks.

"Do I have a projection room?" Ansel is sitting straight up now, "Why I have nothing but state of the art cutting edge projection capability. Follow me!"

Going down a hall lined with photographs of Ansel with the rich and famous, the four come to a door in which Ansel invites them to enter first. Opening the door, Kennedy, Ainsley, and Gemma find themselves in a white twenty-foot-cubed room. It is akin to the Holodeck on the Starship Enterprise in the old Star Trek television series. The floor, ceiling, and walls are all projection panels capable of transforming the room into an incredible virtual reality experience.

"What is it you would like to experience?" Ansel asks with a big grin on his face. He is pretty certain his guests have never seen anything like this. Ironically, they are about to show him things of which he has never seen the likes.

"Can your system interface with this holographic device?" Ainsley asks handing Ansel a small storage device containing a copy of all the evidence they witnessed in Ames.

"I am sure it can, let me plug it into the system," Ansel says taking the small device over to a high-tech panel on the wall. "What am I looking for?"

"This device contains a week's worth of presentations, we will only view a few so you get the idea regarding the seriousness of our visit," Kennedy says.

When Ansel turns on the system and plugs in the small storage device, the entire room comes alive. In front of the three is a long list of things that could be viewed, but time is of the essence.

"We are going to view four topics which should give you all the evidence you need to know the urgency of our mission. Let's look at the Malthusian Theory, Devolution, the Hand of God, and Invasive Species," Ainsley suggests. "This should just about rock your world."

"Good choices cousin," Gemma agrees.

For the next two hours, these four enter an unbelievable world of virtual reality. Not once during the past week did Kennedy, Ainsley, and Gemma experience anything so stark, so vivid, so real, and so horrific. At the end of each presentation the four had to force themselves to continue on to the next. The cousins knew they were achieving the desired impact as they could hear Ansel gasp and see the agony on his face. At the conclusion of the final segment on invasive species, the four quietly returned to the large living area.

"Was that real, or just some Hollywood trick?" Ansel asks in disbelief.

"It couldn't be more real Ansel, and we need your help," Ainsley pleads.

"What can I do? What is it you want me to do?" Ansel asks once again at the edge of his seat.

"We want to put on the most colossal world tour ever! We want to inform and activate people with the truth," Kennedy notes.

"That sounds costly," Ansel tells them.

"Not as costly as it will be if we fail. We have the most talented, intelligent, and caring people working to find a way through all of these issues of catastrophic proportions. They can't do it alone; they need money and they need people to cooperate," Ainsley tells him. "We need your help in bringing together a team of people to mount what could be the last crusade of the human race. We need to do this in a way that reaches multitudes of people, and generates huge amounts of cash to finance the struggle. This means we all do this for free."

"Whoa, free, I have never done anything for free," Ansel says with a laugh.

"Ansel, you just saw the real world as it is and the things to come. Do you really think your money is going to be worth a hill of beans if we fail? If we do not act, and act now, this penthouse could very well crumble to the ground in the near future," Kennedy pronounces. "It is very possible Chicago could become New York!"

Ansel Colioso is now up and standing in front of one of his massive windows looking out and down. He is a smart man, and he knows what recently occurred in New York could eventually be the fate of Chicago. He knows that the people of the world have been lied to for far too long. He knows the wealthy, like himself, have tried to insulate themselves from the impending doom with little concern for those of a lesser social or economic status. He now knows that if the doom arrives in full force, as projected by these three prophetic visitors, no amount of money, no citadel of power, no concrete or metal barrier will protect anyone. He has seen the future, and he is frankly scared shitless.

"Okay girls, I am on board. Let me make a few calls, and let's meet tomorrow to discuss and plan this colossal world tour. This shall be my greatest achievement!" Ansel, never short on hyperbole, proclaims as he stands with his arms raised and his back to the window and world.

CHAPTER 24

MISSIONS OF URGENCY

D R. IVEY ISABELLE HAS SEEN firsthand the marvels and mystery of the Universe. Such revelations constantly put in question her devotion to science as the one gateway to the truth. She has always found it difficult to peer through the lens of the world's great telescopes into the infinite beyond without wondering if there were not some all-powerful being at the conductors stand, directing it all like some grand symphony. Now, she has shared her greatest observation with her brother, sister, and cousins, and gained their confirmation and support for what she calls, the Hand of God.

Ivey is now on a mission to bring together the greatest religious leaders in the world to witness what she has seen. This is no ordinary mission as these leaders come from very diverse backgrounds, cultures, and articles of faith. In many cases, these leaders spread messages of division which often lead to hostilities by one against another. Ivey does not understand all of this. She has not spent much time thinking about it, but now, she has been given the task of bringing these leaders of faith together to witness what her brother, sister, and cousins, feel could be undeniable proof of a Supreme Being.

This rare conclave of family held in Ames left all in attendance convinced that the time has come to leave no stone unturned. What if, Ivey's "Hand of God" is indeed an ominous warning that the end of times is near? What if the decadent and destructive nature of religion, running so counter to what each individual religion professes, were at the heart of the countless doomsday events occurring around the world?

What if the salvation of the human race requires something beyond the realm of science, or what if science and religion turn out to be nothing more than opposite sides of the same coin?

In appealing to these great religious leaders, Ivey needs the assistance of her brother, Senator Joseph, and cousin, Stella Caroline. The Senator and Stella have connections beneficial in reaching out to leaders of all faiths.

While Senator Joseph and Stella also have a political mission, they are committed to bringing these religious leaders together for what could be the greatest and most important revelation of all time. Religious history is littered with stories of God's presence in conveying a message to humanity. Devine revelation is critical to the validation of religious belief. Moses and the Ten Commandments, Christ, Mohammed, Buddha and many stories serve as testament to Devine Revelation.

Never in human history has misery, suffering, devastation, death, and destruction consumed so much of the world at the same time as in 2039. If ever there were a time for divine intervention, now is the time. Could it be possible God selected Dr. Isabelle as his messenger? Does God recognize the unique devotion, intellect, talent, and compassion of Dr. Ivey Isabelle, her brother, sister, and cousins, to make them the instrument of his will?

There is no time to seek an answer to these questions, there is only time to act. If it is true, then they must successfully bring these great religious minds and leaders together for the purpose God intends. It seems so unnatural, and yet feels so natural to find science as an instrument of faith.

After the meeting in Ames, Jack jumps a flight to Nashville. He needs to get a firsthand look at the state of government. He is hoping for some time with the president. He plans to return to Ames the following day.

Ivey and Stella decide to remain in Ames and await Jack's return before the three of them head to their grandparent's home in Belmond. Grandma and Grandpa have lived in the same home in Belmond for the past 28 years. While they are advanced in years with Grandpa 90 years old and Grandma 80 years old, they are in good health. They always love to see their grandchildren. Grandma and Grandpa are extremely proud of each and every one of their grandchildren. They feel so blessed to have such wonderful and talented grandchildren, and they believe in their unique ability.

At Grandma and Grandpa's, these three unlikely missionaries of the divine, will find an environment suitable for the planning they are about to undertake. They know their grandparents will see to it they have whatever they need over the next few days. They will ask to set up their planning in the library which contains a full array of hard copy and digital material as well as state of the art access for research and communication. They will also have access to the four seasons room with the ever-present pool table which has played host to the annual Christmas tournament for as long as the three of them can remember. On a wall in the four seasons room are three plaques which testify to the winners of the annual Christmas tournaments in pool, darts, shuffleboard, ping-pong, bumper pool, and Wii Bowling. These are great memories even at a time when all memory could possibly be extinguished. Adjacent to the four seasons room can be found the Rock and Roll Bar. Regardless their age, Grandma and Grandpa have a great fondness for Rock and Roll. In 2015, they created their Rock and Roll bar complete with psychedelic posters, framed albums, florescent painted murals and symbols, pictures, black lights, and music, lots and lots of music representing the entire history of rock and roll. Of course, they always keep the refrigerator and cabinets stocked with beverages of all flavors for all ages.

Having called ahead, Grandma and Grandpa know they will be hungry upon arrival and have the finest Ribeye Steaks ready to grill. Grandma and Grandpa's freezer always contains the finest beef raised by their Uncle Robert. Uncle Robert has been raising beef for the past thirty years, and he perfected an organic marbling process using natural corn and grasses that leave the meat with just the right fat content to assure tenderness and flavor. Over the years, Grandpa picked up some of Uncle Jeremy's grilling techniques which produce a perfectly grilled steak. Uncle Jeremy, a master griller in his own right, convinced Grandpa long ago to give up his propane grill for the use of charcoal and flavored woods such as apple, cherry, grape, and hickory.

As the three approach Belmond, they are excited to see their grandparents and enter the home which provided so many wonderful times over the years. The love, pride, and support they find at their grandparents never wanes regardless their age or reason for visiting.

Upon arrival, Ivey, Jack, and Stella receive the warmest of hugs and kisses. They are ushered to their own rooms to get settled in while Grandma and Grandpa anxiously wait for them in the four seasons room.

As the three enter the four seasons room, Grandpa immediately offers them a chair and insists on fetching them their favorite drink. "So, I understand you have been meeting with your sisters, and cousins in Ames this past week," Grandpa acknowledges what he already knows. "Grandma and I are just devastated that the state of the world has become so dismal. We cannot recall a time when the fate of humanity hung so precariously in the balance. I remember as a teenager the fears of a nuclear holocaust, but our leaders always offered us hope that tomorrow would be a better day. My generation had such great promise to turn society and government toward a better world for all people. Instead, we grew up to become nothing more than a reflection of the self-indulgence and greed all too common in humans and societies. Now, with the darker side of humanity having prevailed all these years, we find ourselves in the midst of perpetual calamity."

"Things are certainly in a precarious state Grandpa, but I believe we have a plan that could bring the world back from the brink of extinction," Jack asserts.

"Well Grandpa and I know you certainly don't need our help. Our generation had a chance and frankly, we blew it!" Grandma adds. "We are glad to have you here, and we will do anything you ask to be of assistance."

"We are on what may be an impossible mission to bring the religious leaders of the world together for the purpose of witnessing what I have termed the Hand of God," Ivey reveals.

"We couldn't think of a better and more secure place from which to work than here at the home we all love," Stella proclaims. "Just making it as warm, loving, and supportive as you always do will be a great contribution."

"One of our greatest challenges is finding a place where these religious leaders will be willing to gather without feeling one religion has an upper hand over the others, or they are in some way compromising their faith," Jack notes hoping for a suggestion.

"I don't know of any particular place that would meet your criteria, but it seems to me mountains have always been central to religions and communicating with God. If you could find a mountain which would provide that closeness to God, but not be of any specific relevance to any one religion's history, you might have a chance to lure them there," Grandma shares.

"Many years ago, we traveled through Switzerland and the Alps. One of our stops provided us with an opportunity to experience the Golden Triangle at Lucerne. At the top of Mt. Pilatus on the Golden Triangle, we discovered a large visitor's center with a majestic view of the Alps and Lake Lucerne. I believe Kennedy has also made this trip. She could testify to the potential of this area for such a religious gathering," Grandpa adds.

"While Switzerland has always been predominately Christian, the country values their religious diversity. Historically, the Swiss have sought to remain neutral and at peace with other nations. This might be just the place we are looking for," Stella suggests.

As Grandma and Grandpa bid their grandchildren goodnight, Ivey, Jack, and Stella, set to work on the challenge before them.

Back in Ames, Dr. Abraham, Dr. Jude, Dr. Rae, Dr. Henry, and Dr. Margery, indulge supper again at Hickory Park. As they finish dinner and are about to order dessert, the ring tone on Contessa's cell phone goes off. Quickly looking at the phone, Contessa can tell the call is coming from one of her assistants.

"Excuse me a minute," Contessa says as she rises from her seat, "I think this might be important."

Contessa quickly steps outside to take the call. When she returns, there is a real look of concern on her face.

Having worked closely with Contessa, Noah knows when something troubling is happening. He saw this very same look on Contessa's face when she told him her suspicions about the Mid-Atlantic Ridge. "I can tell something is happening Contessa, what is it?"

"You know how we have long been concerned about the Yellowstone Caldera?" she directs her question to Noah. "Well, our concerns don't appear to be warranted."

"That is fantastic news," Noah responds, "So why do you look like all hell has broken loose?"

"Hannah, can we get access to a university facility where we can use the latest technology to monitor what is occurring in Yellowstone and the surrounding area?" Contessa asks.

Looking puzzled, Edison Jude and Thomas Henry simultaneously ask, "What's going on Contessa. What was your phone call about?"

"Let's not talk about it here. Can we get access to university facilities Hannah?" Contessa asks again.

"Absolutely, I can get us into whatever facilities are needed!" Hannah responds.

"Good, let's get our check and get out of here," Contessa insists.

Once these five world renowned experts are in the car heading for the Iowa State campus, Noah asks again, "What's going on Contessa?"

"My call came from Alonzo. You know Alonzo, Noah, he is one of the assistants who helps monitor geological activity around the globe. He said all of our recent data on Yellowstone suggests that the Caldera is not building, but actually melting from within. He believes the entire Yellowstone Park and beyond could soon become a burning inferno." Contessa reveals. "We need to get to the instrumentation and technology which will help us verify or refute what Alonzo suggests."

Arriving at the Science Institute on the ISU campus, these five experts head immediately to the geological department and its array of scientific and data gathering equipment. Even though each person has a different area of expertise, they all know how to use the equipment for data gathering and diagnostic purposes. After a couple hours of accessing every bit of information possible on the current geological state of Yellowstone, the five have arrived at the conclusion they had hoped to refute.

The subsurface temperature of Yellowstone is increasing rapidly and causing the substructure to liquefy. In most cases this situation would lead to an increase in pressure, which once arrived at critical mass, would result in a volcanic eruption. The good news is a volcanic eruption is not the concern. However, the bad news is bad enough.

Rather than building pressure, the melting substructure is consuming everything around it. What Alonzo reported and they have now confirmed, is this intense temperature is currently being shielded from the surface by a thermos layer very similar to that which allows a heater to give off heat and yet be cool to the touch. As a result, the surface temperature might not increase and at times even decrease giving the impression that things are fine. While the increase in subsurface temperatures and surface dangers are evident to them, a person on the surface in Yellowstone would not recognize it as anything different than normal. However, when the subsurface temperature arrives at the critical point where it corrupts the thermal layer, spontaneous combustion on the surface will result in a cataclysmic event.

"How is it the National Earthquake Information Center is not reporting this situation. Are they blind?" Noah is incredulous at the lack of competency of such an important watchdog.

"It is difficult for them to see what they are not looking for," Contessa asserts. "Then again, someone may be asleep at the wheel."

"We can't wait to play a game of cat and mouse with a federal agency. We need to issue a warning for the evacuation of all people from an area within two-hundred and fifty miles of Yellowstone National Park," Dr. Henry declares.

"This is like Déjà vu," Dr. Abraham says, "We made a very similar request prior to the activity along the Mid-Atlantic Ridge. We all know the response we got to that warning."

"Perhaps the powers that be will pay a little more heed this time," Dr. Jude suggests, "We certainly cannot sit back and let this catastrophe occur without attempting to issue a warning. We need to contact the senator," as Edison often calls his cousin Jack.

"Noah, give Jack a call and let him know our assessment of the situation in and around Yellowstone. Ask him to intervene with the president to get an evacuation warning issued for the Yellowstone area," Hannah declares to her cousin.

Leaving the room, Noah speed dials Jack who is in Belmond at

Grandma and Grandpa's home. Recognizing the incoming call, Jack immediately answers, "Noah, why the call at this hour of the night?"

"Jack, we need your help. After hours of examining a situation in Yellowstone National Park, Hannah, Contessa, Edison, Thomas, and I are convinced something catastrophic is about to occur. We need the president to issue an evacuation order for this area, and we are hoping you can help make this happen," Noah says with great urgency in his voice.

"Noah, the president is worthless. I can give him a call, but I won't get through because of that stonewalling bastard Peet. Even if I get through, the president won't act of his own accord without eating up days or weeks," retorts the senator. "This is a very troubling situation. You are damned if you do and damned if you don't. The president and especially Peet, will want to weigh the situation from every possible political angle. Unless you feel confident that a decision on this can wait, the president and his political hacks are not an option."

"What do you suggest we do Jack? We cannot just sit back on our hands and allow hundreds of thousands of people to perish," Noah says with alarm.

"Let me make a call to Christine Mathews at FOX News. As you may know Christine was born Chris Jr. to Chris Mathews, the famed air head for MSNBC. As an adult, Chris Jr. declared himself a woman, had a sex change, and emerged as Christine. I have been a champion of civil rights for all people regardless, as long as their rights don't infringe on the rights of others. Christine owes me a favor for my support which has benefited the transgender community," the senator says. "Give me 30 minutes, and then make a call to Christine and reveal your findings. Like all news people, she will eat up the idea of being the first to break the news."

"I am sure your assessment of the president is correct Jack, but don't you think you should at least make the call?" Noah wonders.

"Hell Noah, the president's Chief of Staff Peet, has him so wrapped up, the only position I have with the president, is no position. Furthermore, the president's actions or lack thereof has put the people of this nation at risk. I consider such behavior treasonous to the American people. As for the party, it is nothing more than a money pit for maintaining power and control. The party doesn't exist for the good of the nation, but rather considers the nation an instrument to be manipulated for the good of the party," Jack announces.

"You sound like a man prepared to seek the White House my cousin," Noah says insightfully.

"Let's not get ahead of ourselves Noah. First off, the White House is no more. Second, you have an issue far more important than politics. Give me 30 minutes and make the call," Jack insists.

"Hello Christine, this is Senator Joseph."

"Senator, to what do I owe the pleasure of this call," Christine inquires.

"Christine, will you keep this call confidential. Five of my cousins have made a very important discovery regarding the Yellowstone National Park area. You may know them for their expertise in their individual fields, Dr. Noah Abraham, Dr. Edison Jude, Dr. Hannah Rae, Dr. Thomas Henry, and Dr. Contessa Margery," Jack continues.

"I am very familiar with the work of each one," Christine acknowledges, "In fact, I recently interviewed Contessa Margery regarding the events along the Mid-Atlantic Ridge. I also did an in-depth piece on Dr. Rae's Theory of Devolution as the antithesis of Evolution less than a year ago. I would welcome hearing from them, and I will keep my sources confidential."

"Thanks Christine!" Jack closes.

Based on Jack's advice, the five scientists decide Contessa should make the call to Christine Mathews. During their recent interview, Contessa and Christine hit it off in a positive and friendly way. Christine appreciated Contessa's openness about the happenings leading up to the cataclysmic events along the Mid-Atlantic Ridge. Contessa has established a gravitas much needed at this time.

"Hello this is Christine Mathews," came the voice on the other end of the phone.

"Hello Christine, this is Contessa Margery calling you from Ames, Iowa."

"Contessa, how are you? Your cousin, Senator Joseph, told me you would be calling."

"Christine, do you remember how the government and other

agencies ignored the warnings about the Mid-Atlantic Ridge?" Contessa asks knowing full well the answer.

"Indeed, I do," Christine responds almost leaning into the phone.

"And you know the devastation which occurred and the millions of lives lost as a result," Contessa unnecessarily states the obvious.

"I know that all too well," Christine assures anxious for what is to come.

"Well, we have hard evidence that something equally horrendous is about to occur in the Yellowstone National Park region. We certainly do not want to start a panic, but we firmly believe all people within 250 miles of Yellowstone National Park need to evacuate. We believe a massive geological event will occur within days, if not sooner. People need to leave their homes and possessions and move to a safe place outside the 250 mile perimeter. Please urge people to evacuate in an orderly and safe manner," Contessa urges Christine.

"Why is this not coming from the president, a federal agency, or the state governors?" Christine asks.

"We tried that route with the Mid-Atlantic Ridge to no avail. For decades the federal and state governments have been blowing off warnings about the environment and other hazards. We have frankly run out of faith in their ability and willingness to protect the people. We are turning to you because Senator Joseph said we could count on you," Contessa reveals.

"I will need to issue any statement as coming from an anonymous source which will lead to disclaimers," Christine notes.

"Please don't do that, we ask you to use our names to give credibility to the announcement. Let people know we tried to warn them about the Mid-Atlantic Ridge, and now we are warning them about this. Use our names, use our titles, use our accomplishments, use anything to get people to listen. This will make it more difficult for the government to refute," Contessa pleads.

"I will do as you wish Contessa, but I cannot guarantee the government will not come after you," Christine shares.

"Let them come Christine, we are trying to saves lives. I hope to God we are wrong, but we are certain something awful is in the works," Contessa attests.

"Hope to God is an interesting line coming from a pure scientist as yourself Contessa," Christine adds as she begins to close the conversation.

"There is so much more to this than we could ever begin to discuss," Contessa assures, "Perhaps we will someday get a chance to discuss all of this in-depth, God willing."

As the receiver on the other end goes dead, Christine Mathews finds it odd that Contessa Margery invoked the name of God twice in closing. As a news anchor, Christine knows she possesses the scoop of a lifetime as well as a grave responsibility. She also knows that should she consult the powers that be at the station, they may very well put a lid on this story. She faces what could be a career altering decision. Right or wrong in issuing this warning, the management at FOX might very well terminate her employment. She knows there is no choice. Senator Joseph has been a true and loyal friend to her and the transgender community. Contessa Margery and her cousins are willing to put their careers and lives on the line, so how could she shrink from this moment out of self-concern?

Returning to her team, Contessa informs them that their warning will be issued on the FOX News Morning report by Christine Mathews. They all know that once the warning is issued by FOX news, the story will be picked up by DNN, MSNBC, MSCBS, and all other national, international, and local news networks. The team agrees that the use of their names is imperative to the credibility of the report. They also know that soon after the announcement, they will be inundated with requests for more information. This unexpected turn of events is but the opening salvo in what will become a comprehensive attempt to educate the world about Devolution in an effort to cause a radical change in human behavior.

After talking with Christine Mathews, Senator Joseph returns to the Four Seasons Room at his grandparents in Belmond. Informing the group of the Yellowstone situation and his end-run maneuver with Christine Mathews. Ivey and Stella agree he had no choice.

"Have you ever thought about challenging the president in next year's election?" Stella asks her cousin. "If we are going to see the nation and world through these dark times, the people need a new voice of leadership. A voice which speaks to them as a father would his children, a voice which comes from someone who is selfless and courageous in facing the ordeals ahead, a voice which gives faith and hope for the future."

"It is interesting you suggest this Stella, our cousin Noah made the same kind of statement to me," the senator reveals. "I just don't know if I am the person for this challenge. I would hate to fail the people; I'm not sure I'm worthy."

"It is for this very reason you are the person brother," Ivey declares. "Humility is the fountain from which people will draw their strength. To have a leader they know and trust, acting in their interest with no self-serving motive will give them hope. To have someone with the courage to face such adversity despite his own self-doubt, will give them strength."

"It is getting late cousins, and we have much to do tomorrow," Stella reminds them, "Perhaps we should call it a night."

CHAPTER 25

ACTS OF COURAGE

A S THEY AWAKE TO A new day, all of the cousins in Atlanta, Chicago, Ames, and Belmond catch the FOX News with Christine Mathews.

"Good morning, this is Christine Mathews with some urgent and breaking news to report. Last night I was contacted by Dr. Contessa Margery, one of the world's foremost geological experts out of the University of Michigan in Ann Arbor. Contessa is currently at Iowa State University with her cousins, Dr. Noah Abraham, a world-renowned expert in Environmental Science and invasive species; Dr. Edison Jude, is considered the world's foremost expert on reptiles; Dr. Hannah Rae, a professor of Agricultural Science at Iowa State University. Dr. Rae has published an acclaimed and yet highly criticized Theory of Devolution, and Dr. Thomas Henry, an expert in Quantitative Paleo-Biology. Dr. Henry received a Nobel Prize for his Thesis on Regeneration."

"I apologize for the lengthy bibliographic information, but our viewers need to know the credibility of the source from which this announcement is based."

"What the hell is Christine doing?" the network producer Claudius Censor asks a nearby cameraman. "Why is she going off script? Let's go to commercial and find out what is going on," he demands.

The cameraman continues to air the broadcast because Christine previously informed him of the severity of the announcement. She did not like putting a colleague in harm's way, but the cameraman's loyalty is to Christine and creating an informed public.

"Contessa Margery and her illustrious cousins are asking all people within two hundred and fifty miles of Yellowstone National Park to orderly evacuate to a location outside that perimeter," Christine announces.

"Someone cut this program immediately!" the producer demands, but the cameras continue to roll.

"According to these world-renowned scientists, Yellowstone National Park is nearing a critical point of meltdown. There is no threat of an eruption, but the subsurface temperature is nearing a point where it will break through the barrier shield which is currently protecting the surface from the intense heat," Christine shares with the viewers.

In Nashville, Christine's broadcast is being viewed by the nation's leader and his Chief of Staff Peet.

"What the fuck is going on?" Peet declares pounding his fist on a nearby table. "Who the hell authorized this broadcast? Mr. President, you need to put an immediate stop to this before the entire Yellowstone region turns into chaos."

The president immediately picks up the phone and gets the owner of FOX on the line. "Dingleberry, this is the president. Are you aware of what is being broadcast over your network? I want it stopped immediately or you will be held liable for the chaos which ensues."

Back at the studio, Christine continues, "Please take heed these are the same scientists who tried to warn the government of the catastrophe resulting from the collision along the Mid-Atlantic Ridge. These scientists are convinced that Yellowstone National Park will soon turn into a burning inferno. Do not take time to be concerned about property or possessions. Evacuate immediately but please do so in an orderly fashion," Christine pleads.

"Mr. President" Dingleberry responds, "I had no idea. I would have thought the producer would have shut this down."

"Obviously he has not, and I want you to get to the bottom of this. I want an immediate retraction," the president demands.

"Mr. President" Chief of Staff Peet stands holding his suit jacket in a Napoleonic fashion, "The five scientists mentioned in the broadcast are all cousins of Senator Joseph. I would bet my career he is behind all of this."

"If this is true, I will have that assholes head on a platter. Mark my word," the President declares.

"I have further breaking news regarding Yellowstone National Park and the surrounding area. The National Park Service just announced that fires are breaking out in and around the epicenter of the Yellowstone Caldera. The reason for the fires is yet to be determined. They are closing all entrances to the park. People are to begin the process of evacuating from the park. FOX news will keep you posted. This is Christine Mathews reporting."

———

In Atlanta, Dr. Olivia Kae is about to meet with Dr. Masterson, Mayor King, and Governor Hickenlooper regarding her breakthrough discovery of a way to neuter the ability of the Mosquito to carry deadly diseases. As she reviews her notes on the data regarding her research, and the argument she intends to make for testing the DNA altering fog in Atlanta, she receives a call from her colleague Dr. Rooh.

"Dr. Kae, I know you are preparing for a very important meeting, but I think you should know what we are observing."

"Please Dr. Rooh" Dr. Kae urges her colleague. "I cannot go into this meeting with anything less than full disclosure."

"As we studied this last batch of hatched mosquitos, we found something possibly every bit as significant as altering the disease carrying DNA structure," Dr. Rooh says with obvious excitement in his voice.

"What is it Dr. Rooh, what have you observed?"

"Dr. Kae this last batch of hatched mosquitos not only are incapable of carrying disease, their needle nose has been softened to the point they are incapable of penetrating even the most vulnerable skin. Dr. Kae, this last batch of mosquitoes has been reduced to nothing more than a bug," Dr. Rooh reveals.

"This is incredible news Dr. Rooh, do you believe it suggests our fog essentially reduces the mosquito to nothing more than a common house fly?" Dr. Kae asks.

"It may very well be the result of your tireless effort to defeat this flying demon," Dr. Rooh responds.

"Thank you Dr. Rooh, this solidifies my presentation," Dr. Kae says in closing.

Dr. Olivia Kae no sooner gets off the phone with her colleague when Dr. Masterson, Mayor King, and Governor Hickenlooper enter the room for their meeting. As the three individuals, who hold the fate of her research and possibly the human race in their hands, take their seats at the far end of a long conference table, Dr. Olivia Kae begins.

"Thank you for taking time to meet with me this morning," she begins. "As you know, our nation and the world are facing astronomical crises every single day. Millions of people are losing their lives due to every imaginable catastrophe with every passing moment. The globe is warming, as it has been for decades, and now after years of ignoring the facts, we are confronted with the very doom we have created through our inaction," Dr. Kae says setting the stage for her revelation.

"What you say is quite true Dr. Kae, but what is it you are seeking from us?" Dr. Masterson asks.

"My dear friends, you have been working for the public good all your lives. In recent years, you have witnessed the death and devastation which occurs from natural disasters, war, starvation, and disease. You have seen and felt the horror that plagues the Earth first hand. You know the demonic nature of the world's deadliest enemy, the mosquito. Well, I am here to tell you, unless we squash this devil with wings, the people of this planet are doomed to die in the most gruesome of ways. The warming planet plays host to not only the traditional mosquito, but to a larger, more aggressive, and dangerous mosquito," Dr. Kae says with all the seriousness of someone delivering apocalyptic news.

"What you say may be true," Mayor King responds to Olivia's warning, "So; do you have something beneficial to offer?"

"I do, my colleagues and I believe we have discovered a chemical agent which alters the mosquito DNA and renders it incapable of carrying disease," Dr. Kae reveals.

"What is your proof and what is your suggestion?" Governor Hickenlooper asks.

"Our proof comes after months of testing a chemical substance which can be added to the traditional mosquito fogging process. What we have discovered is the DNA of mosquito larva subjected to this chemical substance is altered, rendering the mosquito incapable of carrying disease. Furthermore, the treated mosquito population will only reproduce offspring with the same altered DNA. One use of the chemical substance on a mosquito population, and we render them harmless," Dr. Kae shares with conviction.

"This is all very exciting, but what do you need from us?" asks Governor Hickenlooper.

"Before we put this into wide spread use, we need to use it on a target population to validate what we have determined in the lab. We would like to combine our chemical substance with the fog used to control the mosquito population in Atlanta. If we do this and validate our findings, we will be on the road to victory in the war against this deadly pest," Dr. Kae pronounces.

"What if this turns out to be harmful to humans or other animals?" Mayor King wonders.

"This is where what I am about to tell you gets sketchy. I and five other colleagues have exposed ourselves over a lengthy period of time to this chemical substance without any adverse effects. We have also exposed a diverse range of animals with the same results," Dr. Kae shares knowing this could be the straw that breaks the camel's back for support.

"Are you telling me you and your colleagues exposed yourselves and animals to this chemical substance without seeking the authority to do so?" Dr. Masterson asks with a voice of grave concern. "Do you know the ethical questions this raises?"

"I know this, and I take full responsibility," Dr. Kae responds. "We are not talking about the approval of some pill to combat some ailment; we are talking about the survival of the human race. There is no time for protocol. We either defeat the mosquito, or we face a certain doom! Let me mention one other discovery which needs to be validated. It is a distinct possibility that our chemical substance not only neuters the mosquito, but softens the stinger/needle to a point that renders it incapable of penetrating even the most vulnerable skin."

"What do you think Mayor King, it is your city?" asks Governor Hickenlooper. Governor Hickenlooper is a Renaissance Man, he has never hesitated to sail against the wind. He knows and shares Dr. Kae's sense of urgency.

"Great success does not come without great risk. I know we are talking about the population of an entire city, but Atlanta is a city infested by mosquitos, and our people are dying awful deaths every day because of this wicked winged menace. Dr. Kae is offering us hope. If what she says is correct, Atlanta could be the first step in putting an end to what is possibly the greatest threat facing the people of the world. I say let's get this done as soon as possible," the mayor responds with a flare reminiscent of her famous grandfather.

"I agree," interjects the governor. "This is not a time for timid behavior or a time to stand on protocol. Dr. Kae and her colleagues have shown great courage, and it is now our time to stand with them."

"Dr. Kae you are to work with the city maintenance officials to see that your chemical substance is blended with the fog we spray across the city. Let us pray to God the hope you offer us today will bring Atlanta and eventually the world protection from this deadly doomsday bug," Dr. Masterson orders glancing at Mayor King to ensure he is not overstepping his authority.

⸺⸺⸺≫◆≪⸺⸺⸺

Having started their day earlier than the rest, Dr. Jude and Dr. Henry are putting the finishing touches on what they call the Reptilian Corollary to the Theory of Devolution. These two experts in cold blooded animals alive and extinct have been working on this corollary ever since Dr. Rae shared the Theory of Devolution with them. At the heart of their corollary is the idea that as the Earth warms, it is cold blooded animals that thrive. In warm and tropical climates, it is snakes, lizards, alligators, crocodiles and other reptiles that flourish.

Dr. Jude has several years of observation and documentation to support the expansion of reptiles. While his most recent studies have occurred in South Florida, he has observed the large reptiles of the deep south moving north as the climate changes. In fact, large reptiles such as the Burmese Python, alligators, and Kimono Dragons have been found as far north as South Carolina, Georgia, Tennessee, and southern Missouri. Dr. Abraham is equally interested in their corollary due to the fact the Burmese Python and Kimono Dragon are invasive species introduced to the United States by exotic pet owners. As the climate has warmed, these once exotic pets released into the wild by careless and incompetent owners have flourished into a real threat to animals of all sizes and even human beings.

Even more dramatic than the presence of such reptiles is their increase in size. Snakes with a four foot circumference and a length in excess of 40 feet have been documented. Alligators and crocodiles of 30 feet and weighing two ton are rapidly moving into large rivers and lakes. The Kimono Dragon, always a large reptile, has been found at 40 feet in length and weighing four ton. Some scientists try to pass this phenomenon on as an evolutionary process, but Dr. Jude and Dr. Henry believe it is actually a part of Devolution in which species are rapidly returning to a state of existence not seen for hundreds-of-thousands if not millions of years.

Dr. Henry associates the rapid and expanding return of current reptiles to a more prehistoric state to the slower regeneration of Dinosaur DNA into modern living prehistoric reptiles. Unlike most of science which has come to believe dinosaurs were warm blooded animals which evolved into birds, Dr. Henry has undeniable evidence that dinosaurs were actually cold-blooded reptiles. In some cases, these reptiles actually evolved into birds which are modern-day warm-blooded mammals, but in their natural state, dinosaurs were cold blooded reptiles.

In their Reptilian Corollary, Dr. Henry through his Gobi Desert exploration, is on the brink of proving Devolution is pervasive in organic material containing the DNA of extinct living creatures and vegetation. When given the right environment which is happening due to global warming, DNA regenerates into something thought lost to the past. This is at the heart of Devolution.

Arriving in the living room of Hannah's apartment, Dr. Abraham finds Dr. Jude and Dr. Henry hard at work. "I didn't expect to find you two up so early. What has motivated you?" he asks.

Following their stay at the Great Hall, the four scientists took up temporary residence with Hannah Rae while developing a long-term plan for their work.

"We are working on our Reptilian Corollary to the Theory of Devolution," Dr. Jude tells his brother.

"We couldn't sleep, and thought this would be a productive use of our time while we await Christine's FOX news morning broadcast," Dr. Henry reveals.

"Well how is it going?" Noah asks his brother and cousin.

"We think this is an important part of the puzzle. As we piece it together, it all fits into a mosaic which makes complete sense. If nature is rebelling against the abuses of human beings, then why would it not seek to return to its natural state? Everything we are learning are not isolated events, but actually well-connected events aimed at the same goal, the re-establishment of Mother Nature's dominion over the Earth," Edison says with complete and convincing confidence.

"The concept of Mother Nature is more of a mythological thing, more symbolic of nature itself," Noah suggests.

"That all depends," says Thomas. "We all witnessed Ivey's incredible evidence she called the "Hand of God." What if the "Hand of God" and "Mother Nature" are one and the same?"

"Good morning everyone," Hannah calls out as she enters the room, "I do believe it is time for the news. Where is Contessa?"

"I am right behind you. You didn't think I would miss Christine's report?"

As these five scientists turn their attention to the holographic screen in Hannah's apartment, Christine Mathews begins her report.

⸻⸻ ❦ ⸻⸻

High above the Chicago skyline, Kennedy, Ainsley, and Gemma have returned to Ansel Colioso's penthouse to continue their conversation about a world tour. As they enter the penthouse, the smell of bacon tells them that breakfast is in the works.

"Welcome back girls, you are just in time for breakfast. I have been expecting your return, so I have plenty to share," Ansel announces being a gracious host as always.

"Breakfast sounds great," Gemma declares still rubbing the sleep from her eyes, "In fact, what you are fixing reminds us of the breakfasts we get when visiting our Grandparents in Belmond. It also helps that I am hungry."

Grandma and Grandpa loved to make breakfast for their entire family. They rise early in the morning and get the obligatory cinnamon rolls in the oven, bottom shelf at 350 degrees for eighteen-minutes. While the rolls are baking, they pull out three frying pans from the cabinet, trying to avoid the banging of the pans which will awake a hungry gathering before food can be served. Depending if biscuits and gravy are on the menu, a sauce pan finds its way to the stove. The four-burner electric stove is carefully arrayed with just the right pan on the right sized burner. Like an army regime lined up for combat, the pans are followed by the spatula, large stirring spoons, and turning forks. Grandma commandeers one side of the stove, and Grandpa the other side. The pancake batter is mixed, potatoes peeled and diced, and bacon and eggs easy to access. If biscuits and gravy are part of the offering, the biscuits hit the oven as soon as the cinnamon rolls came out, and some home-grown sausage is standing by for the sauce pan. On the counter opposite the stove, they have the plates, juice glasses, and silverware as well as the toaster, butter, and bread. About the time they have everything ready to go, the first of many make the scene, and game on. It is truly a great memory for Kennedy, Ainsley, and Gemma.

"Do you mind if I turn on FOX Morning News? Christine Mathews is one of my favorites," Ansel asks while turning on his incredibly large screen projector and not waiting for an answer.

In a moment, the projector comes alive with Christine larger than life. Sitting with their breakfast, Ansel, Kennedy, Ainsley, and Gemma, witness with surprise Christine's report on Yellowstone while citing the five cousins. They are horrified to think that such a pristine place like Yellowstone could go up in flames. They are hopeful people will pay heed to the warning and safely evacuate before it's too late.

"Your brothers and cousins have done a courageous and selfless thing by prompting this announcement," Ansel acknowledges. "The leaders of our government are so inept! They may very well see this as a threat to their power and leadership. Even if thousands of lives are saved, they are so wrapped up in their own self-interest they very well may take this as an affront. It occurs to me that our mission is now even more important than ever. Your cousins have drawn a line in the sand by taking things into their own hands. We must do everything possible to support their efforts by creating an informed public that stands with them in their effort to save the world."

Little did Senator Joseph, Dr. Abraham, Dr. Jude, Dr. Rae, Dr. Henry, or Dr. Contessa Margery know they had ignited a passion in the heart and soul of the world's foremost fundraiser and promoter. Ansel Colioso is on board with Kennedy, Ainsley, and Gemma, from their discussion the night before, but now with Christine Mathew's report he is all in.

"You guys understand that Christine is going to lose her job over this. I doubt if she survives the day at FOX," Ansel states knowing how the media is in the back pocket of the government.

"I would hate to see that happen," Ainsley says, "She is such a good friend of my brother Jack's."

"Oh, don't consider it bad news," Ansel suggests, "We will quickly enlist Christine to be a part of our crusade. She will jump at the opportunity to be part of a movement led by such a distinguished family. She will be a powerful asset in promoting the events we are going to stage."

"What are you thinking Ansel?" Kennedy wonders.

"We are going to go to every major city in the world with the most colossal show ever staged, and the entire world will hear and listen to the message. We will make it so we cannot be ignored. We will raise so much money and channel it all towards the message, as-well-as helping people in need. We will do this not just because we can, but because we must. I have never been so convinced of an imperative as I am now!" Ansel declares. "So how would you organize such an extravaganza Kennedy?"

"I am fortunate to be in a position to appeal to all the great athletes of the world. We must have the involvement of the greatest of the great. We need to appeal to the legends and current champions of all sports. We will combine a sporting extravaganza with an art festival unlike anything ever attempted or accomplished before!" Kennedy proclaims with bravado and determination.

"Ainsley, you are the musical star, but you cannot do it alone. You need to line up the greatest rock and roll musicians as well as country musicians ever assembled. Again, we want only the best, we need world renown musicians, every one we put on stage must either be a Hall of Famer, or destined for the Hall of Fame," Kennedy conveys with determination.

"Ansel, you must see to it we have the greatest visual artists and literary artists on hand to create a real cultural bonanza," Kennedy attests. "All of these people must be willing to devote their tireless effort to this crusade without any compensation. In fact, they must be willing to cover their own costs and go wherever we go. This is nothing less than a "Save the World" crusade."

"What about Christine?" Ainsley wonders.

"Christine is our ace in the hole and FOX news is our greatest contributor. After firing Christine, she will be the most recognized news person in the world. She will possess a notoriety which will be the basis for our promotion. We will also use her to host all of our festivals," Ansel continues.

"This is a stroke of genius," Ainsley announces feeding Ansel's already over inflated ego. "I think this is brilliant, but what if these people aren't willing to contribute without a cut of the take?"

"If anyone hesitates to be part of this crusade, you tell them all the money in the world will be useless if we are all dead. You tell them in the most direct manner that this is not just some charity project, this may be the last battle for the survival of the human race. All the chips are on the table, and the stakes couldn't be higher. You tell them and show them everything you know, just as you have done with me. You tell them that Ansel Colioso is doing this free and they will understand how critical things have become!" Ansel charges.

Back in Belmond, Christine's report has heightened the urgency of Dr. Isabelle's, Senator Joseph's, and Stella Caroline's mission to bring the leaders of the great religions together to experience the "Hand of God". The cascading events around the world are an indication that time is growing short for the human race. The three agree they must appeal to these religious leaders with a quote from Jesus. While Jesus is not recognized by all religions in the same way, he is recognized by all religions as a great religious teacher. Ivey, Jack, and Stella have agreed to ask each religious leader, "Jesus asked us to love our neighbor as ourselves, so who is our neighbor if it's not each one of us? It is time to put love at the center of who we are as a human race."

Senator Joseph with his international contacts and Stella with her contacts via the United Nations take to the task of getting these religious leaders to Lucerne for this conference. Ivey is responsible for putting together the presentation. Senator Joseph marshals the assistance of his personal secretary Nora and Chief of Staff Arnold in contacting the emissaries of various religious leaders to make arrangements for their attendance at this historical conference. Stella contacts Zach Arthur and Prince Abdul Muntaqim Bolkiah of Brunei from the Island of Borneo for assistance in making her assigned contacts. She believes Prince Abdul who is Muslim will be valuable in contacting and arranging the attendance of Islamic leaders.

The Senator and Stella ask their accomplices to attend the conference and assist them with all the arrangements and needs of these very important guests. Stella is excited by the prospect of seeing her friends Zach and Prince Abdul whom she has not seen for a number of weeks. She especially anticipates seeing Zach; she has grown very fond of him.

Senator Joseph knows he is once again treading on very sensitive ground by taking the initiative to host such a critical conference. He knows that Chief of Staff Peet will portray this conference as proof of the Senator's lack of loyalty to the president and a challenge to the president's authority. He understands this perspective, but knows it must be done. Time is of the essence, and the president and Peet would tie such a conference idea up in bureaucratic knots.

The senator knows he has crossed the line of no return when it comes to his alignment with the president and Democratic Party. His intervention with Christine Mathews to issue the Yellowstone warning, and now his work in arranging such a historic international conference, the senator is shedding the cloak of politics.

It is a grueling day of work, but as the day wears on, it becomes apparent the conference will become a reality. All the leaders of the major world religions as well as many lesser religions have been contacted about the conference. In 2030, Islam became the world's largest religion with 2.7 billion believers followed by Christianity with

2.5 billion, Hinduism with 1.5 billion, Chinese Folk Religion with 900 million, Buddhism with 800 million, Taoism with 150 million, Shinto with 120 million, Falun Data with 70 million, Sikhism with 35 million, and Judaism with 15 million. Beliefs with less than ten million followers include Korean Shamanism, Caodaism, Baha'I Faith, Jainism, Cheondoism, Hoahaoism, Tenriism, and Zoroastrianism.

"It has been an amazing experience," Stella shares with Jack and Ivey. "Everyone we talked to has been praying for some divine intervention. They are not only receptive to attending a conference, but anxious to meet with all of the other religious leaders. They feel our desire for such a conference is the divine intervention they have been looking for. They have no idea regarding the revelations to come."

"My team has received a very similar response," the senator notes, "It is as if one voice has been answering the prayers of these religious leaders."

"Isn't that why we are bringing them to Lucerne?" Ivey asks, "Are we not going to show them something so startling and so dramatic as to remove all doubt that we are one?"

As word of the final arrangements arrive from Prince Abdul Muntaqim Bolkiah of Brunei from the Island of Borneo, the three leaders sit for a drink with their grandparents. They will be departing in the morning, and they want a little time with Grandma and Grandpa. As Grandpa delivers the drinks, he has the Beatles "Here Comes the Sun" playing in the background. The music feels so appropriate to the ray of hope shining on the world at this moment.

Jack, Ivey, and Stella appreciate the fact that their grandparents are not intrusive with their work. Grandma and Grandpa do more than just tell them how much they believe in them; they show it through their trust and faith. They know they can always count on their grandparents when needed.

Grandpa suggests the five of them play a game of cutthroat before calling it a night. The Beatles are still playing, at the moment the song "Come Together" seems an appropriate anthem for the days ahead. Grandma lets them know there will be eggs, bacon, hash browns, pancakes, biscuits and gravy, coffee, and juice in the morning before they depart. For the next hour, the five of them find many reasons to give each other a hard time, laugh, and relax.

CHAPTER 26

THE WARRANT

I N MODERN TIMES, ONE THING holds true about the news media; which is, news cycles come and go with regularity. Although the Earth-shattering events of the Mid-Atlantic Ridge are but a couple of short weeks ago, and the devastation continues to take its toll, the news media has moved on by regulating this horrific disaster to daily news snippets. The fact the east coast of the United States lay in ruins including the nation's capital city doesn't matter, it has become old news. Despite the declaration of martial law by the president, rendering the Constitution of the United State meaningless, the topic and controversy infrequently appear except as editorial fodder for the talking heads. The news cycle does little for people. A little knowledge is dangerous, and too much knowledge is really dangerous. Since the news media is controlled by those of wealth and power, they make sure the news cycles will not allow time for public discussion or reaction. Keep the news moving and the people will stay off the streets.

Over the years as war, disease, and natural disaster claimed more and more lives, property, and possessions, any concern of the general population is paid little heed. Such calamity is the status quo. People grew up playing electronic games and watching entertainment intended to indoctrinate and desensitize the masses to the horrors of life. It only made sense that the vast majority of victims are the poor and middle-class living paycheck to paycheck on the cusp of danger. Race, sexual orientation and other minority designations do not matter. What matters is the size of your savings account and personal holdings. Society has become a socially and politically engineered system based on economic power.

Politicians backed by big money spread bullshit as if it is manna from heaven. Candidates for office wear a party cloak as a means of perpetuating the myth of choice. In the end, almost all of them are self-serving bastards eating from the trough of greed and corruption.

However, something unexpected happened with the Mid-Atlantic Ridge catastrophe which consumed the entire eastern seaboard. Some of the richest people and some of the most valuable property fell into ruins. Of the millions of people who perished along the eastern sea board, many of them belonged to the wealthy and privileged class. The once untouchable have been proven vulnerable.

FOX news fired Christine Mathews as expected. The firing hit the news media world like a fire storm. Everyone wants to know more about the five scientists and their prediction that Yellowstone National Park and the surrounding area is going up in flames. Every syndicated news agency tries to get ahold of the story, but FOX buried it under orders and threats from the president through Chief of Staff Peet.

There aren't many good or respected journalists remaining after years of being no more than talking heads for a political agenda. Unlike journalists of the past who valued integrity and sought out the truth, journalists today work for a paycheck and want to keep their job. These journalists know if they stray from the dictates of the station or news agency for which they work; they will meet a fate much like Christine Mathews.

None-the-less, there are always those who seek out the truth. They may work under the cloak of darkness, but they are there lurking in the shadows searching for the truth like a dying man seeking one last breath. The government and FOX might bury a story, but the names of the five scientists are now clearly known.

"Hello Contessa, this is Christine Mathews."

"Christine, great report this morning! From what I understand, people are evacuating the Yellowstone Park and surrounding area. I must say, for my cousins and me, we are sorry about you losing your job," Contessa offers her regrets.

"Contessa, I need to keep this short. I have it from a good source that the Justice Department has been ordered to arrest you and your cousins and confiscate all of your data," Christine warns. "Please go into hiding, if they catch you, you will be crucified."

"Thanks Christine, you have my number. Stay in touch!" Contessa closes.

"Who was on the line Contessa?" Noah asks certain it was Christine as he heard part of the conversation, "It seems rather serious."

"That was Christine Mathews, she says she has it on good authority that the Justice Department is sending agents to arrest us and confiscate all of our data and equipment," Contessa informs the others. "She is begging us to go into hiding in hopes this will blow over."

"You mean blows up," Edison interjects. "This thing will not blow over until we are vindicated by the occurrence of our prediction."

"It doesn't matter how it blows over, we need to find ourselves a secure location, and find it fast," adds Thomas. "The feds don't screw around. They are probably on their way this very minute."

"I know just the place," Hannah informs the team. "There is a secret passage behind a fake boiler in the sub-basement of the old library which leads to a complex of rooms. In the late 50s, the Board of Regents secretly created a bomb shelter for top university officials. Everyone who knew about it has long forgotten or is dead."

"If it's so secret Hannah, how do you know about it," Edison asks a bit teasingly. "Was this some kind of secret rendezvous point for you and a beau?" he adds with a mischievous smile.

"I know about this because I dated a guy who was a historian for the university. He told me about this mysterious secret place, and one time we went looking for it. What we found are impressive rooms complete with furnishings and all kinds of supplies, but that is all," Hannah shares with a firm look on her face.

"Sure Hannah, we all buy that," her brother Thomas says with a laugh. "We all buy that, right guys?"

"If this guy knows you know Hannah, how can we be sure it will be safe?" Noah asks a bit concerned it might not be so secure. "What if the feds learn of your relationship and question him?"

"First off Noah, it was a date, not a relationship. Second off, he died in a car accident a few years ago," Hannah says putting an end to the conversation. "Look guys, we don't have much time. These are forgotten rooms equipped with power, water, sewer, and non-perishable supplies. There are even old data lines we can use to maintain contact with the outside world."

"We don't have much choice," Edison declares, "We either lock ourselves away in these secret rooms or the feds will lock us up and throw away the key."

"Let's get moving," Noah orders. "Hannah how far is it to the old library."

"Ironically, it is just across the street. Luckily for us, there is a tunnel which runs under the street connecting this building with the first floor of the old library. We should be able to make the move quickly and undetected," Hannah reveals.

"Contessa, you gather up all of the data storage devices. Edison, Thomas, and I will cart the critical equipment we need to continue our work. Hannah, grab all of the technical wire and equipment we will need to connect with the outside world. Don't take anything but what is absolutely essential. When the feds arrive and find us gone, we do not want them to think we took a lot of stuff, or they will figure out we are nearby. Let's get moving! As soon as we are ready, Hannah, lead the way," Noah directs his brother and cousins in the same manner he directed his high school basketball team as point guard.

Within a matter of minutes, these five scientists have everything they need to establish a working lab while in hiding. It is their good fortune that neither building is very busy. Moving quickly and quietly, they successfully exit the science building and hustle through the tunnel under the street arriving in the old library building on the first floor. As Hannah goes to turn a corner leading to the elevator which will take them to the sub-basement, she sees a construction worker down the hall. Saying something to the team, Edison immediately comes forward giving everyone the sign to be completely quiet. Using his cell phone, Edison manages to pair with the construction workers cell phone which also gives him the person's name. Edison dials the number and ques the construction worker's phone to indicate a lack of signal. Edison is counting on the curiosity of the construction worker. Hopefully, he will seek out a place where he can get a signal and redial the number. People are pretty much married to their phones and usually drop anything to answer or return a call. When the construction worker dials the number, he will get an infinite busy signal.

As the team waits patiently, they hear the construction worker's ring tone. Next, they hear the construction worker attempt to answer his phone. Sure enough, the construction worker turns down the hall and up the stairs to seek a good signal. When this occurs, the team moves swiftly to the elevator and the sub-basement. Once in the sub-basement, the elevator is programmed to return to the first floor avoiding suspicion. Access to the secret passage behind the fake boiler is tight and difficult, but the team enters safely. Unless you know about this passage, there is no way you suspect it exists. Once inside the passage, they close the entrance and breathe a sigh of relief.

As they move into the bomb shelter, the team is dumbfounded by the facility. These rooms, prepared for top university officials, are furnished for some fine living. True, the furniture, kitchen equipment, televisions, and other furnishings are vintage late fifties and early sixties, but they are top of the line. The bedrooms are small, but there are enough bedrooms to accommodate ten people. This means there is enough non-perishable food supplies to last a long time. The team finds shelves upon shelves of canned meats, vegetables, fruits, bottled water, and copious amounts of alcohol. They won't be living in luxury, but they have all of the essentials needed for an extended stay.

Once inside the main room, the team immediately get to work setting up their monitoring equipment, as well as equipment needed to receive news and communicate with the outside world. Thank goodness each member of the team possesses unique technological skills. With each stage of set up, they double check each other to make sure what they are doing cannot be traced back to this room. Using their technological savvy, they set up remote clouds, which sends anyone attempting to trace their activity on a wild goose chase.

Four things that concern them is the water, sewer, electrical, and air usage. These things have not been in use before, and the maintenance crew might eventually wonder why they are seeing usage from an undetermined location. The team knows such a clue would probably take a long time to trace, but they might be there a long time. The team decides there needs to be one outside-the-room activity to disconnect the metering of water, sewer, electrical, and air so their use goes undetected. Thomas Henry's time working with his dad on the farm equips him with a basic knowledge in all these areas. So, Thomas, Noah, and Edison sneak out of the room in the wee hours of the morning to do the work.

Working quickly, they complete everything but the air which must be done from the mechanical room in the basement. Moving quietly, the three promptly head for the mechanical room. As they quietly slip into the room, Noah spots a blanket peeking out from behind a boiler at the far end of the room. Edison, always cleaver, signals for the guys to move around the far side of the room for a closer but undetected look. There on the blanket is a naked coed with what appears to be an elderly professor doing the old nasty. Smiling at his brother and cousin, Edison gives the signal for them to back away. Edison begins to pound lightly on a pipe with a hammer and using a screw driver makes a scratching sound on a vent. Sitting up, interrupting their sexual dance, the two intently listen. Now, Eddie makes the sound of footsteps. Sooner than you can say boo, these two naked jay birds scoop up their clothes and head bare assed, one tight and firm and the other wrinkled like a raisin, out of the room leaving the blanket behind.

With the coast clear, the three share a chuckle. "I always suspected the lesser capable coeds would do just about anything to get a grade," Thomas remarks.

"Yea, I think that old geezer was having the time of his life. We're lucky the old fart didn't have a heart attack," Edison adds with a quiet laugh.

"Okay, enough fun, let's get to work," Noah orders.

Safely back in the secret room, the guys share their encounter with Hannah and Contessa at breakfast the next morning.

"You guys surely aren't naïve enough to think that girls who struggled in classes don't trade a little sex for a good grade. Hell, it happens all the time. We had this one girl in our sorority, who the fraternity guys considered drop dead gorgeous, but she was dumber than a stump. She screwed her way to a four-year degree. I don't know what happened to her after that, but I imagine she has taken care of the boss in any job she has ever held," Hannah says seeking to educate her brother and cousins.

"Surely Dr. Abraham, you have been approached by good looking young women in your classes," Contessa suggests.

"Now that you mention it Contessa, I do believe that has happened on several occasions. I feel a bit silly for not recognizing it for what it was. Of course, even if I knew what they were up to, I would not have fallen for this ploy," Noah responds. "I am far more ethical than that."

"Sure Noah, good looking coeds don't appeal to you," Edison teases.

"On a more serious note, what if these two report strange noises in the boiler room," Hannah wonders, "It could give rise to unnecessary attention."

"Seriously Hannah, you think a professor is going to share that with anyone when he would have to explain why he was in the boiler room at two o'clock in the morning," Thomas says trying to alleviate her concern. "As for the coed, all she wants is a good grade, not trouble."

With a new day, the team checks all of the equipment to ensure it is functioning effectively, efficiently, and safely. They are anxious for news, so they check the five black and white twenty-five-inch televisions they wired for reception. The first news they get is from Coyote Blitzer on DNN.

"This is Coyote Blitzer with breaking news from DNN, your first in news. This morning, the governors of Wyoming, Utah, and Montana ordered all people to evacuate from Yellowstone National Park at a perimeter of 250 miles from the center of the park. The governors have ordered their respective National Guards, currently serving as part of the president's order of martial law, to redeploy at the direction of the governor. As we reported last night, wild fires starting from what appears to be spontaneous combustion are burning out of control near the epicenter of the Yellowstone Caldera."

"Once the heat breaks through the epicenter of the caldera, it is only a matter of time before the entire Yellowstone area is ablaze," Contessa says as if talking to Coyote Blitzer.

"That will only be the beginning. I expect we are in for an event of Biblical proportions when valleys are raised up and mountain brought low. The Yellowstone National Park area is going to get so hot it will cause spontaneous fires a couple hundred miles away. The heat will change the climate in ways we have never seen," Hannah remarks. This is Devolution gone wild!"

"In other related news," Coyote continues his broadcast, "The five scientists Noah Abraham, Edison Jude, Hannah Rae, Thomas Henry, and Contessa Margery, who independently shared the warning and advice to evacuate Yellowstone are being sought by the FBI. The President of the United States has ordered their arrest on charges of sabotage. We have our legal editor Anus Reno with us for a special assessment of the situation from Ames, Iowa. Anus, is the son of former Attorney General Janet Reno who once said "There is a special place in hell for women who don't vote for Hillary Clinton. Anus, can you hear me?"

"The FBI is looking for the five scientists being sought by the federal government. As of right now, they have done a thorough sweep of the ISU campus and surrounding areas. In searching the office and research area of Dr. Hannah Rae, they found some items missing, which suggests these five scientists might have been tipped off regarding the president's order for their arrest."

"So, there is no sign of their whereabouts?"

"That is correct Coyote. The questioning of colleagues and friends has begun, but as of right now, the FBI has nothing to go on."

"Anus, since the warning broadcast on FOX yesterday morning, the Yellowstone Caldera has started to burn, and it looks like these five scientists may be correct with their prediction. Three governors are not taking any chances by ordering the evacuation, as the scientists advised, according to the Christine Mathews broadcast. Now the FBI is searching for these five scientists, and Christine has been fired. Does the President of the United States or the owner of FOX Broadcasting have a case to make against these five scientists and Christine?"

"That is a good question Coyote. If these five scientists are correct,

Christine's warning may have saved hundreds of thousands of lives. While the president certainly has grounds to arrest these five, I think he would have a hard time making anything stick. In fact, if their prediction comes true, and their warning saves lives, the president might have a hard time not declaring them heroes."

"What about Christine?" Coyote asks.

"Christine Mathews has shown great courage knowing the possible consequences. FOX might threaten Christine Mathews career, but it is possible public sentiment might say otherwise. We have it from a good source that Christine may be headed to Chicago where she will work with Ainsley Anabelle, Kennedy Kay, Gemma Juniper and Ansel Colioso on the greatest entertainment and philanthropic project in history. Colioso is prone to hyperbole, but this is no joke, the greatest show on Earth is coming to your town, and everything gained will be used to save the planet." says Anus.

"Something interesting is occurring Anus. We just learned that our five fugitive scientists along with Kennedy Kae, Ainsley Annabelle, and Gemma Juniper all belong to the same family," Coyote reveals.

"That is not all Coyote," Anus jumps in. "There are four others belonging to this illustrious family including Senator Jack Joseph, U.N. Assistant Stella Caroline, Astrophysicist Ivey Isabelle, and top research specialist at the CDC, Dr. Olivia Kae."

"I am not certain Anus, but it seems this nation and the world might be at a Cross Roads. Never before in history has there been such a family with the talent and ability to lead humanity from the darkness into the light. Do you realize the relationship between those who are stepping forward to provide leadership? Do you know that each and every one of them possess a unique intellectual ability combined with talent, determination, devotion, and a relentless desire to serve? Such a family connection is incredible!" Coyote declares.

"Your assessment is correct Coyote; however, this illustrious group also represents a serious threat to the status quo and those desperately clinging to power. It appears there may be a very treacherous road ahead," Anus offers his reservation.

CHAPTER 27

THE ESSENCE OF SECRECY

S AFE IN THE SUB-BASEMENT SECRET room of the old library building on the Iowa State University Campus, the five cousins work feverishly to get all their equipment up and running. Modifying the outdated connectivity existing along one of the cement walls Edison Jude, the tech savvy member of the team, works feverishly to bring things to life. The team brought with them three hi-end laptop computers, five state-of-the-art handheld devices, and a seismograph. Edison is also working to create a secure channel by which they may communicate with the outside world, in particular their cousins and Christine Mathews.

The seismograph they possess is able to identify and monitor any shifting in the earth's lithosphere, which is the rigid outermost shell of the planet (the crust and upper mantle) that is broken up into tectonic plates. The Earth's lithosphere is made up of seven or eight major plates and many minor plates.

In most cases, this group of isolated scientists must rely on connectivity to outside sources to gather data for interpretation. They all possess the highest level of clearance at their respective institutions. Edison focuses on gaining access to land-based instruments which will connect them to satellites linked to ATSR instruments such as the Infra-Red Radiometer and the Microwave Sounder. These instruments will help them keep a finger on the ability of substances to stay solid in relationship to temperature and pressure. They are also seeking to connect with fluid inclusion equipment as well as high frequency acoustic equipment.

By tapping into Global Positioning Systems with telescopic capability, they will be able to monitor the movement of animals while cut off from the world in their secret hide-away. The threat of invasive species including reptiles is of serious concern. Monitoring their movement and behavior is critical to finding a management strategy.

These highly knowledgeable and talented scientists possess proof that Devolution is occurring around the globe. People of the world have a right to know what to expect as the Earth struggles to reestablish equilibrium by reverting back to days gone by. It is not necessarily a pretty picture, but it is something that can be successfully negotiated if people know how to respond.

So now, they are relying on a very talented and tech savvy Edison to establish connectivity between a very archaic system and some of the most sophisticated equipment in the world.

"How's it going Eddie," Noah inquires.

"It is slow, but not impossible. I must not only increase the power and speed of the system, but I must teach it to relate to all of our equipment for which it currently has no frame of reference."

"So how can we help?" Noah asks.

"Be patient, all of this requires 100 percent of my concentration. The smallest slip up and I have to start all over again."

"Is there anything we can do?" He wonders.

"You and Contessa must remain ready to give me your codes which will allow us to connect remotely to the online science equipment at the University of Michigan. When I want that, I will need it immediately."

"What about me?" Thomas asks.

"Yes, you too," Edison responds. "I will need your codes for Virginia Tech so we can diversify our access."

"I assume you will want my codes also," Hannah says.

"Actually not, I am concerned about our proximity to your equipment and the potential for detection. I will however connect with the online science equipment at the University of California in Berkeley."

"So, once we are connected, we are okay," Thomas inquires.

"Once we are connected, we will be able to gather data and monitor environmental and geological activity around the globe. However, there is always the potential, no matter how improbable, of someone discovering our link. I am doing everything possible to keep our signals robust, but undetectable. We will only access them in the evening when no one should be around, but even if they are, it would take quite a stroke of luck to detect us."

These five scientists know the big picture plan which came out of the Ames conference, but they do not know where their cousins are at in the execution of this plan. They cannot afford to go without communication. Establishing a secure channel is a risky but necessary thing that must be done. If they make a mistake which leads to their discovery and arrest, all could be lost.

"I believe I have arrived at a plan for a secure channel we can trust," Edison informs the team. Edison is no rookie when it comes to establishing secure channels. When he worked on board the submergible in the south Atlantic off the coast of Florida, his team always maintained a secure channel. "Our channel will change every 24 hours with the last transmission giving our cousins and Christine the contact information for each subsequent channel."

"Why are you so confident this plan will protect us from detection?" Noah asks his brother.

The odds of anyone detecting our secure channel are no better than that of winning the lottery," Edison assures the team. "Even if someone were to stumble upon our channel, the odds of them tracing our location before the channel changes again are even greater than the lottery. I don't know how to make it any more secure than that. Let's give it a try."

"Hello, Kennedy this is Edison Jude."

"Eddie, is that really you, where are you?" Kennedy exclaims with excitement. "Do you know there is an all points bulletin out for the arrest of the five of you? According to the news, the FBI is doing a search of Ames and ISU at this moment," Kennedy shares what Edison already knows.

"I cannot reveal our location, but we are safe. I have you on a secure channel which will notify you of our channel change every twenty-four-hours. This will allow us to stay in communication. What is the status of your work?" Edison asks.

"We are in Chicago working with Ansel Colioso to put together a "Save the World Tour" which will be nothing short of phenomenal.

The whole purpose is to use a festival extravaganza to educate people to the truth and raise funds to help alleviate suffering around the world," Kennedy reveals.

"How soon will this tour begin?" Edison inquires.

"We plan to line up all of the participants in the next two weeks and open the tour right here in Chicago hopefully the week after," Kennedy responds.

"Thanks Sis, let's keep the communication open when necessary. We will be working overtime to put together the kind of information which will be valuable for you to communicate on tour. Take care," Edison closes and he is gone.

"Okay, we need to hear from Olivia. Who would like to place the call," Edison asks?

"We would both like to talk with our sister, if possible," Hannah says referring to Dr. Henry and herself.

"Of course, why didn't I think of that before, give me a minute to set up a speaker so we can all hear and take part in the conversation," Dr. Jude says getting to work setting up a speaker system.

"That won't make us less secure will it," Hannah Rae asks.

"Not unless someone can hear through these walls, and if that is possible nothing will keep us secure for long. However, no need to worry about that, I have determined these walls are three-foot thick concrete lined on the outside by six inches of steel. We are completely sound proof," Edison informs.

"Hello, this is Dr. Olivia Kae, can I help you?" Olivia answers from her office phone.

"Hello Olivia, this is Hannah and Thomas along with Noah, Edison, and Contessa contacting you from our beautiful hideout somewhere in the world."

"Oh my God, Hannah, is that really you?" Olivia says with obvious delight. "Are you alright? You haven't been arrested, have you?"

"We are fine Olivia. We have established ourselves in a very secure location. We have you on a secure line which will notify you of a channel change every twenty-four hours," Hannah tells her sister.

"Be careful you guys, the President has issued a federal warrant for your arrests," Olivia warns.

"Olivia, this is Thomas. Can you give us a quick update on your work?"

"Oh Tommy, my favorite twin, I miss you so much. Remember my presentation in Ames and the progress being made. Well, we made a breakthrough! I have passed all the tests with the CDC, Mayor King, and Governor Hickenlooper. I am currently working with the city maintenance crew in Atlanta to set up a trial run on the city yet this week," Olivia reveals. "We have made a second and most unexpected discovery with our vapor approach. We believe it also renders ticks incapable of carrying disease. I wish I had time to tell you everything."

"That is fantastic Olivia, keep us posted on your work," Hannah insists as she closes the conversation.

"I just received a coded message from Stella," Contessa shares. "Believe it or not, Stella, Senator Joseph, and Dr. Isabella are heading for Mt. Pilatus just outside of Lucerne, Switzerland. They have made arrangements to meet there in three days with what is the largest and most diverse conclave of world religious leaders ever assembled. They are trying to keep this as secretive as possible hoping not to attract the attention of the media or world political leaders."

"We must all be careful," interjects Noah, "We are threatening the powers that be with our warnings, ideas, and soon to come, solutions. If threatened, they will make every effort to stop us."

<hr />

High on Mt. Pilatus, the Swiss Government, acting in secret on the special request of United Nations Ambassador DiCaprio, are working round the clock to ensure the Hotel Pilatus-Kulm and Hotel Belleuve are prepared to receive their illustrious guests in style and comfort. The Hotel Pilatus-Kulm and Belleuve provide inspiring views of Lake Lucerne, the city of Lucerne, and the Swiss Alps. Furthermore, the Restaurant, Queen Victoria, is preparing to provide nourishment for these special guests, and the conference room provides a magnificent backdrop for this historic and crucial gathering.

As Senator Joseph, Nora, Arnold, Dr. Isabelle, Stella, Zachary Arthur, Prince Abdul, and Ambassador DiCaprio arrive atop Mt. Pilatus via the world's steepest cogwheel railway, they find a crew from the University of Iowa's Van Allen Institute installing the most sophisticated and powerful telescope and equipment for peering into the vastness of space. The Director of the Van Allen Institute is a great admirer of Dr. Isabelle. He tried to attract her attention more than once when they were taking doctoral classes, but she was always too busy to notice. He would do anything for her, and so her request to keep such an installation secret came easy for him.

Excusing herself, Dr. Isabelle inspects the installation and equipment immediately. This component is critical to her presentation. It is one thing to show recorded images, it is another thing to show the images in real time. The rest of the entourage settle into their rooms before going to the conference room to make arrangements for receiving their illustrious guests.

"Thank you for bringing Nora and Arnold, Senator Joseph. Their organizational skills are invaluable," the ambassador emphasizes.

"With Stella in charge of all of the arrangements, Nora and Arnold should have it easy. Stella's attention to detail is amazing!" the senator stresses.

"Look at this view Zach," Stella exclaims as the two of them stand looking out at the awe-inspiring vista of the Alps.

"It almost makes you forget all of the trouble, turmoil, chaos, and catastrophe going on around the world," Zach reflects. "It is good to be here with you Stella."

"I have missed you Zach, but we have so much to do in so little time. Perhaps when this is over, we can find a little time to ourselves," Stella suggests grabbing Zach's right hand with her left and giving a little squeeze to accentuate her comment.

"That would be nice Stella, so what do we need to get done first?"

"Would you start by checking with the hotel and restaurant to make sure they are completely ready for the arrival of our guests? I have a checklist here that you might find helpful," Stella says holding out a clipboard with a checklist attached. "Don't forget to make sure that the hotel and restaurant know that none of our guests are to be charged for any costs related to their stay."

"How do you plan to pay for this Stella?" Zach wonders giving her a quizzical look.

"We have three very talented cousins getting ready to launch a "Save the World Tour". Once they get started, I have no doubt the money will roll in freely to support and bankroll the many endeavors ahead," Stella responds with sheer confidence. "I am going to check on Nora and Arnold."

"Nora, I gave the hotel the layout for the conference room as you requested," Arnold announces.

"Thank you, Arnold, now would you take this list of attendees and ask the hotel printing office to produce the name placards for the tables as well as the name tags?" Nora asks.

"Absolutely, anything to help," Arnold responds.

"You know this is the riskiest thing we have ever attempted," Nora says quietly with all seriousness. "We are making an end run around the world community to meet with this conclave of religious leaders. We are fortunate Ambassador DiCaprio has the confidence of the Swiss Government. We are also lucky the Swiss Government has a long history of neutrality and supporting peaceful initiatives. They also recognize the urgency of this mission."

"I know," Arnold responds, "It is our good fortune to work with a courageous and selfless leader like Senator Joseph. He is unwavering in his commitment to saving the planet."

"Let's hope we don't end up in hiding like his five cousins," Nora whispers.

"They are truly a great family aren't they Nora? Where would the world be if not for their determination, dedication, and commitment to finding answers and solutions to the many things threatening civilization despite the personal dangers, obstacles, and harm they face," Arnold muses.

"Let's get moving Arnold lest we let them down. We have much to do before our first guest arrives," Nora reminds him as she begins organizing all of the registration material.

At the quickly established observatory, Dr. Isabelle inspects the telescope installation learning it will not be operational until the time of her presentation. She is concerned by such a narrow window. "What if something occurs and the telescope fails to function?" she asks the chief engineer of the project. "You will put us all in a precarious position if this telescope does not work. We will soon host forty-three of the world's top religious' leaders for my presentation and demonstration. If all goes well, we may witness a paradigm shift unparalleled in human history. If this does not work, we are doomed."

"Dr. Isabelle, I guarantee this telescope will do exactly as you wish. If you have the correct coordinates, everything should work perfectly," the engineer assures.

"Well, I would feel much better if I could give it a trial run before actually using it for my presentation," Ivey points out.

"I know you would doctor, but we are doing this on a tight schedule. Under normal circumstances, we would never be asked to accomplish such a significant task in such a short amount of time. You must trust that the right people are in the right places," the chief engineer reminds her.

"Okay, since this conference is going to involve a lot of people of faith, I guess I best have faith in your ability to make this happen," Ivey says as she begins to walk away.

"Thank you, doctor, we do appreciate that," the head engineer's comment trails behind her.

With the morning sun peeking, the Alps radiate a colorful spectrum across the mountains and valleys as the audio equipment gives way to Cat Stevens "Morning has Broken". It is a beautiful day, and the first of the anticipated guests should arrive on the cogwheel train by early afternoon. They are expecting 43 religious leaders representing 17 of the world's most recognized religions with a total of 6.65 billion members. They have also invited three well-known and well-written Atheists.

Being able to gain agreement for attendance from all of these religious leaders in one full day is nothing short of miraculous. Certainly, the state of the world convinced the religious leaders to take part in this conference. With the religious leaders on board, everything is proceeding on Mt. Pilatus as planned. Soon the leaders, free from the interference of their normal delegations, will begin to arrive.

Manning the registration area, Nora flashes a smile of satisfaction when she sees the Dalai Lama approaching. Having risen to this position as a boy, the Dalai Lama is one of the most respected religious leaders in the world with a Buddhist following of five-hundred-million people.

Soon after the Dalai Lama, other conference participants arrive on the cogwheel and line up for registration. Shaman Byeong-Ho representing the eight-million followers of Korean Shamanism. Ryu Mi-yong II the leader of three-million Cheondoism followers registers next. Pope Francis II, head of one-billion-two-hundred-million Roman Catholics around the world, registers. Mohammed Ali al-Baghdadi II, the leader of the Islamic Caliphate talks respectfully with S.E. Cupp an atheist commentator while waiting to register. S.E. Cupp is followed by the High Priest of the Japanese Shinto Religion of one-hundred-million members. The Hindu leaders of Swami Alvar Shankara and Baba Ram Dass representing one-billion-one-hundred-million members arrive together. As the first day of registration comes to an end, the Archbishop of Canterbury and the President of the Church of Jesus Christ of Latter-Day Saints arrive on the final cogwheel to register.

Looking back at the registration book, Nora smiles with a sigh. It is a good beginning, and by all indications, they are going to have full attendance and representation. Closing down the registration area until 8:00 the next morning, Nora rushes off to report to Senator Joseph.

That evening, the team gathers in a small conference room to review the day and prepare for tomorrow. They are excited about the things to come. They all agree it is time to retire to their rooms knowing a big day lay ahead.

Arriving at their post early the next morning, Nora and Arnold are accompanied by Stella looking to assist and greet some of the arriving dignitaries. By 7:30 a.m., they can hear the cogwheel ascending Mt. Pilatus with the first group to register. As the Cogwheel doors open, Stella immediately recognizes the Greek Patriarch of Jerusalem Theophilos V. Rushing out to greet his eminence, the Patriarch breaks into a huge smile and embraces Stella as if she were his own. While they only met the year before, Stella endeared herself to the Patriarch with her sincerity and understanding regarding the history and contemporary issues engulfing the Holy Land.

"Stella my child," the Patriarch says softly holding her head close to his chest, "It is a breath of fresh air and a true sign of God's goodness to see you again."

Gently pulling away, Stella looks up at this tall man with a smile and a tear, "I too am blessed to see you again your Holiness," knowing all too well the trials and tribulation the Patriarch has endured in his post.

Patriarch Theophiles V has always believed the Holy Lands belong to all faiths. Counter to many in his own faith as well as the Jewish faith, his Holiness works to make Jerusalem an international city free and open to all. Facing much opposition, and even threats of harm, he stands firm.

Next in line is Huynh Phu So III, the Great-Grand Nephew of Hoahaoism founder Huynh Phu So. Hoahaoism is a religion with two-million followers. Stella met Huynh Phu So III at a United Nations function less than a year ago.

The line is now growing, and Nora sees and recognizes a number of guests including the Grand Imam of Al-Azhar, and Muhammad Ahmad Hussein the Grand Mufti of Jerusalem.

Calling Stella over, Nora quietly asks who the two leaders are in line behind the Grand Mufti? Stella is not certain, but she believes they are the Venerable Jetsun Kahndro Rinpoche of Tibet who has lived the past ten-years in Sri Lanka, and Mrs. Fariba Kamalabadi representing six-million followers of the Baha'I Faith.

The growing line of these most holy people is overwhelming. Each person represents millions of followers of different faiths, and yet these leaders stand calm and peaceful in their diversity. All of them are able to speak a bit of English which makes limited communication possible while standing in line patiently waiting their turn to register for the conference.

"Where have you been, we have been working for over an hour?" Nora asks Zach who has just arrived to help out.

"Ignore his tardiness, Zach is a bit of high maintenance when it comes to getting around for the day," Stella shares in his defense.

"Well high maintenance or not, we have serious work to do here and we can use all available help," she says with Zach taking no notice because he has spotted someone he would like to greet.

Bounding from the registration area, Zach heads down the line of dignitaries arriving at a tall man in an impressive black robe covering his head and body holding an ornate staff and sporting a long black beard.

"My dear friend," Zach exclaims as he holds out his hand, "It is so good to see you again."

Zach is referring to the Ecumenical Patriarch of Constantinople Andrew II who recently ascended to the head of the Eastern Orthodox Church. Zach and the newly anointed Patriarch had been childhood friends at a time when his parents vacationed in Istanbul.

"Zachary, it is wonderful to see you here for this very unusual gathering," Andrew II says. "I truly hope this will be a worthwhile time."

"Oh, it is going to be worth your time your Holiness. This could be the single most important time of all times," Zach says confidently.

"Zach, the most important time was the life and time of our Savior Jesus Christ," the Patriarch announces.

From the very beginning, the Patriarch Andrew II has been a controversial figure. In selecting the name Andrew, the founder of the Eastern Church, Andrew II broke with tradition. During his short reign, he has been outspoken breaking with many traditions in an effort to find common ground between all people.

"You will not be disappointed my friend," Zach assures, "What you are about to experience is right up your alley."

Andrew II winces a bit at the phrase "up your alley", he is not certain he understands the slang, but he knows Zach, and knows it must be okay.

Behind Patriarch Andrew stands Pope Joseph III of the Coptic Orthodox Church of Alexandria. Next in line are British Atheists Alastair Campbell and Nick Clegg, followed by Li Li Hongzhi daughter of Falun Dafa founder Li Hongzhi. Li is followed by three Confucian Leaders known as Sages of Rights, two Taoist Priests, and one Patriarch of the Faith, representing over 900 million followers of Chinese Folk Religion.

Knowing the cogwheel train stops for no one, Nora and Arnold go to lunch while Stella and Zach keep the registration going. As Nora and Arnold walk into the restaurant, they are overwhelmed by all of the religious leaders sitting together at tables talking with civility and respect. They recognize that each leader has a device provided by the conference which allows for voice interpretation regardless, the language. Technology is a wonderful thing, and because of these devices, these religious leaders, regardless of nationality or language, can speak freely with each other without the communication barriers due to language.

"This is unbelievable. Arnold, I feel like we should bow as we enter and pass each table," Nora quietly shares.

"I think we instinctively are Nora," Arnold responds as they both offer small bows as gestures of respect.

Arriving at an available table and taking a seat, Nora leans toward Arnold and asks, "Do you think this will make a difference for the world?"

"If God is not paying attention now, I don't know what we can do?" Arnold responds taking a bite from his grilled Turkey and Swiss sandwich.

Acting a bit panicked as if she had just thought of something important, Nora asks, "Did we make sure all of the food served would not offend any of our guests?"

"Zach did as Stella prescribed," Arnold assures, "Everything offered to eat is non-offensive as are any of the cooking ingredients, utensils, or drinks. We offer only a religiously and culturally sanitary dining experience."

In Arnold and Nora's absence, Stella and Zach check in Rabbis Elazar Eidelstein and Asher Povarsky of the Rosh Yeshiva along with Rabbis Baruch Markovitz and Meir Deutch representing the fourteen-million followers of Judaism. They also welcomed Pope Pham Cong Tac representing Caodism's seven-million followers, and Arjan Singh the leader of Sikhism's twenty-eight-million followers. Zach explains to Stella that the leader of Sikhism has no title because the religion's Guru is the Granth Sahib which are the writings of the religions ten Gurus. Not since 1708 has Sikhism had a human Guru.

With Arnold and Nora's return, Stella and Zach slip off to lunch. Most of the delegates have arrived, but there are some very important religious leaders still not present.

Stella and Zach opt to take their lunch on the balcony of Stella's room. Stella stocked her refrigerator and room with food, which would allow her to eat and work at the same time. On the balcony, these two young people who have found themselves at the epicenter of the most important conference in human history enjoy a magnificent view of the Alps.

"Zach, why do you think Judaism has historically commanded such a prominent place in the religious community?" Stella wonders knowing they are safe to talk freely.

"I'm not sure Judaism commanded a prominent place in the world before the Holocaust. Sure, Judaism gave birth to Christianity, but it also gave birth to Islam. But, after World War II, it not only became a prominent religion, but a very controversial nation carved out of very controversial lands," Zach offers.

"Was the world so blind as to believe they could impose their will in a land where wills run deep as the desert sand? To take the Holy Land and make it the very heart and soul of the Zionist State seems to be only asking for problems. It defies rationale," Stella reflects.

"Well, you know what they say about hindsight. The world was a different place after World War II, and the western powers felt invincible in shaping the world to their will. If they had known then what the world knows now, perhaps they would have found a different answer for the Jewish question," Zach proposes.

"Maybe, but it all seems to defy reason," Stella shakes her head in disbelief.

"Following the war, the allies were ashamed of their slow response to the Holocaust. Furthermore, the Jewish lobby inside the United States controlled a great deal of money and power. To appease what the Old Testament claims is a vengeful God, the best answer seemed to be to return his people to the Promised Land."

"Well, with nearly one-hundred-years of war and savagery behind us, the whole idea seems like folly to me," Stella concludes. "We need to get back to the registration area and help complete the registration process."

Upon returning to the registration area, Stella and Zach find that Nora and Arnold have registered the Secretary General of the World Evangelical Alliance Efraim Tendero, the President of the World Methodist Council Frances Alguire II, President of the Lutheran

World Federation Bishop Munib Younan, and President of the Southern Baptist Convention Dr. Steve Gaines.

"Wow," Stella observes to her fellow registers, "We have three-hours before registration closes. How many leaders remain to register?"

"We have Ford-maker Acharya Sudharma Swami of the four-million worshipers of Jainism, the leader or Yoboku of the five-million strong Tenriism religion, and a Zoroastrian priest. We also await the Ayatollah and Grand Ayatollah representing the Shia Muslims," Nora reports.

"What is the significant difference between an Ayatollah and a Grand Ayatollah?" Zach asks.

"Ayatollah means "Sign of God" which is a very prestigious title, but Grand Ayatollah means "Great Sign of God". The Grand Ayatollah is expected to publish his Juristic book called Resalah, where he addresses the vast majority of daily Muslim affairs," Arnold jumps in to answer the question.

"So, who are the two Ayatollahs we are expecting?" Stella asks.

"We are expecting to receive the Grand Ayatollah Abdol-Hamid Masoumi-Tehrani II who is the son of the Ayatollah by the same name. Like his father, he is very open to other religions and just in his ways. The other is the Ayatollah Sayyid Ruhollah Musavi Khomeini II the grandson of the Grand Ayatollah by the same name," Nora reveals.

"It is interesting that so many religious leaders are the descendants of previous leaders," Zach observes.

"It is not so surprising Zach, once fame, fortune, position, and prestige are gained in just about any of life's endeavors, the family puts a great deal of effort into the continuation of it from generation to generation. It is not always what you know and can do, but who you know and what they can do for you. It seems to be universal from culture to culture," Stella reveals the wisdom of someone far older.

"Here comes the cogwheel everyone, prepare to greet our final guests. I think we might have this done before 4:00," Nora announces.

As the four of them stand ready to greet their guests, the dignitaries arrive and approach with a calm dignity fit for the occasion. The Ayatollahs are stern but gracious. They have a divine air about them which convinces Arnold the conference will be a huge success. With registration complete, Nora invites the team back to her room for drinks. Because many religions forbid alcohol, any alcoholic beverages must be kept in private. Tomorrow, the conference begins! They can feel the dawning of a new day on the horizon.

CHAPTER 28

LUKE 3:5

"D R. ABRAHAM WOULD YOU COME look at this?" Contessa Margery asks with a sense of urgency. The trembling in Contessa's voice captures the attention and interest of the others.

"What is it Contessa, you sound rather startled and look a bit undone," Dr. Abraham asks as he leaves his work station and walks across the room to where Contessa is monitoring a computer. As Noah nears Contessa's work station, he can see Contessa's hands visibly shaking.

"Oh my God," Dr. Rae exclaims upon viewing Contessa's screen. Hannah's ominous exclamation causes Dr. Henry and Dr. Jude to abruptly leave their work areas and rush to where Contessa is sitting.

"What do you think cousin, do you see the same thing I am seeing?" Contessa asks Dr. Abraham. These two have worked closely together for a few years, and Contessa knows Dr. Abraham will not mince words if he agrees or disagrees.

Closely examining the computer screen, Dr. Abraham reaches to access the finger control which allows manipulation of the screen. Running the screen up and down several times in an effort to confirm what he is seeing. "This is the most unbelievable thing I have ever witnessed. We were confident our assessment about Yellowstone becoming a burning inferno was correct, but did we really believe it would become a melting inferno!" Noah attests.

"What do you mean brother? Evidently I am not looking at the right thing," Dr. Jude asks trying to get a good look at the screen's contents.

"Look right here at these numbers. These represent the intense substructure temperature. Now look at these surface temperatures at Mt. Haynes, Canyon Village, Lewis Lake, and Steam Boat Point on the east shore of Yellowstone Lake. All of these points are on the edge of the Yellowstone Caldera. The rapidly rising temperatures suggest the inferno has broken through the thermo layer," Noah proclaims in a most ominous tone.

"What do you predict Noah?" Dr. Henry is looking for a better understanding of the existing situation.

"Well, I can only," Noah starts before being cut off by Contessa.

"I'll tell you what will happen. The temperature at the identified points has reached 700 degrees Centigrade or 1,292 degrees Fahrenheit in the past hour. The entire Yellowstone area is engulfed in a towering blaze. Yellowstone Lake is boiling and will be totally evaporated in two hours. As the temperatures continue to rise, all of Yellowstone will literally melt from the intense heat. As the temperatures increase to 1200 degrees Centigrade or 2,192 degrees Fahrenheit, the mountains of Yellowstone will melt like gigantic ice cream cones!" Contessa declares.

"Is that right Noah, is it possible this is truly happening?" Dr. Henry asks hoping to get a different response.

"Contessa is our geological expert and I don't doubt her assessment one bit. But, what does this mean for people is the big question?" Noah responds.

"If people evacuated the full 250 miles announced in our warning, they should be out of harm's way of the substructure heat which has broken through the thermo layer. Of course, this is dependent upon the substructure heat staying isolated to the Yellowstone Caldera," Contessa says confidently.

"What if it does not stay contained to the Caldera?" Hannah asks with desperation in her voice.

"I don't think we can assume it will stay contained to the Caldera. I believe the only safe thing for people to do is evacuate all of Wyoming, Montana, Idaho, northwest Colorado, northeast Utah. And this needs to occur immediately!" Contessa declares as if delivering an order. "At the very least, such intense heat at the surface will cause ground fires incapable of being contained for perhaps hundreds of miles.

Edison Jude has moved to the bank of televisions the team set up in the bunker as a means of staying updated with events in the outside world. The televisions are only used intermittently during the day as a means of guarding against anyone discovering their location.

As the televisions come to life, they discover not one of the networks is airing information regarding the Yellowstone Caldera. "Are the networks really that out of touch, or has the government squelched reporting on the caldera because they are so miserably wrong?" Dr. Henry muses.

The team notices that DNN is still running a bottom banner identifying these five cousins and scientists as fugitives. On a positive note, they are relieved to see that the news media has been so consumed with doing the work of the government they have not noticed the events occurring on Mount Pilatus.

"There is no time to waste, someone must sound the alarm regarding what is occurring in Yellowstone. We have got to alert the news media and we need to do this immediately," Edison Jude declares.

"Who can we trust?" Dr. Henry asks, "I am not concerned for our own safety, but seriously, if we are put out of commission the whole damn country is in trouble."

"I agree cousin, but if we cannot deliver what we know to the general public to keep them safe from the calamities to come, of what use are we? It is truly a catch 22," Edison responds.

"I say we deliver our information and warning to Coyote Blitzer," Noah recommends.

"He's a weasel, I doubt he has the courage to air anything without prior approval from on high, especially if it comes from us," Edison retorts.

"No, he is Coyote, but ironically, he has a young son named Weasel," Noah says trying to inject a little humor into a most dire situation. "Look, we must act, and Coyote is the most opportunistic news person in the country. If we deliver this to him, he won't be able to resist being the first with a breaking story of this magnitude. All we have to do is let him know if he passes this up, we will find someone who will broadcast it," Noah assures.

"How do we do this without giving away our location?" Hannah asks.

"That's why we have Edison," Contessa jumps into the conversation. "Edison is the most tech savvy of our team, so let's get it done! What do you say Eddie?"

"I will send an encrypted message to DNN with attention to Coyote Blitzer. I will use an espionage trick I learned from a friend which makes the message too tantalizing not to open. I will then construct it so accessing the actual message is totally dependent upon Coyote opening it. Once it is opened, we will have his full attention," Edison says as he works feverishly at the computer.

"That sounds great brother, but it also sounds like a long process when we have very little time," Noah voices with concern.

"Hell Noah, it is almost done. Give me two more minutes, and all I have to do is press send," Edison assures.

"Whatever got you so interested in technology Edison?" Hannah wonders.

"As a kid, I was always amazed at how everyone turned to Grandma for tech support. She had an understanding and way with computers which I admired. I remember thinking how I wanted to be able to do the things she could do when I got older. So here I am," Edison reveals.

"So, one way or the other, Grandma is the sixth member of our team," Contessa announces. "Do you remember how she always joined in on just about any tech game just to be able to spend time with us?"

"Yea, I remember how she would play Pokémon Go and Hay Day for hours just to challenge us. She was so consumed by the games that Grandpa and Dad thought she needed an intervention," Hannah recalls giving them all a good laugh.

"There, it has been sent. It should be at DNN by now, so let's see how long it takes good old Coyote to make breaking news with this one," Edison says sitting back in his chair with his hands behind his head.

"Let's have a drink and take a break to see if our efforts bear fruit," Thomas Henry suggests.

The team no sooner returns with their drinks than an event of news media proportions occurs. Rowdy King is in the midst of her news segment when Coyote Blitzer bursts onto the stage to commandeer the broadcast.

"What the Hell is going on?" Rowdy demands.

"I have a critical breaking story," Coyote announces.

"Then give it to me," Rowdy insists, "This is my news segment, so give me the story."

Ignoring Rowdy's dictates, Coyote stands his ground and begins to report. "I have just learned via what I will call an anonymous source."

"Get the hell off my set Coyote, if it is breaking news, it is mine to report," Rowdy shouts while attempting to push Coyote off the set.

"Go to commercial," demands the producer as the screen changes to a commercial for the newest sexual enhancement pill for men and women. The networks know that no matter the catastrophe, sex sells.

"What the frick is going on?" Noah snaps. "Were trying to inform the public about a calamity of unbelievable proportions, and the flipping news anchors want to fight about who gets the credit."

"Well at least we can enjoy the commercial," Thomas says tongue in cheek as a man and woman demonstrate the latest in sexual liberation.

The two minutes interrupting the announcement seems like an eternity. Finally, the screen is back at DNN and the only person on the screen is Coyote Blitzer. Rowdy King is not far away because you can still hear her protesting in the distance.

"We apologize for the delay of this very important breaking news. Remember, you heard it first here on DNN, the first in news" Coyote begins.

"Seriously dumb shit, you're sitting on news vital to the safety of millions of people, and you're still worried about getting and giving credit. Get on with it!" Edison shouts at the screen.

"We have it by an anonymous but highly credible source that the Yellowstone Caldera is in full melt down. This means the substructure temperatures have broken through the thermo layer previously protecting the surface from searing heat and have reached temperatures which turn rock into lava at critical points around the perimeter of the caldera. The exact reach of this inferno is difficult to predict, but it could be hundreds-of-miles. Our source is calling for all people living in Wyoming, Montana, Idaho, northeast Utah, and northwest Colorado to evacuate for safety purposes. Since Rowdy is not with us at the moment, let me show you the map. Everyone living inside the dark line needs to evacuate now!" Coyote declares.

"Our source did not quote the Bible, but did say this event could level the mountains and fill the valleys in Yellowstone. As a biblical reference, we turn to Luke 3:5 "Every valley shall be filled in, and every mountain and hill made low. The crooked ways shall be made straight and the rough ways smooth." Our source could not predict how much molten lava would flow out of Yellowstone to neighboring regions, but did suggest the flow could be significant and the heat index disastrous and fatal for anyone who does not heed this warning. Furthermore, expect ground fires to breakout anywhere within a several hundred-mile radius of the Yellowstone Caldera."

"Great job Edison, your message not only got through, but it protected our identity," Hannah commends.

"Oh, I didn't protect our identity," Edison reveals, "Coyote protected our identity, but I was able to protect our location. I felt if we wanted this warning reported, we needed to stand behind the message, so I signed off on it."

"Imagine that," Contessa says, "Who would have guessed that Coyote Blitzer would protect our identity. Perhaps, we are beginning to turn the tide on our battle to save the planet."

"I wouldn't get too excited Contessa," warns Noah, "We are still in hiding, and we have a hostile government ready to lock us up if they ever find us."

"How can this be Noah, as awful as it is, we have been proven right. Our actions have saved millions of lives. Surely the government must back off now," Contessa argues.

"We are a threat to the authority and power of the government as well as those who control the political system," Thomas reminds Contessa. "Until those in power come to their senses, or there is a power shift, we will remain in exile."

Six-hundred-ninety-one-miles to the southeast in Nashville, Tennessee, the provisional capital of the United States, the threat to the five scientists hiding in Ames is very real.

"Goddammit Mr. President, I know our fugitive scientists are responsible for the most recent warning. They are calling for people to evacuate three full states and part of two others. Who the hell do these rogues think they are, doing an end run around protocol?" Chief of Staff Peet says to the president.

"I am not pleased with Coyote Blitzer, but he claims the breaking news came from an anonymous source. Can we be so sure our outlaw scientists are still functioning and responsible?" the president wonders.

"Where the hell else would it have come from Mr. President? And, Coyote Blitzer needs to meet the same fate as Christine Mathews. I can get the President of DNN on the line for you Mr. President. You should have Coyote's head on a platter," Peet tells the president with a hint of pleasure in such an execution.

"No, we cannot do that Peet, Coyote's father Wolfe served the Democratic Party far too well to do that to his son. If you recall, Wolfe mastered the art of coming across objectively while delivering powerful subliminal messages to his viewers. Send someone to DNN to have a talk with young Blitzer. Let him know this was strike one, and there will be no strike two," the president orders. "Also, Peet, get our communication people working on taking credit for this announcement. I do not need people thinking we were asleep at the wheel again."

"Brilliant idea Mr. President, I will have them on it right away. As for Coyote Blitzer, I'll do as you order, but I think your loyalty to his father is misplaced. Coyote did this of his own free will knowing full well what happened to Christine Mathews. I do not trust young Blitzer," Peet conveys to the president.

"How is it we missed the Mid-Atlantic Ridge Disaster and now Yellowstone?" the President asks Peet.

"We're spread too thin Mr. President, there is only so much money and resources to go around. Besides, your donors want you to focus on protecting their vital foreign interests which requires a huge military investment. Science and the environment have taken a back seat for the past several decades. The wealthy contend they can protect and take care of themselves when it comes to environmental concerns. No one has given a shit about the common people for a half century, and frankly they still don't. Your constituency is the all-mighty dollar," Peet reminds the president.

"Well, our lack of concern for the environment and science sure helped my constituency on the east coast recently," the president offers sarcastically.

"Listen Mr. President, regardless the situation, it still comes down to maintaining control and power. Despite all the financial and material losses on the east eoast, your constituency still control power with their pocketbook, and as long as you act in their best interest, they will keep you in power," Peet declares steering the president toward indifference and self-interest.

"So, you think we're doing well?" the president asks.

"Look Mr. President, we are in control. Your declaration of martial law secures stability across this nation. You are doing what is necessary to hold this nation together at a very challenging time," Peet says slapping his boss on the back.

"Yea, we are holding it together alright with armed troops in every city. I never thought such a thing would ever happen, let alone on my watch. Go take care of business Peet, I need to rest," the president commands as Peet exits the room and the president lays down on the couch in his make shift office.

Back in Ames, the fugitive scientists are at work monitoring all of their other concerns. Convinced that Devolution is a reality, they have much work to do in finding answers to the rapidly developing situations around the globe.

Dr. Abraham and Dr. Jude are working as a team to address the concern of new and gigantic predators that are threatening to spread into urban areas and jeopardize entire populations. Noah and Edison are developing a plan to contain and control these predators. The containment aspect of their work is based on ensuring these monsters have plenty to eat. It is a fact that when predatory animals have plenty to eat, they will not seek out unnatural sources of food. They will stay within the territory where they can readily find food. It is only when food becomes scarce that predatory animals extend their territory into human populations. Their plan is to produce a food source which when eaten by a predator releases a hormone that renders the predator sterile and unable to produce offspring. If this is done incrementally, a controlled propagation of the predator will be achieved. This is a difficult thing to do while in exile, but with their communication capabilities, they can still collaborate with colleagues at their respective universities as long as their colleagues remain discrete and loyal. While Edison is certain their communication links are untraceable, he would hate for a disloyal colleague to alert the authorities. For this reason, they are highly selective with whom they work. The fact is no one other than Dr. Henry possesses the knowledge and talent of his two cousins to find solutions for the challenges they face. However, their colleagues at the remote locations have access to the labs so important to testing their ideas. With little else to divert their attention, Noah and Edison have established a common schedule for working and sleeping which allows one of them to be working 24-7.

———— >◆< ————

Dr. Henry focuses on the Reptilian Corollary believing somewhere in this phenomenon is the answer to containing what could become the unleashing of monsters upon the earth. With the help of Dr. Jude, he has hopefully established a link with his team in the Gobi Desert. It is time to test this uplink and get the latest dinosaur news.

The communication tent in the Gobi Desert is silent, so Dr. Henry leaves a coded message to contact him which only Reza will understand. Reza is as diligent, trustworthy, and loyal assistant as you will ever find. Thomas knows if the uplink is successful, he will hear from Reza soon.

Before he can get up for a cup of coffee, the light on the communication device turns green. It is Reza, and Thomas quickly picks up the phone.

"Reza, this is Dr. Henry, it has been too long, but circumstances here require we be prompt and discrete in our conversation. Please tell all quickly."

"Dr. Henry, I have wanted to speak with you for many days now."

Thomas can sense the excitement in Reza's voice. "The first egg hatched doctor! It was an Oviraptor about the size of a small bird."

"What do you mean was Reza?" Thomas asks urgently.

"It lived about ten hours and then died. We had nothing to feed it. We kept it in a box and tried to nurture it with a fluid, but we had no idea what to use. I am so sorry Dr. Henry," Reza explains apologetically.

"Reza, don't be sorry. My God, this was the first birth of an Oviraptor in millions of years. This is astounding, mysterious, and a bit frightening at the same time. What is the condition of the other eggs?" Thomas asks anxious to know more.

"They are all progressing along the same lines as the first and if they continue, they should hatch in less than two weeks. What do we do Dr. Henry?" Reza pleads for help.

"Listen carefully Reza, if this is occurring in a controlled setting, we have no idea the full extent this may be occurring in nature. We are observing the impact of climate change around the globe, and we are discovering the emergence of extinct mammals and reptiles, as well as a pattern of immense growth. We have no way of knowing how fast this will progress, but we are working around the clock to find a way to contain and control what is happening," Thomas tells his trusted assistant.

"Dr. Henry, there is one other thing," Reza seems anxious to share with Thomas.

"What is it Reza, we must be quick," Dr. Henry urges.

"The other day we uncovered several new nests at Flaming Cliffs. We have reason to believe they may include Citipati, Sinosauropteryx, and velociraptor eggs," Reza reveals.

"Have these been excavated? Do you have them at camp?" Dr. Henry pointedly asks his assistant.

"No, but we are near extraction. What do you want me to do doctor?" Reza pleads in clear desperation about what direction he should take.

"You cannot stay there Reza. I want you to follow these exact directions. Get the team together now. Assign a group to pack everything including the remaining eggs for transport. While one group is packing, I want you to send another group to Flaming Cliffs and extract as many eggs from these nests as can be accomplished in no more than a half day. Get everything packed and get to the Chinggis Khaan International Airport in Ulaanbaater. At the airport, ask for Oyuuachimeg, he is our friend and the owner-operator of a transport plane. He will ask no questions. Tell him you need to get to Virginia Tech University in Blacksburg, Virginia immediately upon my directions. That is all he will need, and he will do the rest," Thomas dictates.

"Okay Doctor, I think we can be at the airport by late tomorrow afternoon. Is there anything else?" Reza asks.

"Under no circumstances let anyone know your cargo. Also, Reza, the body of the dead Oviraptor is to be packed and brought with you," Thomas directs.

"But Doctor, it is already starting to decay and smells," Reza says hoping Thomas will rescind his command.

"We need that body Reza, find a way to make it happen," Thomas says in no uncertain terms. "Best of luck Reza!" with that the transmission goes dead.

Dr. Henry immediately asks Dr. Abraham and Dr. Jude to join him for a conversation about what he just learned. The three of them agree this development could be the missing link in their effort to contain and control the spread of aggressive and dangerous species around the globe.

Across the room, Dr. Rae has accelerated her efforts to establish a global link for monitoring soil, water, and air. Because of her access to many earth probes as well as satellites, she is able to see things which no one else understands because they will not accept the Theory of Devolution. So much of her Theory of Devolution is based upon the microscopic and atomic level of soil, water, and air composition. What she has witnessed and believes is happening is only recognized by her closest assistants who over the past couple years have come to understand and believe what she is theorizing.

Dr. Rae has gone silent with her assistants for security purposes. She could try to pull a ruse and contact them as if she were far away, but Dr. Jude feels such an effort is too risky. Hannah must continue to monitor and do her work in isolation without outside help.

Dr. Hannah Rae discovers that Devolution in the soil is increasing at an alarming rate. The scenario of seeds being rejected by the soil is still not happening, but significant yield reduction is occurring. She knows the majority of large family farms and corporate farms will increase the use of chemical and putrid fertilizer combined with advanced GMO seeds. Such a desperate strategy motivated by economics with no concern for land husbandry will accelerate Devolution. It is just a matter of time and the land will be in full rebellion. Global famine is on the horizon if farmers do not listen to her warnings or recognize the consequence of their actions. The fate of water and air is not far behind with such irresponsible and short sightedness by people who have taken control of the Earth.

"Could I get everyone's attention for a few minutes?" Hannah requests of her cousins.

"Absolutely, what's up Hannah?" Contessa responds, "Hey guys, come over here for a minute."

As everyone gathers, Hannah struggles to start, "As you know, my Theory of Devolution has been called everything from Voodoo to quackery by most of the scientific world, and those who acknowledge its possibility have little standing in the scientific community."

"You're wrong on one thing Hannah," Dr. Abraham interrupts, "Everyone here as well as your sister and other cousins are all in on your Theory. We believe it is not only true, we believe it is happening."

"I am grateful for that Noah, but my challenge is convincing the world that Devolution threatens to destroy the Earth unless something drastic is done, and done now," Hannah says adjusting her glasses and wiping her forehead.

"You're wrong on that also Hannah," her brother Thomas Henry soberly adds, "We are all in this together. I think I speak for our entire family; Devolution is real and it is a holistic phenomenon occurring at all levels all around the globe. Devolution is impacting every aspect of the Earth and placing human survival in the balance. It is our challenge to convince the world, and convince them we must!"

"Thank you, but here is the crux of the challenge. When it comes to the soil, water, and air, nobody gets too excited. Well, I now believe a massive assault on the soil is imminent, which will result in food shortages leading to global famine. Such a prediction will go unheeded. It won't even make breaking news. Millions of people are going to die of starvation and no one is listening. I don't know what to do," Dr. Rae buries her head in her hands giving a hopeless sigh.

"Here is what we do guys. We remember Kennedy, Ainsley, and Gemma are out there preparing to sound the alarm," Dr. Jude reminds everyone. "It is easy to feel isolated here in this living tomb, but we must remember that there are seven other brothers, sisters, and cousins out there working to carry out our plan. We have every reason to be hopeful."

"Eddie is right on target," Contessa adds, "We soon won't need breaking news; we will be breaking news! I am confident that Kennedy, Ainsley, and Gemma are well on their way to putting together a delivery system for our message which cannot and will not be ignored. We need to get the message to them, and they will take it from there."

"You're right everyone, we need to put together information for Kennedy, Ainsley, and Gemma, and they will package it for consumption in a way that will turn the tide in humanities favor," Hannah recognizes. "Thank you!"

CHAPTER 29

THE REVELATION

Ⓗ IGH ATOP MT. PILATUS, THE hour has arrived for the revelation
which Senator Joseph, Stella, and Dr. Isabelle hope will unite the
world religions in a common cause to save the planet. Dr. Isabelle has
inspected the powerful telescope installed at the peak of Mt. Pilatus and
believes it is ready to do the job of peering into the far regions of the
universe. She did not have time to look, but she did test the mobility of
the telescope to do as she commands from inside the conference room
where the religious leaders will sit awaiting her revelation.

In Greek Mythology, after the Titan's lost the war between Zeus
and the Gods, Atlas was forced to hold up the Heaven's. The place
where Atlas stood to perform his task was what the ancient Greeks
considered the westernmost end of the world. The ocean near him was
called the Atlantic meaning the "Sea of Atlas" in his honor.

Like Atlas, Ivey resolves to bear the weight of responsibility with
determination and perseverance. She knows her presentation will make
all the difference.

As the distinguished guests enter the conference room, they discover
no table assignments. Senator Joseph, Stella, and Ivey decided that the
best seating arrangement is one chosen by the delegates themselves.
So, as the guests entered the room, they are given their table placard to
display wherever they choose to sit. The senator, his sister, and cousin
know this organizational strategy is risky, but they feel any attempt to
assign seats will give rise to unnecessary conflict. As they stand at the
door, welcoming each person with all the dignity and grace accorded

their esteemed position in the religious world, they are met with smiles reflecting individuals who know and understand the sincerity of their efforts.

In providing suitable accommodations, each delegate's room has an incredible view of the Swiss Alps from an eagle like perch. Each room is carefully prepared to compliment the sacred nature of the occupant's religion. Even the atheists have rooms of a totally secular nature. The dining accommodations provide each guest with eating options suitable to their religious and cultural preference. All the preparations reflect the highest consideration and respect for each delegate and their religious beliefs. This is noted and appreciated by all the delegates.

And so, these religious icons file into the room with all the civility and reverence expected of men and women of their stature. At each table they find glasses, pitchers of water, and bowls of fresh delicious fruit and nuts. Sitting on their chairs are the devices which enable them to instantaneously translate all languages into their native language. These marvels of technology are easily programmed through a voice command for the guests preferred language.

At the front of the room are 30 foot-tall-floor to ceiling windows providing an incredible view of the Alps as the sun begins its descent over the mountains. As these leaders take their seats in quiet conversation, a group of seven Golden Eagles, like some omen of good will, provide a demonstration of magnificent flight just outside the windows. After five minutes, these eagles depart as if on cue and the entire room responds with polite applause.

Stella is ready to offer the welcome, and Senator Joseph is next providing a state of the world, after which the show belongs to Dr. Isabelle. Off to the side of the large windows stands a podium and all along the expanse of windows at the top is a screen measuring 60 feet wide by 30 feet tall. If all goes as planned, this gathering of religious leaders will not only witness a glorious display of the Universe, but what Ivey Isabelle calls the "Hand of God".

No program is provided the gathering, because this moment is not about any person, it is about a revelation. No mention has been made regarding what Ivey called the Hand of God because there is no reason to risk offending any one of these religious leaders.

As the last of the delegates arrive and find their seats, Ambassador DiCaprio leans over and tells Stella she will be amazing. Zach likewise gives Stella a wink and a smile. There is no touching or any behavior which might be misconstrued as inappropriate by anyone in this magnificent gathering of Holy people. Looking at his cousin, Senator Joseph quietly says, "Okay Stella, it's show time!"

The phrase "It's show time" has long been a family saying. It comes from years ago when Great-Grandpa Maske admired Pistol Pete Maravich, a phenomenal shooting guard for LSU and later in the NBA. Pistol Pete was once asked what he thought about before a big game? Pete answered, "It's show time!" So, the family borrowed from Pistol Pete not only the saying, but the attitude which comes with it.

Stepping to the podium decked out in a dark blue floor length dress with her long flowing brunette hair, Stella in all her nervousness smiles. The room spontaneously responds with a polite and genuine applause of affection. In just two days, the delegates have been gathering, Stella has displayed a grace which resonated with each religious leader. She knows each religion inside and out, and she conducts herself accordingly in the presence of each leader. Regardless the leader, they could not help but be overwhelmed by Stella's simple charm and respectful manner.

"Good evening, it is such a pleasure to be in the presence of so many leaders of faith!" Stella opens. Out of courtesy, she had even approached the atheist delegates to see if referring to them as leaders of faith would be acceptable. They concurred that while their faith is of a different nature; their convictions were a matter of faith.

"This must be the greatest assemblage of interfaith leadership in the history of the world. I am overwhelmed at your willingness to attend this conference. Your recognition of humanities predicament, and willingness to cast aside your differences, is the first step in what I pray will be a united effort to save humanity," Stella continues.

"This planet is our home, not just a segment of it, but all of it. The globe is interconnected in every possible manner. In this year of 2039, what occurs on one side of the globe has ramifications for the other side. Our precious environment provides the sustenance which supports all human life regardless of differences. We have not been very good caretakers of the blessings of such a miraculous home. There is nothing to be gained by laying blame, and there is no redemption in struggling against one another."

"So, this evening we begin by offering you an experience which we believe and hope will be life altering for you and more importantly all of mankind. Welcome and thank you for attending," Stella concludes.

There is no doubt in the entire room that Stella spoke from the heart. She had won them over personally, and now she set the stage for the things to come.

As Stella steps away from the podium, Senator Jack Joseph steps to the microphone. He is not greeted with the same courtesy as Stella, but he is recognized as a political leader of the United States. This does not put him in a bad light, but it does not generate the kind of response offered Stella.

"Your eminences, I stand before you a humble man of no station but citizen of the Earth. My purpose is to intentionally set a tone of seriousness because as you know, we live in the most serious and dangerous of times," Jack begins knowing his introduction is not needed.

"I recall being a young lad of 12 but 23 years ago. My parents, grandfather, grandmother, uncles, and aunts, taught our family the critical importance of being good stewards of the Earth. I recall my grandfather running for U.S. Congress with my father as his campaign manager, touting the importance of taking care of the environment. Just over a quarter of a century ago, they warned about the dangers of global warming and so many other abuses which are endangering our air, water, soil, and so many other things critical to the sanctity of life. I remember my grandfather talking about the Great Himalayan Glacier Basin and the geo-political ramifications of water shortage in Asia, India, and the Middle East. Most people especially politicians felt too removed to care," Jack offers somberly.

"Over the past quarter century, we have allowed the Earth to fall victim to many abuses. It is not like the signs have not been everywhere. Weather patterns have led to increased violent storm activity. The warming planet has led to food shortages, water shortages, and disease. As the human condition deteriorates, nations are not looking for ways to work together to solve problems, but rather increase hostilities which adds to human misery. In the last few years, natural disasters have wrecked havoc on the planet in unimaginable ways. Most recently, the activity along the 10,000-mile Mid-Atlantic Ridge devastated the east coast of North and South America as well as the west Coast of Portugal and Africa. Volcanic eruptions in Iceland are spewing huge ash clouds across northern Europe blocking out the Sun and threatening a long cold winter. Now, as we speak, the Yellowstone Caldera is actually liquefying and laying waste to hundreds of millions of acres in the Rocky Mountains of the United States," Jack pauses to allow his comments to resonate.

"Here is the biggest tragedy of it all, billions, not millions, but billions of people have perished for one reason or another because we have failed at our one crucial task of taking care of this planet. Every day, hundreds of thousands of people of every nation and faith die because of famine, disease, dehydration, natural disasters, and war. In the last nine years alone, 3.5 billion people have died because of the previously mentioned reasons. In 2016, the total population of the world was approximately 7 billion people. In 2030, the total population of the world was approximately 9.5 billion people. In 2039, the total population of the world is approximately 6 billion people," Jack again pauses to allow time for contemplation.

"Now let me share one other bit of information regarding those who have perished. Other than the recent natural disaster along the East Coast of the United States, nearly 100 percent of those who perished due to famine, disease, dehydration, natural disasters, and war are of the poor and middle class. In fact, should anyone of the upper class perish, it is due to them being in the wrong place at the wrong time during a natural disaster. Why is this important? It is important my friends because the people of the upper class do not care as long as they and their small empires remain safe. The upper class of all nations and societies have buttressed themselves in fortifications safe from the torrent of afflictions which currently plague the Earth," Jack solemnly reveals.

"I am not sure you are aware, but Stella is my cousin and Dr. Isabelle is my sister. We believe humanity may be entering the end of days. It is the most awful of prospects. We not only need your help, but we believe you as leaders of faith are a critical part of the solution. We are hoping after you witness what Dr. Isabelle has to offer, we may find a unity of purpose. Thank you!" Jack concludes.

As Jack departs the podium the room is silent and the huge curtain begins to descend across the windows. Ivey Isabelle steps to the podium in a gray blue floor length dress very similar to Stella's. There is a clear resemblance between the two young women, who are cousins. Ivey has her hair pulled back in a pony tail. She is wearing a broach which symbolizes peace and love. Behind her smile, she is wearing the weight of her mission. She is hoping all goes well with no technological glitches. However, in the event something happens, she possesses an electronic copy of her "Hand of God" presentation used during the family conference in Ames.

"Good evening, I am Dr. Ivey Isabelle and I am an Astrophysicist with a doctorate from Harvard University, Cambridge, Massachusetts, United States of America. For the past four years, I have been peering at the Universe from over 18,500 feet at the Atacama Observatory in the Atacama Desert in Chile as an employee of the University of Tokyo.

My job involves looking as far into space as possible in search of the outer regions of the Universe. As a result of my job, I see some absolutely amazing things of beauty and wonder. Several weeks ago, I came across something very startling; something which caused me great consternation. I could not believe my eyes. I actually became grievously ill and found it difficult to sleep. Each night, I returned to my telescope, and each night I encountered the phenomenon of my disbelief and despair. Each night it was there," Ivey pauses as everyone sits in complete silence.

"Just over a week ago, I was part of a family conference in Ames, Iowa with my brother Jack, my sister Ainsley Annabelle, and my cousins to discuss the current state of the Earth and determine what we individually and collectively can do to save the planet. I am fortunate to belong to a very illustrious group of people all of whom possess incredible knowledge and talent. At that conference, I presented what I believe you will see. It is from that presentation that my family identified the conference you are attending as a top priority if there is to be any hope for the human race," Ivey pauses again.

"What I am going to do is take you on a little journey into the cosmos. I am going to, if the technology does not fail, show you in real time things that very few people have ever seen other than in pictures. After I have acquainted you to the vast infiniteness of space, I will take you to the place of which I have spoken. So, let's get going. Would someone please turn off the lights? Do not be startled, this journey is best accomplished in darkness. I believe there are very soft lights at your table if it makes you more comfortable. These table lights are so soft they will not impede the presentation. Now the lights," Ivey directs as she hits a switch and the entire thirty-by-sixty-foot screen comes alive.

"The telescope I am using is mounted at the peak of this very mountain upon which we sit. What you are looking at is Saturn. What a beautiful sight and we are getting a gorgeous look at its rings. Saturn has 60 moons and it takes Saturn 30 Earth years to orbit the sun. Saturn is 760 million miles from Earth at the nearest point and just over a billion-miles from Earth at the farthest point. Traveling at the speed of light, it would take you just over an hour to get from Earth to Saturn."

"As we move through the Milky Way, let's take a look at the supernova remnant known as Simeas 147 or the Flaming Star nebula. This supernova is 3,000 light years from Earth and resulted from an exploding star 30,000 years ago. The brilliant red design is the result of hydrogen gas. This nebula itself is 150 light years across, just think of the immensity?" Ivey challenges.

"Let's now jump to what scientists call NGC 2174 or the Monkey Head Nebula located six-thousand-four-hundred-light-years from Earth. Keep in mind a light year is the distance that light travels at 100,086 miles per second in one year. Examine the beauty of this nebula loaded with colors and character. If you were traveling at the speed of light, you could arrive at this nebula in 6,400 hundred years," Ivey continues to emphasize time and distance.

"Now hold on, we are going to jump to the outer regions of the Milky Way. This brilliant light show represents billions of stars in our galaxy? We are still relatively close to Earth at 25,000 light years away. So, while we could travel to Saturn in just over an hour at the speed of light, it would take us 25,000 years to reach the edge of the Milky Way Galaxy. So, the edge of the galaxy is actually an unimaginable distance," Ivey takes a moment to allow those gathered to process this information.

"We are now viewing The Rho Ophiuchus Cloud Complex, one of the most beautiful sections of the night sky in the Milky Way Galaxy. Just look at the incredible blues, reds, greens and yellows. The complex features of this stunning nebulae are huge clouds of interstellar gas and dust. The red areas you see are created by light emitted from hydrogen gas. The sensational blue reflection nebula surrounds the Rho Ophiuchi triple star which are the three very bright spots in this complex," Ivey is masterful in her presentation always giving the audience time to take in what are very common sights to her.

Now let's travel outside the Milky Way to the Spiral Galaxy known to scientists as M83 or the Southern Pinwheel which lies 15 million light years from Earth in the constellation Hydra," before Ivey can say more, the room which has been silent to this point emits the sound of wonder. Continuing, Ivey adds, "The bright center of this galaxy is larger than the entire Milky Way." As these religious leaders take in this gigantic pinwheel of reds, pinks, purples all spinning against the background of dark space you can hear the quiet chatter of amazed minds.

"I only have a couple more places to show you before we arrive at our destination," Ivey shares knowing how important it is to keep an audience informed of what to expect.

"We are now jumping 130 million light years into space to the constellation Canis Major. Here are two galaxies NGC 2207 and IC 2163 interplaying for the same place in space. This celestial dance has been going on for eons, and at some point, the gravitational force of both galaxies will cause them to merge. The heat involved in these beautiful and yet violent events rises into the millions of degrees Fahrenheit," Ivey shares. "The contradiction we see in space is the incredible beauty which results from the most violent conditions."

"We are now looking into very deep space at a massive galaxy cluster called Abell 2744. This view is not impressive for its beauty but rather the fact we are looking at some of the youngest galaxies in the Universe. Every single light regardless the size represents a young or newly forming galaxy," Ivey assures her audience.

"Well enough for the field trip, let's get to the destination," Ivey declares.

"A quarter century ago, the long defunct Hubble Space Telescope managed to photograph a patch of sky called the eXtreme Deep Field or XDF. We are not talking about something millions of light years away, but 13.2 billion light years into a Universe thought to be about 13.7 billion years old," Ivey reveals.

"In the past 25 years, telescopic technology has made incredible advances to the point that we tonight are able to see real time into space in a way never accomplished in human history. For the past four-years, I have been peering into deep space searching the edge of the Universe. Over the past four-years, I have seen and discovered many phenomena which offer insight and understanding. However, as I mentioned at the beginning of my presentation, I experienced something a while back which I consider life altering," Ivey leads into the anticipated revelation. "Here we go!"

The screen displays the faint light of the deepest regions of the Universe as the telescope outside adjusts to the directions it is given. Then, it begins to appear. Ivey is expecting what she calls the "Hand of God", but the fact is, God is offering more than a hand.

As the telescope struggles to give focus to such a far distance, the image on the screen begins to take the shape of a face with an outstretched arm and hand. The audience is absolutely silent, and Ivey is spellbound. This is looking to be far more than she had anticipated. The image is not exactly clear, but it is without a doubt a face with an outstretched arm and a hand held up with the palm indicating "stop".

"My God, my most Holy God," a voice cries out from the religious dignitaries in the room.

"Is this real?" calls out another, "Or is this some hoax being perpetuated upon us."

"This is not a hoax, this is real, but it is not what I expected," Ivey announces, "I saw what I called the "Hand of God", I did not see God."

"It is God! But what is he trying to tell us?" another member of the audience exclaims.

At about this time, a technician arrives in the room and immediately goes to the podium to speak with Dr. Isabelle. "Turn up the volume," he says, "The image has a voice."

With these directions, Ivey adjusts the volume on the equipment to more clearly pick up what is usually the static sound of space. She waits but hears nothing. Then it comes, it is nothing like anyone has heard before, but the translation equipment is able to convert it to the native language of all in attendance.

"Please save the Earth, let love and peace guide you," is the message repeated over and over.

Every person in the conference room drops from their chair to their knees. With their heads bowed they listen to the refrain over and over. You could hear a pin drop as every religious leader prays in their own way to the revelation before them. Then, the voice goes silent and the image fades from the screen.

Ivey asks for the house lights to be gradually brought up. As she looks out amongst the gathering, she sees faces torn by an experience only proclaimed by a handful of men in the history of the world. Now, she stands before an assemblage shaken to the core by a common revelation regardless the religion. No one doubted they had just been in the presence of God, and charged with the task of saving the Earth.

As the lights arrive at full illumination, Ivey, Jack, Stella, and the others are overwhelmed by the sight. All of the dignitaries left their seats and are circulating through the room hugging and blessing each other. All the barriers which once divided them collapsed, and a common bond emerged. Ivey, Jack, and Stella are delighted and yet overwhelmed at what just occurred.

After a half hour in which no one noticed the passage of time, the dignitaries begin to return to their seats each engulfed in the continence of love and peace.

Stepping to the microphone, Stella suggests adjournment and a return at 10:00 a.m. in the morning to talk. To her amazement, the Grand Ayatollah stands to address what he now calls his brothers and sisters.

"We are all blessed," he begins. "Allah has chosen us, not one person or one religion, but us as a collective of leaders to do his will. I know that each person here is overwhelmed to the core by this most Holy experience. I pray tomorrow we all arrive back here to do God's work as asked."

Before Stella gives closure, the Greek Patriarch of Jerusalem Theophilos V stands to thank Stella, Jack, Ivey and the others for their divine intervention in bringing about this revelation. He then suggests that when they convene tomorrow that Stella, moderate their conversation. His suggestion is met with overwhelming approval.

"Thank you for your confidence, and I will strive to serve you as God wills. Now I suggest we adjourn until tomorrow, and may God go with you!" Stella offers as a benediction.

CHAPTER 30

WALKING THE TALK

"DR. KAE, I TRULY URGE you to not take part in the experimental use of our vapor here in Atlanta. What if we discover harmful effects to humans? We cannot afford to lose your leadership, knowledge, and talent in our fight against the winged infidel from hell," Dr. Rooh protests. Olivia Kae is determined to place herself front and center with the experimental use of the vapor by driving behind one of the maintenance trucks spaying the city.

"Look Dr. Rooh, we are about to use this vapor on the entire city of Atlanta based on our test results and belief that it is totally harmless to humans. How do you think it will look if the head of the research and development team is hesitant to be part of this experiment?" Olivia counters.

"Then let me or any other research assistant take your place. You are irreplaceable in this fight, and we would be set back by years if we lost your contributions," Dr. Rooh implores.

"First off Dr. Rooh, your assessment is totally in error. I have worked with all of you, and I believe you are highly capable of picking up the pieces and moving forward in a successful manner should this experiment negatively impact my health and ability to function. But the fact-of-the-matter is, I have every confidence this will work, or I would not have urged the leadership of this state and city to go through with this experiment. They have put their political and personal lives on the line because I believe we have the solution to neutering the mosquito. I must take the lead!" Dr. Kae pronounces in defiance of any protest.

"Then I must join you Dr. Kae. If you are so confident, you surely won't protest or block my involvement at your side," Dr. Rooh states.

"I guess you leave me no choice, welcome aboard Dr. Rooh," Dr. Kae relents to Dr. Rooh's determination. "However, if me and my top assistant are going to stand front and center during the application of our vapor to this city, we need to put everything in order which would allow our team to pick up and move on should something go wrong."

"Ha, so you admit that something could go wrong," says Dr. Rooh.

"Seriously Dr. Rooh, you know that no great endeavor is ever taken without some risk. But in this case, we have done our due diligence. We have tested this vapor on human subjects as well as animals with no adverse effects. So now, thanks to the courage of some great leaders, we are going to test it on a city of 750,000 people. How does that make you feel?" Dr. Kae retorts.

"May God be with us," Dr. Rooh solemnly responds.

"Dr. Kae, the phone is for you," says one of her other assistants.

"Dr. Kae, this is Mayor Char King."

"Mayor King, are we ready to put Operation Good-bye Mosquito" into action?" Dr. Kae asks.

"I am calling to wish you the very best. We will begin fogging the city at dusk. I have asked all residents of the city to remain inside with their doors and windows closed. The maintenance people fogging the city will be wearing Hazmat suits. I wish you would agree to do so also," the mayor urges.

"I can't do that mayor. This is the boldest experiment ever taken with such a large population, and I must instill confidence by exposing myself to the fog and vapor. I would like you to know that my assistant Dr. Rooh is going to join me," Olivia tells the mayor.

"What if something goes wrong Dr. Kae, we cannot afford to lose your brilliant mind and leadership in our fight against this insidious demonic creature," Mayor King says desperately hoping Dr. Kae will exercise some precaution.

"Mayor King, if my mind is so brilliant, then we will not fail. If my leadership is so important, then I must lead now by my actions," Dr. Kae responds. "Dr. Rooh and I will be at the Central Atlanta maintenance building an hour before dusk."

"God be with you Dr. Kae, I will be praying," the mayor assures her as she hangs up the phone.

"God be with us all," Dr. Kae says silently to herself.

Back in their sanctuary deep in the basement of the old library on the Iowa State University Campus, Dr. Hannah Rae receives a message which says DNN will be airing breaking news at six o'clock central time. It is five-fifty-five, and Hannah doesn't want to miss what might be going on. Turning on the bunker televisions, she announces to the others that DNN is flashing Breaking News.

"Good evening, this is Anus Reno filling in for Rowdy King who is on paid leave. This is Breaking News from DNN first in the news business. We have just learned from the office of Georgia Governor John Hickenlooper Jr. that the city of Atlanta will be fogging the city for Mosquitoes at dusk this evening. The governor along with Atlanta Mayor Char King have approved a request by Dr. Olivia Kae with the recommendation of CDC Head, Dr. Masterson, to fog the city with a vapor created by Dr. Olivia Kae and her team of research and development experts at the CDC. The mayor's office is telling all residents of the city to close all doors and windows, as well as shut off all air conditioning and other units which pull outside air in. It is advised that residents adhere to this directive until midnight as a precaution while allowing the fog, containing the vapor, to settle," Anus reports.

"Let's now turn to our expert panel for a discussion about what is going on in Atlanta. We have assembled Amelia Bedelia Borcher, daughter of the famed CNN know-it-all Gloria Borcher, Dr. Stupta Gupta, son of the famed CNN medical expert Dr. Sanja Gupta, and Nerda Gergen, daughter of the famed CNN political contributor David Gergen. Let's start with you Amelia, what do you think of the action about to occur in Atlanta?" Anus asks.

"Look Anus, what we have here is a case of government overreach which could endanger the lives of thousands of Atlanta citizens. Evidently Governor Hickenlooper and Mayor King have little concern for their jobs. This is just a bad idea," says Amelia projecting a know-it-all persona reminiscent of her famous Mom.

"What do you think Stupta, and why would your parents give you such a name?" inquires Anus.

"First off, you are not in a good position to talk about first names. But let's consider what is going on. The mosquito is the most dangerous creature on Earth. It has the capability of transmitting a multitude of deadly diseases. The Earth is warming at an increasing rate, and the mosquito is growing bigger and more prevalent around the globe. If we do not find a way to control this evil beast of death, we are in real trouble. I am personally acquainted with Dr. Kae and her research, and let me tell you, she is the greatest hope for finding a way to control the mosquito. If she is recommending the use of a vapor, I would tend to believe it is safe. If I am right, Dr. Kae is putting herself front and center during this test," Stupta says offering an objective and insightful assessment.

"Thank you Stupta, I too heard that Dr. Kae is going to ride along with one of the maintenance crews fogging the city. If my source is correct, she and an assistant will not be wearing Hazmat suits like the maintenance workers. So, Nerda what is your assessment?" Anus asks.

"I think we should all sue our parents for our birth names. As for what is about to occur in Atlanta, I hope it works. Mosquitoes are becoming an increasingly deadly pest. In many areas including Atlanta, the resources of hospitals are stretched by those suffering from deadly diseases due to mosquito bites. If this works, we will be on the cusp of defeating the deadliest enemy to face the human race," Nerda adds.

"Anus, if I can add a bit more insight into what is going to occur in Atlanta. In my last conversation with Dr. Kae, she noted that the vapor has been tested as harmless to humans and animals. The vapor which will be added to the usual mosquito fog used to control mosquito larva is intended to alter a DNA gene in the mosquito which would render the mosquito and all subsequent larva from being capable of carrying disease. If I understand the situation, the vapor also softens the mosquito needle so it is incapable of penetrating human skin. As a bonus, another source of mine at the CDC suggested the vapor may very well have the same effect on ticks as it does mosquitoes. What I am saying is if this works, the world may soon become a much safer place for us all. It would be a good idea if we all pray for success in Atlanta today," Stupta reveals.

"Fantastic," exclaims Dr. Henry who happens to be Dr. Rae's twin. "What a great report other than the stupidity of Amelia Bedelia Borcher. That entire Borcher clan has their head up their ass."

Switching off the television set, Hannah offers her brother and cousins a high five. For once a report suggesting progress is being made in the fight to save humanity. "Let's all pray that things go well and Olivia remains safe," she adds at which the five join hands in silent hope that all goes well for Olivia and her team.

In Nashville, the reaction to the news from Atlanta is not so positive. Chief of Staff Peet must once again inform the president that things are spinning beyond his control. While they all would truly welcome a successful way to neuter the mosquito, the president does not appreciate being upstaged at any time on anything.

"Peet, get our communication people on this immediately. If this vapor is for real, I want the spin coming our way. I do not want anything said until we know the results, but if it is successful, I want our people prepared to release statements which suggest we knew and approved of this all along. Do you understand what I am saying Peet?" the president is clearly irritated that so many independent agents seem to be at work.

As the news is airing, Olivia and Dr. Rooh make their way from CDC Headquarters near Emory University to the maintenance building adjacent to the Public Safety Headquarters at 226 Peachtree Street SW not far from downtown Atlanta. They are traveling in a bright red self-driving 2036 Ford Mustang convertible along an eight-and-a-half-mile journey which will take them less than ten minutes.

As they pass the Carter Center and the Jimmy Carter Presidential Library and Museum, they recall those days long before their time when President Carter warned of the dangers of an energy crisis and used his executive power to lower the national speed limit to 55 miles an hour. They chuckle considering they are moving along at just over 85 miles an hour. They are pleased to find the roads vacant. This means the citizens of Atlanta listened to the warning of their governor and mayor. Further down the road, they pass signs indicating the location of the King Center and the Martin Luther King Jr. National Historical Site. Olivia points out that 71 years after the death of Martin Luther King Jr., his granddaughter is engaged in the fight to save humanity. As they zoom past the sky scrapers of downtown Atlanta, Dr. Kae and her assistant near their destination.

At the maintenance shed, they coordinated their plans with the two men who will be driving the truck they will follow. They will follow the maintenance truck spraying the Mechanicsville section of greater Atlanta with the top down at a distance of two blocks back. The purpose for the distance is to assure they don't get drenched by the fog and vapor. The driver assures them that at two blocks they will get full exposure. They will not be wearing any protective gear. The spraying is set to begin all across greater Atlanta at 8:00 p.m. and be completed by 9:00 p.m.

At the completion of the spraying, Dr. Kae and Dr. Rooh will report to the CDC Lab for 48 hours of observation. If any ill effects are going to occur, they will be detectable within this time frame. As for the mosquito, the time frame is ten to fourteen days if they allow the current larva to attain maturity. However, in the morning an expedition from the CDC research team will gather larva samples from various Atlanta locations. By examining the larva, the team will be able to determine if the vapor did indeed neutralize the DNA which allows the mosquito to carry and spread disease. The team will also search for tick specimens for the same purpose. By doing this, Dr. Kae and her team will be able to determine if the vapor successfully accomplished the desired result within a couple days.

It's hurry-up and wait, but if the result is as desired, the fog and vapor will be shipped around the world post-haste. It is a situation filled with apprehension, anticipation, and high hopes.

CHAPTER 31

THE GREATEST SHOW
ON EARTH

IN CHICAGO, KENNEDY, AINSLEY, GEMMA, and Ansel are working feverishly to put together a premier lineup for their Save the World Tour. The purpose of the lineup is to attract people by the droves. It is Kennedy, Ainsley, and Gemma's job to identify those who will donate their time and talent to take part in this extravaganza, and Ansel's job to promote the tour. With her organizational skills, Kennedy will make sure all arrangements are in place. Ainsley, as the top musical performer in the world will lead the star-studded lineup. Gemma will ensure that the medium is all about the message.

So far, Kennedy has enlisted the involvement of some of the world's greatest athletes. Sam Alexis Woods, the daughter of golf Hall of Famer Tiger Woods, and a world class golfer on the LPGA circuit will be present to electrify the audience with her magical golf antics around the green. She can put the golf ball in the cup as mysteriously as a magician pulls a rabbit from a hat.

Kennedy convinced former Olympic basketball players and NBA shooting stars Ryan Curry son of Steven Curry, Michael Jordon Jr. the grandson of Michael Jordon, Pariah Bird the grandson of Larry Bird, Shaq Miller son of Reggie Miller, Pistol Maravich grandson of Pete Maravich, and Kevin Durant Jr. son of Kevin Durant to forgo an NBA Season to be part of the "Greatest Show on Earth". On the tour, these NBA stars will display their basketball wizardry through demonstrations and competition.

In appealing to the gymnastic world, Kennedy lined up thoroughbred Olympic Gold Medalists Alyona Feldman, Great-Granddaughter of the famed Russian gymnast Larisa Latynina; Yuliya Petrov the Granddaughter of Russian star Svetlana Khorkina; Elena Conner the fifteen-year-old phenomenon and Granddaughter of Nadia Comaneci; Radka Odlozil the Granddaughter of the great Czechoslovakian gymnast Vera Caslavska, and Daniela Cummings the Granddaughter of Romanian Daniela Silivas. All of these gymnasts are going to devote an entire year to being part of this World Tour to save the planet.

Probably the most aggressive and challenging of Kennedy's pursuits is the Platform Diving Exhibition she plans to make a part of every tour stop. She has successfully obtained the best divers in the world to devote their time and talent to the World Tour. The diving lineup includes diving legend Greg Louganis's adopted son Darian Louganis; Alberto Marino the Great-Grandson of Italy's famed Klaus Dibias; Lucas Mitcham adopted son of Australia's celebrated diver Matthew Mitcham; China's renowned female diver Wu Minxia's daughter Lixue Minxia; Fu Leung the Granddaughter of China's illustrious Fu Mingxia; and Dierch Stein the Great-Granddaughter of Germany's fabled Ingrid Kramer.

Kennedy is just getting started; she has designs on obtaining the participation of the greatest power hitters in baseball; ball handlers and scorers in soccer; strong men and women in weight lifting; and those with lightning-fast reflexes in table tennis. What she didn't expect is the onslaught of talent from so many different sports that want to be a part of this World tour. Word of the tour is spreading at Mach speed, and everyone wants to be associated with this effort to save humanity.

"We are going to be able to put on a sporting exhibition which will attract the interest of thousands and saturate a three-day schedule with brilliant performances. This is going to be something to behold," Kennedy announces to Ainsley, Gemma, and Ansel with a big smile of satisfaction.

"How are you doing Ainsley?" Ansel inquires.

"I don't think you will be disappointed. I have lined up the finest musicians in the world representing a wide range of musical genre. We will wow spectators with rock and roll, country, hip-hop, the Blues, and even some classical," Ainsley reports.

"Let me tell you about the real coup when it comes to involvement. I have every single Beatles son or daughter on board for this challenge. Sean Lennon, Julian Lennon, Dhani Harrison, Zak Starkey, James McCartney, and Beatrice McCartney are coming together as a rock band to perform all of the Beatle's classics. Paul McCartney's other daughters are also on board with Mary volunteering to be the tours official photographer, Stella heading our fashion exhibit, and Heather coordinating the visual arts. This alone will draw thousands of fans to our extravaganza!" Ainsley justifiably boasts proud of this accomplishment.

"Don't forget yourself cousin, you were just named the most popular recording artist in the world. You alone will draw thousands of fans," Kennedy proudly reminds her cousin.

"Thank you, Kennedy, but let's talk about the incredibly diverse talent I have on board. I think you will be amazed," Ainsley says anxious to share what she has achieved.

"I have some of the greats in rock music ready to devote their time and energy to this cause including Miley Cyrus, Ed Sheeran, Taylor Swift, and Jakob Dylan. You add to the list Issac Bartlett grandson of Eric Clapton, Gabriel Jagger son of Mick, Rushawnna Guy daughter of Buddy Guy, Evan Olav Naess son of Diana Ross, and Jaden Smith son of Will Smith and wow! All of these children of famous people of the past are established as contemporary greats," Ainsley says with excitement.

"What about country Ainsley, not everyone is tuned into rock and roll," Kennedy asks showing her personal preference.

"Oh, we have country my cousin," Ainsley announces. "I have a commitment from some of the greats in country music namely, Eric Church, Garth Brooks, Kelsea Ballerini, Kacey Musgraves as individual artists, and the country bands Little Big Town and A Thousand Horses."

"You girls have done extremely well. Our challenge is going to be providing a venue to accommodate the thousands upon thousands of people who will attend," Ansel declares rolling his eyes.

While publicity is your bailiwick dear friend, you leave accommodations to me," Kennedy says with a smile.

"Don't you worry about publicity," Ansel replies, "I now have 32 of the world's top promoters and handlers working round the clock to make sure every person on this planet knows about the Greatest Show on Earth!"

"Before we get into schedules and time frames, might I finish informing you of the talent I lined up to be part of our extravaganza?" Ainsley begs.

"Most certainly cousin, finish before our conversation changes direction," Kennedy allows.

"Diversity is critical to our appeal, so I have brought into our fold the Punk Groups: Against Me! Paramore, and Chromatics. I have also lined up the Berlin Philharmonic, Vienna Philharmonic, Tokyo Symphony Orchestra, and the Orchestre de Paris to round out the music," Ainsley boasts.

"The logistics for this is mind boggling," Ansel says placing his left hand on his forehead. Some of these things are a huge challenge, but moving an Orchestra let alone four isn't manageable."

"Relax Ansel; I am working with the Orchestras to schedule only one per venue. The way I figure it, before we are done, we might not need to move an Orchestra if each city provides their own," Ainsley assures. "As for everyone else, they understand and agree that it is their responsibility as well as cost to move with our schedule."

"Nothing like this has ever been attempted before. It is truly going to require a miracle to pull it off," Ansel responds.

Playing to Ansel's over the top ego, Kennedy proclaims, "Ansel, we came to you because you are the master. You and I have worked together in the promotion and organization of Olympics, and this is going to be very similar only on the move. If anyone can pull this off and do it in a world class way, it is you!"

"I agree," Ainsley chimes in knowing Ansel's ego needs stroked, "You are the only person in the world who can truly bring this all together. Besides, you will be working with the best people in every profession. Being on the move and making things work is what all our performers are about. We just need to put things together and provide the venue, and they will take it from there. However, one thing is for sure, we could not do this without you!"

"We don't have much time," Ansel says with a renewed sense of energy and purpose, "We need to get this extravaganza nailed down and we need the message. All of this is for not if we fail to successfully deliver the message."

"Let me assure you on a couple other things before we talk about the message," Ainsley interjects. As I previously mentioned, I have arranged for Stella McCartney to be in charge of all fashion aspects of our extravaganza. Well, Elizabeth and Georgia May Jagger have come on board to assist Stella. I also noted that Heather McCartney was heading the visual art aspect, well Molly Lackey daughter of Carole King, Frances Bean Cobain, and Amber Jean Young are working with Heather. You give these people a spot to work, and they will do magic!

"What about the schedule and message for our extravaganza?" Kennedy asks.

"Gabriel Jagger suggested we use the Rolling Stones "Gimme Shelter" as the tours anthem," Ainsley reveals. "What do you think?"

"I think it's a fabulous idea," says Ansel, "It is just a shot away."

"I love rock and roll, but Gimme Shelter is an extremely intense song. I know we have Christine Matthews to be our ring leader, but who could we get to follow "Gimme Shelter" with the message?" Gemma wonders.

"The message must be all around and ever present if it is going to resonate and be effective. Even all our entertainment must reflect the message, so I am uncertain as to what you mean?" Ansel has a quizzical look on his face.

"While everything we do must reflect the message, we need someone to speak directly to what this is all about. The address does not need to be lengthy, but we must offer it intermittently so everyone attending hears it clearly and therefore relates everything around them to the message," Gemma reveals her vision regarding the message.

"I believe I have the very persons for the job," states Ainsley taking a very serious posture to make her point.

"Who would you suggest Ainsley," Kennedy says raising her eyebrows in interest.

"It is not who Kennedy but whom," Ainsley smiles. "I have had a conversation with these sisters, and I believe Natalie Rae Hynde and Yasmin Kerr would be willing to tag team in providing the message. Natalie Rae and Yasmin are both activists with huge credibility. They have both spent lots of time on the front lines of protests and done more jail time than Eldridge Cleaver. Natalie's parents are Ray Davies of the Kinks and Chrissie Hynde of the Pretenders, and Yasmin's parents are Jim Kerr of Simple Minds and Chrissie Hynde. I don't know how you get more powerful than this for credibility in delivering the message."

"Wow, I know these girls," Ansel struggles to contain his excitement. "They will command an audience to hear every word they speak simply by their presence. Bravo Ainsley, Bravo!"

"I can't refute an endorsement like that," Gemma says with a smirk, "Get them on board!"

"Here is our challenge, and I know Kennedy faces the same thing. As word gets around about the Save the World Tour, there will be celebrities, entertainers and notables coming out of the woodwork wanting to be a part of the scene. It is a good challenge, but what do we do?" Ainsley wonders knowing they are dealing with big egos that bruise easily.

"Let's see how this all evolves," Ansel cautions, "But this might be our answer to preventing burnout. Even though most of these people are accustom to the hectic pace of touring and performing, the pace often becomes overwhelming. What we are preparing to do will certainly test the human limits. The more talent we have to tap, the more we can offer everyone time to re-energize. This is certainly a case where more is better."

"Good point Ansel, I suggest we create a data base of all interested parties and develop a strategic plan for their use. There is no reason to keep anyone who can contribute to the quality of our extravaganza from participating. If there is one thing, and actually there are many, which we have learned from our family, it is inclusion is good," Kennedy notes.

"Kennedy makes a great point, but there is a pitfall in all of this. We must beware the vultures. The vultures are those who present them themselves as altruistic, but actually possess an ulterior motive. We do not want anyone involved who is looking to further their own agenda.

Everyone involved must be about the message and only the message!" Gemma could not be more adamant.

"I have an idea," Ainsley blurts out of nowhere. "Gemma is highly skilled with a computer, and she could create a database for us of all the resources including people that need to be managed. Such a database would be invaluable in making sure nothing gets overlooked. While we do not want disingenuous involvement, we need to ensure that all talent has an opportunity to be involved."

"Great idea Ainsley! Gemma would be perfect to provide this critical organizational component," Kennedy agrees.

"What do you think Gemma? Are you up to this challenge?" Ainsley leans her head to the side with a smile as if to say, sure you are.

"Actually, this makes good sense. By managing this type of database, I can make sure everyone who takes part in the Save the World Tour understands their role as the medium for the message," Gemma is an easy sell. She has an incredible work ethic, and loves a challenge. The more responsibility she has, the more energized she is.

"The schedule for the first leg of the extravaganza is set girls. While this is a bit of a rush, we begin here in Chicago in two weeks. From there we move to Los Angeles, Manila, Tokyo, Beijing, Bangkok, Istanbul, Rome, Moscow, Berlin, Madrid, Paris, and London, each on consecutive weeks. I have people in each of these cities working overtime to promote the Save the World Tour," Ansel boasts.

"I will mobilize the organizational gurus in each of these cities to ensure the venue is set for the extravaganza," Kennedy adds.

"How can we possibly make this work on such a massive scale? It is no small feat moving things and getting them set up week after week?" Ainsley asks knowing the challenge and massive undertaking it is for her concert tours. "This will be like moving a small city."

"Isn't that why you have me?" Ansel asks indignantly. "I am the master of promotion and staging. I am connected all over the world girls, and believe me everyone owes me something. I will be calling in all my chips on this one. We are currently rushing against time here in Chicago, but while we speak, my people, and they are my people, are hard at work in every one of our cities preparing for the first leg of the Save the World Tour."

"You are the magic man Ansel," Kennedy says offering him one of her rare but genuine hugs.

"Furthermore, we have every major broadcast network bidding for the rights to broadcast this tour. I suggest we segment our network contracts so we maximize the funds generated for the Save the World Foundation. What do you think?" Ansel asks.

"How would we segment this?" Ainsley wonders not having a great deal of insight into how the business works as she leaves most of these details to her business manager.

"If we segment this too much, we will get low balled in any bidding competition. If we want to maximize profits from competition, we must make it so low bidders lose out," Kennedy suggests.

"What seems as important to me as the profits from bids is the guarantee that whoever is awarded the broadcast rights are required to air the festival in its entirety for all of their contract time. Furthermore, they must agree to make the message the centerpiece of their broadcast," Gemma asserts.

"Gemma is right, we don't want some network purchasing the rights and then using the time for some other purpose. We also need to be guaranteed the right to run a cyber bank for the solicitation and accumulation of donations to the Save the World Foundation," Kennedy attests.

"These are all important points," Ansel acknowledges. "We must make these stipulations part of the contract. What I would suggest is we create four time slots, 8-noon, noon-4, 4-8, and 8-midnight. We take closed bids with the bidders knowing that the highest bidder gets first choice of time slot, and so on. I believe this creates an inclusive process and would lead to maximum financial benefit."

"How can we doubt you Ansel, you are the master. Make it happen!" Kennedy pronounces trying to keep the conversation moving.

"I agree," chimes in Ainsley.

"Now, about the message," Kennedy pivots to move the conversation along.

"Ah yes," says Ansel leaning back in a high back chair while staring out the window at the incredible Chicago skyline. "Save the World from what?"

"Save the World from humanity for God's sake," Ainsley says jumping to her feet and moving in front of Ansel. "Save the World from the unbelievable abuse of human beings. Save the World from Global Warming, pestilence, starvation, dehydration, disease, war, and annihilation."

"Ainsley, Ansel gets it. He didn't get on board with us on this grand venture for no reason," Kennedy rushes to Ansel's rescue.

"I'm sorry," Ainsley says backing away from Ansel's chair. "I am a bit more than anxious to hear from my sister, brother, and our cousins who are so important to the message we must bring to the world. I do hope we hear some definitive things from them soon."

"I am sure we will Ainsley, we must be patient," Kennedy assures her.

CHAPTER 32

DNA

In Ames, a young custodian finds his way to the sub-basement of the old library looking to remove a centrifugal pump from an unused boiler to replace a malfunctioning pump in the liberal arts building. In examining the boilers, he notices that one of the boilers was never equipped to run. In fact, with its placement so close to the wall, it would have been impractical to maintain. This seems odd, but he was sent to retrieve a part so he moves on to a fully equipped boiler. As the custodian works to remove the pump, he stops to listen. A sound has caught his attention, and he cannot determine its source. It sounds like people talking, and it seems to be coming from the ventilation system.

Inside the bunker, Dr. Henry tells everyone to be quiet. He can hear something going on outside the room. As everyone listens, they detect the sound of tools being used coming through the ventilation system. It occurs to them that if they can hear someone working outside their bunker through the ventilation system, then someone outside could hear them in the same manner. Reminiscent of those younger years when their parents would suggest they play the car game of seeing who could be quiet the longest, they go into silent mode. Unlike those car games, they remain in dead silence until they are certain the coast is clear.

Gathering up the centrifugal pump, the custodian makes his way out of the sub-basement and the old library building. He is still mystified by the phantom boiler and the sounds coming from the ventilation system. Arriving at the liberal arts building, he mentions his experience to a co-worker over a cup of coffee.

"That's an old building buddy," the co-worker advises his friend. "You know these public institutions waste a lot of money in a lot of ways. As for your voices, an old building like that must have ghosts," he adds with a grin and a friendly punch to the shoulder.

"I don't believe in ghosts, but you're probably right, it was nothing," the young custodian agrees.

Back in the bunker, Dr. Jude, Dr. Henry, and Dr. Abraham learn that Reza along with the dinosaur eggs and the decaying body of the Oviraptor are safe and secure in the Paleobiology Lab at Virginia Tech University in Blacksburg, VA. By some miracle, the devastation caused by the Mid-Atlantic Ridge catastrophe spared Blacksburg and Virginia Tech by 50 miles to the east.

Dr. Jude arranged for his top assistants in Herpetology from the University of California at Berkeley to fly to Blacksburg to join Dr. Henry's team. Dr. Abraham did the same with his top assistants in Invasive Species from the University of Michigan in Ann Arbor to join the Virginia Tech team.

What these three scientists need is vital information to process as they seek to find a way to contain and control the spread of dangerous predatory species around the globe. Noah, Edison, and Thomas truly believe the secret lies in the DNA structure of the most ancient creatures to live on Earth. They know it is their good fortune to possess dinosaur eggs and the actual corpse of an Oviraptor which they believe is the product of Devolution.

With Reza acting as the contact and Virginia Tech team leader; Noah, Eddie, and Thomas engage the Herculean task of finding a solution to the rapidly growing problem of gigantic and highly aggressive predators. Their effort is risky on two levels: First, if the authorities discover what is going on at Virginia Tech, they will move in and confiscate the eggs and corpse as well as shut down the lab. Second, by using the established communication between the Ames hideout and the Virginia Tech lab, the scientists in hiding risk being discovered, arrested, and put out of business. Despite the risk, the work must be pursued or vicious predators will soon threaten a large part of civilization.

For the time being, the abundance of food in remote and less populated areas is curtailing the spread of these giant beasts. However, with a diminished food supply, these beasts will soon move into populated areas and threaten human beings. Furthermore, attempting to control these beasts through the use of armaments will only drive them outside their established territory, toward populated areas. Many of these creatures are highly intelligent. They quickly recognize danger, and figure out ways to protect themselves. Populated areas not only protect them but provide an abundant food supply.

Dr. Abraham, Dr. Jude, and Dr. Henry believe a ban on hunting is key to maintaining an ample food source for these gigantic beasts and containing their spread to unwanted areas. Furthermore, hunters place themselves in harm's way. Should they encounter one of these beasts, they will not live to share their horrendous story. They are now in a race against time to find a means to control and contain these beasts. One thing they are confident in is the fact that all creatures maintain territorial patterns unless they have cause to do differently.

"This is robust data we are receiving from the lab at Virginia Tech," Dr. Abraham proclaims as he peers through the lens of a highly sophisticated microscope. The DNA of the Oviraptor gives me a reason to be optimistic about our search."

"This is incredible data. Now if we can only isolate the reproductive DNA, we might be able to determine a way to control the propagation of these beasts," Dr. Henry adds as he too gazes into the Microscopic world of the Oviraptor.

"The work we are doing here is not all that dissimilar to the work accomplished by Olivia and her team at the CDC in Atlanta. If they could find a way to alter the DNA of the mosquito to render it incapable of carrying disease, we can surely find a way to alter the reproductive DNA of invasive species," Dr. Jude says with determination as he examines the data in search of a clue.

"Well let's hope that Olivia and her team are successful with their Atlanta project. Forty-eight-hours seems like a hell of a long time when waiting," Noah says taking a deep breath.

In Atlanta, Dr. Kae and Dr. Rooh are being examined every hour on the hour for any adverse signs from their exposure to the fog and vapor used on the mosquito population. So far; so good!

Dr. Kae's team is waiting for the test results of their harvest of mosquito larva exposed to the fog and vapor so they will know if the DNA structure has been altered as hoped.

⟫◆⟪

In the Ames hideout, Contessa has just received the schedule for the first leg of the Save the World Tour. She is concerned.

Interrupting Dr. Abraham's work on the invasive species, she shares her concern. "Noah, we just received a communication from Kennedy, Ainsley, and Gemma, about the Save the World Tour. They are planning tour stops in Los Angeles, Bangkok, and Rome."

"So, why the concern Contessa, these seem like logical stops on a world tour," Noah asks while maintaining half his attention on his discoveries under the microscope.

"Right now, these three cities are perhaps the most susceptible to a major Earthquake of anywhere in the world. The San Jacinto Fault which connects to the San Andreas Fault is becoming more volatile every day. The Phayao Fault which impacts Bangkok is showing increased signs of activity. With the nature of the ground under Bangkok, a major quake could literally swallow that city. Rome seems a bit safer, but still, the African plate and the Eurasian plate in the Alps have increased activity and movement over the past month. All these things add up to a potential nightmare for any one of these cities," Contessa says looking at her computer screen and putting her left hand over her mouth.

"All you can do is alert Kennedy, Ainsley, and Gemma about your concerns. We can't run the world tour and accomplish our work here. I know they will appreciate and take your concerns seriously," Noah says as he returns to his work.

⟫◆⟪

In Chicago, Kennedy, Ainsley, and Gemma receive Contessa's concern about their tour schedule. They take her warning seriously and have a conversation with Ansel.

"Who are we to question your cousin Contessa? She foresaw the Mid-Atlantic Ridge and Yellowstone catastrophes, and saved hundreds-of-thousands of lives in the west with her warning. We probably should have checked with her before setting up our schedule," Ansel declares.

"So, we will make the changes?" Kennedy asks.

"I do not see how we can change the Los Angeles event. I have people working overtime to be ready for that tour stop in four weeks. If we cancel this stop it will interrupt the tour, and possibly cause panic in southern California. Is that what you want to do?" Ansel displays his frustration and anxiety.

"No, that is not what we want to do!" Ainsley declares. "There are millions of people living in harm's way, and what does that say about us if we hesitate to take our message to them?" Ainsley asks throwing up her hands.

"You're right Ainsley," Kennedy offers in agreement, "If we get the message to these people, perhaps we can actually save lives and begin to turn the tables in our effort to save the world. By displaying the courage to be there, we add powerful credibility to our crusade."

"I agree girls, but don't we need to let all our people know that this tour stop has innate dangers?" Ansel asks.

"Absolutely, everyone needs to have the opportunity to buy in or opt out of this particular stop. However, since so many of our people live or own homes in the Sun Shine State, I am confident they will be solid on being a part of this stop," Ainsley says bringing her fist down firmly on a small nearby table.

"Careful Ainsley," Ansel erupts, "That is a 16th century antique table from Vienna. I don't think you want to pay for it."

"So, what do we do about Bangkok and Rome?" Kennedy inquires.

"We should keep Rome simply because of its huge religious and cultural significance," Ansel suggests, "But I believe we can change Bangkok to Damascus. What do you think?"

"I agree with keeping Rome, but why Damascus, is it not in the heart of the Middle Eastern conflict?" Kennedy draws back with a puzzled look.

"I never did care for the scheduling of Bangkok, but Damascus provides us with an opportunity to go into a war-torn area with our message of saving the world. Perhaps your cousin Stella could convince Ambassador DiCaprio to appeal to these countries for the secession of hostilities during the time of our tour stop. If so, it could be a real coup for our crusade. If not, we could always cancel," Ansel rationalizes.

"I like it," Kennedy approves.

"So, do I," Ainsley says as Gemma nods in agreement.

"Then it is set!" proclaims Ansel.

Amongst all the things going on, Dr. Rae is hard at work putting together a simple and concise message which can be used by the tour to convince people that the Theory of Devolution is real. The message will emphasize the things people must do to counter act Devolution and move the Earth back into balance.

Hannah Rae can sense it all coming together. She prays day and night for the success of her little sister in Atlanta. She anxiously awaits word from her three cousins in Lucerne, Switzerland. She is confident Noah, Eddie, and Thomas will achieve a successful breakthrough on dealing with and containing predatory creatures. She values Contessa's unique insight into the geological activity all around the globe. She is hopeful that the world tour her cousins are about to initiate will provide the platform for the message which promises to save the world.

CHAPTER 33

TENETS OF LOVE AND PEACE

HIGH IN THE SWISS ALPS the morning sun welcomes the delegates to a warm clear blue sky. The eagles which graced the delegates with a commanding performance outside the conference room windows the night before reappear as if by popular demand. As the delegates seat themselves, the eagles dip, weave, and soar to Cat Stevens' "Morning Has Broken" with the vista of a snow-capped mountain range in the background.

Standing at the door welcoming each delegate as they enter the room, Senator Joseph, Dr. Isabelle, and Stella sense that something significant occurred during the night. Each delegate emits a radiance suggesting a transformation from the night before. As the delegates enter the room, they walk with arms around each other as you would expect from brothers and sisters. The conversations amongst the delegates are quiet and reverent.

With the arrival of everyone, Stella steps to the podium and receives an extended and respectful applause. "Good morning!" Stella offers with a melodic and poetic sound to her voice. "Before we get started, I want to point out that each table now has a microphone. Only one microphone can be activated at a time to facilitate your conversation. With that, I hope everyone is rested and ready for a new day!"

No sooner has Stella finished and the Dalai Lama rises to speak, "My dearest friends and representatives of God. Last night, God appealed to us to save the Earth with love and peace. Last night during my sleep, the same face of God appeared to me asking that we start anew by casting aside our old ways." As the Dalai Lama shares these things, the conference room comes alive with the murmuring of quiet comments at every table. As the murmuring quiets down, the Dalai Lama continues, "I have spoken with many of you this morning, and it seems that all of us may have had the same vision and received the same message during the night. I believe it is our sacred obligation to the living God to become as one."

As Stella and her cousins survey the room, everyone is nodding in agreement. Walking over to her cousins, Stella quietly asks, "What do you think?"

Looking at her in near disbelief, Jack responds, "It seems to me that today the past will be cast aside as this room of incredibly intelligent, reverent, and powerful religious leaders seek to become one belief and one voice."

"I have never felt so overwhelmed with humility," Ivey adds. "Lead them where they want to go, let God work through you," she encourages Stella.

Returning to the podium, Stella begins echoing Ivey, "As I stand before you, I am overwhelmed with humility. I don't know if I am up to the task you have entrusted to me, but I put myself in God's hands and ask that his will be done."

As Stella gazes over the assemblage of religious leaders, Sayyid-Ruhollah Musavi Khomeini II stands to speak, "I have long known that we are brothers and sisters of one seed rising out of the Garden of Eden. I have long wondered why and how brothers and sisters of the Father Abraham can remain so hostile toward each other knowing their common linage? Last night it became clear that the one and only God is providing us one more chance. I am convinced that we must now depart from the past and chart a new course toward love and peace as our God has asked. To do less would be to invite the end of the world."

"I welcome the words and the wisdom of our Brother Sayyid-Ruhollah. Over the centuries we have all lost our way and allowed hate to consume our belief and control our actions toward one another. There is only one God and one way which God revealed to us last night. We must bond together with a message of love and peace if we are to save the Earth," Francis II declares.

"All across the world millions of people are dying from wars perpetuated by hate and ignorance. We have lost our way, and as a result, our people flounder not knowing which way to turn. God has asked us to turn them toward love and peace, and the realization that we are all one. Our differences should not separate us, but bind us together in a beautiful fabric which we call the human race. It is now our sacred duty to save the Earth!" proclaims Baba Ram Dass.

"Before last night, I was not a believer. Now, sitting here today, I have no doubt that God is real. I suggest we compile a list of things we believe in common as the basis for bringing people together as one in love and peace," adds S.E. Cupp.

"Yes, we need a list of tenets which will provide all people with a guide for a loving and peaceful existence," Urges Fariba Kamalabadi.

"Is there anyone who sees things differently? Is everyone agreeable that it is time to begin anew?" Stella asks from the podium.

Looking around the room, she sees heads nodding in agreement. She can hear the soft murmur of chatter, but it appears no one is in dissent.

"So, let us begin," Stella declares. As individuals offer suggestions, we must all agree if it is to be accepted. If anyone has reservations about any suggestion, they must speak up. After each suggestion, I will pause for two minutes before moving on. When we are done, what is created must meet unanimous approval so we move forward as one."

"I suggest we begin with a very basic precept upon which I believe we can all agree," offers Alastair Campbell. "As you sow, so you reap. Sow love, reap love. Sow peace, reap peace."

After a pause, Pham Cong Tac stands and suggests, "Nature obeys us as we obey nature. This planet is our home, and we must care for and respect our home."

"Love for all with none attachment," says Li Li Hongzhi. "Our love for each other must be unconditional."

Theophilos V adds, "Lead an ethical life. Do unto others as you would have others do unto yourself. It is the Golden Rule."

I suggest, "Operate in the present time" says Huynh Phu So III. "It seems that so many problems come from dealing with the past or worrying about the future. If we all just take care of the here and now, the past and future will be taken care of."

Efraim Tendero has been patiently waiting for an opportunity to make a suggestion. Over his lifetime, he has noticed how so many people are inflexible to other people, ideas, or ways of life. He feels this inflexibility contributes to a great deal of mistrust and hostility. Seeing a chance to speak Efraim advocates including "Hardness must go, relax, tension is self-centeredness. Find beauty in diversity".

As Stella stands at the podium observing the graceful and unified manner in which these delegates are establishing tenets for the human race, she feels the presence of something divine. Later, when she asks Jack, Ivey, Zach, Ambassador DiCaprio, and others if they experienced the same feeling, they all confirm a feeling of great promise as if God was actively guiding the proceedings.

"Stella," called out Mohammed Ali al-Baghdadi II, "I have something to offer."

"By all means, please do," Stella responds.

"Don't be discouraged, we can do the impossible. Through the grace of God, human beings are the distributer of Divine Power. We must live in accordance with a conscience of good will towards all," Ali al-Baghdadi II puts forth.

"This is most inspiring," beams Asher Povarsky, "We are truly experiencing the blessing of a good and gracious God. What I have to advise comes from years of observing, and too often perpetuating the negative and hurtful results of loose lips" he reveals before suggesting, "Let all speech reflect the goodness of the human heart and the grace of a loving God."

"I am enthralled by our accomplishments today. We are establishing universal truths important to the realization of one world and one people," adds Andrew II who then submits his contribution, "Never need or desire anything so badly you can't do without. Replace cravings and greed with an attitude of generosity and sacrifice."

Muhammed Ahmad Hussein notes that "Our ability to do the right thing must be combined with our willingness and determination to do so."

"We must see that the results of our deliberation are published in a pamphlet entitled "The Tenets of Love and Peace", this pamphlet along with our testimony must be the transfiguration of faith around the world. I offer the following tenet for inclusion, "We are born equal and we leave equal, therefore, we should all live equal," pronounces Steve Gaines.

"I am overwhelmed by the wisdom pouring forth from this august gathering. We are truly on the path to a new and better world," shares Joseph III. "I would like to make the following contribution, "The universe, galaxies, and planets are all in harmony. There is a divine balance in every cause and every effect."

Not hearing any further contributions, Stella says, "It has been a very productive morning with many contributions. I sense the delegates would like to break for lunch before we continue."

"Just a second Stella, I would like to offer a tenet for consideration," requests Abdol-Hamid Masoumi. This is an age-old tenet, but one I believe is critical to the establishment of one world and one people. "As we judge, so are we judged. As we condemn, so are we condemned."

As she has done all morning, Stella shows the utmost patience awaiting any response to Abdol-Hamid Masoumi's suggestion. After a full two minutes pass, she asks, "Does anyone else have something to offer before we break for lunch? This has been a most inspiring morning. We will gather this afternoon at 2:30 which will give everyone time for lunch, reflection, and perhaps a short nap. God bless you all and we stand adjourned," Stella declares.

Over lunch, Jack, Ivey, and Stella consider the unbelievable notion that religion, science, and secularity could merge into something so Holy. They recall the surreal pronouncement of their brothers, sisters, cousins to go forth in pursuit of this most mysterious and otherworldly phenomenon. Now, as the people of the world stand on the very precipice from which they must turn back or forever perish, comes God. While looking into the depths of space, the face of God appeared with the pronouncement to save the Earth. Something beyond definition, which defies explanation, occurred holding the promise for a new world of love and peace.

"I have Nora compiling a New Testament for Life on Earth. It will contain all of the names and contributions of the most Holy of God's representatives to ever assemble. Nora will see that Kennedy, Ainsley, and Gemma get this material immediately," Jack says returning to a more senatorial posture.

"Might I suggest we call this list of tenets something other than a New Testament which sounds too Biblical. We have come so far to alienate anyone with words. What if we stick with "The Tenets of Love and Peace" as suggested by Steve Gaines? When he made this suggestion, everyone seemed in agreement," Ivey offers.

"The ambassador told me this morning that he is going to personally present these tenets to the United Nations General Assembly," Stella informed.

"No one can tell the other the best manner in which to reveal this information because it must be revealed. I believe there will be a unanimous agreement to call our tenants "The Tenets of Love and Peace". These tenets must be spread across billions of cyber lines to the very chapel of the human heart. People need to know that they may rest at night and arise heartened each morning knowing that God is at hand," the Dalai Lama notes as he quietly came across the three at lunch. "It is out of our hands now," he adds.

Standing with the Dalai Lama, the Grand Ayatollah stresses that a video of the heavenly experience must be allowed to speak for itself. Any publication of the tenets must be free from names and acknowledgements which only serve the human ego, not God. Such acknowledgements seem innocent at first, but over time they become the source of division. God wants us to be one! Let our tenets accompany the video, but attribute them to divine inspiration and intervention. Upon witnessing, people will see and know the truth."

"My brother is wise in his recommendation," the Dalai Lama shares his support.

"Brother, make sure Nora gets this out to Kennedy, Gemma, and our dear sister immediately! Follow the advice of the Grand Ayatollah, no one can feel slighted if everyone is slighted. Make sure the recording of God's intervention accompanies "The Tenets of Love and Peace," Ivey directs.

CHAPTER 34

COMING TOGETHER

As Kennedy, Ainsley, and Gemma, wrestle with the technicalities of the world tour; they receive word that Olivia and her team in Atlanta have successfully developed a vapor which neuters the ability of Mosquitoes and Ticks to carry disease. Olivia and Dr. Rooh suffered no ill effects from their exposure to the vapor. A study of the larva samples determined that they are one-hundred-percent neutered of disease carrying capability. By using the vapor worldwide, the evil demon of death will soon be nothing more than a pesky pest.

As Kennedy, Ainsley, and Gemma discuss the magnificent news, they receive news from Lucerne.

"Things are starting to develop extremely fast cousins," Kennedy, (whose experience in the track world emphasizes the speed of things), points out.

"Do you think?" Ainsley responds incredulously, "We have received two earth shattering proclamations. Furthermore, of these pronouncements, one is of science and one of religion."

"This is exciting," Kennedy notes, "But we have five incredibly brilliant family members who have yet to report. If they confirm what we are sensing, our message will be one of great hope."

As Dr. Abraham, Dr. Jude, Dr. Rae, Dr. Henry, and Dr. Margery study the data arriving at their stations every minute, they grow ever more suspect that a terminal global catastrophe looms on the horizon. They have yet to hear of the success in Atlanta or the transformation in Lucerne.

The five of them are unwavering in their belief in Devolution. It has come to be the very basis for the regeneration of nature. People must embrace the truth about the relationship between humans and nature as practiced by the indigenous people around the globe. Take nothing more than what can be used and replaced; to do anything other is to rape the Earth of its self-sustaining ability and perpetual benefit to subsequent generations. Find harmony, achieve harmony, and maintain harmony.

People must learn to live with all creatures of the Earth. As humans intrude upon the territory of another creature, a chain of predators may follow. Give all life forms room in which to live where the natural cycle of life is allowed to unfold, and they will maintain themselves as part of a healthy ecosystem.

As man returns to a harmonic relationship with the Earth, the Earth will heal itself and bring forth an environment of abundance and plenty for all. The secret is to stop abusing every aspect of this world, and nature will reward mankind tenfold.

For Noah, Edison, and Thomas, a huge concern centers on the proliferation of gigantic reptiles and mammals around the globe. These are invasive creatures of the creepiest and deadliest nature.

Until the temperate zones of the Earth return to normal, life around the globe may never know normalcy because of the invasion of gigantic reptiles. These creatures have ravenous and insatiable appetites which make anything or anyone prey.

In areas with tropical climates, snakes of massive size can slither through an open doorway down a vacant hall and into a room to quickly lay claim to any unsuspecting human being. In these same areas, a huge Komoto Dragon, alligator, or crocodile may lumber in offering no avenue of escape. Humans and reptiles do not mix no matter the size.

In the northern regions of the world, human populations are threatened by the emergence of Sabre-Toothed Tigers, gigantic Eagles, Giant Short-Faced Bears, Dire Wolves, and Hell Pigs. Should these vicious and aggressive mammals find their way into populated areas, humans are in for a nightmarish existence. The sheer strength of the Giant Short-Faced Bear or Hell Pig could easily break through a door and invade a house should the creature become desperate for food.

If something is not done to control and manage these prehistoric beasts, they will make any area they possess uninhabitable. This consideration leaves open the questions of, what will these creatures do when the food runs out, and what will humans do when these creatures invade populated areas?

Knowing they must find an answer fast, Noah, Edison, and Thomas pour over the data coming in from the lab at Virginia Tech. They know these vicious and gigantic reptiles have become too numerous to control. They reproduce far too many offspring to manage. They also know that while mammals don't reproduce in such numbers, their population is growing as is the need for food. Noah, Edison, and Thomas must find a way to inhibit the ability of these reptiles and mammals to reproduce.

They are currently engaged in a process of sending directives to their assistants at the Virginia Tech Lab and receiving data reflecting the results of their directives. They do not believe in failure, but rather look at things through a lens described by Thomas Edison as the discovery of things which do not work. "I believe our best opportunity to finding a universal solution to controlling the reproductive ability of all these reptiles and unwanted mammals is the dead Oviraptor and eggs," Dr. Henry asserts. "If evolution is real, and the Oviraptor clearly fits the phylum Chordata, we may find the answer in this prehistoric DNA."

"I think you could be right cousin, but what aspect of this complicated DNA should be the focus of our lab assistants?" Dr. Jude inquires rubbing his weary eyes after staring at the computer screen for so long.

Dr. Abraham has been carefully listening to his brother and cousin. He has been searching for that one common denominator within the phylum Chordata. "I suggest we direct those in the lab at Virginia Tech to abandon all other avenues, and focus on the ability of the female to produce eggs."

"You are definitely onto something brother. If the lab can isolate the nucleotide responsible for egg production, we can use CRISPR (clustered regularly interspaced short palindromic repeats) Cas9 to remove the targeted DNA strand and disrupt the linear sequence rendering the female incapable of producing eggs," Dr. Jude declares as a eureka moment.

"Hopefully, the still borne Oviraptor is female which would simplify this challenge," Dr. Henry notes, "But if not, they will need to access the DNA structure of the eggs to find a female. I will send instructions off to the lab immediately."

In sharing their ideas with Hannah and Contessa, they stumble across a dichotomy in their plan. A significant part of Devolution is the belief nature is rebelling against the abuses of human beings which include the genetic engineering of crops and animals. They have already crossed this line of thinking when Dr. Olivia Kae and her team created a vapor which altered the genetic ability of mosquitoes and ticks to carry disease. Now, Noah, Edison, and Thomas are proposing to use genetic engineering in an attempt to curtail and control the propagation of large, vicious, aggressive predators.

"It seems like a "Catch 22," Hannah suggests. "It is a troubling consideration knowing that GMO crops and animals, along with chemicals of every sort, have led to the ruination of the land, air, and water. It seems there is a downside to your plan."

"I am not sure about the downside, sister," Thomas Henry interjects, "But unless we do something, these creatures could become a global infestation."

"Thus far they have not invaded highly populated areas, but if they increase in population and run out of food, they will invade and take over populated areas," Noah Abraham delivers with the force of someone who understands the horror and magnitude of such an invasion.

"Listen everyone," Edison Jude demands, "We have instances where these creatures have moved into populated rural areas and either wiped out all human life, or caused them to evacuate. We have reports of people trying to hold these creatures off with all kinds of weapons to no avail. These creatures are vicious and they are ravenous. They kill and eat everything in their path."

"There is always a time for pragmatism, and this seems to be the time," Contessa asserts. "We don't know for certain where any of this is leading, but we do know what the results will be if we do nothing."

"I think we are all in agreement," Hannah affirms. "Hopefully your resolution will work, and also find favor with nature."

"Speaking of nature," Contessa exclaims, "We are going to move forward full throttle in communicating the principles of Devolution to Kennedy, Ainsley, and Gemma in Chicago. They are gearing up with the "Save the World Tour", and we need them to deliver the full message if we are to pull the world back from the abyss."

"We will continue to work overtime in search of a solution for the invasive species problem with the hope of good news before the beginning of the tour," Dr. Abraham assures.

———

As Senator Joseph, Dr. Isabella, and Stella, fly from Lucerne, Switzerland to Chicago where they will link up with Kennedy, Ainsley, and Gemma, they catch a broadcast of DNN with breaking news.

"This is Coyote Blitzer bringing you Breaking News from the number one source for news. The CDC has just announced that Dr. Olivia Kae and her research team have successfully developed and tested a vapor which applied to mosquito larva and ticks will render all successive generations incapable of carrying disease. This vapor is currently in rapid production, and will be shipped for use around the world. It is projected that within a year, the global mosquito population could be rendered nothing more than a harmless pest."

"Wow," Stella exclaims offering her fellow travelers a high five, "Olivia has done it! The days for this demonic carrier of the most dreaded and awful diseases are numbered."

"This is incredible news," Ivey notes, "I am so proud of Olivia!"

"We just received more breaking news," Coyote announces. "While we do not have all the particulars, it seems that a secret conference of the world's religious leaders on Mt. Pilatus overlooking Lucerne, Switzerland concluded this afternoon. In a most dramatic announcement with all of these leaders standing in unity, the Dalai Lama declared a new day and a new way dedicated to love and peace under the watchful eye of one God. The Dalai Lama spoke of a transformation brought on when the delegates witnessed the face of God, and hearing the commandment to heal the Earth with love and peace."

"There it is girls," Jack Joseph affirms, "There is no turning back, God is on our side."

Looking out the airliner at 35,000 feet, the sky is black as coal. The Earth below looks distant and dark with just the lights from large towns and cities marking the way. Jack, Ivey, and Stella lean back in their seats. For the moment, they can smile knowing that tomorrow brings a new day.

Before these three weary travelers doze off for a well-deserved rest, Coyote Blitzer steps forward with one more bit of breaking news.

"I have with me tonight via satellite a former DNN newscaster and now the official spokesperson for the "Save the World Tour" Christine Matthews. Good evening Christine, it is so good to see you again!"

"Good evening Coyote, it is good to be with you!" Christine responds.

"Christine, what is this "Save the World Tour?" Coyote begins.

"Coyote, the "Save the World Tour" is the brain child of a unique family of brothers, sisters, and cousins. Kennedy Kay, Ainsley Anabelle, and Gemma Juniper, working with world renowned promoter Ansel Colioso are putting together a three-day extravaganza the likes the world has never seen. The entire purpose of the "Save the World Tour" is to share the things being done, and the things that need to be done to save the world from time ending calamities."

"When will this all take place, and what will be the cost," Coyote asks thinking he will reveal the downside of the tour idea.

"The tour starts right here in Chicago in two weeks, and there is no charge for admission. Free will donations will be solicited, and all proceeds will be used to provide relief for people in need around the world, as well as promote the message of saving the world," Christine beams her famous smile at the thought of such generosity.

"What about the entertainers and the cost of putting a show like this on the road?" Coyote asks thinking he has her on this one.

"Every single person involved in this tour is donating one-hundred-percent of their time and talent. All of the identified sites for this extravaganza are preparing the venues at no charge. All of the entertainers are putting their portion of the show on the road at no charge. Everyone involved in this tour are doing it because they know a failure to act will doom our planet," Christine declares.

"Okay, that is very impressive. What is the itinerary?" Coyote asks residing to the fact there is nothing controversial to discover.

"In just over two weeks, the first leg of the tour begins in Chicago. The extravaganza will be held over three full days running from Friday through Sunday. The tour will then move to Los Angeles, Manila, Tokyo, Beijing, Istanbul, Damascus, Rome, Moscow, Berlin, Madrid, Paris, and London on subsequent weeks. We are currently working on the second leg of the tour, and we will announce these locations soon," Christine assures Coyote as she signs off.

"It is all coming together just as we had hoped at our meeting in Ames," Jack says, "I just wish we could get our cousins and your sister Contessa out of hiding! They have been wrongly accused of acts completely counter to the great service they have rendered humanity."

CHAPTER 35

THE MESSAGE

IN NASHVILLE, PRESIDENT ARMSTRONG AND his loyal Chief of Staff Andrew Peet maintain constant vigilance over the state of the United States, world, and the president's political future. Martial law continues to divide the nation with public sentiment opposed to such a heavy-handed approach. In many states especially along the Eastern Seaboard and across the Northwest, governors battle the president for control of the National Guard. Recognizing the political fallout which will occur should he press for nationalizing the National Guard in these states, the president has yielded and sent federal troops to enforce martial law.

The east coast lay in ruins with no possible recovery for decades. The northwest remains a blazing inferno due to the Yellowstone Caldera creating millions of refugees as strangers in their own land. Global warming has much of the nation infested in mosquitoes, ticks, predatory reptiles and mammals. The once productive ground of the mid-west so critical to feeding the people of the United States and around the world is becoming increasingly infertile. The water and air quality at home and around the world grows more at risk every day.

Northern Europe is engulfed in smoke, deadly fumes, and ash spewing forth from the erupting volcanoes in Iceland which threatens the lives of millions. In the Middle East, Christians, Muslims, and Jews are at each other's throats fighting the age-old battle for what each claim as their rightful heritage to the Holy Land. Buddhists and Hindus are engaged in a butchery leaving carnage in their wake. The nations of Asia and the Near East wage war over the dwindling water supply coming from an ever-shrinking Himalayan Glacier Basin. The continent of Africa is consumed by starvation, dehydration, and disease. Much of the east coast of South America lay in devastation from the Mid-Atlantic catastrophe, and the remainder of the continent struggles against the onslaught of disease and gigantic predators. The oceans of the world continue to swell. The rising seas swallow islands and claim land mass important to humans and many animal species.

With the federal government in exile from the ruination of Washington D.C. during the Mid-Atlantic cataclysm, the president struggles to make Nashville the temporary seat of power. A great deal of his political and financial base submerged with the skylines of Boston, New York, Washington D.C., and Miami, leaving him to operate from a position of weakness. As is the case so often with weak leaders, the president, based upon the misguided advice of his chief of staff, strikes out against anyone who threatens him.

In an attempt to solidify his position, the president gathers the members of Congress with the most significant connections to big money and special interests. In secrecy, cloaked by martial law, the president and his collaborators adopt a plan focused on securing the well-being of the upper echelon of society. They have determined it is time to cut their losses and secure the survival of those who will be needed to rebuild the country and world. They have no solutions to offer, so they create a ruse to foster a calm populace as Armageddon engulfs the world. The public face of government remains optimistic while the private face prepares to abandon all those deemed unworthy of saving.

<hr />

Having made the 4,038 mile flight from Lucerne to Buffalo, New York, Jack, Ivey, and Stella must stop at the Buffalo-Niagra International Airport to switch flights. Jack reveals to his traveling companions that he is going to take a flight to Nashville to get a feel for things occurring at the federal level. He is also going to lobby Attorney General Loophole and National Security Advisor Shadey for a ruling which would allow his five cousins to come out of hiding.

Upon landing in Nashville, Senator Joseph learns that Chief of Staff Peet has left the city for the day. Senator Joseph seizes on the opportunity to visit with his one-time friend President Armstrong.

"Senator Joseph, so you decided to rejoin the government," the President says in greeting.

"I have never left the government, Mr. President, but I get the feeling my government left me," the senator suggests standing tall as he gives the president a firm look in the eye.

"Why senator, your government would never leave you. Your leadership is too important to dismiss," the president retorts. "Besides, it was your cousins who decided to go rogue and abandon all established channels for communicating natural disasters."

"You know full well that if my cousins had not acted of good conscience, we all may have died when the east coast met the fate of Atlantis. My cousins have done nothing wrong. Their actions were in the public's best interest. To have followed the bureaucratic process regarding the Yellowstone Caldara would have delayed warnings by days or weeks and resulted in the death of millions of people," the senator defends his cousins at near shouting level.

"You don't know that senator, and your absence is only proof that you have had little interest in being a part of the solution," the president proclaims.

"The solution my ass, you have fallen under the misguided advice of your chief of staff. You have changed as a person and a leader President Armstrong. I urge you as an old and one-time friend, call off the dogs from my cousins so they can surface and serve the public interest," the senator demands.

"I cannot do that Jack. I suspect you and your entire family are behind all of the efforts to undermine my government," the president declares.

"Your government! This is not your government, but the government of the people of the United States. You would be wise to remember this before it's too late," the senator reminds the president as he turns to leave.

Departing the presidential residence, Senator Joseph heads immediately to the office of Attorney General Loophole. Upon arrival, he is surprised to find National Security Advisor Shadey visiting with the attorney general.

"Greetings senator, it is good to see you again," the attorney general announces while offering a seat.

"Gentlemen, let me get right to the point," Senator Joseph says refusing to sit. "You have been arguing with my attorneys for far too long about the unlawful warrant for the capture and arrest of my five cousins. These individuals may have violated presidential protocol, but they have not broken any law. It is time to rescind the warrant and allow my cousins to come out of hiding."

"Senator, we are acting under presidential orders. We are currently operating under martial law which means the president dictates the law. Your argument holds no weight," Shadey informs the senator.

"Okay, here is what is going to happen," the senator commands, "You are going to have a visit with the president about the hazards of continuing to hunt down my cousins. You are going to make it clear to him that if he does not rescind the warrant, I am going to blow the whistle, and reveal the manner in which this corrupt and autocratic government is prepared to sacrifice the very people it alleges to serve."

"Are you threatening the president and the government, senator?" asks the attorney general.

"The only threat I am making is the truth. I have a significant voice, and I am not afraid to use it. Is that clear?" the senator responds.

As he departs the attorney general's office, the senator looks about with suspicion. He has ruffled the feathers of a heavy-handed federal government, and as far as he knows, he could become the target of an unwarranted warrant. Catching a taxi, he heads for Nashville International Airport and the 377-mile flight to Chicago. Boarding the plane, Senator Joseph is hopeful his pressure tactics will yield good news for his cousins. He is anxious to arrive in Chicago and rejoin Ivey and Stella. He smiles knowing he will see his sister Ainsley, as well as his cousins Kennedy and Gemma.

As Jack departs Nashville, Ivey and Stella have arrived at Ansel Colioso's apartment and reunited with Kennedy, Ainsley, and Gemma. After meeting Ansel and hearing the plans for the "Save the World Tour", they captivate Kennedy, Ainsley, Gemma, and Ansel with their experience in Lucerne. Ansel is an avowed atheist, and he is enthralled by the attendance of his good friend S.E. Cupp at the Lucerne Conference. Is it possible that what Ivey and Stella are sharing is real?

Kennedy, Ainsley, and Gemma are thrilled at the prospect of having such a broad and overwhelming message for the "Save the World Tour". By having the world's religious leaders standing together as one, there is hope that the fires of aggression stoked by religious divisions may calm and bring an opening for peace.

Landing at O'Hare International Airport, Jack is picked up by his Chief of Staff Arnold who traveled on to Chicago with Ivey and Stella. As they race through the streets to the Willis Tower and Ansel Colioso's Penthouse Suite, the senator fills Arnold in on the details of his meetings in Nashville. Arnold too is concerned that once the president's Chief of Staff Peet hears about the senator's visit, he will push to silence the Senator with an arrest warrant.

"These are very difficult and troubled times Arnold. You were with us in Lucerne, and you witnessed the Divine Intervention which occurred on Mt. Pilatus. We must act in good conscience and trust God's will," the Senator reminds his chief of staff. "Now hurry on and get us to the Willis Tower!"

Arriving at Ansel's Penthouse Suite, Jack is met with hugs. Everyone wants to know about his side trip to Nashville. As he shares his reception and conversation with the president, as well as Attorney General Loophole and National Security Advisor Shadey, everyone voices concern for his safety. Remaining stoic in his demeanor, the Senator makes a statement reminiscent of his Uncle Robert, "It is what it is."

"I sure wish Olivia were here," Ivey says obviously longing to see her cousin.

"Let's give her a call," Stella suggests.

"Hello Ivey, it is wonderful to hear from you," Olivia answers the phone in delight.

"Olivia, I have you on the speaker phone with Kennedy, Ainsley, Gemma, Jack, and Stella," Ivey informs.

Before Olivia can respond, the cousins in Chicago break into the "Hurrah" song. "Hurrah for Olivia, Hurrah for Olivia, we are all in the crowd yelling Hurrah for Olivia, one, two, three, four, who we going to yell for, Olivia that's who!"

As the song comes to an end, they can hear Olivia giggling on the other end of the phone, delightfully remembering this childhood song which Grandma and Grandpa would sing to provide their grandkids with positive reinforcement.

"Thank you everyone, it has been a long journey, but it looks like we have achieved success. We have the vapor in full production, and it will soon be shipped around the globe to terminate the insidious and deadly nature of the devil's winged demon," Olivia proclaims with a weary tone to her voice.

"You have been working extremely hard for a long time to achieve this success, why don't you take some time and join us in Chicago," Ivey pleads.

"I can't do it Ivey! I must oversee the production of the vapor until we have a large enough supply to begin shipping," Olivia leaves no doubt about her determination.

"We are preparing to kick off the "Save the World Tour," Kennedy reveals, "It would be wonderful if you could be with us at that time."

"I have been following the news, and it sounds like all of our planning in Ames is coming to fruition. I pray every day for the light of hope and the emergence of my sister, brother, and cousins from hiding. We must stay focused and use every success to advance our mission to save humanity," Olivia says with confidence and determination in her voice. "It has been good to hear from you, but I must get back to work."

"Take care cousin," comes a closing in unison from Chicago.

As the group closes their conversation with Olivia, they realize they are receiving a transmission from Dr. Hannah Rae over the secure channel.

"Hannah, how are you guys holding up in seclusion?" Jack asks his cousin hoping for good news.

"We are doing fine, but seclusion is no fun! However, we are too busy to be concerned about our isolation," comes her reply.

"To what do we owe this transmission?" Ainsley wonders.

"We know you are preparing for the "Save the World Tour", and we need you to include our message based upon what we know and believe," Hannah informs them with a sense of urgency.

"We are working on a unified and comprehensive message now," Kennedy tells Hannah. "Please send us what you have as soon as possible so it can be included in our message!'

"We have been running the data day and night, and we are absolutely certain that Devolution is real. No matter how you might define Mother Nature, she is in full revolt against the practices of human beings when it comes to the land, water, air, and the animal kingdom. Unless humans abandon the current abuses of CAFOs, putrefied fertilizer, chemicals, GMO seeds and animals, antibiotics, human waste disposal, the pollution of streams, rivers, lakes, the oceans, and the air, the Earth will soon be uninhabitable for the human race," Hannah reveals.

"But Hannah, this alarm has been sounded for decades to no avail. Why will it resonate now?" Ivey asks.

"Because it is happening," Hannah responds. "All around the world, the Earth is refusing to produce crops in land that has been abused and planted with genetically engineered seeds. Genetically altered domestic animals are failing to grow to maturity and unable to reproduce. Medicated animals are dying from the very medicine they are receiving. The surface water and ground water are nearing the point of no return when it comes to human consumption. Even purification systems are finding it impossible to render the water consumable. In heavily populated areas of the world, people are developing serious breathing problems and dying because of the foul air. The depletion of the ozone continues to warm the planet giving rise to increased ocean levels, violent storms, and geological disasters. Deadly invasive species are spreading around a warming planet, and beasts extinct for millions of years are experiencing resurrection. Humanity is experiencing the truth every day!"

"How do we put this in a message so people will change?" Ainsley asks.

"We are putting the data together in an easily digestible format for publication. These things are happening now, and people will relate from their own personal experience or that of someone they know. The "Save the World Tour" must incorporate a message about good Earth husbandry. We are convinced that if people change the manner in which they treat the Earth, the Earth will return to a state which will support human life as long as good husbandry practices are maintained. We need to publish and distribute millions of these documents," Hannah stresses.

As Hannah expounds on the articles of Devolution, it occurs to Kennedy that there are threads of commonality between the Articles of Devolution, and the Tenets of Love and Peace coming from the conference on Mt. Pilatus. During their Ames Conference, the cousins talked about the possibility of science and religion actually being one and the same. As things unfold, it occurs to Kennedy that this may very well be the truth.

As the group sits down in Ansel's plush living room suite to consider the central theme of the "Save the World Tour", they focus on the products of the Mt. Pilatus Conference and the Theory of Devolution.

"It seems to me that the commandment of love and peace revealed on Mt. Pilatus refers to the relationship that must exist between human beings, as well as the Earth and all of its creatures," Kennedy offers the group.

"I wholeheartedly agree," adds Stella. "As I listened to Hannah, I heard the tenants of "As you sow, so you reap", "Nature obeys us as we obey nature. This planet is our home, and we must care for and respect our home" as things which also reflect the Articles of Devolution."

"What Stella has offered goes hand in hand with "The Universe, galaxies, and planets are all in harmony. There is a divine balance in every cause and every effect." What we are experiencing is the manner in which human behavior interferes with divine balance," notes Kennedy.

"It was not only 'as you sow, so you reap', but furthermore, 'Sow love reap love. Sow peace, reap peace' which speaks to love and peace with our planet," Ivey affirms.

"I believe an important aspect of the harmony which exists between the Tenets of Love and Peace and the Articles of Devolution is "Never need or desire anything so badly you can't do without. Replace cravings and greed with an attitude of generosity and sacrifice," Ainsley contributes and then adds, "A huge contributor to the abuses of the past has been greed. The rush by some to own and control everything has given a few the power to pervert our relationship with each other and nature for their own benefit. We can only achieve love and peace through a spirit of generosity and sacrifice."

"There is everything to gain by melding the Articles of Devolution with the Tenets of Love and Peace," Senator Joseph confirms, "Whenever and wherever we can combine the power of science and religion, we will have a greater impact on human behavior. We need to include within the main message "Don't be discouraged, we can do the impossible. Through the grace of God, human beings are the distributer of Divine Power. We must live in accordance with a conscience of good will towards all. Our ability to do the right thing must be combined with our willingness and determination to do so."

"We also need to deliver the good news of Olivia's accomplishment in making the mosquito and tick no longer capable of carrying disease. This alone will eliminate much human suffering and save millions of lives," Ivey asserts.

"I sure wish we would hear some good news from Noah, Edison, and Thomas," Kennedy adds.

CHAPTER 36

EMERGENCE

SITTING IN THEIR AMES HIDEOUT, Thomas receives a message from Reza at Virginia Tech saying the Oviraptor carcass is male. This is not good news as Reza also indicates that none of the assistants in the lab have any idea how to access the DNA from the semi-petrified eggs. They have identified three eggs which are female, but their inability to extract a DNA sample leaves them at a standstill.

Noah, Edison, and Thomas have reached the tipping point in their work. They cannot advance their theory without accessing the DNA of a female Oviraptor. Thomas is certain he can extract the sample if he had access to an egg. It is too dangerous to have an egg sent to them, plus they do not have access to the equipment needed for extracting a DNA sample.

Looking at Edison and Thomas, Noah turns to Hannah and Contessa, "Girls, we must leave this sanctuary in order to pursue a solution to the invasive species conundrum. We must go to Virginia Tech to solve this problem ourselves."

"If you leave and get caught, there will never be a solution," Hannah responds.

"We have accomplished a great deal in this secret fortress, but our situation no longer allows us the latitude to remain in hiding. It is time for us to emerge, but that does not mean we need to be foolish or careless in our escape," Edison reminds the girls.

"If some of us leave, we all need to leave. For Hannah and Contessa to remain behind puts the identity of their location in jeopardy. We cannot afford to lose any of our team members," Thomas insists. "If we are going to emerge, we need to have a plan to minimize our chances of being detected."

"One thing we can do is leave the equipment running to emit a faint but evasive signal as to this location. This will cause the authorities to hone in on this area, but create a difficult puzzle to solve. When they finally find this location, we will be long gone with no trace as to our whereabouts," Edison suggests.

"That is fine," says Noah, "but how do we get out of here without being discovered, and how do we get to Virginia Tech without detection?"

"We need disguises," Contessa proclaims, "We need to make sure if we are seen, no one pays us any attention."

"I know just the thing," Thomas offers enjoying the intrigue of being on the lamb. "While we were outside this room the other night when the professor was about to do the dirty deed with the coed, I noticed a custodial closet full of clothing. We could use this clothing for our disguise."

"Brilliant," exclaims Noah, "Nobody pays any attention to custodians as they move about doing their work."

"Except other custodians," Hannah reminds the group. "You know what they say about the best laid plans of mice and men."

Of Mice and Men is a reference to the novel written by John Steinbeck in 1937 in which two displaced migrant ranch workers move from place to place in California during the Great Depression. Despite their efforts, many of their plans did not work out. Thus, the phrase, "the best laid plans of mice and men."

"What are our options?" Edison questions. "We need a disguise to get us out of here, and it would be hard to beat custodial clothes. However, when we leave, where do we go and how do we get there?"

"There is an old service entrance on the ground floor," Hannah reveals.

"I suppose your knowledge of this plays into a romantic interlude again?" Edison teases.

"Remember Eddie, the guy is no longer with us," Noah reminds him. "You might want to show some sensitivity."

"No harm Edison," Hannah assures, "The important thing is the service entrance is obscure and easily accessed with little risk of being seen."

"What do we do once we reach the service entrance," Contessa wonders. "Where do we go from there, and how do we get there?"

"I have a friend," Hannah says, "and I believe he can be trusted."

"Ah, another male friend," Edison cannot resist the tease. "How do we know he can be trusted?"

"I have shared a great deal about Devolution with him. He is a scientist, and he holds our entire family in the highest esteem. I know he will help, and I am certain he can be trusted 100 percent," Hannah assures them with confidence.

"So, where will you and Contessa go, and how will Noah, Edison, and I get to Virginia Tech?" Thomas asks his sister.

"Shortly after Ames was settled in 1854, it became an important link to the Underground Railroad. Very few people know this fact because it was so secretive. In fact, Iowa History does not recognize this fact. However, at 804 Kellogg Avenue there sits a beautiful Italianate style structure built in 1885 over the site of Ames' Underground Railroad connection. This is my friend's home. Contessa and I can hold up there. Should it be necessary, we can seek refuge in the secret room below the basement until any threat blows over. My friend will see that we are well taken care of," Hannah informs the group.

"That is good," Noah responds, "But what about us? How do we get to Virginia Tech?"

"It can't happen without some risk, and trusting other people with our mission," Hannah reminds them. "I have a friend, with a private Lear Jet, who I feel confident will help us."

"Wow Hannah," you sure make the rounds. How long have you known this guy?" Edison welcomes every opportunity to tease Hannah. He has always found levity to be good medicine.

"First off Eddie, she is not a guy but rather a very attractive red head," Hannah turns the tables on her cousin. "If I remember correctly, Grandpa used to tease you about the little red headed girl from Charlie Brown. Well, this woman's name is Charlie and she is an excellent pilot. I am confident Charlie will get you safely and quickly to Virginia Tech."

"It seems to me we have a plan," Thomas declares.

"I agree," Contessa voices her support, "Let's get moving."

As Edison works on setting the equipment to continue emitting faint signals in their absence, Noah and Thomas slip out of the room to retrieve the custodial clothing. Thinking beyond their escape, Contessa archives all of the data they need to continue their work if and when the necessary equipment becomes available. The down side of this plan is the need to be off the grid for an undetermined amount of time.

Using a secure channel, Hannah contacts her friend Ray. After a brief conversation, Hannah is confident that Ray is on board with their clandestine operation. Ray has always been an anti-establishment man, so he relishes the opportunity to help Hannah and her fugitive brother and cousins. Closing her conversation with Ray, Hannah immediately contacts Charlie, a consummate woman in every way. Her physical attributes combined with a keen intelligence and razor-sharp wit make her an enviable friend and formidable foe. All Charlie needed to be motivated was a challenge involving risk and danger. When Hannah mentioned the need for deception in filing her flight plan, Charlie couldn't wait to get started. With everything in place, it's now time for the team to get started.

After sanitizing their quarters, the fugitives slip on the custodial clothing including hats and gloves. They do not want to leave any finger prints behind or along their trail. More than a bit nervous, the five fugitives slip out and close the boiler door on their hideout home. Once outside, it dawns on them that they are now past the point of no return. All they can do is move forward and hope for the best.

As they make their way to the ground floor service entrance at the back of the building, they check every hallway before turning a corner, and they look back to ensure no one sees them disappear down the next corridor. They all breathe a sigh of relief when they reach the service entrance and find Hannah's friend Ray arriving just in time. Climbing into his 2029 Ford Cargo Van, these five brilliant scientists, fugitives from the federal government, hunker down in the cargo bay for a run to the airport at 2501 Airport Drive on the west side of Highway 69 on the south side of Ames. As they navigate down South University Boulevard, they pass a federal vehicle doing a routine scan of the University campus.

When the federal vehicle turns around with lights flashing, Ray tells the five to hide behind the boxes in the back of the van and remain quiet. Pulling over, both federal agents exit their vehicle and walk toward the van with one on each side.

"How are you doing tonight?" the agent on the driver's side says as he points his flash light in the window and toward the back of the van.

Ray is a cool-cookie, he has dealt with the authorities many times during his young life and he is adept in handling this situation. "About as well as expected for working the graveyard shift," Ray responds. 'You know the saying, no rest for the wicked."

"Tell us about it," the agent on the driver's side responds. "It would be nice to get out from under these late-night details."

As the agent continues to quiz Ray, the other agent is running his flash light up, down, and around the passenger's side window trying to get a look. Ray pays this person no heed not wanting to give any cause for alarm.

"Do you have any identification?" the agent asks as he attempts to lean inside Ray's open window.

"Right here Sir," as Ray hands the agent a card which identifies him as a university employee.

"So, what is your business tonight Mr. Chavez?" the agent inquires. "What causes a doctoral assistant to be out at this time of night?"

"I am delivering supplies to the Administration Building," Ray says. "I make these runs to pick up a little extra cash," Ray reveals in an effort to beat the agent to his next question. "With the rising cost of everything, a guy can't have too much cash."

"What kind of supplies could be so important that they need to be delivered in the middle of the night?" the agent continues to interrogate Ray.

"These are publications from the printing office that are needed in the morning for registration," Ray says. "Would you like a look?" Ray asks knowing if he beats them to the punch with this question, there is a high probability it will defuse their curiosity. "Perhaps you might want to pick up a class or two while you're here in Ames?"

"What do you think?" the agent who has been talking to Ray asks his partner.

"I have no interest in taking a class," the other agent responds.

"I'm not talking about taking a class idiot, do you think we need to take a look at his cargo?" comes the specific question.

"I think we are wasting our time," is the response.

"One last question, have you seen anything suspicious this evening?" the agent asks.

"Not a thing, just another night at Iowa State," Ray assures.

"Let's go," one agent says to the other and they walk slowly back to their car glancing at the van every so often.

"Stay low and do not move," Ray tells his fugitive passengers. "We are going to make an unscheduled turn toward the Administrative Building in the event these characters decide to follow".

As Ray pulls away, the federal agents follow him at close proximity. Ray holds his breath as he turns toward the Administrative Building hoping they do not follow. He exhales a deep sigh of relief when they go straight. However, he must now chart a course which will not intersect with these agents again.

⸺⸺≫◆≪⸺⸺

Ten minutes later, they find themselves arriving at the airport. The pilot, Charlie, has made arrangements for the van to pull onto the tarmac for the loading of passengers. Noah, Edison, and Thomas look at each other in astonishment when they see the Learjet 45XL awaiting their arrival. Edison has some familiarity with the Learjet and he informs Noah and Thomas that they will probably be cruising 510 miles per hour at an altitude of over 50,000 feet. We will arrive at Virginia Tech in no time he assures.

As Noah, Edison, and Thomas quickly exit the van and climb the short staircase into the plane, they are greeted by a gorgeous blue eyed red head in a light brown flight suit, that hides some impressive attributes. As they pass Charlie, she specifically greets Edison and requests him to go to the cockpit. Edison is a bit taken aback that she knows his name, and he is mystified by her request. He is unaware that Hannah has set him up so Charlie would not only greet him personally, but make him the designated copilot.

As Noah and Thomas get comfortable in the plush seats. They soon become familiar with all of the technological amenities of the aircraft, While Edison waits patiently at the entrance to the cockpit.

"Hi Edison," Charlie greets him again as she approaches the cockpit. "Please enter and take the seat to the right."

Edison still dumbstruck by her directions and sheer beauty does as he is told. "Why am I sitting here in the cockpit?"

"When I filed my flight plan, I had to indicate a copilot. Hannah indicated this must be a top-secret flight, and I am aware of your situation. So, I had to falsify a copilot. Air control cannot tell who is in the copilot seat, but they can tell if it is occupied," Charlie informs him with a smile.

"Why make me the copilot, why not one of the other guys?" Edison asks as he reveals his nervousness at being in the copilot seat so close to this beautiful woman. He knows it will be a quick flight, at less than two hours, to travel just under 1000 miles, but what if he has to make conversation with Charlie. He has never seen anyone so incredibly attractive.

"I chose you because I have followed your career as a world-renowned expert on reptiles. I am also very intrigued by your Reptilian Theory. I have so many questions, and I thought we could pass the time in conversation," Charlie reveals flashing Edison a big and somewhat flirtatious smile. "Besides, you will enjoy and appreciate the view from here."

Edison reflects on the fact that he is already enjoying the view. Strangely, his thoughts turn to that day years ago when he and Noah were in the Canoe on the Little Sioux River. Here he is years later on another grand adventure, only this time it is his traveling companion that increases his respiration, not the sight of a Mountain Lion. However, he finds it possible to relax knowing their conversation will be about areas of his interest and expertise.

"Ok passengers, this is your pilot, we are moving to runway three in preparation for takeoff. Make sure your seats are in the upright position, and your seatbelts are fastened. If you have not ridden in a Learjet before, don't be startled by the force and speed of our takeoff. We will climb to 50,000 feet to avoid a storm system and take advantage of the jet stream. With good fortune, we will arrive in Roanoke, Virginia in less than two hours," Charlie notifies her passengers. "Okay, here we go!"

As the jet releases itself from the grip of the Earth, Noah and Thomas settle in to relax with an ironically apocalyptic onboard movie and a drink. Edison remains a bit tense being alone and in close proximity to Charlie in the cockpit. She is wearing an unfamiliar fragrance both sweet and mystifying. Upon reaching 50,000 feet and cruising speed, Charlie turns on the automatic pilot. As Charlie takes off her head set and pivots her seat toward Edison, he cannot believe the situation in which he finds himself.

"See that lever near the floor and to the right of your seat?" Charlie instructs. "It is no different than any other lever for turning a seat. Pull up on it and rotate your seat towards me so we can talk."

Edison is quite nervous and fumbles with the lever with no luck. Charlie has already unbuckled her seatbelt, "Here let me help you," she says leaning across Edison to reach the lever and turn his seat. As she leans, her long red hair brushes across his face leaving a sweet fragrance. As her body stretches to reach the lever, it comes in contact with his causing him to draw back. As the seat releases and turns, Charlie returns to her seat. Sensing Edison's discomfort, she offers him a big smile revealing her perfectly aligned white teeth and a shrug suggesting everything is cool.

Charlie's pleasant personality combined with an unquenchable curiosity quickly puts Edison at ease. Before he knows it, they are nonstop talking reptiles and Reptilian Theory. Edison finds himself wondering how someone of such exquisite beauty could find reptiles so fascinating. Every once in a while, their conversation is interrupted by turbulence, but like the jet, the time just flies by.

As they approach Roanoke, Charlie puts her seat back to flight position and instructs Edison to do the same. This time, Edison successfully maneuvers his seat into position.

"This is your pilot, please turn off all electronic devices, return your seats to the upright position, fasten your seatbelts and prepare for landing. We should be back on the ground in less than 15 minutes. Once we have landed, a 2035 Ford Mustang will pull alongside the plane. It is imperative that you grab all your belongings and depart immediately to the vehicle. I do not know the driver, but Hannah assures me he will take you to your destination at Virginia Tech," Charlie informs her passengers.

As the plane comes to a stop on the tarmac, Noah, Thomas, and Edison grab their belongings and head for the exit. As Edison is about to exit, he hears Charlie, "Edison, be safe, and I will see you again for the return flight," as she flashes her irresistible smile and adds a rather flirtatious wave. All Edison can think to do is wave back as he disappears down the stairway and into the car. As Charlie arrives at the exit to offer one more wave to this fascinating man and scientist, all she can see is the back of the car as it speeds away.

CHAPTER 37

THE KEY

As THEY SPEED OUT OF the airport for the 30 minute drive to Virginia Tech, the driver does not say a word but sticks to his business. The three fugitive scientists remain silent hoping they are in the right car with the right driver as the Virginia landscape quickly passes by. On route, they pass numerous historical sites and monuments from the American Revolution and Civil War era. Noah thinks about how the survival of the nation hung in the balance during these critical times in history. He recalls the words of Thomas Paine, "These are the times that try men's souls." He considers the courage and risk required to prevail under such horrendous circumstances. Now, he, his brother, sister, and cousins must persevere against what appears to be insurmountable odds.

Cruising along, Edison does not mind the silence, his thoughts are on Charlie and the serendipitous manner in which they met. Looking out the car window, Thomas recognizes many of the landmarks from his days as a doctoral student at Virginia Tech. Noah has never been to Virginia and turns his thoughts to their mission ahead.

When they are within 20 miles of Virginia Tech, the driver decides to break the silence. "Gentlemen, federal agents have been keeping a close eye on Virginia Tech in the event any of you decide to surface. If you will reach under your seats, you will find everything you need to disguise yourselves. The good news about the federal agents is that they are lazy and rather incompetent. Once you are disguised, we should be fine."

As Noah, Edison, and Thomas reach under their seats, they pull out clothes, hats, and facial disguises. Noah chuckles as he finds a full beard among his items as well as a broad rimed hat. Edison smiles at the thought of wearing a Van Dyke with long hair. Thomas has a neatly trimmed mustache to go with his bald head and baseball cap. The three of them quickly change into the clothes and add the facial features. They are surprised at how well the facial hair attaches in a very natural way. When their transformation is complete, they honestly cannot recognize each other!"

As they turn the corner to enter the campus, they see a blockade ahead. "Is that for us?" Noah inquires.

"Yes," comes the response, "But that blockade has been there ever since the president put a warrant out for your apprehension. I come this way all the time, so these fools know me," the driver explains as they pull up to the blockade.

"Well Mr. Jamison, how are you today?" one of the sentries greets.

"I am doing well Agent Campbell. How are you?" Jamison asks.

"Enough with the pleasantries, I see you have passengers. I do not recognize these individuals," Agent Campbell shares his curiosity.

"What do you think Agent Campbell; I picked these three academics up at the airport. They are here for the literary conference this weekend. I am sure they are very interesting," the driver says sarcastically.

Bending over the agent takes a good look in the window glancing at each of the passengers. "Well, they look literary enough to me. Have a great day Mr. Jamison!"

With that, the gate opens and the driver with his three fugitive scientists quickly slips by. "I am going to turn toward the Liberal Arts Center, but I will circle around to the Science Building. We will have you safely inside in a matter of minutes."

Thomas smiles at the thought that his sister, Hannah, is so well connected. She made all the arrangements to get them safely out of hiding and to the lab at Virginia Tech in a matter of a few hours. Hannah is very ingenious and clever.

Entering the lab, the three scientists are met by Dr. Henry's assistant Reza. "Dr. Abraham and Dr. Jude, I would like you to meet Reza, the best Paleobiology assistant in the world. Reza has been leading the research team since they all arrived here at Virginia Tech. Fill us in on your progress Reza."

"Dr. Henry, as you know the Oviraptor cadaver is a male. We have identified three eggs as female Oviraptors, but we have been unable to extract DNA," Reza responds with a sense of desperation.

"What seems to be the problem Reza," Dr. Henry further inquires.

"While the eggs are regenerating as with the first egg, which resulted in the birth of the male oviraptor, we are unable to penetrate the egg to extract a DNA sample," Reza says holding the palms of his hands upward suggesting he knows not what to do.

"Have you thought about breaking the egg open?" Dr. Abraham asks, "The outside of an egg usually is impenetrable."

"We have not done this because we have not wanted to destroy any developing embryo," Reza says, "Were we wrong in not doing this?"

"We need a DNA sample of a female Oviraptor more than we need a new born Oviraptor. The Oviraptor is of the phylum Chordata which has a genetic link to reptiles and mammals. We must gain access to the Oviraptor DNA. We must break open an egg and hope access to the genetic code lay inside," Dr. Abraham stresses as he moves toward the lab table containing the eggs.

"Dr. Henry," Reza protests, "These eggs are too valuable to just break open."

Looking at one of the assistants standing around the table, Dr. Henry asks, "Is this one of the female eggs?"

The assistant nods in agreement.

"Then get a hammer and break this egg open immediately," Dr. Henry orders.

Returning with a hammer, Dr. Henry takes it from the assistant's hand and gives the egg a sharp rap which causes the egg to split in half revealing a soft inner core. "Alright, isolate the nucleotide responsible for egg production," Dr. Henry instructs the assistant.

As Thomas, Edison, and Noah watch the assistants at work, they shake their heads at the incredible risk and distance traveled just to crack an egg. They watch closely to ensure the procedure is completed with the greatest fidelity. They smile as the egg producing nucleotide is successfully extracted.

"Okay, now use the CRISPR Cas9 39 to remove a strand that will disrupt the linear sequence and render the female incapable of producing eggs," Dr. Jude declares at this critical moment.

With the successful extraction, our three innovative and ingenious scientists have a prototype for testing. They are going to fast track this testing process because urgency is at hand. "So, my dear colleagues and cousins, what is the most effective delivery system when dealing with carnivorous beasts?" Dr. Henry asks clearly knowing the answer.

"We need to implant the mutated DNA in a host. As the host is eaten by a predator, the mutated DNA will enter the blood stream of the predator via the digestive system. Once in the blood stream, the mutated DNA will act as an invasive species attacking the female predator's ability to produce eggs. This means the host must be something enticing to the predator. Of course, from reptile to mammal this may vary greatly," Dr. Jude notes.

"I know this seems simplistic, but let's try it on a female cat and host mouse. If the cat is a mature female and it eats a host mouse, the DNA make up of the cat should change to the mutated version rendering the cat incapable of producing eggs. We should have results in twenty-four hours. Let's do the same thing with a snake and mouse to include a reptile in our extremely short study," Dr. Henry suggests.

"We need results and we need them now," Dr. Abraham says moving around the lab table. "There is too much at jeopardy if we fail to get this right. Yet, if we prolong what we believe is true, we could sacrifice all that we hope to gain. Time is of the essence. Let's do as Thomas suggests."

"Someone, bring a cat, snake, and two mice in here immediately," Reza commands the lab assistants.

Within minutes someone produces a female cat, snake, and two lab mice. "Perfect," Dr. Henry thanks the lab assistant, "Now inject the mice with the altered DNA and put the cat and a mouse together. Do the same with the snake and mouse. In the morning we should know the result," Dr. Henry shares with great anticipation.

In just a short amount of time, less than the time needed to travel from Ames to Virginia Tech, the three fugitive scientists successfully complete the first phase of their mission. With time on their hands,

Thomas suggests the three make their way to a local haunt for some food and beverage.

"Venturing out in public seems like an unnecessary risk Thomas," Noah suggests.

"We have been cooped up in hiding for a long-time cousin. I think we deserve a little relaxation. Besides, we have some rather impressive disguises just waiting to serve this purpose," Thomas reminds Noah and Edison in a determination to hit the town.

"They are good disguises Noah. As long as we are careful, what can it hurt?" Edison proclaims sensing a need to unwind.

"Good, then it is done," Thomas declares. "Let's get Jamison to be our chauffer and help steer us out of harm's way."

———————>≫◈≪<———————

Leaving the lab, the three fugitives put on their disguises and pile into the limousine driven by Jamison.

"Take us to the Horny Hog," Thomas directs Jamison.

"The Horny Hog," Noah retorts in surprise. "How ironic we should visit an establishment named after Eddie," he says with a smile and chuckle.

"What is that suppose to mean?" Edison fires back a bit defensively.

"Just busting your chops little brother, frankly Thomas and I are a bit more than jealous of your private flight with Ms. Charlie," Noah reveals. "Besides, we're hoping a few drinks will loosen your lips and provide us with some insight into our angelic pilot."

As they enter the Horny Hog, Thomas suggests they sit at an obscure booth along the wall. Noah and Edison, peer through the dimly lit room searching for the essence of this establishment. It is a typical college bar complete with pool tables, foosball tables, and darts. The bar is busy with men and women of the Greek societies. The three of them settle back and smile at the antics of college men attempting to gain the attention of young coeds. None of them joined a fraternity during their college days, but they all recall Grandpa's stories about his fraternity days as a Phi Sig at Wayne State College in Wayne, Nebraska.

One of the down sides of sitting in an obscure location is the lack of service. Each time the waitress attempts to get to their booth, she is stopped by another customer seeking assistance. Finally, Thomas decides to take matters into his own hands and goes to the bar.

"What can I do for you?" the woman behind the bar asks Thomas.

"Could I please get three bottles of Coors Light," Thomas asks.

"I don't believe I have seen you in here before," the woman asks.

"No, my friends and I are attending a literary conference on campus," Thomas responds.

"You sure have a familiar voice," the woman notes. "It has a very distinct quality. Are you sure you haven't visited this bar before?"

"No, this is my first trip to Virginia," Thomas assures her as he lays down a ten-dollar bill, grabs the bottles and says, "Keep the change."

Back at the booth, Thomas relates his encounter with the bartender to Noah and Edison. "Maybe we should forgo the beer and return to the lab," Noah suggests. The three men have cots awaiting them in a room off of the lab as a means of keeping them out of public view. Ironically, they currently sit in one of the most public places, a bar.

"I don't think she is going to be a problem. She said I sounded familiar, but she never indicated who I sounded like. Furthermore, the college crowd is keeping her rather busy," Thomas says attempting to reduce Noah's concern.

"Come on Noah, we're in disguise, and no one is going to identify us by our voice. We deserve a little down time," Edison pleads.

As they sit enjoying the bar environment, they find the young coeds a welcome distraction. They entertain themselves with a little game in which they attempt to predict something about someone in the bar, preferably a female. They might guess whether she is from the farm or city, her major, her age, or anything else to keep the conversation lively and entertaining. If one of them feels their prediction is correct or someone else's prediction is wrong, they put a dollar on the table and everyone must play.

This game not only makes for good fun, but it engages the three with the bar crowd. In most cases, the individuals they encounter are good sports.

"You see that brunette over by the shuffleboard table. She actually has short hair. Her long ponytail is a hair piece," Thomas asserts.

"Now how the hell could you know that?" Edison challenges by putting a dollar on the table. "What do you say Noah?"

"I say Thomas knows something we don't, so my dollar is on Thomas being correct," Noah says. "Okay Eddie, you challenged so you need to entice the young lady to our booth."

Getting up from the booth, Edison has forgotten he looks like an aged literary professor rather than the young handsome scientist he is. "Excuse me," Edison says moving into the young brunette's space. A bit startled, she gives Edison a quizzical look as if to say who the hell are you?

"My friends and I wonder if you would be so kind as to answer a question for us," Edison asks.

"I guess I could do that," she answers with a slur revealing she has had several drinks.

Back at the booth, Thomas compliments her appearance before asking about a hair piece. With a smile, she easily removes her ponytail confirming Thomas' prediction. Since Thomas was right and Noah agreed with Thomas, Edison paid a dollar to each.

As their game progresses, the guys get more daring with each drink. Tonight, the coeds validate everything they had ever heard about sorority girls being a whole lot of fun. For a brief time, Noah, Edison, and Thomas forget they are fugitives.

"Since Edison is the big loser tonight, let's give him the final prediction with whatever amount he may want to wager," Noah suggests to Thomas.

"Sure, why not. Just like Home Run Derby, it is all or nothing," Thomas says recalling a game they use to play as kids.

"Okay guys, I predict the very pretty short blonde at the table with her sorority sisters will give Noah a kiss if I ask her," Edison boldly proclaims.

Thomas takes a good look at Noah and his disguise and says, "Nobody is going to kiss that hairy mug."

"I agree with Thomas; you're going out on a limb with this one," Noah announces.

"You said I could determine the amount of this wager. Well, I am down ten dollars, and I really want to finish big, so the wager is ten dollars," Edison throws down the gauntlet. "Let me get her over here."

"No, you don't! How do we know you won't set us up by seeking her cooperation?" Noah reveals his suspicion that Edison is up to something.

"Let's see if the waitress can get her to come over here?" Thomas suggests.

After asking the waitress to run interference for them, the short young blonde coed staggers her way to the booth. Arriving at the booth, Edison initiates the request, "Hi Mavis, you appear to be having a good time tonight."

"How do you know my name?" she asks while struggling to stand.

"Oh, I'm in the knowing business," Edison responds. "You look like you might need a seat, please join us for a minute. Slide in next to my colleague, he won't mind," as he offers her a seat next to Noah.

"Are you guys important or something? You look important so why do you want to talk to me?" Mavis says leaning close to Noah for a good look.

"Yea, I would say we are important Mavis but tonight we are just having a good time," Edison reveals. "You look like you're having a good time. In fact, you impress me as someone who is a good sport."

"I am, life is too short not to be a good sport and have fun. Fun is me," Mavis informs.

"Good, so here is the situation. My friend sitting next to you has never been kissed by a pretty girl. When I asked him of all the girls in this bar which one is the prettiest, he said it was you. So, I am wondering Mavis, if you are such a good sport, would you give my friend a kiss," Edison asks.

With Edison's question, Mavis turns to Noah and throws her arms around his neck. She then proceeds to plant a long and passionate kiss on his lips. Drawing away from the kiss, Mavis looks Noah in the eyes and asks, "Is there anything else you might want?"

Delighted by the kiss, Noah is shocked by the question. "No thank you Mavis," Edison jumps in to remedy the situation. "Thank you for being a good sport."

As Mavis stumbles back to the table from which she came, the three scientists' chuckle at the unpredictability of college students and college bars.

"How did you know she would actually give Noah a kiss?" Thomas demands.

"I don't know what they have been shooting for drinks, but I have been watching that group for over an hour. Anyone who knocks down as many shots as Mavis loses all inhibition. The kiss was not in question. However, her ability to walk from there to here was. So, I believe you each owe me ten dollars," Edison says with great satisfaction.

As they are finishing their drink before heading back to the lab, the woman who had been tending bar approaches the booth. Looking at Thomas, "I know you say you have never been in this bar, but I have heard your voice before. I now know why it is so familiar. You sound just like the fugitive scientist Thomas Henry but you don't look anything like him."

"I'm not a fugitive and I'm not a scientist," Thomas declares. "We are just three literary professors trying to have a good time."

"I understand that, but I just couldn't get over how much you sound like him. Besides, if I ever had the chance, I would like to shake his hand as well as the hands of his sisters, and cousins. They are such an amazing family, and we are very fortunate to have so many ingenious people with such dedication and courage fighting for our survival," she attests. "Well, I will let you be, but I just wanted to say thank you!" as she holds out her hand to Thomas.

As the woman returns to the bar, Noah says, "It is now past time to go."

CHAPTER 38

CREATURE CONTROL

T HE NEXT MORNING, THE THREE fugitive scientists are in the lab as the research team arrives for the day. Observing the cages, the mice are gone.

"Test the DNA structure of the cat and snake," directs Dr. Abraham.

When the test results arrive later that afternoon, it reveals that by eating the infected mice, the cat and snake's DNA structure has been altered to prohibit the production of eggs. Noah, Edison, and Thomas know they have not done the prerequisite studies required for scientific certainty, but the results validate what they believe based on experience and sheer intuition. This is the time to act! Any delay could cost millions of lives.

"We must focus on control not elimination," Dr. Jude tells his brother and cousin. "In order to eliminate, we would need to saturate the food chain beyond the reach of our intended target. If we can control our targeted beasts by creating sanctuaries, we could achieve ecological harmony."

"Begin mass production of this mutated DNA immediately," Dr. Abraham orders. "We will identify strategic areas for delivery based upon infestation. We will identify the prey worthiest of carrying the mutated DNA depending on predator preference of food source. We will saturate each area with the DNA mutated prey knowing that the end result may be 20 percent with each saturation. If this is done incrementally, we will witness a significant reduction in predators. As predator's decrease and the food source increases, the geographical territory of a predator will become restrained and predictable. Once we reach a manageable predator to food source ratio, "we will be able to maintain established sanctuaries."

"This is surreal," Dr. Henry exclaims. "Imagine a world where prehistoric and ancient beasts can exist without endangering human beings and civilization. The scientific and ecological possibilities are beyond amazing."

"Dr. Abraham," Reza is looking for Noah's attention.

"What is it Reza?" Noah asks.

"We have been working for several hours, and we do not possess enough actual DNA to mass produce the mutated version," Reza reveals.

"This is not acceptable. You're telling me we have discovered a way to render these monster reptiles and mammals incapable of reproduction, but now lack the means to make it happen," Dr. Abraham is clearly agitated. "We need a solution and we need it now. If we fail to deliver on this solution, thousands and eventually millions of people will meet a grizzly fate."

"Dr. Abraham, I am the head of technology here at the lab. I believe we can replicate a synthetic version of the mutated DNA which will have the same effect as the actual mutated DNA."

"That's fantastic news, how soon can you make this happen? We need to get started on mass production!" Noah's mood has swung from agitation to exhilaration.

"We can get on it first thing in the morning and put it into mass production by mid-afternoon," the technology head suggests.

"Bullshit man, we're not planning a picnic here," Noah retorts. "The world depends on us. I want you and your team working on this throughout the night. When I return in the morning, I expect to see this synthetic mutated DNA in full production," Noah demands.

Having achieved a mutated DNA, there is nothing Noah, Edison, and Thomas can do but wait. As Noah, Edison, and Thomas find refuge on their back-room cots for the night, they are eager to see their discovery put to use in securing the safety of human beings. They are also excited about the possibility of managing the existence of reptiles and mammals not seen on the Earth for millions of years.

Our brilliant scientists know they have only one chance to get this right. Once unleashed on civilization, there will be no turning back. These vicious mammals and reptiles will bring devastation to everything and everyone in their path. Whole communities and cities will be laid waste in a blood bath of carnage.

Now, at this moment, the opportunity exists to maintain these aggressive predators under a controlled environment. Why eradicate something of such importance if management is possible. Why would nature restore them to the Earth unless it was a second chance at life?

The risk is great, and the responsibility weighs heavy on these three scientists. They are confident of success, but only if they are in time.

Noah finds it difficult to sleep knowing there is nothing they can do until the technology team completes their task. Waiting is not his strong suit, and he wants to know how things are going in the lab. It is 3:30 a.m., and Noah walks out to the lab for a look.

Trying not to disturb Edison or Thomas, Noah prepares to start his day. "Is it time to get up?" Edison asks half asleep.

"No, it's only 3:30 in the morning, but I cannot sleep. I am going out to the lab for a look. I'll see you and Thomas later," Noah whispers.

Arriving in the lab, Noah rushes in to find everyone hard at work. "How are things going?" He asks the head of technology.

"We are just completing the synthetic model. We will then run the synthetic model through a digital test to make sure it replicates the mutated DNA 100 percent," the technology head reveals with a hint of caution.

"Are you concerned about your ability to achieve success?" Noah asks.

"I am not; we have been in the business of making synthetics for a full range of purposes for a long time. However, this is our first attempt to create synthetic DNA. I don't want there to be any doubt about our success," he assures Noah. "If things go as expected, we should be in full production by 6:00 this morning."

"Excellent! I have every confidence in your ability to obtain the desired result. I appreciate the effort of you and your team," Noah says pumping his fist in a determined manner.

When Edison and Thomas arrive in the lab, the mass production of the mutated DNA is in full swing. Noah asks for everyone's attention,

"We have a huge and urgent mission to accomplish. Thanks to all of you, we have developed a synthetic mutated DNA which when ingested by a reptilian or mammal predator renders the female predator incapable of producing eggs. This means we have a method for controlling the propagation of very vicious and dangerous beasts. Congratulations!"

"Now that we are done patting ourselves on the back," Thomas adds, "We must mass produce this synthetic version of mutated DNA by the thousands if not millions. So, your challenge here at the lab is to keep the wheels of production moving."

"What we will do," Edison says, "Is leverage our contacts to generate, in sufficient numbers, the ideal prey to act as hosts for this mutated DNA. We will have these animals brought into a local stockyard where they can be infected and shipped immediately to the identified areas."

"But professors, what if the wrong predator eats the infected prey?" Reza asks.

"Excellent question," Noah jumps in to respond, "We will coordinate with trusted colleagues to see that the infected prey is delivered into the heart of the predator's territory well away from human civilization."

"But that is no guarantee a human will not eat the infected prey," another lab assistant notes.

"Here is the situation," Thomas delivers to a fully aware group of assistants, "As you have been previously informed, we are dealing with predators that have the capability of making short work of adult human beings in a very gruesome manner. We are talking about curtailing an infestation of beasts with a voracious appetite that could lay waste to whole communities. If we do not act soon, the horror brought on by an invasion of these hungry predators will be unlike anything we have ever seen."

"Thomas is right," Edison says supporting his cousin's depiction, "The carnage these beasts could indiscriminately inflict on a human population would be grizzly. By implementing this strategy to control the population of these beasts, and by ensuring an abundant food supply, they will not threaten human beings or populated areas. These are territorial creatures that only want food and to procreate. If we can get them under control, we could establish sanctuaries for their study without needing to eradicate them from the Earth a second time."

"Look, we understand the downside of what we are doing, but at the moment we have no other choice. To do nothing is to sentence populated areas to the butchery which would be inflicted by these beasts. We need to move forward with what we have, and continue to strive to find a mutation of the DNA which will not adversely affect human beings should they use an infected animal for food," Noah recognizes.

"Let's stay focused folks," Thomas urges the team, "The areas in the United States and around the world where this will be used first have already experienced and seen the horror of these beasts. We will inform the public fully of our effort and warn them against eating the meat of any of the animals being used as prey. Furthermore, we will try to use animals for prey which are not normally used as human food. However, you must understand that if the prey is not attractive to the predator, we are defeating our entire purpose."

"As you work, you must do it subtly as to not attract the attention of the authorities who could shut this project down," Edison warns. "Keep in mind, the safety of thousands if not millions of people are in our hands. We must not fail!"

"We will work closely with the local stockyard where truck loads of animals are rolling in and out 24-7. I know the owner of the stockyard from my days here at Virginia Tech," Thomas acknowledges. "We will make this project lucrative for his business. As long as we act with caution, we should stay under the radar. Reza, we are putting you in charge of this operation. We will communicate only with you, and you are to keep us apprised of the progress."

"We are all dedicated to the mission professors, you can count on us!" Reza responds.

Knowing everything is in good hands, Noah, Edison, and Thomas contact Charlie waiting at the airport about their readiness to return to Ames. Within a half an hour, an airport delivery truck arrives to pick up the three fugitive scientists. As they travel to the airport hidden in the back of the truck, Edison wonders if he will once again be copilot, or if he has been replaced.

As they pull onto the tarmac, they feel the truck come to a stop. As the back hatch opens, Edison sees Charlie's beautiful flowing red hair.

"Hey guys," Charlie greets, "You ready for a return trip? Edison, are you ready to be my copilot?"

"Yea Eddie, are you ready to be her copilot?" Thomas teases.

"You're just jealous," Edison retorts.

"Damn right I am, look who I have to ride with?" he says with a smile and a wink.

As Edison gets settled into the copilot seat, Charlie turns "Is everything okay Doctor, was your stop successful?"

"Don't call me doctor, my name is Edison or Eddie," he responds, "Why yes, we had a very productive and successful trip."

CHAPTER 39

FREEDOM

Attorney General Loophole has slipped away to Hidden Lakes State Park 18 miles southeast of Nashville to do a little fishing. The attorney general likes this lake because of the seclusion and privacy it offers. The trail to reach Hidden Lake starts at a gravel lot and winds through a tall grass field before entering the woods. It is a picturesque journey which features a few creeks and a deep thick vegetation of foliage. The lake eventually emerges as the trail arrives at a rocky bluff. The trail continues down the bluff to lake level where an old wooden dock stands. The wooden dock is missing a couple of planks, and is supported by poles leaning to the right and left, looking like palace guards after a little too much to drink. The dock stretches 30 feet into a lily pad covered water, which allows an angler to play the far edges of the lily pad where the big fish lie. Few people are aware that Hidden Lake is home to an abundance of Large Mouth Bass, and the attorney general has landed some trophy fish during his fishing ventures to the lake.

Standing on the end of the dock, Attorney General Loophole and his fishing companion, a young advisor, are catching largemouth bass with every other cast. Out of the thick covering of the woods emerges a deer that enters the water but ten yards from where they are standing. No sooner has the unsuspecting deer wadded into the water, when a gigantic snake, hidden in the shoreline rushes, strikes with lightning speed. The snake engulfs the deer's head up to its front legs and begins to constrict the deer with its massive body.

The startled attorney general and his young advisor drop their rods and reels, and sprint for shore hoping there are no other gigantic snakes nearby. The attorney general catches his foot in the rickety old deck. As the force of his body twists to the left on the same side as the snake, Loophole plunges head first into the water. In panic mode, the attorney general comes to the surface yelling for help. His young advisor without thinking twice about the snake, turns around to rescue his boss. Fortunately, the snake is already too busy to care, and there doesn't seem to be a second snake in the vicinity. Grabbing the attorney general by the left hand with his right, the young advisor, with an ability to press 300 pounds in the weight room, lifts Loophole quickly to the dock where a drenched attorney general shows amazing speed, despite a twisted ankle.

Two secret service agents standing guard on the shore rush to meet the horrified attorney general. They hustle him up the bluff and back along the trail leading to the parked limousine, with the young advisor following close behind. With their side arms drawn, the agents push the injured attorney general along while scanning the woods for any sign of danger. Loophole doesn't mind their pushing, he just wants to get back to the limousine before he, or any of his companions, become supper for another hungry snake.

Arriving at the limousine, the agents shove Loophole and his young advisor into the vehicle securing the doors. "What the hell was that?" the attorney general asks while trying to catch his breath. Wasting no time, the Limousine speeds away leaving a trail of dust and flying gravel. Loophole is in such a panic mode; he fails to thank his young assistant for saving his life.

Sensing an opportunity to have an impact on something which has troubled him for some time, the young assistant begins. "Attorney General Loophole, do you remember the president's story about Senator Joseph warning him of these incredible beasts. The senator had learned about these beasts from his cousin, Doctor Abraham?"

"I remember something of the sort, but the president called it a bunch of scientific baloney. The rise of mythological beasts threatening humanity," the attorney general responds with a scoff.

"Well, that was one of those beasts, Sir. Think if that snake had not been busy with the deer? It might be you with your head in its mouth," the young advisor presents.

"What are you trying to say?" the attorney general asks his eyes still bulging from the fear evoked by witnessing such a violent attack.

"I just wondered if you remembered the president's story Sir," the advisor says obviously hesitant to say more.

"Speak freely son," Loophole commands still trying to catch his breath.

"Well Sir, I have been reading a lot of Doctor Noah Abraham's work on invasive species and the Reptilian Theory being developed by Doctor Edison Jude and Doctor Thomas Henry. What you witnessed, they predict, will become commonplace and could spread to populated areas if it is not addressed," the young advisor says.

"You can't be serious son! The Earth is being invaded by gigantic snakes," the attorney general says with skepticism despite his first experience just moments ago.

"Snakes are just a part of the theory, and if the truth be told, the theory is rapidly becoming a reality. They not only predict, but have proof of beasts of prehistoric dimensions increasing in numbers throughout the world. Just saying," the young advisor shares hesitantly.

"How do you know this and the government doesn't?" the attorney general asks a bit indignantly.

"The government knows, but just refuses to believe. There is an entire social media underground where this information and more is being shared in hopes of saving humanity," the young advisor discloses.

"Why is this underground information and not common knowledge?" the attorney general asks.

"May I continue to speak freely?" the young advisor nervously requests.

"Please do, I have just seen something out of a sci-fi movie, and I want to know what is going on?" the attorney general demands.

"Well frankly Sir, this government forced five of the world's foremost thinkers and scientists into hiding because they acted to save lives rather than follow established protocol. Everything they have been doing since the warrants for their arrest were issued has been circulating through the underground. In cases where the mainstream media has tried to inform the public, news anchors like Christine Matthews, have been censored and even fired due to governmental pressure," the young advisor bravely shares.

"Are you talking about Senator Joseph's cousins?" the attorney general asks.

"I am Sir. These five scientists hold important keys to reversing the pestilence which is consuming the Earth. However, because they are in hiding, they must do everything in secret, which limits their ability to find and implement solutions to the problems facing humanity," the young advisor replies. He has done everything but suggest rescinding the warrants on these five fugitive scientists.

"Driver, take us directly to the home of Federal Judge Douglas Holmes! By God it is time we get a court order declaring the warrants on these five scientists unconstitutional and null and void," states a determined attorney general.

"What about the president Sir, should you not confer with him first," the young advisor wonders.

"The president lost his senses a long time ago. I should have had the courage to stand up to him before. I am the attorney general, and I have seen this beast up close. Now is the time for action, not consultation. This could cost me my job, but it is the right thing to do," the attorney general declares.

Arriving at the Nashville home of Federal Judge Douglas Holmes, Attorney General Loophole spills the beans to the judge and requests a ruling.

"Well Mr. Attorney General, you seem like the lion in the Wizard of Oz. You have finally found your courage. I have been wondering just how long it would take for someone of authority to seek an injunction on these unjustifiable warrants. If the president was doing his job, these fine citizens and leaders of the scientific community would never have had to do an end run around the government to save millions of lives," the Judge declares. "However, we are under martial law, and I am not certain an injunction would do much good when the Constitution is being ignored."

"You seem to be rather knowledgeable about the situation Judge," the young advisor notes.

"Look son, I am a direct descendent of the great jurists William O. Douglas and Oliver Wendell Holmes. It is my solemn duty to know what is going on in our country and around the world. Do you find it odd that someone of my status and stature would be tuned into the media underground?" the Judge asks.

Knowing a rhetorical question when he hears it, the young advisor remains silent.

"So, are you going to issue an injunction Judge?" Attorney General Loophole inquires.

"Do bear's poop in the woods?" the Judge responds and directs his clerk to draw up the injunction papers which will nullify the president's warrant on the five fugitive scientists. "You do know under martial law the president can declare this injunction null and void. You also know that if the president chooses to recognize the Constitution, this injunction can be overturned by any member of the United States Supreme Court. Of course, I only know of two who might do this. I urge you to contact them immediately with your story and justification for seeking this injunction. Furthermore, ask them to contact me before taking any action."

"I know who you are talking about Judge, but they will not take action unless requested by the president. Proper procedure would require such a request come through me," the attorney general responds.

"Don't be a simpleton Loophole, you are talking about an out-of-control president and his menacing sidekick Peet. Get out ahead of this thing and stay there," the Judge advises.

When the clerk returns with the injunction, the Judge quickly signs it and sends the Loophole on his way. "Good luck to you."

Attorney General Loophole has his office issue a press release revealing the injunction overturning the warrants. DNN picks up on it immediately. Feeling safe in the living room at 804 Kellogg Ave in Ames, Hannah, Contessa, and Ray are watching an old rerun of the Big Bang Theory when bold letters spelling out "Breaking News" comes across the screen quickly followed by the face of Coyote Blitzer.

"We have breaking news to report; remember it came to you first from DNN the first in news. The Office of the Attorney General of the United States has just issued a press release stating that Federal Judge Douglas Holmes has issued an injunction on the presidential warrant for the arrest of the five fugitive scientists."

As these words come from the holographic projection, Hannah and Contessa can hardly believe their ears. "Did I just hear him correctly?" Contessa exclaims exuberantly.

"My God," Hannah says jubilantly, "We are free, we don't need to hide any longer."

"Dr. Noah Abraham, Dr. Edison Jude, Dr. Hannah Rae, Dr. Thomas Henry, and Dr. Contessa Margery, all internationally renowned scientists responsible for saving the lives of millions of people, are free," comes the report.

The news of the injunction reaches Noah, Edison, and Thomas as they are preparing to land at the Des Moines International Airport. Charlie and Edison can hear Noah and Thomas give out a shout of jubilation at the news. Charlie turns to Edison and offers him a smile reflecting great pride and affection. Edison returns the smile and let's loose with a big sigh.

As the DNN broadcast continues, "While this is certainly great news for these five scientists, everything might not be roses. Let's get a report from our legal consultant Anus Reno. Anus, what does this all mean for these five scientists?"

"Thanks Coyote, well the injunction from the Federal Judge is certainly good news. As long as the injunction stands, the five scientists have no cause for worry. However, an injunction can be declared null and void by the president under martial law, or the president can seek to overturn the injunction by appealing to a Supreme Court Justice," Anus reveals.

"But doesn't it bode well for these five scientists that the injunction was sought by the Attorney General of the United States?" Coyote asks.

"Yes, and No, if the attorney general acted on the authority of the president, this should be a done deal. However, if the attorney general acted of his own accord, and the president does not agree with his actions, the president could act to overturn the injunction," Anus informs.

"What is the likelihood of that happening Anus?" Coyote continues to investigate.

"That is a great question Coyote. We have to wonder if the president is willing to act counter to his own attorney general. How important is it, and of what benefit is it to keep these five scientists in hiding? Anus adds.

"Well, it does not look like the five scientists are out of the woods yet. How long do you think it will be before it will be safe for them to come out of hiding?" Coyote asks as if giving them a warning.

"We should know in two or three days if the President is going to act of his own accord or seek the action of a Supreme Court Justice. In situations like these, in which they are going to be asked to overturn the actions of one of their own brethren, the justices do not appreciate procrastination," Anus suggests.

"Charlie, this is Hannah. Did you guys get the news on the injunction?"

"Yes, we did, isn't it great news?" Charlie responds.

"Did you also catch the conversation between Coyote Blitzer and Anus Reno?" Hannah inquires.

"Yes, we did that also, is seems like good news is always followed by cautionary news. The guys want to know your plan," Charlie asks.

"Ray is on his way to the Airport to pick up Noah, Edison, and Thomas and bring them back to Ray's. We need to continue laying low until we know what the president is going to do," Hannah informs.

"I got that and will let the guys know. Over and out, this is Charlie."

Prior to landing, Charlie asks the tower for permission to taxi to an area behind the main terminal reserved for small personal aircraft. As she begins her maneuvers for taxing, she is relieved to see Ray's van turning into the small aircraft area to receive her cargo. As she comes to a stop, Edison unbuckles and prepares to leave the cockpit.

"You know Edison; I admire you, your brother, sister and cousins for the courage, sacrifice, leadership, and hope you are providing humanity. I am not the most educated person, but I recognize the world is in real trouble and your family is putting it all on the line to bring us back from the abyss," Charlie offers her sincere sentiment.

"Thank you, I have enjoyed our time together. Thanks for allowing me to be your copilot," Edison answers.

"You can be my copilot anytime Doctor Jude," Charlie says with a big smile and offers Edison a hug. "In fact, I have grown quite fond of you," she whispers.

"As I have of you," Edison responds. "Perhaps our paths will cross again!" as he turns to exit the cockpit.

"That would be nice," Charlie calls out as Edison steps into the passenger section, grabs his bag, and heads down the stairs toward the van.

Charlie hustles to the hatch hoping to get one last glance of this brilliantly personable man who has managed to capture her heart. Arriving at the hatch, she watches as Edison begins to climb into the van, and then pauses as he senses someone watching. He turns toward the plane and sees this goddess of the sky waving and smiling. He smiles and offers a big wave before disappearing into the van.

"Is everyone set?" asks Ray.

"Yea, I believe we are all set except for Edison who seems to be floating on cloud nine," Thomas teases.

"Okay, were off," Ray announces as the van zooms across the tarmac toward the exit leaving Charlie and her Learjet behind.

CHAPTER 40

REUNION

IN CHICAGO EVERYONE IS EXCITED about the prospect of seeing their brother, sister, and cousin's safe and back in the fold. So many things are happening. It feels like they have arrived at the right place, just in time. There is a real feeling of optimism in the air. This wonderful family of incredible personal and collective intelligence and talent are the catalyst for hope. After decades of wandering in the wilderness, there shines the light of promise for a new day.

As they receive word on their fugitive cousins, they remain confident their cousins will soon be free. Senator Joseph says the president does not have the personal courage to deal with an attorney general who could make matters more difficult as an adversary. "It is a matter of time," the senator tells everyone.

A matter of time also means the Chicago kickoff of the "Save the World Tour" is rapidly approaching. How wonderful it will be if they can all be together for the beginning of this monumental extravaganza. The Tenants of Peace and Love are already resonating around the globe through the witnessing of the conference disciples. Devolution revealing its ugly head around the world cries out for a renaissance of conscientious behavior. The cousins discover that God and science are not only real, but one and the same. The die is cast, and the time has come for the difficult work to begin. It is time to ask humanity to save the Earth as well as themselves.

2039

When Rabbis Markovitz and Ali al-Baghdadi II made a joint appearance to witness a new age with One God and One World, peace fell over that part of the world which has existed in turmoil and chaos for millennium. Instantaneously, some miraculous force engulfs the world with the witnessing of each conference disciple. Millions of believers make the transformation from hatred to peace. There are no hidden secrets about the revelations from the conference on Mt. Pilatus. All glory belongs to God and humility to those blessed to gaze upon his face and hear his cry to save planet Earth. The chosen ones previously treated their religion and faith as a reason to divide humanity in a very destructive manner. Now they are commissioned to carry the Tenants of Peace and Love to the followers of the religions they lead. The dramatic message declaring all religions and faiths as one under the Tenants requires great courage. But they witnessed and saw the face of God. They heard his command. Their testimony combined with a video of the revelation left nothing in doubt, God is calling, and the people of Earth will either respond or perish.

The Save the World Tour will bring front and center those things which need to be done if the planet Earth is to avert a cataclysmic event leading to the extinction of the human race. Every single moment of this three-day extravaganza with every single performance will serve to highlight the message that God and science are one. God needs the people of Earth to be free but committed to caring for each other and the planet with which they have been blessed. Peace and Love must prevail. Human beings must cast aside religious theology which creates hatred and causes hostilities between God's children. Human beings must cast aside greed and self-interest for the benefit of all. Human beings must treat the Earth and all living creatures with respect. Human beings must accept the reality of Devolution and practice good husbandry of the land, air, and water, which assures their purity and productivity. Global warming must be reversed! Only the Earth in balance will bring an end to the geological and environmental catastrophes which have led to billions of deaths and unbelievable destruction. The Earth in balance will result in climate stability, and return regions of the Earth to their most productive state. The tour will recognize Olivia's amazing victory over Satan's insidious winged angel of death. The tour will highlight the successful work of Noah, Edison, and Thomas in containing and controlling the rise of predatory beasts. Most of all, the tour will give all glory to a loving and gracious God.

The entire purpose of the tour is the message. Pulling together all of these very talented people is intended to captivate interest and bring people to the revival tent where the message will be loud and clear. Whether it is enough to change human behavior and save the Earth is yet to be seen? The hard work and miraculous journey of the twelve cousins will never be known. This is intentional and essential. If true change is to come, which will save the planet, it must result from an internal desire and willingness of people to change. The tour is the medium by which the message will be spread from continent to continent and around the globe. Kennedy, Ainsley, and Gemma teamed up to make this happen, and their unique talent and leadership along with their friendship with Ansel prevailed in putting together the greatest show on Earth.

As the cousins gather in Ansel's penthouse, Ainsley receives word from Gabriel Jagger that his father Mick, at the age of ninety-five, would like to perform the tour's theme song "Gimme Shelter" at the opening show in Chicago. Everyone is ecstatic at the thought of this rock legend making such an appearance.

"We have just taken this show over the top," Ansel declares. With a kickoff like this, we are assured that the entire entertainment world will be onboard. "What an amazing thing to happen, Mick Jagger has not performed in ten-years. His health has been frail, and yet, he has found a mission in this tour spreading this message. We cannot and will not fail."

Back in Ames, after three days of waiting in seclusion, Thomas, Noah, Edison, Hannah, and Contessa agree it is time to come out of the shadows and join the others in Chicago. They want to be present for the kickoff of the Save the World Tour, and they have received a note from Jack suggesting the coast is clear.

"Ray, would you mind going down to the Dodge dealer and lease an electric 2038 Dodge Caravan complete with all the bells and whistles for our trip to Chicago?" Hannah asks.

"I am sure they are going to want one of you guys to sign the lease, insurance papers, and other documents as the designated driver of the vehicle," Ray replies.

"I realize this Ray, but we have been in hiding for so long, it seems rather risky and causes us to be a bit edgy about it all," Hannah responds. "If you would do this for us, it would be greatly appreciated."

"I don't know, I will be liable, and by doing this I am committing fraud," Ray says displaying a nervous edge of his own.

"Ray, you have already committed a number of crimes including aiding and abetting us these past several days. Are you really going to turn paranoid on us now?" Hannah asks sarcastically.

"I'll go," Noah jumps into the conversation. "I am ready to get the hell out of hiding, and I have leased several vehicles over the years."

"Are you sure?" Ray asks, "I guess I could do this." Ray knows that for all the good he has done, this last statement of reservation cast him in a less than positive light with Hannah. Ray has liked Hannah for some time and he hopes the feelings might one day be mutual. He now has doubts.

"No, you have done more than enough. You have put yourself at great risk to help us and we are extremely grateful. You are a good friend and very courageous," Noah asserts sensing Ray needs some help. "If Senator Joseph is correct, we are out of harm's way. There is no time like the present to find out."

"I'll give you a ride to the dealership," Ray volunteers.

"I appreciate that, let's go," Noah proclaims. "I will be back with a van in a short bit, everyone be ready for a road trip."

As Noah approaches the dealership, the salesman recognizes him from the many pictures which have been published and posted everywhere.

"Professor Abraham, what an honor to meet you!" the salesman greets. "Are you sure you should be out in public Sir?'

"We recently received a message suggesting it is safe for us to come out of hiding, so here I am," Noah responds.

"Well let's be safe Sir. I admire everything you; your brother, sister, and cousins are doing to save our planet. There is no reason to take unnecessary risks," the salesman adds. "What can I do for you?"

"Do you have an electric 2038 Dodge Caravan complete with all the bells and whistles that I can lease?" Noah inquires.

"Professor, I happen to own this dealership and I have the very vehicle you are looking for," the Salesman says. "Let me get the keys and I will have someone bring the vehicle around immediately."

Returning with the keys, the owner offers the keys to Noah.

"What about the paperwork?" Noah inquires.

"Consider this my gift to you and your family for all of the sacrifice and risk you have taken to serve humanity," the owner declares. "The world has lived in fear for far too long and now after all the things your family has done, we have hope."

"I can't accept this," Noah protests.

"You have no choice Professor, either graciously accept my gift and be on your way, or go and do your business elsewhere," the owner declares.

"Thank you, I don't recall getting your name," Noah admits somewhat embarrassed.

"Abraham, my name is Abraham," the owner responds. "There, the vehicle is out front and ready to go. There is a temporary tag in the back window so you shouldn't have any problem. Here is the paperwork which gives you title and testifies that the vehicle is under dealership insurance."

"Thank you, Abraham," Noah says offering an outstretched hand of gratitude.

"Safe travels Sir," Abraham calls out as Noah heads for the van.

Arriving back at 804 Kellogg Ave., Noah finds the others still gathering their things.

"Come on, we need to get moving," Noah commands.

"We didn't expect you back so soon," Contessa explains, "We are moving as fast as we can."

"Nice wheels," Edison exclaims, "Things must have gone well."

"No time to talk now, I will explain everything once we are on the road," Noah says with all urgency. "Time is of the essence."

"Why so anxious Noah, did you steal the vehicle?" Thomas wonders.

"No, I did not steal the vehicle. I just think we need to hit the road. I don't know about you guys, but I am anxious to feel the freedom of the open road and see our sister and cousins," Noah announces.

As the last one tosses their belongings into the vehicle, they all offer Ray their sincerest appreciation for his help and friendship.

"Hannah," Ray says turning to face her, "I am sorry about my hesitancy with leasing a vehicle this morning. I don't know what came over me?"

"Listen Ray, you and me have a wonderful history, so let's keep it that way," Hannah says as she gives him a hug and kiss on the cheek which causes Ray to blush.

As they begin to climb into the van, Edison calls out "Shotgun". It is a habit which goes back to his youth. He always found himself competing with Kennedy and Noah for the passenger seat.

With everyone in the van, they pull away from the curb with arms waving goodbye to their host. Ray stands on the sidewalk in front of his home waving and wondering what lay ahead for these five very brave scientists.

Heading south on I-35, they are all more than a bit nervous. They have not enjoyed this type of freedom for some time. They all chuckle at the irony of their close confinement in the van with the only real difference being they were heading down the road.

"I suggest we all relax and enjoy the ride," Contessa advises. "We have 358 miles to travel, which will take us five and a half hours, just to get to Chicago."

"I am anxious to see everyone again. I hope my Twin, Olivia, is there also!" Thomas reveals.

"Hey Noah, you never told us the story of leasing this van," Edison recalls.

"I'll tell you the story, but then how about everyone grab a pillow and get comfortable and leave the driving to me," Noah asserts.

Arriving in Chicago, Noah uses the vehicles voice activation system to enter Ansel's address into the vehicles GPS. Exhausted, everyone else slept through most of the trip. Awakening, they are all surprised to not only be in Chicago, but well on their way to Willis Tower and Ansel Colioso's Penthouse Suite. With only ten minutes to go, Noah texts Kennedy about their imminent arrival. Kennedy texts back the parking instructions and the means by which they can access the Penthouse Suite.

As the five one-time fugitive scientists ride the elevator to the top of Willis Tower, they are impatient to see their sisters and cousins. It has been a wild journey from their conference in Ames to this day and moment. As the door opens to Ansel's Penthouse Suite, they find Kennedy, Ainsley, Gemma, Jack, Ivey, and Stella waiting with open arms. It is a joyous reunion to find the eleven of them back together again.

As things begin to settle down, Thomas stands looking around with a sad and disappointed look. He hoped his sister Olivia would also be waiting for their arrival.

"Are you okay Thomas?" Ainsley asks knowing something is wrong.

"I miss my twin Sis, I hoped she would be here," he says as tears fill his eyes.

At that moment, he feels a hand on his left shoulder. Turning he sees Olivia standing with open arms and tears streaming down her cheeks. Thomas embraces his twin sister too emotional to say anything. They embrace for a long time, both trying to gain composure. Finally, Thomas pushes back from Olivia with tears still present, "How dare you," he proclaims. "What a rotten trick."

With this the tears dry up and turn to laughter.

"I didn't think you were here," Thomas says.

"I wasn't, but my assistant Dr. Rooh insisted I take time to join everyone for the kick off of the "Save the World Tour". He didn't really give me much choice, so here I am," Olivia explains. "We thought it would be fun to surprise you."

"Well, your surprise just about caused a heart attack. I am so glad you are here, and we are all together again," Thomas proclaims.

CHAPTER 41

SAVING THE PLANET

WITH THE COUSINS ALL TOGETHER again, and the wheels of change in motion, they begin to discuss the promise of a new world free from disease, disaster, war and human abuse. They have worked together as a team, and they have been blessed with divine intervention. It had not previously occurred to them, but now it is so simple to see. They were chosen for this role in human history, and they are humbled by the prospect and the burden it bears.

"Think how all this has come together," Kennedy challenges as she takes a sip of Champaign. "Not long ago, we were searching for answers to the most-dire situations."

"Most of us thought the answers would only be found in science. What a foolish notion," Noah interjects. "It turns out that science and God are inseparable".

"It was not a foolish notion Noah," Ivey comes to his defense. "Religion around the world has been a mess. Theologies based on peace and love wallowing in hate and war do not offer much reason to believe".

"The revelation on Mount Pilatus set all concepts and pretexts of religion on its head. God chose this family as an instrument of transformation, and now the great religious leaders of the world are God's messengers. One God and one message," Stella proclaims with a twinkle of excitement in her eye.

"I think it is a little too soon to be excited," Thomas advises, "We have much work to do and many miles to go before we can rest."

"I agree, Thomas, I am not suggesting our work is done. What I am saying is that God is with us," Stella assures.

"We have put together the most amazing extravaganza for getting out the message to billions of people," Ainsley proclaims giving a strum on the guitar slung around her neck. "This is a multimedia phenomenon like no one has ever seen. We are going to highlight the video from the Mount Pilatus conference so all present and around the world can experience the solemn inspiration only possible by witnessing the one and only living God. Once this is accomplished, our message will flow to people like the purest of water coming from a mountain stream."

I would like to raise a toast to all of the fine work Kennedy, Ainsley, and Gemma have put into making this "Save the World Tour" extravaganza possible. Bringing together the people, the resources, and the logistics is nothing less than astonishing. Here is to Kennedy, Ainsley, and Gemma!" Hannah proposes.

"Thank you," Kennedy responds, "But we owe a great deal to Ansel. He chose to believe in our mission when he could have dismissed us."

Ansel has never felt such closeness to a group of people. He has always been motivated by the bottom line which allowed him to live in a penthouse and own antiquities. Now, his heart is filled with something unexplainable. He has discovered the unique magic of peace and love.

"We have accomplished a great deal, but until we prevail in converting people all around the globe to the need to be better stewards of this planet, our mission remains in jeopardy," Contessa proclaims standing in front of one of Ansel's massive penthouse windows looking out across Chicago's vast skyline. "Out there is where the change must occur. People are addicted to a lifestyle made possible by abusing the resources of the Earth, and the wealthy pose our biggest challenge."

"Much has happened recently which serves notice to people everywhere that the Earth is doomed unless human's change. As a family, we have gravitas and credibility earned through unselfish action. We have put our own lives in jeopardy while attempting to save millions. We now stand ready to take our message to the world through a cultural extravaganza of which the likes has never been seen," Edison reminds everyone.

"Our message, but most importantly Gods," Olivia adds. "Not too long ago, the sky was dark and ominous. Tomorrow the sun rises on a world full of possibilities and hope. We must never forget that we may be the messengers, but it is the message which must prevail."

"It seems to me we are missing something. Humans have made positive changes before only to backslide as greed and power return to the forefront of society. How do we guard against the shortcomings of humans and the evil of power and greed?" Noah poses the question with a clear idea to the answer.

"We are missing something," Contessa adds sensing where her cousin Noah is heading. She has worked closely with Noah and has a sixth sense about what he is thinking. "We need a political linchpin with the charisma and courage to galvanize people behind a movement of legislative change to codify our care of the Earth."

By now, everyone is looking directly at Jack. Sensing the attention, Jack throws his hands into the air, "What?"

The nation and the world are waiting for a leader, a leader with courage, compassion, and vision. God and science are one! We need a leader who will acknowledge this fact, and stake claim to the moral high ground. It is time Jack!" Edison declares.

"This is not a good idea guys," Jack states shaking his head. "We are about to set off on the most historic tour in human history. We are attempting to change the attitudes, beliefs, and habits of the people of Earth. We don't want to muddy the water with politics."

"It might not be what we want to do Jack, but it is exactly what must be done," Thomas fervently declares turning to everyone in the group. "We are a three-legged stool missing the third leg. If we do not control the political agenda, we could very well tip over in failure."

"Please consider my perspective. For too long, politicians have been playing fast and loose with leadership. The road of history is littered with the false promises and corruption of self-righteous leaders advancing their own interest. Money has been king, and the people have been defenseless against the rich and powerful. Trust in our political systems is all but lost. Politics is not the third leg of the stool!" Jack has never felt so convinced of something in his life.

"So, what is the third leg Jack?" Thomas wonders.

"It is the people!" Ainsley declares. "This World Tour, this crusade for the Earth, offers the people a chance at redemption."

"The three-leg stool is God, science, and the people," Olivia proclaims. "Without the people, the stool definitely will not stand."

"Politics is never far away," Jack assures, "However, politics must follow the people, not the other way around."

"Jack is correct!" Ivey affirms her brother's conviction. "The hearts and minds of the people will determine the fate of our planet. If the Save the World Tour is successful, the people will usher in a new day for the planet Earth."

"We all need faith. God has not brought us to this point only to abandon us. We are not offered an easy path forward, but we are offered a path," Stella pleads for her siblings and cousins to believe.

"The die is cast. We have already seen a reduction in religious tensions around the world due to the testimony coming from the Mt. Pilatus experience. This is just the beginning of a long arduous endeavor," Noah proclaims. "So, let us begin!"

ABOUT THE AUTHOR

It has been the authors lifelong desire to write a book. Over the past 70 years, family and career pushed this desire to the back burner of life. Now, with time and experience, the author is taking a literary leap.

Over the years, the author adopted the idealism of Robert Kennedy, the pragmatism of Oliver Wendell Homes Jr., the transcendentalism of Walt Whitman, and the cynicism of Demetrius. These four forces of human thought have greatly influenced the authors journey in telling this story.

Early in life, the author learned to love and value all of God's creation while hunting, fishing, and trapping with his Father. He learned the importance of faith from his Grandmother. He learned to appreciate and value the arts from his Mother. He learned to not take things or himself too seriously from his Grandfather.

The author has spent his lifetime as a professional educator with a deep interest in history and politics. He loves to travel, and in 1975 moved to Tehran, Iran to teach at the American School. Throughout their life together, the author and his wife have traveled extensively throughout the continental United States as well as Alaska and Hawaii. They have taken their adventures to Canada, Mexico, Panama, Britain, Italy, France, Switzerland, Greece, Turkey, Peru, and Ecuador including the Galapagos Islands.

The author has long been a writer of articles about education. He has written volumes about his travels for personal reflection. Now, he writes for you with the hope that you will enjoy his story as much as he enjoyed writing it.

ABOUT THE ARTIST

Growing up, Justin would attempt to redraw the art of his favorite album covers of his favorite bands. Not seriously considering art a part of a career choice, he ignored his high school art teacher's advice to pursue graphic design. Instead, he went to work after high school traveling as a roofer throughout the US.

After some years, Justin decided to go back to school. He earned his bachelor's degree toward being an artist. Creating his very first album cover (and all their covers since) for the local rock band, Brutal Republic. Over the years, Justin has struggled but never quit creating art. After a failed attempt at a tattoo apprenticeship, Justin worked at creating his company, Abstract Entity Art by Justin Pritchard. Justin regularly sets up vendor spots at local wineries, breweries, and live music venues as he strives to be known throughout Iowa. He has created signage for a local bait and tackle shop, as well as assisting in the creation of high school art scholarships in Fort Dodge. Justin frequently donates his art works to aid with various benefits.

Using mainly ball point pens, gel pens, colored pencils and markers, his art often takes more hours than a 40-hour work week. Creating a style that speaks to intellectuals, and fits between rock and rollers, country, hip-hop, bluesy, and the young and old. With each creation, Justin continues to push his talents to new boundaries. Each piece of art has its own unique story.

Other works of Abstract Entity Art by Justin Pritchard can be viewed via Facebook at Facebook.com/JamosMolokai

Printed in the United States
by Baker & Taylor Publisher Services